THE SISTERS AND THE SWORD

THE SISTERS AND THE SWORD

A NOVEL OF THE
PENDRAGON PROPHECY

SAM DAVEY

DIVERSION
BOOKS

Diversion Books
A division of Diversion Publishing Corp.
www.diversionbooks.com

Diversion Books and colophon are registered trademarks of
Diversion Publishing Corp.

For more information, email info@diversionbooks.com

First Diversion Books Edition: June 2026
Trade paperback ISBN: 9798895151471
e-ISBN: 9798895151488

Design by Neuwirth & Associates, Inc.
Cover design by Dylan Marcus McConnell
Cover illustrations by Jonathan Sainsbury // 6x9 design
Map design by Sioux Bradshaw

Printed in the United States of America

1 3 5 7 9 10 8 6 4 2

Diversion books are available at special discounts for bulk purchases in the US by corporations,
institutions, and other organizations. For more information, please
contact admin@diversionbooks.com.

For my children

ORKNEY ISLES
ORKNEY And the Isles
Loch Harray
Ring o' Brodgar
Loch Stromness
Stromness
N
S
W
E
Lands of The Norther Lords
Mercia
Lindsey
Welsh Marches
Caerloo
Caer Lundien
Kaoney Island
Deira
Gewisse
The Isle of Avalon
Cornwall
Ynas Weith
Lyonesse

CHAPTER ONE

THE QUEEN AND THE WISE WOMAN

The unicorn was old. Its golden hooves had lost their sheen, and its flanks, now dull and threadbare, were worn by years of loving caresses. It lay still, head resting in trusting submission on the lap of the maiden who had tamed him, and as she stretched out her hand, once pale and finely wrought, the mottled marks of age were there for all to see. The sun had faded the fabric of her dress from a brilliant emerald to a green so pale that it was becoming increasingly hard to make out where her outline ended and the forest behind her began.

"I don't know why you insist on hanging this old rag-tag of a tapestry in our chamber, Morgause. It is certainly no longer pleasing to the eye, and I doubt it will be effective in keeping the draughts at bay this winter." The speaker was a tall, thin man with a weather-beaten face and hair that had once been a fierce, flaming red. The eyes that now rested on his wife were quizzical, but not unkind.

She had her back to him, and he was not sure if she was looking at the tapestry or through the window, where the sun was beginning to set behind the Ring of Brodgar, the ancient standing stones casting long shadows across the loch.

Her hair was loose and fell below her hips in tawny, polished waves. He noticed that she had removed her kirtle; it lay in a thoughtless heap on the floor, half covered by blankets that had tumbled from the unmade bed. She was dressed in a simple undershift, and her feet were bare.

Without saying a word, Morgause walked across to the window, resting her hands upon the stone sill and shaking out her hair. He could see the outline of her body clearly through the flimsy linen. Despite having borne him four sons, she was still beautiful, and as the years advanced, they had done little to diminish his desire for her.

When she spoke, her voice was soft. "If you hate it so, I'll get rid of it. I know it is old now, tattered and past its best, but it is all I have left to remind me of home. The castle at Tintagel and my poor mother."

"But is this not your home, Morgause? You have lived here since you were but a bairn. Has Orkney not welcomed you and taken you into its heart? You are my queen, the mother of my sons and, as Uther is still unwed, first lady in the land. I cannot understand why you still hanker for a tiny piece of Cornish soil."

As he spoke, he walked towards her and she leant against him, resting her head upon his shoulder. He circled her in his arms and together they looked out across the causeway at the evening star, shining in the purpling sky. The air was still, the rose-tipped clouds framing the ageless monoliths. As they watched, a pair of curlews alighted on the nearest stone and turned towards each other, their beaks forming delicate arcs, until, startled perhaps by the call of an owl, they rose as one and flew away across the loch.

"Is there anything to match this in your Tintagel?" he asked her. "Any place as powerful or as beautiful?"

At this, she turned within his arms and raised her face to his. "No, my lord, you are right. I was simply being foolish. I love our Isles of Orkney and am proud to call them my home." She kissed him and soon he forgot all about the tapestry, the standing stones, and even why he had found his wife undressed and his bed dishevelled a good hour before sunset.

But Morgause forgot nothing, and whilst her husband slept, she lay awake, her eyes staring at the pale outline of the unicorn upon the wall.

SHE HAD BEEN BUT six years old when her parents, Gorlois and Igraine, the Duke and Duchess of Cornwall and Lyonesse, had sent her on the long sea voyage to Orkney. She had been affianced in early childhood to Lot—newly crowned King of Orkney and at that time a young warrior of some five and twenty summers. It was an advantageous political union, brokered by Igraine's father, Amlawdd, King of the Welsh Marches, who hoped in this way to consolidate an alliance between Cornwall, the Marches and the increasingly powerful kingdom of Orkney.

At the time of the betrothal her parents had expected to keep their pretty eldest daughter at home with them until she had reached marriage-able age, but when Uther Pendragon, High King of Britain, fell in love with Igraine, civil war had broken out. Concerned for the safety of their daughter, Igraine and Gorlois had accepted the offer of chaperonage and safe passage made by Lot's brother, Urien, and Morgause had been des-patched in haste to Orkney upon the ship, the *Llyr's Daughter*.

Her mother had tried to make the small cabin as comfortable as pos-sible, and Morgause could still remember her delight when, on entering the tiny room that was to be her home for the many weeks of the long sea voyage, she had seen the familiar unicorn tapestry upon the wall. Igraine had made it in the early years of her marriage to Gorlois, and before she had given it to her daughter it had hung in their private chambers in Tintagel. The young Morgause had never failed to be delighted by the graceful creature. She loved to stroke its soft white nose and dreamt of the time when she would be as beautiful as the lady in whose lap the unicorn had laid its head.

She thought about the day when the *Llyr's Daughter* had finally arrived at the port of Stromness. Waiting for her on the quayside was a tall, red-haired man, flanked by soldiers in full battledress. The emblem of the two-headed raven, symbol of the Northern tribes, was emblazoned on their shields and flew above their heads on the banners that pulsed proudly in the strong sea breeze. She noticed that the air had an edge to it, a biting chill that was unfamiliar and made her pull her cape more tightly around her. Beside her were Avice, her nursemaid and companion, and Einar, a young boy about five years her senior. Originally from Norway, Einar was King Lot's cousin and ward and had journeyed south with Urien as his page boy and squire. But as the civil war erupted, Urien had decided that the lad, though keen, was too young and inexperienced to take his chance upon the battlefield and so had sent his brother's ward back to Orkney.

Morgause recalled standing on deck, looking at the stark yet dramatic landscape that was now to be her home. She was used to cliffs and stony promontories, but at this time of year the Cornish headlands were softened by the yellow, pink and blue of rock flowers. Here, there seemed to be no such softness, just a grey, granite outcrop standing hard against an unfor-givingly bleak, steel-grey sky.

The tall man had dismounted and walked towards the harbour's edge, finally pausing at the end of the gangplank. Avice pushed her gently towards him, but Morgause hung back, not wanting to leave the ship.

She knew that she must go to him, that she had no choice. Avice had told her many times that etiquette demanded that she—Lot's bride and future queen—must walk away from the ship, which was symbolically Cornish territory, towards him and the Isle of Orkney. It would not do for him to mount the gangplank. But she could not do it. She wanted to run back to her cabin or hurl herself into the air, taking the form of a seabird as the servants whispered her mother was said to do. Anything but take that first step down the wooden walkway towards him.

He had taken off his helmet and passed it to one of his companions. He was so tall and so old. He looked nearly as old as her father. Morgause remembered being frightened, her lip trembling, feeling certain that she was about to cry and bring disgrace to herself, when she felt a warm hand take hers and heard Einar whisper, "Don't worry, I'll look after you." She felt Avice give her another push and gripped Einar's hand tightly. "Walk down with me," she said. "Don't make me go alone." And so, he had.

At the bottom of the gangplank, Einar had let go of her hand and propelled her gently towards the tall man who had got down on one knee, so his head was at a level with hers.

"Greetings, Lady Morgause." His voice was low and, she had thought, kind. She noticed that unlike his brother and the Orcadian soldiers she had met in Tintagel, he did not speak with a northern accent; indeed, his voice was more like her father's. She remembered that he had not been raised in the Northern Isles but had spent most of his early years in Brittany at the court of King Budic, like so many of the rebels who had fought with Uther against the Saxon tyrant, Vortigern.

He bent forwards and took her hand, raising her small fingers to his lips. "It would seem my brother did not lie. You are as lovely a girl as I have ever seen." He turned to Einar with a smile and ruffled his hair. "And how are you, cousin? It seems I have you to thank for bringing my bride safe to Stromness and helping her make her first steps upon the soil of Orkney." With that, they mounted their horses and made their way up from the harbour to the old stone house that Lot had furnished for her, which was to be her home until she became a grown woman and could join Lot as queen in truth of Orkney and the Northern Isles.

"Aye," thought Morgause, her lips twisting in a dark smile of remembrance. "And it was Einar who was first with so many other things." She felt a glow of pleasure as she remembered his fumbling caresses, those furtive, stolen kisses that made them both weak with a desire they were at first far too scared to give in to. And then, finally, the week before her marriage ceremony to Lot, it was Einar who took her for the first time and initiated her in the delights and torments the Goddess bestows upon those who serve her.

It had been over twenty years since she had left Tintagel, and fifteen since Lot had placed the crown of Orkney on her head. And Einar was still with them. He had not returned to his family in Norway, although his mother had sent summons on more than one occasion. When asked about his reluctance, he was always ready with an excuse, and so far, no one had guessed the real reason was his obsession with the queen.

It must be said that Morgause had for a long time found his passion amusing. It was flattering to be so adored, and he was a vigorous and imaginative lover, very different from her staid and perhaps overly respectful husband. But Morgause was beginning to find Einar's devotion rather claustrophobic, and her diminishing ardour had the result of making Einar behave more and more recklessly. He had repeatedly urged her to fly with him, saying that if Lot knew about them, he would renounce her, and they would be given shelter in Norway with his family. They could finally live what he had called "a simple life" together as man and wife.

The idea had frankly made her shudder. The thought of a simple life did not appeal at all to Morgause, who loved the pageantry of life at court. She also recognised that the passions and pleasures of a stolen affair are enflamed by the frisson of secrecy and are likely to sputter out when given the blessings of convention. As to the notion that Lot would just accept their betrayal and allow them to sail away unchallenged to the shores of Norway . . . Well, Morgause had a more practical head upon her shoulders than her passionate but unworldly lover, and knew that, kind and reasonable as he seemed to be, Lot was more likely to order their execution than suffer the shame of being cuckolded by his cousin.

Musing on this, she reflected that Lot had nearly caught them that evening and if his attention had not been distracted by the unicorn tapestry, he would almost certainly have seen her pushing Einar's surcoat out of sight beneath the bedstead. There was no doubt about it. Einar was becoming a liability, and as she fell asleep, soothed by the regular, gentle breathing of her husband beside her, Morgause began to consider exactly what she was going to do about it.

IN THE SUMMER MONTHS, THE days are long in Orkney, and it was now nearing the midsummer Solstice. Morgause had been asleep for only four or five hours when she felt the first rays of sunlight gentling her eyelids and rousing her. She got out of bed, being careful not to wake her still-sleeping husband and pulled her shift over her head. Grabbing her shawl and pushing her feet into a pair of soft, sheepskin slippers, she made her way downstairs. She could hear noises from the kitchens and knew that soon the castle servants would be about, carrying fresh water to the upper chambers and lighting the fires in the Great Hall, making ready for the household to rise and begin their day. But she saw no one and soon she was walking away from the shadows of the high stone walls, towards the causeway known as the Ness of Brodgar, a thin strip of land separating the great Lochs of Stenness and Harray, providing a natural walkway to the ancient settlement and, beyond it, the mighty, mysterious ring of standing stones.

Although the sun was now almost risen, there was a chill in the air, and the coarse grass was damp with dew. There are few songbirds on the Northern Isles, and Morgause could hear nothing but the occasional call of a lone gull slowly circling the still waters of the loch. She knew exactly where she was going and walked quickly, almost to the edge of the Ness, before turning to her right and walking inland. Soon she came upon a group of stones that seemed as ancient and immovable as the loch itself. Standing tall, grey and scarred with age, the stones were ranged around a single, massive monolith. It rose from the heather to the height of three men and was broad and solid, looking as if it had jutted forth from the innermost heart of the earth. Near its base was a large, ragged hole that framed the loch and through which the other stone circle, the Ring of Brodgar, could be seen, silhouetted against the early morning sky.

This was an ancient place, a place of mystery and elemental magic. Unlike her mother and her sister Morgan, Morgause had not been schooled on the Lake Isle of Avalon. She remembered, and made use of the magics her mother had taught her when she was a young girl in Tintagel; how to use the scrying bowl to conjure visions, to ask for guidance from the Goddess or how to brew simple potions and healing remedies, but she had little formal training in the subtle complexities of the Mysteries. Despite this, Morgause had long recognised the power that resided in this place, this ancient ring of stones, and knew that it was older than the Mysteries of the Goddess, older even than the magics the Roman conquerors had brought with them to the shores of Britain. Here was a power as strong as it was primitive; a power primeval in its force, and as dark and dispassionate as the earth itself.

Today, however, her business was not with the stones. Faintly inclining her head in a gesture of respect, she made her way around the edge of the circle towards a rocky outcrop on the southern edge of the loch. Here, the ground fell away sharply, creating an escarpment at the bottom of which was a small house, partially built into the face of the rock and not much more than a stone's throw from the shore.

Winding down the cliff was a narrow track, chiselled out of the rock and almost invisible to anyone who did not know of its existence. Morgause, however, was familiar with the pathway and made her way down unhesitatingly. It felt colder at the bottom of the cliff. The sun had not yet risen high enough to cast its rays on the shaded valley and Morgause pulled her shawl tightly around her. As she approached the dwelling, she became aware of a warm glow from the open firepit situated to the left of the doorway, and the welcoming smell of baking bread.

As she watched, a boy of perhaps ten or twelve summers emerged from the cottage, carrying a tray containing three loaves, risen and ready for the oven. Seeing her, he started, almost dropping his burden, before righting himself and greeting her with a shy smile. "Guid mornin', Yer Majesty. It's fair guid tae see ye." The boy blushed as he spoke, unable to stop himself from staring at her night shift and the long, untamed tangle of her hair. Young as he was, he thought he would never again see a woman as beautiful as his queen.

Remembering his manners, he placed the tray on the ground and bent forward in a deep bow. "And how kin ah hulp ye, Yer Majesty?"

"Good morning, Donal." Morgause smiled and gestured towards the loaves that were already showing signs of wilting in the chill of the morning air. "Please, see to your tasks. I have no wish to spoil your bread." As she spoke, she stepped forward, towards the door of the cottage. "Are your mother and father within?"

"Faither is oot on th' loch, th' broon trout ur movin' 'n' he dreems tae catch a fair few this mornin', bit mah mither is in the ben—'n' she'll be richt glad tae see ye."

Morgause smiled again and made her way into the little house. The boy watched her for a moment, before running his hands through his tangle of coarse, curly black hair and shaking his head, as if to bring himself back to the reality of his morning duties. He saw the door close behind her and knew that he would not be welcome whilst she was inside discussing whatever it was that she had come to talk about with his mother. Disconsolately, he stooped to pick up his tray and took the loaves to the oven, where he exchanged them for the batch he had put in earlier, which were now a little overdone.

He placed the loaves to cool on the rock his mother had positioned beneath the wooden shelf she had made his father add to the back of the oven in the early days of their marriage. Until then, the generations of people who had lived and worked in the stone cottage on the shores of the loch had always had to run the risk of their fresh-made bread falling victim to the ever-watchful seabirds. But his mother had a way of finding solutions to problems that other people regarded as just the inevitabilities of life. It was one of the things that Donal now knew to be unusual about her, the things that made the other boys unwilling to call for him or include him in their games. The things that probably helped explain why the Queen of Orkney and the Northern Isles had just appeared at his doorway dressed only in a nightshift and a simple woollen shawl.

The boy made his way down to the water's edge and began to walk slowly through the still, brown shallows, scanning the surface of the loch for his father's small fishing boat, hoping to join him in his morning's work. No one would be welcome indoors whilst the queen was paying her visit.

Donal had learned over the years that his mother's behaviour towards visitors followed two very distinct patterns: When neighbours or family called, such as his older brother, Conn, and his new wife, Aoife, or one of his father's brothers, his mother would usher them into the house with smiles and a warm embrace. But when certain other people came, not just the queen, but the strangers who appeared perhaps once or twice a year from the other islands, and even a man who he later discovered had travelled from Norway, his mother closed the door on Donal and his father.

Donal's father, Cormac, had always lived in the house on the lochshore, as had his father, and his father before that; a line that reached so far back that it made his head spin to even try to think about it. As the eldest son, Cormac had inherited the house, and his brothers had moved away, marrying girls who lived in the small hamlets and villages that flourished the lochside. But Donal's mother did not come from one of these small, local settlements—she did not even come from Orkney, but from a place far away, an island that, according to her, was as different as it was possible to be from the stark, cold and ruggedly familiar landscape that he loved.

He knew by heart the story of how his parents had met. It always made him feel warm inside to think that they had begun their lives in such different places, but had found each other and made each other happy, and from that happiness had come Conn and himself. As he walked, he could hear his mother's softly musical voice telling him the tale, which always began in the same way.

"When I was a little girl, Donal, I lived far, far away, on an island called Corsica, where the sea is as blue as the sky at Solstice and the summer waves are warm and gentle. I would play on the sand with my sisters and brothers, and swim, and sometimes, in the summer, we would sleep out under the stars, for the nights were warm and it was too hot to be indoors.

"I had two sisters and two brothers, and their names were Abigay, Adelet, Carlu and Jaquet. I was the littlest and although my proper name was Anilla, they all called me Annie or Little Anna." Donal's mother would always smile when she said this and then she would pause, before going on with the story.

"One by one, we all grew up and my brothers and sisters began to leave home. First Carlu, then Abigay fell in love and married. They didn't go very far away; they settled close to our village, and we would still see them every day. Then Jaquet met a girl from the other side of the island and went to live many miles away, and we didn't see them very often; but when we did, at festivals and name days, it was wonderful." At this point in the story, his mother would always put her hand to her throat and smile, closing her eyes for a moment.

"So now, there was just Adelet and me left at home. Sadness came when my father died, but Mother told us that he had lived a long and happy life and that we should not grieve too much. Then Adelet left home, and it was just me and my mother. We were very close. She taught me everything she knew, the wisdom of the old days, how to cook, how to take care of people. Healing and plant craft, too. I was happy. But I started to long for a home of my own. A family of my own. A child of my own." When she said this, his mother would always reach out and stroke Donal's hair and run her finger along the side of his cheek.

"But there was no one I wanted. No one I wished to fall in love with, and I thought that I would never find the happiness I was looking for.

"But then, one winter's day, something happened. I must tell you that for many years, traders had been visiting our island, ships from Sardinia, Phoenicia and even great Rome itself. On this day, it was cold and blustery, just a few weeks after Samhain, and there was a great storm. One of the Phoenician ships had got into trouble, running aground on the rocks outside the harbour. Although my brothers and other brave Corsicans risked their own lives to try to rescue the sailors from the waves, many of the men were drowned. Carlu, rowing out in his small fishing boat, pulled a man from the waters and brought him back to my mother's house.

At first, we thought he would not live, but my mother refused to lose hope and eventually, the stranger began to thrive. He stayed with us for many weeks, growing ever stronger, cherished and strengthened by my mother's care, and soon it became clear that he had begun to love her.

My mother was still a young woman, not much older than I am now, and she was very beautiful. He begged her to marry him and to go with him to his home in Phoenicia, but that was hundreds of miles away, on a long, long journey across the seas, and she did not wish to leave her home and her children.

Eventually, he accepted the fact that she would not marry him, and he prepared to leave. His ship had been repaired and was now fully loaded with the goods that he wished to take back across the seas to trade. The last few days passed sadly. My mother's heart was breaking. She did not know what to do, and so I went to visit my brothers and sisters. I told them that I thought they should come to see our mother and tell her that, although they would miss her, they could not bear for her to lose the happiness she had now found. They agreed, and together we spoke to her, and finally convinced her. This was hard for my brothers and sisters, but even harder for me. They were married and by now all had children of their own. Unlike them, I had no one but my mother."

At this point, she would raise a finger to her eye and wipe away a single tear.

"And so, they were married, right there on the beach, and all of us laughed and sang and wept at their wedding. They were to depart the next day, and I went to bed early, crying myself to sleep because I knew I would miss her so much. I had not thought my mother would hear me. But I was wrong. I felt her arms around me, and she held me close to her, even though by now I was a woman grown. 'Little Anna,' she said to me, again and again, 'My little Anna, I cannot leave you. I have spoken to my husband, and we will take you with us. Wherever we go, you will go, and we will not be parted until you are ready to leave me.'

"And it was as she said. I sailed with them on that first voyage, visiting first Qadis in a distant country called Iberia, and then on to Brittany, where my stepfather sought trade with the merchants at the court of King Budic. We went ashore, and within a week I had met your father, who was then a sailor under the command of King Lot of Orkney."

Donal would always reach out and give her a hug when she said this familiar name, pleased and relieved that the story was going to end as it always had, with the marriage of his mother to his father, their journey home to Orkney, the birth of his brother and, some years later, himself.

He smiled again to himself as he thought about the unfamiliar land that his mother had come from: Corsica, an island he would never see except through the words of her stories, which was so different from the place she now called home. He knew that his mother was not like other people. She was clever and powerful; she had seen things that no one else he knew had seen. Was it really so surprising that the Queen of the Northern Isles came visiting in the early morning, her hair unkempt and her eyes still heavy from sleep, in her urgency to talk with Anna, the woman from Corsica, who was known to the fishermen of Orkney as the Dream Hunter?

INSIDE THE STONE HOUSE, MORGAUSE pushed aside the spiced ale that Anna had just placed on the table in front of her. "You know I can't stand that stuff. If you have no wine, I will just take water. But that is the least of my worries. Sit down and stop fussing." Anna, who had been reaching for a jug of chilled water, had her back to the queen, her face set in a disapproving frown that she did nothing to conceal as she placed the jug and two beakers on the table. She reached out her hand to remove the unwanted ale, but Morgause moved faster, dashing the mug to the floor and taking hold of the older woman's hand.

"Now stop all these foolish niceties. You know I did not come here to break my fast. I will be expected back at the castle within the hour, so don't waste my time. Sit down and listen to me." With a sigh, Anna took her seat on the other side of the rough wooden table. She sat up straight, ignoring the soft lambswool pillow on the settle behind her, and folded her hands neatly in her lap. Morgause reached out across the table, an expression of hurt incredulity upon her beautiful face. "I don't understand why you say you can't help me. You've never refused me before, Anna. What's so different this time?"

"You know very well, Your Grace. Yes, I've helped you before, and been glad to do so, but I have always told you that there are lines you don't cross, powers you don't call on . . . not if you want to sleep easy in your bed."

The queen smiled. "Are you frightened, Anna—with me to protect you? You know the king will do anything I ask of him. Help me, and I will make sure he continues to overlook those strange visitors who seek you out, bringing gold to your coffers, not one ounce of which, I believe, has been surrendered in tithes." She got up from the table and made her way to the great dark-wood dresser that ran along the whole length of the rear wall. Along the bottom shelf was an array of burnished cooking pots and pans. There were three great saucepans and a number of polished jugs and serving vessels. Ranged on the shelves above were bowls and plates, some made of wood, simple and rustic, but others fashioned from pewter or beaten copper. On the very top shelf, there was a small collection of fine glazed pottery that could only have been purchased from a Mediterranean trader.

"Your house has many comforts, Anna. These plates are as fine as any we use at the castle, and I hear that your husband has recently commissioned a new boat. It would be a shame if he suddenly found that he did not have the means to pay for it." Morgause pulled her shawl tightly around her and resumed her seat at the table. She shook out her hair, pulling it over one shoulder and began to give her attention to braiding it into a long, single plait.

"There is no need to be frightened of what I am asking you to do . . . but I would counsel that you should indeed be worried if you persist on refusing me." She continued to twist her hair slowly, weaving one strand on top of another, her fingers moving deftly until, at last, the braid was finished. Neither woman spoke. Morgause poured herself some water and leant back in her chair.

There was no sound but the crackle and spit of the logs on the fire and the distant call of the seabirds whirling above the still waters of the loch. Eventually, Anna looked up.

"Yes, I know that you could ruin me, Morgause. But that is not what frightens me. I have helped you before, and there are things I know, stories I could tell, that I think you would rather remain untold." And now it was the older woman who leant forward, reaching out her hand to the Queen's. "But I do not want to take that path. It would be a sad day if you and I become enemies. Remember, you have been my pupil, and I have taught you well and with a good heart. Listen to me. The Wild Hunt is not a power we should seek to command, but one we serve."

Morgause shrugged away the hand that tried to take hers with an impatient gesture. When she spoke, her voice was cold, and her expression implacable. "No, you listen to me. I am your queen, and it is my right to command you—and your duty to serve me as I desire. You will summon the Mazzeri, lead the Dream Hunters to the kill, and rid me of this troublesome fool. Do you understand me?"

"I understand you well enough." Anna rose to her feet and made her way to the door. It was clear to her that she had no other choice. She must obey a direct order from the queen and all she could do was try to minimise the danger to herself and those she loved. When she spoke, it was with care, enunciating the words with ritual solemnity. "I will do this at your behest, and in your name."

"And when will the time be right? How soon can you summon the hunters?" Morgause was eager now, her eyes shining with the pleasure she always felt when she had managed to get her own way.

"The hunters will ride when the moon is full. Three nights from now. You do understand, Morgause, this is at your behest, and in your name?"

"Yes, yes, it is as I wish it. Exactly. Now, thank you, Anna . . . you see, that was not so hard." Morgause leant forwards and placed a kiss upon the older woman's cheek. "We should not quarrel. Now, I must get back to the castle before Lot misses me. I'm so glad that we were able to come to an understanding." And with that, she was gone, leaving Anna to clear up the shattered fragments of the broken beaker and to brood upon the promise she had made.

CHAPTER TWO

THE DREAM HUNTERS

It was less than a week until Solstice and although it was now nearly midnight, the sky was not yet dark. There were few clouds, and only the evening star was visible, shining bright and clear just above the walls of Stromness. Although it was fully risen, the full moon hung low against the purple horizon. Strangely and remarkably, it was red, a blood moon. To the four boys lying on their backs in the rough grass at the edge of Loch Harray, it seemed as if they would only need to climb to the top of the tallest of the standing stones to be able to step up, and on to its strange, craggy surface.

"Do you think we could do it?" asked the youngest child, a skinny boy of about six summers with an untamed shock of red hair that he was constantly pushing out of his eyes "I would love to go to the moon."

"Why don't you run along and see? At least it will mean we don't have to listen to your idiotic chatter for the next few hours." The speaker was a tall lad of around eleven or twelve, with a face that would have been handsome were it not for the lack of warmth in his eyes and his expression, which was that of an almost perpetual sneer. He sat up and gave his brother a none-too-gentle kick.

"Stop that, Agravaine, and don't be so silly, Gareth. You know that Mother told us to wait here for her." Gawaine, the eldest of the brothers, was now nearly fourteen. Although not as tall as Agravaine, he was well made, with broad shoulders and an air of confidence that made him seem older than his years.

"But we've been here a long time, Gawaine. It's cold, and I'm bored." Gareth had got up, moving himself out of range of Agravaine's feet and fists. There was a slight quiver in his voice.

"I said you were too young to come out tonight. You should've stayed at home with Avice if all you can do is blub. You're only just seven. I wasn't allowed to stay out when I was your age, and I think it's really unfair of Mother saying you could watch the Hunters when I'm older than you and I've never seen them." The speaker was a pale, slender child with a freckled face and startling green eyes. His name was Gaheris, and he was little more than a year older than Gareth. Gaheris had only very recently stopped sleeping in the nursery, and now that he had a place in the dormitory with the older boys, he did everything he could to distance himself from the little brother who only a few short months ago had been his favourite playmate and companion.

Gareth stood his ground. "I'm not blubbing, I'm just cold," he said. Although his words were defiant, it still sounded as if he were trying to hold back tears. Gawaine sighed, knowing that Gareth would be teased unmercifully by the other two if he began to cry. The last thing he wanted was for his mother, when she finally arrived, to find them in the middle of one of the quarrels that seemed to characterise the relationships between the red-headed, tempestuous brothers.

"Come here, shrimp, you can huddle inside my cloak." Gawaine sat up and smiled at Gareth. At this, the little boy immediately flung himself at his oldest brother, who tousled his hair fondly before pulling the folds of his cloak around him.

Above them, the purple began to darken and slowly the other stars came out, tiny pinpricks of distant light in a sky bathed in the rich, red glow of the moon. Gaheris moved closer to Gawaine, whereupon he too was enfolded in the welcoming warmth of the cloak and soon, the three brothers had fallen asleep. Only Agravaine remained awake, watching and waiting for their mother.

It was cold, so he got to his feet and began to walk along by the edge of the water. Every now and then he bent down, picking up a stone and sending it skimming across the still surface of the loch. Looking across to Stromness, he could see the dark shape of the castle. There were no lights in any of the windows, save the warm, tawny glow of the fire in the Great Hall. He wondered how late it was, and what had happened to their mother. Like Gawaine, he had come prepared. He was dressed warmly, and his travelling cloak hung, weighty and reassuring around his shoulders.

Although he was not cold, Agravaine liked his comforts and did not fancy a damp, weary night on the rough grass.

He turned northwards, away from the castle and scanned the lochshore, out to the causeway and beyond. He could just make out the dark outline of the standing stones and thought he could see movement beyond them. Strange shapes seemed to be stirring in the shadows, but nothing was clear, and he knew that it might just be a trick of the uncanny and somehow sinister red moonlight. Wrapped in his thoughts, Agravaine was not minding where he put his feet. Catching the toe of his boot on something hard and sharp, he stumbled and would have fallen into the water had not his natural agility enabled him to right himself. Muttering one of the curses he had picked up from hours spent hanging around the stables with the castle farriers—but which he was not yet confident enough to use in front of his brothers—he looked down to see what had sent him off balance. Sticking out of the damp, marshy soil was what seemed at first to be an old tree branch, but when he reached down and grasped it, its surface was hard, cool and smooth to his touch. It did not feel like a tree branch, not even one that had been buffed and weathered by the pounding waves.

Intrigued, Agravaine pulled harder, but whatever it was, it held fast. Refusing to accept defeat, he grasped tighter, moving the thing up and down, to left and right, using his feet to hold the object in place, but still, it would not work loose. Determined now, he adjusted his grasp and began to pull, bending backwards so his whole body acted as a lever to force whatever it was from its burial place. He felt something deep within the soil give way and he stumbled backwards on to the marsh grass, his treasure, whatever it was, grasped firmly in both hands.

It stank, with the cloying smell of decay, and Agravaine thought he was going to vomit. Turning his head away, he gulped deep draughts of cool night air and soon was able to swallow down the bile and take control of himself. Looking down, he could now see that the thing he held in his hands was a long bone. The part he had stumbled over and had originally mistaken for a branch or tree root had been cleansed by the action of wind and water, but farther up, where it had been buried in the marshy soil, clumps of rotting flesh still remained. He could see frayed strips of dark, red-brown hide that had ripped asunder when he had pulled the leg from the corpse of the dead creature. It was a thigh bone, long and slender, and he was sure that the animal whose rotting remains he had uncovered was a red deer.

Then he remembered the last Dream Hunt. It had been dark that night, and bitterly cold, two or perhaps three years ago. He and Gawaine had been deeply asleep in the room they shared above the Great Hall, but he had woken immediately at his mother's touch. She had held a candle in one hand, and had smiled at him, raising a finger to her lips to warn him to stay silent as she went to the other bed to rouse his brother. She was so beautiful, her skin pale and luminous, her hair hanging loose around her shoulders. Agravaine loved her more than anyone else he knew. More than Gawaine, more than Lot, his tall, uncompromising father, and certainly more than his stupid little brothers.

Gawaine had awakened, and the two boys had hurriedly pulled on their boots and britches and tugged their warmest jerkins over their heads. Their mother pointed to the travel cloaks hanging on their pegs behind the door and once they had flung them around their shoulders, the three of them set out.

The night was cold and the frosted grass crackled beneath their feet. Their breath came in warm clouds and Agravaine, wishing he had remembered to bring his lambswool gloves, wrapped his hands tightly in the folds of his cloak. Above them, the sky was clear, the stars small pricks of light around the horned moon.

Their mother walked fast and the two boys had to trot to keep up with her. Every now and then, she would reach down and touch their shoulders or ruffle their hair, urging them forwards, encouraging them to keep up with her. At first, they had headed towards the loch, but before they reached the strand she had turned and made her way through the standing stones towards the small, shadowy house that stood alone on the shoreline. Agravaine had been there before. His mother had sent him once with messages for Anna, the strange, dark woman who had married one of his father's fishermen.

He had known that the local boys thought she was a witch. They taunted and threw stones at her son Donal and made signs to ward off the evil eye if they ever caught him on his own, but not one of them would have dared to say a word if Anna herself had been present. Yet Agravaine had not been scared of her. She had opened the door and looked him up and down appraisingly, before smiling a slow, knowing smile and holding out her hand for his mother's note. She was standing in the doorway now, her cloak held tight around her, her black curls whipped into elflocks by the wind. But this time, she was not smiling, and she had not moved aside to make them welcome. "Why have you brought these boys? What we do tonight is not entertainment for children."

Her voice had been firm and accusatory and Agravaine remembered how startled he had been to hear anyone address his mother in this way. But Morgause had paid no heed to the lack of deference in the other woman's tone. When she replied, she had spoken as if to an equal "Anna, you disappoint me. I would have thought that you of all people would recognise the need to ensure our children understand the power and responsibility their destinies place upon them. Do you not wish Donal to follow in your footsteps?"

"No, I do not," Anna had spoken with quiet certainty. "Donal has gone to his brother's, with Cormac. These matters do not concern them. What I do, I do because I choose to, but it is a burden I am loath to pass on to my children."

He remembered that his mother had raised her eyebrows and pursed her lips. "Hm. You would rather your son become a fisherman, a humble worker like his father, than a master, a Mazzeri?"

"I would rather he know peace."

Morgause had said nothing, and the two women had faced each other in silence until eventually Anna looked away. When she had done so, her gaze had fallen upon the two young boys shivering on her doorstep. She seemed to come to a decision; shrugging her shoulders, she had stepped back into the house and gestured for them to enter.

He remembered how relieved he had been to walk into the warmth. It had been dark inside, but although the candles were unlit, a fire was still burning in the large stone fireplace. He and Gawaine had made their way to the inglenook and without waiting to be asked, had thrown themselves down on to the thick rag hearthrug and begun to warm their frozen fingers.

His mother followed them. She was clearly familiar with her surroundings, hanging her cloak on a hook to the right of the door before pouring herself a drink from a pewter jug on the dresser. She took a sip and settled herself at the table before asking. "And is everything prepared?"

"Yes. See, I have it here." Anna took a small box from her pocket and placed it on the table. She opened it and their mother bent her face towards it. "This smells rather better than I remembered. Have you changed something?" The other woman shook her head. "No, this is as it should be. In fact, it reminds me of the salves my mother used to make, back home in Corsica. I used the herbs your sister brought with her on her last visit. I think we will find that plants grown on the lake shores of Avalon may well be more effective than the sad scraps I have managed to cultivate."

"Oh, if it comes from Avalon, I have no doubt that it will be potent. My sister is no fool when it comes to plant-lore, and as heir apparent to the Lady of the Lake, she can command the best." As always when Morgause spoke of her sister, pride and resentment mingled. "Shall we begin? There is still much to do, and the moon is already nearing her peak." Agravaine remembered that his mother had sounded eager, excited and clearly unwilling to wait for very much longer.

"But what of the boys? It is true that I would rather they were not here, but as you have brought them, you must at least explain to them what we are doing, and what it is likely they will see. Most importantly, Morgause, you must tell them that they are on no account to leave these walls until they can do so safely. The Wild Hunt is not for children." Whilst she talked, Anna had picked up the box and, after having made sure it was sealed, had placed it in her pocket. A look of anger had flashed across his mother's face, followed by one of frustrated resignation as she went over to join him and Gawaine by the fire.

"Now, my darling boys, this is a very special night, a very important night, and you are both extremely lucky that I have allowed you to be part of it." Morgause had knelt down between them. Agravaine remembered her putting her arms around their shoulders as they stared into the dancing depths of the fire. She had often told them tales of the Mazzeri, the Dream Hunters who can leave their bodies and join the Wild Hunt, but tonight, she had said, they would get the chance to see a real Dream Hunter and to watch the Wild Hunt chase its prey across the causeway.

She had laughed at his wide eyes and held up her hand, refusing to answer any of his or Gawaine's excited questions. "No boys, I don't have time for your chatter. Watch, and you will learn." She had got to her feet in one smooth, fluid movement, ruffled their hair and returned to the table, only turning to say "And don't leave this house, whatever you hear, whatever you see. You must stay here. Do you promise?"

And so, they had watched as his mother and Anna, the Dream Hunter, drank deeply from a flagon of spiced wine. Anna had taken the little box out of her pocket and given it to Morgause, who rubbed a quantity of whatever it contained on her eyelids, before passing it back to the other woman, who did likewise. They sat close together, shoulders touching, and Agravaine noticed that Anna had reached out and taken his mother's hand in hers.

It was dark within the stone house, and silent. Nothing seemed to be happening, and both boys had just begun to drowse on the hearthrug when Anna raised her head and let out a single, unearthly call in a language Agravaine did not understand. Then his mother looked up, and she too raised her voice, calling out words that the two boys did not recognise, but which caused the hair on the back of their necks to prickle unpleasantly. Agravaine remembered moving closer to Gawaine, farther away from the table, until they both sat with their backs hard up against the comforting solidity of the wooden settle.

Now the two women were making noises that did not sound like language, strong, deep ululations that seemed to match the flickering dance of the flames within the hearth. As the boys watched, shadows began to form on the walls and ceiling, strange shapes appeared, horned beasts with slender riders, the squat forms of hunting dogs, noses down, seeking the scent of their quarry. Round and round the shadows raced, faster and faster in the flickering firelight until, with a loud crack, the door of the house burst open, and the spectral cavalcade charged out, into the night.

Agravaine looked towards the table and saw that both women had slumped forward, their heads motionless and heavy upon their arms. Before he could move towards them, wanting to touch his mother, to make sure she was alright, he heard his brother's voice, hoarse and low, calling him from the doorway. Together they looked out across the loch at the dark, looming outline of the Ring of Brodgar. Something was moving, running fast, away from the baleful shades of the standing stones. An animal; was it a horse without a rider? But no, it was too small. As it came closer, Agravaine saw that it was a doe, full grown and strong. Her head flung forwards, eyes wide in terror as she raced towards the shore.

The air was suddenly filled with tumult. A hunting horn sounded, harsh and urgent above the baying of hounds, and then the night was filled with the riders of the Wild Hunt. Over the causeway they came, some across the rough grass, fast and fearless, leaning low in their saddles. At first, Agravaine had thought that the huntsman all wore horned helmets, but as a cloud moved away from the moon and the hunt's path veered close towards the lochshore, he could see clearly they were bareheaded. Each rider was a horned man, and the horns were sharp and terrible. Above them, raced the shadow riders, insubstantial phantoms, but just as determined to play their part in the Hunt. Onwards they charged, speeding through the air. The mouths of the pale horses stretched, foam flecked as their ghastly riders urged them forwards. And there, at the front, were two horses—one grey, one white—rising above the causeway, pale hooves skimming the waves of the loch. Their riders were women, bareheaded and uncloaked, their long tresses streaming out behind them as they rode onwards, faster and faster, determined that the deer would not escape.

Agravaine realised that he was holding on to his brother's arm, gripping him tight as they stood on the threshold, staring with astonished eyes at the figures in the sky. For the woman who was leading the hunt was his mother, Morgause, and behind her was Anna, a look of grim determination on her face and the bow of a huntress strapped upon her back. Hardly able to believe their eyes, the two boys swivelled round and there, silent and unmoving, the two women still sat, heads bowed low across the table, their shoulders rising and falling almost imperceptibly, with the measured breathing of deepest sleep.

The hunt had almost passed now, but Agravaine could still see the fleeting form of the doe as she ran desperately towards a scrubby copse of trees upon the headland, perhaps hoping to find shelter and safety beneath their branches.

He couldn't remember whether he or Gawaine had first stepped over the threshold, forgetting the warnings they had been given to remain within the house, but soon they were running together, following the hunt, leaving the two women alone at the fireside in their strange, silent sleep.

Rather than taking the path chosen by the riders of the Wild Hunt, who were keeping close to the lochshore, the two boys ran across country, heading towards the small clump of trees where they had last spotted the deer. Above them, the spectral horses raced and reared. One rode in close to Agravaine. He could see the rider, pale and emaciated, and his mouth twisted in a snarl. His face was grey, the skin stretched taut across his bones, but his lips were full and red as blood, and when he opened his mouth, Agravaine could see strong white teeth, each hard and sharp, and filed to a point. The rider reached out his arm, pale fingers with long, yellowed nails clawing at Agravaine's cloak as if to pull him up into the sky. But Gawaine had seen the danger and had moved quickly, pushing his brother to the ground just in time, so that the rider's claw-like fingers had closed on nothing but air as his horse carried him upwards and away.

Shaken, but still determined to find out what was happening, the two boys ran to the edge of the thicket. The dogs had done their work well and the deer had stopped running. She was standing, eyes wide with terror, her haunches hard against a tree trunk, the hounds milling round her and baying, nipping at her flank if she tried to push past them. The Wild Hunt was almost on them, and not wanting to be seen, the two boys had hidden themselves as best they could in a small ditch behind a clump of gorse bushes. The huntsmen reined in their horses and stood, strangely silent, watching the terrified animal, but not making a move towards it. Above them, the spectral sky riders were also still, their horses stamping noiselessly on the air, whinnying and snorting as they recovered from the chase.

As the boys watched, two of the horses, one white and one grey, came forwards. The woman on the white horse, the one who looked just like their mother, dismounted and the dogs fell back, becoming silent as she passed. The woman on the other horse remained in the saddle. Raising her bow, she put an arrow to the string and took aim.

Her aim was true, and the deadly flight struck the doe on her flank, causing her to tumble and fall heavily on to the bracken. The dogs continued to circle her, but to the boys' surprise, did not move in for the kill, and as the woman with the face of their mother walked towards the fallen creature, the dogs fell back, their tails down and heads held low as she passed.

The boys crept closer, still under cover of the hedgerow, and watched the woman pull a short, cruel-looking dagger from her belt. She raised it high, holding it above her head with both hands. It glinted in the moonlight, and the woman closed her eyes, her lips moving, uttering words the boys were not close enough to hear. And then she thrust downwards, plunging the knife into the deer's throat, dragging it sideways, almost as if she wished to sever the neck from the body as the creature's lifeblood spewed upwards in a dark, sticky fountain. As they watched, a change came upon the creature. Its features seemed to shimmer and shift and suddenly, they were no longer looking at the face of a roe deer, but that of a girl, staring at them with wide, terrified eyes, her mouth stretched open in a silent, petrified scream.

They recognised her instantly. It was Aileen, one of the kitchen maids, a pretty wench who had a reputation for being rather generous with her favours. But she was not pretty now, and Gawaine had looked away, frightened and repulsed by this strange half-human creature. Agravaine crept closer, his curiosity and determination to see what his mother was doing far outweighing any sense of revulsion. She was kneeling now beside the creature, her head slightly on one side as she watched the blue eyes glaze over, and the blood oozing from the gaping wound slowly cease to flow as its heart stopped beating.

She had been joined by the other woman, the archer, who reached forwards, dipping her fingers in the pool of blood. The woman who looked like Morgause turned her face towards her companion and smiled. Reaching out her hand, she took the other woman's fingers in hers and smeared the blood across her face, drawing lines of red across her high, pale cheekbones. Then she had opened her mouth and held the fingers to her lips. Gently, delicately, with a look of delicious pleasure on her face, she licked away the remaining droplets. When she was done, they leant towards each other and their mouths met in a kiss that seemed both tender and triumphant.

Agravaine could not tear his eyes away and tried to move closer still. He had pushed himself forward, over the soft, slightly damp bracken, but as he did so, his elbow caught on an old branch, and it snapped beneath him. The sharp noise broke the silence and the eyes of the woman who looked like his mother flew open and stared directly at him. Horrified, Agravaine at first felt himself unable to move, furious with himself for being so careless, dreading what his mother would do to him for having disobeyed her.

And then something happened that he would never have expected. The woman had thrown back her head and laughed, loudly and exultantly.

There was no joy or happiness in the sound, and it sent shivers of cold fear racing through his body. But now that their eyes were no longer locked together, Agravaine felt the strength returning to his limbs, and he pushed himself backwards through the hedgerow to where Gawaine was waiting. Without saying a word about what they had seen, the two boys turned away from the woodland and ran, racing fast across the uneven marshland, back towards the lochshore. The door of the old stone house was ajar, and they dashed inside, closing it firmly behind them, before making their way to the comfort of the hearthside and the last embers of the fire.

They had clattered into the house, paying little mind to the noise they were making, their breath coming in short, panting starts that they were unable to control. They had thought to find the place empty, but it was not. The two women, Anna and their mother, remained exactly as they had been when they had left them, slumped forward and motionless on the table. Gingerly, Gawaine moved towards them, one finger to his lips and his hand held out behind him, indicating to his brother that he should stay still. Agravaine was usually unwilling to follow his brother's commands, but on this occasion, he was only too happy to shrink back onto the settle. The older boy had reached out and touched his mother, his hand brushing the exposed skin of her pale, slender neck. It had been cold to the touch.

Gawaine had moved forward, splaying his fingers more widely in the hope of feeling the rhythmic pulsing of a vein. Agravaine had watched, the terror rising in his throat as he thought about what would happen next. How could they tell their father that their mother was dead? How would they explain what had happened, how they had come to be in Anna's cottage in the dead of night? And then Gawaine had gasped and uttered a single, strangled word, "Mother."

She had slowly turned her head and smiled up at him, reaching out to capture his hand within her own as she did so. Her mouth had been smeared with blood. The other woman, Anna, was now also awake and there was a look of triumph on their mother's face.

"Did you see her?"

"Yes, but I did not know her."

"She was but an ill-mannered chit from the kitchens. And now she will die?" Mother asked Anna.

"Aye, within three days," Anna had replied. "Once a Dream Hunter has taken her, there is only one conclusion."

Their mother had smiled and risen from the table, wiping the blood from her face with her sleeve. She walked towards the settle by the fire. "Well, my little men, you have seen at first hand one of the special gifts our Anna brought with her from Corsica. Now you have seen what it is to be a Mazzeri, a Dream Hunter. It is a power that even Avalon does not possess, and now she has given it to me."

"But what happened, Mother?" Gawaine had spoken quietly, uncertainly. "What did we see? You were here, but you were out there too." And Agravaine had been unable to help himself, blurting out. "Mother, the deer, what was it? I saw, I saw . . . a face, a human face . . . it looked like Aileen."

"I told you not to leave this room." Morgause had advanced angrily towards the boys and cuffed them both sharply, cutting Agravaine's face with her rings. But as they cowered away from her, she had suddenly laughed and reached out, rumpling Gawaine's hair and gently stroking the red weal on Agravaine's cheek.

"I should have known you would not obey me. You are brave boys, and I would not have you otherwise.

"So . . . tonight you ran with the Wild Hunt and saw the Mazzeri at work. As you witnessed, Anna and I did not leave this house. But we were there, in our dreams, as was that foolish child from the kitchens—Aileen did you say?" Agravaine had nodded.

"And once the prey has felt the Dream Hunter's knife upon their throat—or arrow in their heart—they have but three days to live.

"I do not know why she was chosen. She must have offended the Mother in some way. But we will have to find another girl to keel the pots."

"The Mazzeri do not choose their quarry. We are the servants of the Old Ones, and do their bidding," Anna had spoken quietly, "To be a Dream Hunter is a gift, but it is also a burden."

Morgause had laughed, "Perhaps to you it is a burden, because you have not sought to take control of the forces you wield. But that is not my way. I am of the royal line, and I will learn to command these powers in the name of the Goddess."

Anna had said nothing to this, and soon Morgause and the boys made their way homewards. As they walked towards the castle, they had seen a small group of dogs standing close together, silently guarding something by the side of the loch. It was the body of the deer. Agravaine had been surprised that the creatures had not been devouring the slaughtered doe, but when he mentioned this his mother had said, "The hounds recognise the scent of enchantment. This flesh is not for them, and nor is it for the pot. They will guard it tonight, and in the morning, I will send someone to dispose of it."

The three of them had walked on and said nothing more. When they reached the castle, their mother had kissed them softly on the mouth before sending them to their beds.

Agravaine could still remember the iron taste of blood lingering on her lips. Looking at the long thigh bone and rotten flesh that now lay at his feet, he shivered. As his mother had told them, the kitchen girl, Aileen, had indeed died less than three days after they had witnessed the Wild Hunt. For many months, the memory of the tortured deer with a human face had haunted his dreams and kept him from his rest. Did he want to witness this again?

The castle was not far away, and the glow of the fire in the Great Hall seemed very welcoming. He had almost decided to return to the comfort of his bed, when a sudden sound made him look out, across the causeway.

It came again, closer this time, a sharp, harsh noise that began as a bark, but which ended with a high, uncanny scream. Then he saw them, shadows racing across the causeway, two small creatures, red fur bloodied by the light of the moon, the tufts of white at the end of their tails shining clear in the starlight. And behind them, the hunt.

Through the standing stones they came, some on horseback, some running alongside, and as Agravaine stared, he realised that not all of them were human. There was a tall figure with powerful legs and a heavy, barrel-shaped body whose head was that of a bull, with long, fearful horns. Beside him raced a man on horseback, but in the strange, eldritch moonlight, his face was green. There were ivy leaves in his beard and hair and instead of a helmet, from his head appeared the antlers of a stag.

He knew without doubt that once again, he was in the presence of the Wild Hunt. On they charged, across the causeway, and at their head were two women, dressed in robes of white and silver. They were mounted on horses whose coats were blacker than midnight, and whose eyes shone blood-red in the light of the full moon.

Agravaine began to run, back along the loch shore to where his brothers were now stirring, pulled from their sleep by the clamour. Gawaine got to his feet, arms still tight around Gareth. The air was now rent with noise. The screams of the two foxes as they ran for their lives along the headland, the deadly bellowing of the man with the bull's head, the yips and barks of the hunting dogs, and above it, a sound that was to the boys the most disturbing of all, the shrill peal of their mother's excited laughter.

Gareth was huddled in close to Gawaine, arms around his elder brother's waist, face pushed into his chest. His shoulders were shaking and although there was too much noise for Agravaine to hear him, he was certain his youngest brother was howling with fear. Gaheris stood a little apart, but when he saw Agravaine he ran to him and flung his arms around him, his green eyes wide with terror in his small, pale face.

The hunt was getting closer now, the spectral horses with their skeletal riders swooping down across the lake like monstrous bats. Agravaine pulled his cloak tight around his brother and turning to Gawaine said, "I don't care what Mother says. This isn't for them; they are too young. We have to take them back before she gets here."

Gawaine nodded and the two older boys began to run towards the castle, holding their brothers' hands tightly to prevent them from falling as they raced across the rough marshland path towards the safety and warmth of the Great Hall. Agravaine, taller and more athletic, was the faster of the two. He also had the advantage of running with the slightly older Gaheris and the two of them had already reached the castle wall when the foxes, followed by a pack of baying, slavering hounds emerged from the coppice. Racing towards the loch, they cut straight across the rough pathway the boys had been following, and Gawaine and Gareth were trapped.

Grabbing his brother to him, Gawaine changed course, running back towards the thicket, hoping to take shelter in the bushes. The foxes were now racing along the lochside, hounds closing upon them and the riders of the Wild Hunt approaching fast from the causeway. The man with the head and horns of a bull was forcing his way through the thicket, bellowing as one of his horns became caught up in the brambles, causing him to almost stumble upon the sobbing and terrified Gareth.

The foxes were trapped now, penned against the water's edge, the hounds dancing and baying, running backwards and forwards, snarling and snapping. The riders of the Wild Hunt, led by the two women robed in white and silver, were circling slowly, ensuring there were no escape routes—nowhere for the cornered and desperate animals to run. The man with the head and horns of a bull took his place behind the dogs, pawing the ground with his heavily armoured boots. Gawaine could see the breath steaming from his flared nostrils as he threw back his head and bellowed to the moon.

The two women dismounted from their horses. Gawaine could not see their faces, but he thought the one to the right, who had just taken an arrow from her quiver and fixing it to her bow, was his mother. Suddenly, there was a disturbance. One of the foxes, finding courage in desperation, had run at one of the now riderless black horses, snarling and biting at its fetlocks. The horse had reared, and taking the chance, the two foxes made one last, desperate dash away from the lake, running back towards the thicket where Gawaine and Gareth were hidden. They had almost made the cover of the trees when two arrows flew towards them from the women's bows. Deadly and silent in the uncanny light of the heavy, red moon, both arrows reached their target, and the foxes fell, screaming, not three yards from the bushes that concealed the boys.

Gareth, held fast in his brother's arms had his face turned away from the scene, but Gawaine, despite his terror, was unable to avert his eyes. As he watched, he saw the faces of the dying animals change, becoming human in their final agony. With horror, Gawaine met the eyes of a man whose face he recognised.

It was Einar, a man he had known all his life, who had played with him as a baby and who had first taught him to wield a bow and ride a horse. Einar, his father's ward and cousin.

And now Einar would die within three days.

He glanced at the other face but didn't recognise it. Considerably older than Einar, this man had grey hair and a short, grizzled beard. The eyes that reached for his were blue and piercing, and despite his agony, his face looked noble. This was a man who had known command, and yet here he lay, brought low by the Mazzeri, and he too, whoever he was, would be dead within three days.

Struggling to his feet, Gawaine began to make his way backwards through the thicket, pulling Gareth alongside him. In minutes, they emerged on the far side, just a few hundred yards from the castle. With relief, they ran towards the security of its walls, where they could see Agravaine and Gaheris anxiously waiting.

But as they reached the threshold, they heard a voice calling from the lochside. "I see you, my boys, lurking in the shadows. Did I not tell you to wait for me, here, by the water's edge. Do you think to disobey me?" They saw their mother, once more on horseback beginning to move towards them. Her pale dress was now spotted with blood. Beside her rode the strange man from whose forehead sprung the antlers of a stag, his face dappled and uncanny in the unearthly light of the blood moon.

The boys did not dare to move. Gawaine and Agravaine stood, shoulder to shoulder, pushing the younger boys behind them to try to shield them. Their mother came nearer, but as she did so, the man riding alongside her reached out and took her hand. "Leave them," he said, quietly, but with a voice as deep and dark as the night sky. "They are but children. You are ambitious for them, but they are, as yet too young to learn the old ways." He raised her hand to his mouth and kissed it. "Leave them," he said again. "We have little time before night ends and the sleepers awake. There are things that you and I can do that are not for the eyes of younglings."

Morgause reached up and brushed the man's face, her fingers caressing his jaw and moving down to stroke his collar bone, his chest, his thigh. The boys heard him moan and saw him seem to shudder as, catching her hand, he pulled their mother roughly upwards, towards him.

Not waiting to see or hear anything more, Gawaine took Gareth's hand and pulled him through the archway into the castle courtyard. The boy was spent, almost dropping with fear and exhaustion. Agravaine and Gaheris followed them, and without discussing it, the four brothers made their way to their old nursery, instinctively wishing to stay together for comfort. The two younger boys got into their beds and fell asleep almost immediately. Gawaine and Agravaine sat down upon the hearthrug, covering themselves with their cloaks.

For a long time, they said nothing and just stared into the fire. Occasionally one of them would add a brick of peat, watching it burst into life, and then calm to a gentle smouldering glow, throwing flickering shadows onto the faces of the two boys. Eventually Agravaine said. "Who was it? Did you see?"

"Yes," Gawaine answered, "I saw them both. One was an old man. I don't know who he was."

"And the other?"

Gawaine did not answer.

"Gowie, who was the other? Not . . . not our father?" It had been a long time since Agravaine had called him by his old nursery nickname, and the older boy could hear the shudder of fear in his brother's usually casual voice.

"No. Not our father." Gawaine looked away. He had not even thought of that, and now he took some relief in reassuring himself King Lot was not in danger, and he, Gawaine, did not have to face the pain of his death, or assume the burden of kingship at such a tender age. But the loss of Einar was not a little thing.

Einar was as close to him and his brothers as any uncle and they all loved him. Gawaine reached out and placed his arm upon his brother's shoulder. "It was Einar, Agravaine. Einar."

He saw a look of shock and horror flash across his brother's face, and both felt their tears begin to well. They knew they could do nothing, and so they said nothing, but sat in silence watching the fire until Agravaine first, and then Gawaine, fell asleep.

THE VISION IN THE ROCK POOL

Next morning, all four boys were listless and unsettled. Their mother did not join them in the Great Hall, and there was no sign of Einar, who had a hearty appetite and could usually be relied upon to break his fast with gusto. None of the brothers were particularly hungry, and after eating a few mouthfuls of porridge they silently went their separate ways.

They all had lessons; Gawaine and Agravaine spent the morning with the armourer, learning more about the castle's weaponry and defences, whilst the younger boys spent two unhappy hours being tutored in the basics of addition and subtraction by Finn, the castle steward.

They were all required to spend some time each day practising at the archery butts, and usually they enjoyed this, even though Gareth still found it hard to string his bow. But none of them could concentrate and all felt nothing but relief when the sergeant at arms indicated that they had done enough and could go. It was a beautiful morning, so they decided to beg bread and cheese from the kitchen and spend the rest of the day out of doors.

Normally, they would have headed towards the causeway and the great standing stones of the Ring of Brodgar, but they all had a strong reluctance to retrace their steps from the previous night. Instead, they turned westwards, taking the path that ran alongside the shore of Loch Stenness, heading towards the sea. The water was calm, flat and blue, reflecting the cloudless summer sky.

So far, the boys hadn't said anything at all about what they had seen and heard on the loch shores beneath the Hunter's Moon, and the atmosphere between them was strained and uncomfortable. Gawaine could see how much the experience had unsettled his two younger brothers and was trying to find the right words to begin the conversation when Agravaine preempted him.

"Well, shrimps, how did you like your first serious taste of our mother's magics?" His tone was amused and condescending and Gaheris, always mindful of his desire to appear more grown up than he was, bristled instantly. "I would have liked to have seen more of it. I wish you hadn't pulled me away just when it was getting interesting."

"That's not the way it looked last night. I've never seen a sorrier bundle—perhaps excepting Gareth. You were so terrified I'm surprised your breeks remained dry . . ."

"And I've never seen anyone run as fast as you did, Agravaine," responded Gawaine. "You had no mind to stay and enjoy the spectacle, so don't make Gaheris feel bad about it."

"I still don't understand what was going on," said Gareth. "Who were those people and why did they look so strange? That man, with the head of a bull, and the other one, with the green face and antlers like a stag. Who are they, and what have they got to do with our mother?"

"Oh, our mother is a very unusual and powerful person," said Agravaine, his words managing at the same time to be both mocking and respectful "You know that her mother, the Queen Igraine, was raised on the Isle of Avalon and her sister—our aunt Morgan—is second only to Vivian, the Lady of the Lake."

"Yes," said Gaheris. "I know all that, and I know about the Goddess, and Avalon and the Lady of the Lake, but last night was different. Mother lets me help her with the scrying bowl sometimes, and I like that. It's fun to see things in the water. But last night, that wasn't fun. That was scary."

Gawaine reached over and ruffled his younger brother's hair. "She let me have a go at the scrying a few years ago, but I was no good, couldn't see a thing beside my own reflection. Mother said the magic chooses you; you don't choose the magic, and I am, very clearly, one of the unchosen!"

"She hasn't let me try yet," said Gareth. "She told me that I could have a go at Solstice, but I don't know if I want to. I don't think I like the magics. I don't understand them, and . . . I'm scared."

"Oh, don't be silly," said Agravaine. "Magics like the scrying bowl aren't dangerous. I really like it. I just wish I could do it more often. It only seems to happen when I do it with Mother. I can't make it work by myself."

"I still don't understand," said Gaheris. "The scrying bowl seems safe, but magics like last night are different. Why is Mother doing scary things like that?"

"I think what happened last night is a very peculiar sort of magic," Gawaine replied. "A few years ago, Mother took me and Agravaine to Anna's house, down by the loch, and the same thing happened. They went into some sort of trance, and then those creatures, the hunters, were there, and they chased a deer out along the causeway, and then they killed it. But when it died its face changed. It became human."

"Yes," said Agravaine. "It was one of the kitchen maids, I don't remember her name. But you'll never guess what, a couple of days later, she was dead."

"That's horrible," said Gareth, shivering despite the warmth of the sun. "But that didn't happen last night, did it? It was just a hunt. No one changed into anything, just those poor foxes . . ."

Agravaine was about to speak, but Gawaine held up his hand. "No, nothing like that happened last night." He looked warningly at his sharp-faced brother and shook his head. "Come on, let's find somewhere to sit. I'm hungry." The boys scrambled over the boulders until they found a rock pool, ringed around with large, flat stones that made a very pleasant place to rest.

They ate their bread and cheese, every now and then picking up stones and skimming them over the still waters of the loch. Gareth, though the youngest, was particularly good at this, and Gawaine could see that he was starting to relax and forget the terrors of the previous night. He was more than a little annoyed therefore when Agravaine said, "Do you think Mother will still be angry with us when we get back?"

"I don't know," said Gawaine. "We didn't really do anything wrong. That man, the one with the green face, he told her to leave us alone. Maybe she'll listen to him."

Agravaine snorted at the idea of his mother doing anything that she didn't want to do, even if a man with a green face and antlers had suggested it.

"I know," said Gaheris. "If Mother wants us to know more about the magics, why don't we try some?"

"What do you mean?" asked Gawaine.

"We can try to scry—we know you're useless at it—but Agravaine is quite good, even if he does need help." As he spoke, Gaheris dodged out of the way of a punch that Agravaine was trying to land. "And Gareth hasn't ever had a go. Maybe if we can find out something interesting, and tell her about it, she'd be happy."

"And what makes you think that you can do it?" said Agravaine. "I'm older than you and I can't do it on my own."

Gaheris gave a sly giggle. "Well, I know that I probably shouldn't have been doing it, but I've tried a few times on my own, and I always see something. I'm not always sure what I'm seeing. Last time it was a beautiful lady, a lot like Mother but with dark hair. And a man, old, with grey hair and blue eyes. It's fun. I think we should do it."

Gawaine thought it a rather ridiculous idea, but not wanting to hurt his little brother, decided to keep his mouth shut. Agravaine was torn between a desire to do it and resentment that his younger brother clearly believed that he had mastered the art of scrying. Gareth remained silent, taking his lead from Gawaine.

"Well," said Gaheris. "What do you think?"

"Even if we did try, what are we going to use?" asked Agravaine. "None of us happens to have brought a large bowl with us, and all we are likely to find out here are old lobster pots."

"We don't need a bowl," said Gaheris. "Mother told me that all you need is a flat surface that you can see into. She told me that her mother had used a mirror once and that it could even be done with a shield, if it's well polished. Look." He pointed down at the surface of the rock pool. "The water is flat and still. We can use this."

All four boys looked down and gazed at their reflections. Gawaine was sitting next to Gareth, their two red, curly heads touching. Agravaine was on the other side of the pool, a supercilious smile on his lips as he looked sceptically into the water. Lastly, Gaheris, sitting just beyond Gareth, staring fixedly into the rock pool with a look of happy expectation on his face.

"We need a question," said Gaheris. "You have to ask the Goddess to answer a question for you, and if you are in her favour, she will grant you a vision. Mother said that you need to remember the vision may be of something that has already happened, or something from the future. And she said that it can either be a prediction or a warning. That means that it could be something that will happen, or something we can change. I didn't really understand. But that's what she told me."

"All right." said Agravaine. "Why don't we ask when Gareth will get big enough to string his own bow without needing one of us to help him?"

"Don't be stupid," said Gawaine. "I'm not at all sure that this is going to work, but I'm pretty certain the Goddess isn't going to waste her time on trivial matters like that. And in any case, I seem to remember that you were at least eight before you could string your own bow. No, if we are going to do this, we should ask something that will interest our mother, something that nobody else could tell her."

Agravaine looked sulky, but he knew that Gawaine was right.

"I know," said Gareth. "Why don't we ask her for news of her sister, the Lady Morgan. She hasn't seen her for a long time, and I know she thinks of her often."

The boys agreed that this was a good idea and so, following Gaheris' instructions, they took their places in a circle around the pool, kneeling on the sand and placing their linked hands on the rocks surrounding the water. By now, it was late afternoon, but the sky was still blue and cloudless. There was no wind, and the surface of the pool was utterly still as Gaheris—his eyes closed, his young voice urgent and entreating—began to speak. "Goddess, please hear us, we ask a question not for ourselves but for our mother. Goddess, please tell us . . . what news of Avalon and the Lady Morgan?"

The boys were silent, and in the distance across the loch they heard the whistling stutter of a curlew's call. Nothing was happening.

Gaheris tried again. "Goddess, I know we are young and only boys, but please, we ask for our mother. What news of Avalon and the Lady Morgan?"

Again, the curlew called, and Agravaine looked impatiently across the pool to Gawaine. He was just about to speak, just about to pull his hands away, when the water in the pool began to move. Slowly at first, it rippled. A gentle motion causing small wavelets to form, splashing against the rocks, and then the water began to churn. A whirlpool formed at its centre, spinning faster and faster, foam flying up and splashing the faces of the watching boys. And then, just as suddenly, it stopped. The surface cleared and there, just below the water's surface, an unfamiliar scene appeared. Within the pool the skies were dark, with faint colour at the horizon, suggesting it was either dusk or daybreak.

They were looking at a small encampment, with tents and makeshift stables. All around were horses and soldiers, men busying themselves cleaning weapons and grooming their mounts. The boys looked closer as the vision rippled and changed, taking them onwards, into one of the tents. Up to now, the vision had been silent, but as the scene within the tent steadied itself, the boys began to hear noises: the whinnying of horses, the sounds of men calling out orders.

As the scene shifted again, deeper in and closer to centre of the tent, these outlying noises became muffled, and they were able to hear the faint crackle and sputter of the fire and; just above this, the voices of two people talking quietly and low.

"And how does he fare? Do you see any improvement?" The speaker was a man, with a long, deftly plaited white beard, whose face seemed younger than his white hair would suggest. From this, and from the grey robes and the staff upon which he was leaning, the boys knew him to be a druid. He was standing next to a bed upon which a figure lay, swathed in blankets and motionless.

"No, if anything, he worsens. I have done my best, but I think this sunrise may well be his last." This was a woman's voice and seemed to be coming from the other side of the bed, deep in the shadows.

"That is not good enough. What magics have you tried to break the enchantment? Vivian told me that you were at least her equal, but I am beginning to have my doubts."

"Merlin, you are a fool. This is not magic. Do you not think, with all the protections we have woven round him, with the full might of Avalon defending him, that Uther could be laid low by spells or enchantments?" As she spoke, the woman came into view and all four boys gasped to see their mother's face. But where their mother was golden, this woman was pale, with white skin and a cloud of midnight black hair. The boys knew without doubt who she was, although Gaheris and Gareth had been but babes when they had last seen her. This was their mother's sister, Lady Morgan, the enchantress of Avalon.

She approached the bed and, lowering the blankets that covered the silent, unmoving figure, placed her hand beneath his chin and, none too gently, pulled his face towards her. His eyes were open and his pupils unnaturally large. The boys could only just make out a faint ring of the palest blue at their very edge and Gawaine felt his blood run cold as he recognised the face he had seen upon the dying fox, the night before.

"See, his pupils are dilated and, before I administered a sleeping draught, he was raving like a veritable lunatic." She moved forwards, pulling up his sleeve and exposing the flesh of his arm. It was mottled with an angry rash, scabbed and bloody with itching. She let it fall and turned to face the druid.

"He has been poisoned, and it has taken hold." Her mouth crinkled in a small moue of annoyance. "You called on us too late, Merlin. Had you summoned me yesterday, perhaps I could have done something, tried purges or emetics to void his system, but now, such rough treatment would only speed the inevitable."

The druid sighed and made his way to a small table, where he sat down and poured himself something from a pewter jug. "It is too soon. He cannot die now. We cannot afford to lose the Pendragon with the Saxons still abroad and the country rent by war." He raised the cup to his lips and drank deeply, not looking at the man on the bed or the woman who stood beside him, but staring fixedly ahead.

The woman bent to put the blankets back in place and then made her way to the table. "What are you drinking, Merlin? If I know you, it will be of the finest, and I feel in need of refreshment."

The druid did not look up but gestured to her to take a seat and pushed the jug and a second vessel towards her. She poured and drank, and poured again, before sitting down. "You and Vivian, you have done everything for Uther, smoothed his way, protected him, removed his enemies. But despite all this, he has failed you. Perhaps you backed the wrong horse, all those years ago. Perhaps you should have chosen Gorlois, chosen my father, the great warrior. And who knows, perhaps things would be very different now."

"Morgan, you call me a fool, but you now betray just how little you know and understand. Gorlois had his chance, he made his choice, and we could not unmake it. Your mother begged him to reconsider but he would not. He preferred the Risen God to the powers of the Goddess. He would not bend, and so what other option did we have?"

"And so, you had him killed and used your powers to allow Uther to assume his form, to deceive my mother and dishonour her." Though Morgan's words were dark, she spoke lightly, almost as if reciting a lesson. "And from that union, her bastard son was born, and I was sent away to Avalon."

"As I recall, you begged to leave Tintagel, to go with Vivian to the enchanted Isle."

"I was a child, Merlin, but four years old, when you and Vivian took me from my mother." Reaching for the jug, she poured herself another drink.

"Yes, 'tis true, but you were gifted, and Igraine, though beautiful, did not have the skills needed to teach you. Tell me, Morgan, do you not love the Isle of Avalon? Are you not proud of the gifts the Goddess has given you, the powers Vivian has nurtured within you and in which, by all accounts you now excel? Remember, if Gorlois had decided differently, he would not have allowed you to choose the path you now walk with such confidence and grace. He would not have allowed any schooling at all. You would have grown up learning nothing but tapestry and household management."

"I would have grown up with a mother and a father." Morgan was angry. Her voice was harsh, as she drained her cup, slamming it down upon the table, where it shattered.

Perhaps disturbed by the noise, there came a murmur from the bed. Merlin at once got to his feet.

"He stirs. Come, you must put aside the past. We cannot change it, and we must now think of the future."

They both approached the bed. The man within it was trying to sit up, his breathing short and laboured. Merlin reached behind him and helped to raise him against the pillows.

"Uther, my lord, will you take a glass of water?"

The man shook his head, raising his hand as if to shield himself.

"Here is the Lady Morgan, come from Avalon to help heal you." The man on the bed turned his head, with difficulty, to look at Morgan. "But she is … just a child." His voice was hesitant and strained "Where is Vivian? I would see the Lady of the Lake."

"Vivian is old, my lord, and no longer likes to travel, and the enchanted paths are too much for her now," Morgan spoke softly, and reaching out, placed her hand upon his head. "Uther Pendragon, I think you know I cannot heal you. The poison has taken hold, and nothing I or anyone can do to change its course. But I can help you on your way. You have always been a good servant to the Goddess, and she will smile upon you in your final hours."

Uther said nothing, but reaching out, he grasped her hand, tiny and slender in his own, and held it to his heart.

"You look so like her, so like your mother." He raised the hand to his lips and kissed it, before letting it fall. "Oh, how I loved her. There was never anyone for me but her. And maybe now, if the Goddess wills, my spirit will find her spirit, and we will, at last be together."

"My lord, there is still hope," said Merlin. "Despite what Morgan says, you seem to have regained some strength, perhaps . . ." His voice trailed off as he looked at Uther's face, ravaged by pain, and listened again to the agonised, tortuous breathing.

"No, Merlin, there is no hope." Though low, Uther's words were clear and spoken with decision. "And so, we needs must agree what to do to safeguard the future of this country. Where is the sword?"

"Caliburn? Why, it is in the trunk beside your bed, where you always keep it."

"Then you must shield it with your life. Send it to Avalon, defend it with magics and place it where it can only be used by the one who rules by right, by the will of the Goddess and with the consent of the people." This speech exhausted Uther, who sank back against his pillows, eyes closed, chest rising and falling rapidly as he fought for the breath to speak again.

"And what . . . what of the boy? What of my son?"

"He is safe, my lord, as I promised you, he would be." Merlin sighed. "I had hoped that he would come of age and come to court. Be welcomed by you, his father, and accepted as your rightful heir, through the will of the Goddess. But all these years, we have been at war, and the time has not been right."

The man on the bed made a strange noise. He was attempting to laugh, although this caused him pain. "All your schemes Merlin . . . all your planning. They have come to naught, and I am to die a failure. I have not brought peace. I have never known my son, and I lost the only woman I ever loved."

"But you did your duty."

"I did what I was told. Perhaps . . . I would have fared better . . . if I had simply . . . followed . . . my heart." And with those words, the man upon the bed, Uther Pendragon, High King of all Britains, sank back upon the pillows and breathed no more.

Morgan leant over and gently placed her fingers upon his eyelids to shield his eyes. "Strange," she said. "I liked him more this day, than I ever have before. I hope he will find peace, but his shade may have many years to wait before he meets my mother. Why did you never tell him that she lives?"

"If I had done so, he would have spent his life searching for her, rather than working to rule the kingdom and defeat our enemies."

"Yes, I suppose so. But I will tell her, when next I send news to Carbonek. And what now? There must be a regent, I suppose."

"We must call the allies together, to Caer-Lundein, as quickly as possible. Uther's death will unsettle everything, put hard-won alliances at risk. We must do all we can to bring stability, otherwise we give every advantage to our enemies."

"And who is your choice to assume his mantle? You cannot expect the Lords and allies just to roll over and welcome his little bastard, who you have kept safely out of sight all these years?"

"Arthur is young yet. Vivian and I have discussed this many times over the years and laid our plans long ago. There is only one man who can reign until the true heir is ready to assume his place. The regent will be King Lot of Orkney. You should prepare yourself, my dear. We will be summoning your sister and her husband this very night."

Hearing these words, the boys gasped and Agravaine jumped up, punching the air with his fist. The circle broken, the vision faded from the water, which once again showed nothing but the clear blue reflection of the cloudless skies.

"We're going to Caer-Lundein . . . Our father will be King . . . We're going to Caer-Lundein." Agravaine had grabbed Gareth by the hand, and both boys were dancing with delight, but Gawaine looked across at Gaheris, who seemed quite dumbfounded, and was perhaps a little dazed by the way the scrying had come to such an abrupt end.

"What have we seen, little brother? A vision of the present or of the future? Something true, or only something that might come to pass?"

"Gawaine, I do not know, but I think I was wrong to suggest this. Mother told me that the scrying bowl is always silent, but we heard everything, and I don't know how or why. We have seen things we probably should not have seen, heard secrets that are truly not for our ears. I do not think it was well done."

"Well, there is nothing we can do now to change it, but I agree. I have never liked to meddle with the magics and this has made me even more wary."

Picking up the empty knapsack that had contained their bread and cheese, Gawaine and Gaheris began to walk back along the shoreline, Agravaine and Gareth capering behind them.

But when they arrived at the castle, what they found there sent all thoughts of the scrying from their minds. The household was in turmoil, kitchen maids weeping as they went clumsily about their work, pages and ostlers moving silently through the house and stables without the calls and whistles that usually accompanied their duties. And in the Great Hall, where their father and mother sat side by side upon the dais, sad-faced and unspeaking, there was no fire burning in the grate,

On a bier beside the hearth was a body, still wet from the waters of the loch. Einar, Lot's ward and cousin, kind-hearted, laughing Einar, who had taught the boys to swim and ride, and who, perhaps had loved his queen too well, was dead.

CHAPTER FOUR

A MOTHER'S UNDERSTANDING

After a day of troubles, the castle was now quiet, but Morgause could not sleep. She got out of bed, pulling her robe tight around her, and finding comfort for her feet in the warmth of her slippers. The last few hours had been particularly tedious and unpleasant, and she could not get her mind to settle.

The day that she now knew marked Einar's last on earth had not begun well. The combination of her experiments with the Mazzeri, followed by her private revelries with the leader of the Wild Hunt had left her jaded and overwrought, and she had risen late and ill-inclined for company. By the time she had made her way to the Great Hall, it had been thankfully almost deserted, and she had sat alone, breaking her fast with small beer, bread and honey. As she ate, her feelings of anger towards her children solidified and began to gain strength.

How dare they treat her so shabbily, and with such little respect? She was Morgause, Queen of Orkney, the proven mistress of the Dream Hunters, commander of powers that even her sister, the enchantress, did not possess. All she had wanted to do was share the magics with them, show them that their mother was a person to be reckoned with, even if she had not had training in Avalon. But when she had sought to share with them the glory of her achievement, her sons had shown nothing but weakness and shabby cowardice. They had humiliated her before the warriors of the Wild Hunt, behaving like scared children rather than scions of the blood royal, and had added further insult to injury by running away.

In her mind's eye, she saw them again; four terrified youngsters, clinging to each other in the uncanny light of the blood moon. Her bluff boy Gawaine keeping Gareth, the youngest, close to him, always seeking to protect, whilst Gaheris, desperate to be grown up, attached himself to Agravaine, the sharpest, if not the kindest of the bunch. She softened slightly. They were her boys, and she loved them. They just needed to realise what opportunities she was offering them; chances to see and do things that she had never been given.

Unfortunately, this mellowing of mood was undermined slightly when Morgause asked Avice to bring the boys to her and had been told that they'd taken food from the kitchen and gone out for the day. She'd wanted to talk to them about the previous evening. She'd been too far away to witness the faces of the dying foxes as they transformed into human form, and so was uncertain if her plans to make use of the Dream Hunters had, in fact come to fruition. She wanted to question Gawaine and Gareth closely, to find out what they had seen, and if their testimonies were as useless as she feared they might be, she planned to send Agravaine—the most fleet-footed of her children—with a message to Anna at the cottage.

Still, at least on that score she had received an answer—and more swiftly than she would have thought possible. She knew that the Mazzeri's victims could possibly remain alive for up to three days after their dream-self was vanquished by the Dream Hunters, but death had come more swiftly in this case.

Before the sun had travelled far upon its afternoon descent, the castle had been thrown into disarray by the arrival of a small procession of fishermen carrying their sad and sodden burden into the Great Hall. Einar's body had been found at Firth Bay, on the shore of Loch Stenness. He was fully clothed, and his body had no visible injuries. No one had reported seeing him since the previous afternoon, and it was assumed that he had gone night fishing—a thing he was known to delight in—and had somehow got into difficulties and drowned in the still, cold depths of the saltwater loch.

The rest of the day passed rapidly and, for Morgause, in a flurry of seemingly endless organisation and activity. Einar had been well loved, and the shock of his death had brought forth an outpouring of grief that affected everyone from Lot and his sons down to the lowliest of the pot-boys and scullery maids.

It would seem that he had not been in the water long. His face and body were not waxen or bloated, and there had not been time for him to have become the victim of carrion birds or other despoilers of corpses.

He was still beautiful.

His eyes had been closed, his face peaceful, mouth settled in its usual expression of a rueful half-smile. His hair, drying gently in the warm summer air, fell soft and long around his shoulders.

Morgause could not bear to look at him.

She had given orders for the body to be purified and prepared for ritual burial, which would, by local tradition, take place at sunset on the following day. She had spoken with Finn, the castle steward, and made plans for the immediate preparation of funeral baked meats and the building of the pyre upon the headland, to be lit in Einar's honour and to give thanks to the Goddess.

She had sent word to his family in Norway, and to Lot's brother, Urien, a soldier with Uther Pendragon's army. Einar had been his page boy when he had first arrived in Orkney, and he deserved to be told what had befallen the young boy he had taken under his wing.

The work had been tiring and thankless, and it seemed as if no one else had the wit or willingness to do it. Next, she had instructed Angus, the castle's sergeant at arms, to instigate a search for Einar's boat, and to talk to the fisherfolk and loch dwellers to see if there were any witnesses to the accident. She told them that she wanted their findings on the morrow and would reward generously anyone who could shed light on what had happened.

Finally, she had ordered that the fire in the Great Hall be lit, and supper prepared. She ordered casks of ale to be broached and had flagons of mead and wine brought to the table. Once she had done this, unwilling to be drawn into the roister of an impromptu wake, she had made her way to her chamber.

Several hours passed before, finally, Lot had come to bed and had tearfully fumbled with her, quickly satisfying himself and falling into a mercifully silent slumber. The coupling brought her neither pleasure nor relief.

Now, the night was quiet save for the occasional call of a night-bird seeking its quarry, and the gentle lapping of the waves. The moon, still full, but no longer red, shone brightly across the loch and the tall stones of the Ring of Brodgar, and gave enough light for Morgause to find her way about the castle without a candle. She realised that she was hungry, but still feeling a strong desire for solitude, decided not to visit the kitchen, where even at this hour there would be servants at work preparing the bread and making ready the funeral roasts. Instead, she made her way to the Great Hall, hoping for leftovers.

She was in luck. In normal circumstances, Finn would not have allowed such slapdash confusion, but Einar's death had disrupted much of the castle's habitual routine. Cloths soiled by grease and spilled ale still lay across most of the tables. Platters of uneaten food were piled higgledy-piggledy around the room. She would have serious words with him in the morning. Finn was normally most assiduous in his duties, and he would not be pleased that his queen had been made aware of this dereliction. Nevertheless, the shortfall had worked to her advantage, so perhaps she would not be too harsh when she spoke to him.

She smiled to herself, thinking of the stewards' future discomfiture, and turning up her nose at the half-eaten joints sitting unappetisingly in their congealed juices, she helped herself to bread and cheese. Making her way towards the fireplace, she intended to settle herself within the hearth seat, where the remains of last night's fire still gave out a welcome warmth and light. She would be able to gaze upon the tawny embers as she ate, and take stock. But as she approached, she saw that someone had got there before her.

Curled up on the deep stone bench built into the walls of the vast fireplace was a sleeping figure. It was lying on one side, knees hugged to chest and tightly wrapped in a blanket that revealed only a shock of red hair, a snub nose and a pale, freckled forehead.

Gawaine.

Her eldest child, born within the first year of her marriage to Lot, sent to her by the Goddess when she had been but sixteen years old. He would be fourteen at his next birthday, and he really should have been in bed, in the chamber he shared with Agravaine at the top of the West Tower. What, she wondered, had dragged him from his bed on this of all nights? Being careful not to wake him she edged in beside him and seated herself with her back to the hearth wall. Feeling a stab of hunger, she bit hungrily into her food, only to find that the bread had gone stale, and the cheese tasted well past its best.

In her annoyance, she hurled the wooden trencher and its contents into the fire, inadvertently causing a surge of heat. Without even thinking about what she was doing she reached out and placed her hand over Gawaine's exposed forehand to shield him from the flames. At her touch, he stirred, his sleep-filled eyes flickering in and out of focus. Clumsily, because his legs were wrapped tightly in his blanket, he tried, with little initial success, to right himself.

"Mother . . . Mother . . . where are we? Why are we here?"

"Shush, child. We are in the Great Hall. I am here because I had little supper, could not sleep and was hungry. But what brought you here, I know not."

Gawaine finally managed to scrabble backwards until he was seated at the opposite edge of the hearth seat, with his back against the wall. He crossed his legs in front of him and despite the warmth of the fire, he pulled his blanket tight around him. She could see his feet and legs were bare.

"I couldn't sleep, and the moon was so bright . . . there was no rest for me in my chamber."

"Is that all it is, Gawaine? Are you sure that there is not something troubling you? Something you should tell your mother?"

But he said nothing, hanging his head to avoid catching her eye.

"Gawaine, because of that terrible business with Einar, we have not spoken of the events you witnessed. The Wild Hunt, the two foxes and what became of them. Do you remember?"

He didn't move, just pulled his blanket more tightly around him.

"I had hoped to talk to you yesterday, but when I sought you out, it was to be told that you and your brothers had made yourself scarce. Running away rather than face me, were you?" As she spoke, she reached out and prodded him teasingly, but none too gently, with her slippered foot.

"Come on, Gowie, you're not scared, are you? A big brave boy like you . . ." As she spoke, she leant forwards and tickled his foot, making him squirm and, almost despite himself, giggle. She lunged again for his toes, tickling with one hand, pulling at his blanket with the other again in a mock tug-of-war until Gawaine responded and for a short while, mother and son romped together on the bench until Morgause suddenly let go and Gawaine crashed backwards into the wall, his blanket clasped tightly in his arms.

"You'll have to get up even earlier than this to get the better of me, Gowie . . . but still, that was a good effort. Now tell me, why couldn't you sleep? Was it Einar?"

"Sort of." For the first time, Gawaine raised his face towards his mother. "We knew it would happen, me and Agravaine, after what we saw . . . after last time . . ."

"You mean after the last hunt? The kitchen maid?"

Gawaine nodded, and blinked, desperate not to cry in front of his mother. "Yes. We saw her face. On the deer, just before it died. And this time, on the foxes . . . we saw Einar . . . and we knew it would happen."

"You and Agravaine saw this?"

"No. Just me. I was with Gareth, but I made him shield his eyes, so he didn't see the foxes die. But I told Agravaine afterwards. And so, we knew."

"And the other fox . . . did you see what happened to him? Did you see the other face?"

Gawaine nodded but said nothing. He pulled his blanket even more tightly around him, and rubbed his eyes.

Morgause persisted. "Who was it? Tell me, Gawaine. I need to know."

"I'd never seen his face before Mother . . . and I don't care about him anyway. He was just some stupid old man. But why did Einar have to die? Why Einar? We loved him . . . and . . . and it's just not fair." Despite all his efforts, Gawaine finally began to sob.

For a few seconds, Morgause looked at her son, sitting, huddled into the corner of the hearth-bench, legs crossed, chin tucked into his chest, thin shoulders shaking as he cried tears he had hoped to contain but could no longer control.

At first, she had just looked at him, her face hard and unforgiving.

"Fair. You expect things to be fair. I cannot believe that I would ever live to hear a child of mine say anything so ridiculous. Do you think it was fair that I was sent away from my home and my family when I was younger than Gareth is now? Do you think it fair that I had no mother to protect me, no father to guide me . . . whilst you, you have everything . . . and still you complain."

As her tongue lashed out at him, he shrank further into himself, a pitiful man-child, weeping for his loss.

For a while, neither of them spoke. And then she sighed and moved towards him, reaching out to take him in her arms.

"Hush, Gowie, hush now. No, of course it's not fair."

At first, he struggled against her, holding himself stiff and resisting her encircling arms, but then, with a slight shudder, he gave in and let her hold him to her, to rock him gently, as if he were still a little boy of five or six.

"As you grow to manhood, you will realise that very little in this life is fair. I know it is hard for you to understand, sweeting, but part of growing up is learning to accept. As I did. As you must.

"The Goddess sends us the fate she sees fit, and it is for us to thank her and make of it what we can." She stroked his red hair, feeling it coarse and curly between her fingers, just like his father's.

"It is well that you weep for Einar. He was your kinsman, and you have much to thank him for. But do you think he would want you boys to go about with long faces because the Goddess has called him home?" Gawaine said nothing, but his tears began to subside.

"That's better. Now, I have something that I think will please you. You are but thirteen I know, and not yet a man, and normally, the honour of lighting the funeral pyre would be given to those much older than you. But I shall speak to your father and tell him that you are old enough to comport yourself with dignity and are ready to take on some of the duties that will fall to you as eldest son and heir to the kingdom of Orkney. I will suggest to him that you should be the one to walk by his side in the procession, and that to you should be given the honour of lighting the first flame. Would you like that?"

"Do you mean it, Mother?" Gawaine looked up at her, his blue eyes still wet with tears, but a look of pride and excitement on his pale, freckled face.

"Aye, I do. But you must promise me that there will be no more tears."

He gulped and sought to take control of himself. "I promise, Mother."

"Good." Morgause gave him one final hug and released him. Moving backwards, she resumed her seat against the hearth wall and Gawaine, giving his eyes one last rub, crossed his legs and once again wrapped himself in his blanket.

"Now, we shall say no more on that subject. But there are other questions I have for you and now, I think, is as good a time as any."

"Yes, Mother." Gawaine was able to be calm now.

"Tell me about the other fox. You saw his face. Describe it to me."

"He was an old man, with grey hair and a grey beard. I had never seen him before."

"Is there nothing more you can tell me? You are a clever boy, observant . . . I'm sure you must have noticed more than that."

Gawaine hesitated. He knew that trying to hide anything from his mother was a fool's errand, but he was not sure exactly how to tell her about the scrying and what he and his brothers had seen.

"He had blue eyes, pale blue, and I had no idea who he was Mother, honestly I hadn't . . . but . . ." he paused, not sure how to continue.

"But . . . ? Come on, Gowie, you can tell me. I promise I won't be cross." She moved towards him and placing one hand on his shoulder, she cupped the other beneath his chin, raising his face until he was looking straight into her eyes.

"Listen to me, Gawaine, the magic of the Dream Hunters is old and strange and has powers that even I am still learning. I need to understand why they were abroad two nights ago and who they had been called for.

"There were two foxes; one was for Einar, and that is, as we both know, finished business. But who was meant for the other?

"I will speak with you frankly. There are just the two of us here, no one else in all of Orkney will hear what we say, and if you can help me, I will be grateful. I promise I will not be cross if you have broken a few rules, but I will know if you are keeping something from me, and I will not have disobedience. So tell me, Gawaine. Tell your mother."

He began hesitantly. "We did it for you, Mother. We knew you were angry with us because we'd run away from the Wild Hunt, and we thought we would do something that would make you proud of us."

"Go on."

"We decided to find out something you would like to know, to ask the Goddess to send us a vision."

Morgause gave a sharp bark of incredulous laughter. "You did what?"

"We asked the Goddess to give us news of the Lady Morgan. We asked it for you, because we knew you'd not had word from her for some months, and we thought it would make you happy."

She laughed again. "I can't believe I'm hearing this. Forgive me my son, but there is more aptitude for enchantment in the nail of my little finger than in the whole of you put together—and Agravaine isn't much better. And here you are telling me that you have been experimenting with the scrying bowl . . ."

"You're right. I know I'm useless, and to be honest, Mother, I really don't like it. But it wasn't me or Agravaine, it was Gaheris. And we didn't use a scrying bowl, but a rock pool, out by the lochshore."

And so, he told her of all that he and his brothers had seen and heard—the conversation between Merlin and the Lady Morgan, the anguished words of the dying King, Uther Pendragon.

When he had finished his tale, Morgause got up from her seat on the hearthside and made her way across the hall towards the great window that looked out across the loch towards the standing stones. After a while, Gawaine joined her. The sky was no longer dark, and although the last few, faint stars were still shining at the edges of the horizon, a new day was beginning.

"What you have told me is most unusual. I have never before heard of voices accompanying the visions the Goddess sends us. I will discuss it with Anna—but be that as it may, that is a moot point. What is important is the news you have brought me. Uther Pendragon is dead—or will be within the next few hours—and we are to be summoned to Caer-Lundein."

"Agravaine and Gaheris were very excited about travelling to the city, Mother."

"Well, I'm not sure if they will be coming . . . there is much for me to think on, and it is too soon for anything to be decided," Morgause spoke slowly, clearly wrapped deep within her thoughts. "But we get ahead of ourselves." She turned to face her son, and leaning down, placed a rare kiss upon his forehead.

"You have done well, Gawaine, and I thank you, but now, you should get back to your chamber. There is much to do today, and you will have a big part to play. You need to ready yourself and help your brothers with the preparations." Abashed and slightly embarrassed by this unaccustomed caress, Gawaine simply nodded, grabbed his blanket and made his way swiftly from the room.

Morgause returned to her place at the window, casting her eyes out beyond the causeway and then back towards the ancient stones. She was waiting for the moment at which the first rays of the sun would fall upon the tallest megalith, standing high and slightly raised above its fellows.

The sky lightened, rosy-pink turning to brighter orange, the clouds at the horizon lustrous and ablaze with the glories of the newly rising sun. As its rays shone, sharp and clear upon the stones, Morgause was gratified to see that she had been right. Exactly what she had anticipated was happening.

She looked on eagerly as the sunlight hit the surface of the ancient stone, which began to shimmer and deliquesce, the rough-hewn rock losing its substance and dissolving into formless vapour. As she watched, the elemental haze flickered and glowed with a pale, phosphorescent light, revealing the outline of a doorway through which she could just make out the entrance to a dark and poorly lit tunnel.

A visitor was coming, one of the very few who had the power to walk safely upon the enchanted pathways.

Morgause did not have to wait long before she saw the figure approaching. At first, she could make out just a shadowy shape, but as it came closer, she could see that it was a woman, walking rapidly and with purpose. Within a matter of seconds, the newcomer had made her way through the shimmering doorway, emerging confidently into the warming rays of the early dawn.

The woman gazed about her as if to take her bearings and, appearing to be satisfied, turned to look back the way she had come, nodding her head in a courteous gesture of both gratitude and dismissal. As she did so, the mists surrounding the tunnel entrance started to slowly drift westwards towards the loch. Once again, there was a shimmering, and when the air stilled, the entrance to the passageway had disappeared, leaving nothing but the rough, eternal surface of the sacred stone.

The woman, who was now making her way directly through the stone circle towards the causeway and the castle, was not tall, but very slender, and her hair fell long and loose around her shoulders. Looking up, she saw Morgause and raised her hand in greeting.

Morgause did the same, and then turned purposefully away from the window, making her way out of the castle, towards the courtyard to welcome her sister, Morgan, the enchantress, known to all as the Fae.

CHAPTER FIVE

WELL MET MY SISTER

As always when she visited her sister, Morgan was overcome with the beauty of the Northern Isles. She responded instinctively and with an almost visceral intensity to the magnitude and brilliance of the light, reflecting and rebounding between sea and sky, the fierce energy of the landscape, spare and sculpted in its minimal and essential purity. She loved the lack of fuss and prettiness, the subtle nuances of green and grey, the openness, the sense of being in the presence of powers older and more primal than anything to be found in the delicate, carefully cultivated gardens of Avalon.

Orkney was a place of unfathomed magic, woven deep within the island's core and buried, half-sleeping beneath the rock. She could feel it calling to her, in the pricking of her thumbs, and in the subtle, uncanny thrumming in her brain and blood that never left her when she visited her sister's court. She was sure the forces that dwelt here recognised her, acknowledged a kindred power, and she was certain that they wanted her to wake them.

And she was tempted, oh yes, she was tempted, but Morgan, unlike her older sister, was not impetuous. From an early age, people had been in awe of her, and many had been scared by the things she could do, without any guidance or tuition. Her powers and abilities had swiftly outstripped those of her mother, and at four years old, she had been sent to Avalon to study under Vivian, the Lady of the Lake, to learn discipline and control. And learn it she had.

To call these ancient magics to her, to explore them and master them was a challenge she found most attractive, but one that would require many days of work and preparation, and time was one luxury she did not have.

She had never discussed this with her beautiful, feckless older sister. Fond though she was of her, Morgan had little respect for Morgause as practitioner of the Goddess's arts. She had never been able to spend more than a day or so visiting the Northern Isles, and these visits had always been missions of state or ceremony. On these occasions it seemed to Morgan that her sister was concerned only with matters relating to her appearance, her children or, in the latter years, her romantic entanglements, giving little thought to the sacred rites and rituals beyond that which duty demanded.

Sometimes Morgan envied her sister for what she regarded as the relative simplicity of her life. To have a family, children, to be loved and honoured by a husband who all acknowledged to be a good man—such things would never be possible for one who walked the enchanted pathways. She had been sworn to the Goddess whilst little more than a babe in arms, and in her sixteenth year had freely made her vows of fealty and service. And the Goddess had rewarded her. Her powers now outstripped even Vivian's, and she was recognised as Lady of the Lake in all but name. She could command the wind to do her bidding and instruct the very waves to hold her weight, should she wish to walk across the waters.

Her pathway had been plotted whilst she was but a child, taken from her mother's care and raised to fulfill a high, but very lonely destiny. The vows she had taken meant that she would never feel a child quicken within her or hold her baby to her breast to suckle. She knew this and she accepted it. It was part of the price extracted by the Goddess; with power comes duty, and duty demands sacrifice. But there had been times over the years, as she watched her sister ripen and bloom, when she had held the first born—Gawaine—in her arms and he had grasped her finger and looked into her eyes with such trusting curiosity, that Morgan wondered if the sacrifice was more than she could bear.

As she hastened towards the castle, she recognised just how tired and travel-weary she was. She had not slept for two days, and the strain of navigating the enchanted paths had taken its toll on her body and spirits. She hoped that her sister would be able to provide her with somewhere to cleanse and rest herself before she had to deal with the practicalities of the business that had brought her to the Northern Court.

Given this, she was glad that Morgause was up and about, and she wouldn't have to waste time sending a servant to summon her. When she had first passed through the doorway in the standing stones and seen her sister standing at the castle window, she had thought it a little odd that she appeared to be watching for her, but she assumed that this must just have been a Goddess-given coincidence, and pushed it from her mind.

Within another minute she entered the castle courtyard and made her way towards the doorway—huge and forbidding, stoutly made of seasoned Highland oak and studded with iron. She saw the wicket gate open and her sister, dressed only in night clothes and a soft, fur-trimmed robe, stepping over the threshold, her arm outstretched in welcome.

"Greetings, Morgause, it is good to see you."

"Welcome, Morgan, you look weary, but then, with such news as you carry, I am sure you have not stopped for sleep."

The two sisters embraced, and before Morgause could step backwards, Morgan took her sister by the shoulders, gently holding her at arm's length. "What mean you?"

"Why, you come to tell us that the old villain is dead. Uther Pendragon, poisoned by the Saxons, and nothing that you, Merlin or all the powers of Avalon could do about it." Morgause smiled as she pushed Morgan's hands away.

"That surprised you, didn't it? You didn't think your silly fool of a sister had the means or the power to know what is going on in the big wide world, but things have changed, Morgan. Things have changed a lot."

"Hmm. I can see that." Morgan smiled and reached out her hand to touch her sister's cheek. "What hasn't changed is that you are still as beautiful as ever. In fact, I swear your eyes are brighter and your hair even more lustrous than when last I saw you."

"Don't change the subject. You are here because Uther is dead, and Lot is the only one who can hold the kingdom together. Yes?"

"Morgause, I don't know how you know this, but yes, you are right. Is Lot awake? Has he heard the news?"

"No, he will sleep awhile yet I think, and will have a sore head when he finally does wake up. His cousin and ward, Einar—perhaps you remember him—was found yesterday in Loch Stenness and Lot was not the only one to drown his sorrows. The funeral pyre is to be lit at dusk."

"That is sad news, indeed. I remember Einar as a boy, when we were children in Tintagel. And I think I am not wrong in saying that you had a very special . . . fondness . . . for him?"

Morgause frowned. "We were all fond of Einar, but let us not get distracted." Holding out her hand to her sister, she began to lead her into the castle.

"You look tired to the bone and I'm sure you would welcome the chance to rest. I have much to do to prepare for today's rituals and Lot will be good for nothing until at least noon."

Morgan smiled as she followed her sister. "I would also welcome a basin of water and some herbs for purification. I had little time to gather supplies before I began my journey and have nothing with me but the clothes on my back."

"I will send Avice to you, she is the housekeeper now and will be able to provide you with all you need. We may even have a gown of mine that could be altered to fit you, although you are so skinny that you might do better in some of Gawaine's hand-me-downs."

As they'd been talking, they had made their way into the Great Hall, where Finn was now overseeing the clearing away of the previous evening's detritus, clearly hoping to have had the task finished before his Lord and Lady appeared. After a few stern words of admonition, Morgause sent him to fetch Avice and arranged to meet him in the buttery in an hour's time to review the plans for the funeral.

"Now, I must dress and wake the boys. There is much to be done today." Morgause looked at her sister, who had settled herself on the window seat to await the housekeeper. Reaching out, she touched her gently on the tip of her nose, something she had not done since childhood.

"I'm glad you are here, Morgan."

"Are you, Morgause? That gives me pleasure."

"And I'm glad that man is dead, glad that he died unhappy and frustrated. Glad that everything he hoped for came to nothing."

Morgan looked startled. "Morgause, how do you know these things? You speak as if you were there, as if you had witnessed his death bed, heard his last words . . ."

Behind them they heard a small cough. Avice had joined them. Morgause quickly took charge.

"Now is not the time; you are tired and neither of us are at liberty for discussion. Let us wait until this evening, after the ritual. Most of the court will chose to continue their celebrations here, in the Great Hall, but I will order supper for the two of us in my solar, and we can then talk in private, and at leisure."

And with this, Morgan had to be satisfied.

WHILST MORGAN RESTED, MORGAUSE WORKED. She was closeted with Finn for over an hour discussing the detailed arrangements for the funeral. Einar would be buried in accordance with the rites and rituals of the Goddess, and at sunset, a great bonfire would be lit on the promontory of Loch Stenness. The flames would be tended through the night and would mark Einar's passing from this realm to the lands beyond.

News of Einar's death had spread rapidly across the Island's small communities, and Morgause thought it likely that several hundred people would make their way westwards along the lochshore to the burial site at Unstan, and then onwards to the promontory for the lighting of the memorial pyre. Although a handful would remain behind to tend the flames, the remainder would then make their way back to the castle, where they would need to be fed and watered.

"'Tis a lot to do, Majesty, and with very little notice." Finn was not happy. He had served in Lot's household all his life, travelling with him as a young man to the court of King Budic of Brittany, where they had fought together with Uther and his allies. He had been Lot's household steward for nearly thirty years and prided himself on the detail and rigour of his household planning. He did not relish the idea of opening his well-stocked storerooms and cellars to provide sustenance for scores of unplanned-for visitors.

"Yes, Finn, clearly it was inconvenient for Einar to go and get himself killed without checking first with the household calendar, but I'm afraid there is little we can do about it."

If the old steward was shocked by the irreverence of his queen's words, he did not show it. He had known her since her girlhood and had learned many years ago that there was little to be gained in crossing her. "It all just seems a bit rushed, Your Grace, that's all. It might have been better to leave it for a day or two, so we could have had more time to do it properly." Finn looked at her hopefully, wondering if there still might be time to postpone.

Morgause shook her head. "You forget, Finn, next week it will be Solstice. We do not want our celebrations to be overshadowed with out-pourings of grief—and we need to give Einar a burial with full honours. I see no reason why it should prove difficult to do so—we are well supplied, are we not?"

"Aye, Your Grace, we are—but if we use up too much this evening, we may find ourselves running short for Solstice."

"Then you must send to Shetland and the Isles to replenish. For good-ness' sake, Finn, must I think of everything myself? You know what needs to be done. Please do it."

"As you will, Majesty." Finn scratched his head and, with dutiful resig-nation, began to look around the buttery, deciding what should be set aside for this evening's feasting, and what should be allowed to remain.

Morgause got to her feet. "Good. I knew you would rise to the chal-lenge. And Finn, no need to put out much wine or mead this evening, ale and cider should be sufficient. And now, I need to speak with the sergeant at arms. I'll be in my solar if you need me."

Morgause went first to the Great Hall to see if her husband was there, and she was both unsurprised and reassured to find that he was still nowhere to be seen. A short conversation with one of the housemaids informed her that he had yet to break his fast, and she smiled a satisfied smile as she made her way to her solar; all was as she had hoped.

Lot wasn't getting any younger. He had ruled as King of Orkney and the Northern Isles for over thirty years, and had always prided himself on being able to beat any of his men at hand-to-hand combat—and to drink each and every one of them under the table. But she knew, even if he didn't, that, whilst he was still a fine figure of a man and a force to be reckoned with on the battlefield, he no longer had the same head for drink.

If he had not stirred by the time she had dealt with the sergeant at arms, she would send one of his pages to wake him, but for now, it was kinder—and more suited to her purpose—to leave him to his slumbers.

The solar was her room, warm and comfortable, and modelled as much as possible on her memories of her mother Igraine's private chamber in Tintagel. Like her mother, Morgause always kept a fire burning in the grate, but whilst Igraine, in warm and temperate Cornwall, had been able to burn logs of fragrant apple and rose wood, Morgause frequently had to make do with chunks of peat, whose sour smell she tried to mask with lavender.

Igraine's room had been made beautiful with wildflowers and woodland garlands even in the depths of winter; but it was only in the months of spring and early summer that Morgause could decorate her chamber with small posies of speedwell, veronica and campion. For the rest of the year, she displayed shells and beautiful feathers, and sometimes wave-sculpted driftwood washed up on the lochshores, but like her mother's loved and well-remembered room, the effect was both tranquil and pleasing to the eye.

Like her mother, Morgause always insisted that her room was well-stocked, with a crock of freshly made biscuits, a pitcher of spring water, which the house maid freshened daily, and a flagon of the best, most deli-cately spiced mead. She reached for this, and was about to pour herself a drink, thinking that its potent sweetness would calm and settle her, but then stayed her hand and instead, served herself a tumbler of cold water. The day was young, and she had much still to do—she owed it to herself to keep a clear head.

There was a knock at the door and calling out to bid whoever was outside to enter, she seated herself on the far side of a heavy wooden table. The door was opened by the maid she had spoken with earlier, who looked more than a little flustered. "Here's Angus noo, Your Grace, bit he's brought sae mony folk wi' him, ah don't think they'll fit in yer."

Looking up, Morgause saw a number of people clustered in the doorway: Angus, the sergeant at arms, accompanied by several of his men, a handful of loch dwellers, whose faces she recognised, but whose name she didn't know—and three people who were certainly familiar to her. Donal, the young boy from the lochside cottage, his father, the fisherman Cormac, and between them, appearing to not want to meet her eyes, was Anna.

Morgause caught her breath, and seeking to compose herself, got to her feet. This was not what she had expected. "How now Angus, what need you for such company?"

Angus manoeuvred himself to the front of the cluster, stepping over the threshold into the solar. "I'm sorry fur bringin' wae me sae mony fowk, Yer Majesty, bit Laird Einar's boat wis fun'd jest befo' sunset, and Erland and his family"—here he gestured to the small cluster of villagers standing nervously behind him—"wantae ken whit ye wid wish thaim tae dae wi' it?"

"And you needed to bring them all with you to hear my decision?" Morgause spoke quietly, but the displeasure in her voice was unmistakeable.

"Thay wanted tae come, yer majesty, it's a bonny boat, 'n' ainlie twa summers auld. Thay ken it wid normally be burned oan th' pyre, bit, weel . . ." but then Angus was interrupted by another voice.

"It seems sic a waste Yer Majesty. Laird Einar, he loved that boat." The new speaker was a tall young man, well-made and dark-haired, who pushed his way forward into the room, to stand next to Angus.

The young man continued. "Sometimes, he wid tak' me wi' him, 'n' we wid gang nicht fishing, or, whin th' waither wis richt, we wid catch th' win' 'n' chase th' seagulls."

"And you are?" asked Morgause.

"Arran, Yer Majesty. Erland is ma faither, 'n' Laird Einar, he wis mah friend."

"Your friend? That is quite a claim to make. He was a lord, the cousin of your king, and you, a humble fisherman."

"He wis mah friend. He talked tae me." Arran spoke quietly, raising his eyes to stare directly at the queen.

"Did he now . . . and what did you talk about, I wonder?"

"Mony things, Yer Majesty . . . 'n' some that micht surprise ye."

"Indeed . . . and can you share these with us?"

The young man was silent for a while, as if mulling over what to say next. Finally, and somewhat grudgingly he said. "Nay, Yer Majesty, a' he said wis tellt in confidence."

"Well . . . I'm sure there were no words of treachery or insurrection. I am certain that Einar was loyal to Lot and Orkney, and if he was bragging of his conquests with the fairer sex, well, such things were told in private—and it is in private, I'm sure you agree, they should remain." Morgause held his gaze, and it was Arran, blushing slightly, who was first to drop his eyes.

"Well, Einar was in many ways a law unto himself . . . but surely, you want to honour your friend in death? To give him a fitting memorial, a just tribute, to mark his time upon this earth and honour the Goddess."

"Well . . . aye Yer Majesty, o' coorse ah dae."

"But you think his boat, which by your own words you recognise he loved and cherished, should not be sent to him with his other possessions, burned upon the pyre?"

But before he could answer, yet another figure pushed her way into the room. "Yer Majesty, don't listen tae him." The newcomer was a tall, rangy woman, grey-haired and wiry, dressed in a faded and much darned woollen shift, her shoulders covered by the traditional Orcadian woven hood and stole.

"I'm sorry, Yer Majesty. I'm Bridie, Erland's mah man 'n' yon Arran's mah laddie. Don't listen tae him. Ah ken he wants th' boat, fur his da's is auld 'n' falling tae pieces, bit it isn't fitting. Th' boat shuid be burned. Tae honour th' Goddess. Anythin' else wid bring ill luck."

Arran glowered at his mother but said nothing, and Morgause, who had remained standing through the previous exchange, now resumed her seat. As she did so, her hand went, almost involuntarily, to the heavy silver amulet she had placed around her neck when she dressed that morning. Beautifully designed and intricately made, it showed the symbol of maiden, mother and crone, the three faces of the Goddess.

"I am glad to hear that at least one of you understands what is right and proper. Thank you, Bridie, your words do you credit. Now let us see if we can resolve this."

The older woman mumbled something Morgause couldn't catch, and placed her hands on her son's shoulder, as if to caution him to remain silent.

Morgause let the amulet fall free, and the light caught it, sending silver glisters onto the faces of Angus and the two loch dwellers. When she spoke, it was slowly, and clearly, a queen giving judgement.

"Lord Einar's boat is to be taken to the promontory, where it will form part of the pyre and will be burned tonight, along with Einar's other possessions, in memory of his name and . . ." her hand returned to the pendant, "to honour the Goddess."

Arran started, as if about to protest, and Morgause saw his mother further tighten her grip on his shoulder.

"That is not all. Lord Einar was a generous man, and he made friends with many. In recognition of his friendship for your son, and to say thank you for finding his boat and returning it to us so speedily, King Lot and I will pay for a new boat to be built for Erland and his family—on the condition that it is named in honour of the friendship between Lord Einar and your son."

Morgause looked directly at Arran. "It will be named *Friendship's Vow* and will be blessed and consecrated. I promise you that as long as you remain true to your vows to hold Lord Einar's words to you in confidence, you and your family will be favoured by the Goddess."

At this, there was another slight disturbance in the doorway as a stout man of medium height pushed his way into the room. The man, who Morgause assumed must be Erland, bowed low before her. "Och Yer Majesty," he said, his voice gruff with emotion, "bit yer as generous as yer bonny, how kin we ever gie ye thanks?" Turning from her, he proceeded to enfold his wife and son in his arms, hugging them to him in a tearful and joyful embrace.

"Angus, I think the business with Erland, his family and disposal of Lord Einar's boat has now been resolved. Please instruct one of your men to take them to the Great Hall for some refreshment and then arrange for the boat to be taken to the promontory. I will speak to Finn tomorrow about commissioning *Friendship's Vow* and you shall hear from him before Solstice."

At these words, Bridie immediately proceeded to bob and curtsey her thanks to Morgause and to hurry her husband and son from the room. Angus stepped out into the corridor, barking out his orders to his men, before returning to the solar.

"I'm sorry aboot that, Yer Majesty."

"What's done is done, and it has resolved itself well in the end. But I believe you have brought other people to see me?"

"Aye, Yer Majesty, th' fisherman Cormac 'n' his son Donal. Fae whit thay hae tellt me, ah think thay wur th' lest fowk tae see him alive."

"Well, bid them enter. Let us hear what they have to say."

◆ ◆ ◆

MORGAUSE FELT CONFIDENT THAT SHE now had nothing to fear from Erland and his family. They stood to gain too much, and she was certain that Arran would not repeat his rather clumsy attempt at blackmail. She rather felt that Bridie, his mother, wore the trousers in that household, and Morgause was certain that she would ensure her son kept *Friendship's Vow* to the letter.

Still, she mused, it would not hurt to keep a watchful eye on the lad, and if she had any concerns that his tongue was becoming too unguarded, she had ways and means to deal with that. Her main worry now was that Lot would waken from his alcohol induced slumber and insist on becoming involved in the investigation into Einar's death. It would be far more convenient for her if all the loose ends were tied up before he made an appearance, and she was increasingly conscious that the morning was running away with her.

She became aware that Angus was now ushering Cormac, Donal and Anna into the solar. As Angus closed the door and positioned himself in front of it, Morgause got to her feet, smiling warmly, and indicating to Anna that she should sit.

"Anna, my dear, as always, it is a pleasure to see you; and Cormac, Donal, you are welcome."

Anna took a seat as she was bid, whilst her husband and son arranged themselves somewhat self-consciously behind her. They were both aware that Morgause was a regular visitor to their house by the lochshore; indeed, Cormac was proud that his wife was on such terms with the Queen of Orkney, but he always absented himself when she visited their cottage, and this was the first time he had ever been in such close contact with her.

Like his son, he thought his queen was the most beautiful woman he had ever seen. This made him feel clumsy and awkward, conscious of his darned breeches and homespun tunic that, despite Anna's best efforts, was never completely free of the smell of fish.

Morgause, as always, was very aware of the effect she had on the men around her and smiled inwardly to see his embarrassment and confusion. She decided to be her most charming.

"I'm sorry I cannot find seating for all of you, but this is a small room, and I was not expecting so many people. Now, I understand you have something to tell me, something that has bearing on the tragic death of my kinsman Einar?"

Their tale was short and straightforward. Two nights ago—the night of the Hunter's Moon—Cormac had decided to go night fishing on the far side of Loch Stenness, way beyond the Firth. He had asked both his sons to come with him, but Conn, the eldest, had been disinclined to leave the comforts of his new wife and his hearthside, and so Cormac and Donal had ventured out alone, leaving Anna at home. She had work to do repairing the nets, and she always said she made better progress when the house was empty.

When Cormac provided this detail, Morgause and Anna caught each other's eye, but neither woman had said anything.

At first, they thought they had been the only ones out on the loch. It had been a strange night, the full moon red and glowing with uncanny brightness, and although this gave good light for fishing, many of the loch dwellers felt it was bad luck and preferred to stay indoors. However, Cormac and Donal had been lucky and had made a good catch of plump brown trout. They had even managed to get a little sleep on the boat. The night was warm, and each took turn to keep watch, but as the sky began to lighten, they both became aware of the hunger in their bellies and decided to go home.

As they approached the Firth, they saw another boat coming round the promontory. Its sail was furled, which did not surprise them as there was little wind. They could only make out one person on board, and he was rowing very slowly. The boat was within a stone's throw of the lochshore, which was not unusual as Stenness is a loch where the fish are bound to the shoreline, and was not far out of the shallows when they saw the man drop anchor. But then, rather than ready himself to begin fishing, he simply sat, silent and motionless, looking at the moon.

The water was calm and the sky cloudless, but the moon was now low on the horizon and neither Cormac nor Donal could make out who he was. Still, in a spirit of friendship, they hailed him. At first, he did not appear to hear them and so they called again, and this time, the strangest thing happened.

The man did not acknowledge them, but as soon as he had heard them, he stood up and went to the stern of the boat. There, he raised his hand to the moon, as if in salute, waited for a second, and then toppled forwards into the water.

When they heard this, both Angus and Morgause began to ask questions, trying to understand exactly what it was that Cormac and his son had seen, and Donal was very insistent, saying fervently, "A'm telling th' honest truth, Yer Majesty! He didnae dive or jump, juist toppled intae th' loch, lik' a tree trunk or yin o' th' standing stanes."

Father and son had rowed as fast as they could towards the small vessel, but when they reached it, there was no sight of the person who had fallen into the water. They now recognised the boat as Einar's, and both of them dived into the loch to see if he had got tangled in the weeds or the mooring rope, but they were unable to find him.

Knowing it was Einar's boat, they did wonder if he had been playing a joke on them—it was the sort of light-hearted prank he would have delighted in—and they kept their eyes peeled, thinking that he might suddenly appear several yards out in the depths of loch, or even on the lochside, but after searching and waiting for some time, they decided that they needed to alert others, and widen the search.

They were home just after daybreak, and whilst Donal unloaded the catch, Cormac went to waken Anna, and the two of them set out to alert their neighbours and begin the search. Einar's body was found less than four hours later, cast up on the shore just beyond the Firth.

When Corman and Donal had finished their tale, Morgause thanked them and asked her sergeant at arms if he had any further questions.

"You say thare wis no-one else in th' boat?" Angus asked them.

"No, thare wis nobody else," Cormac confirmed.

"And did he seem scared?"

Both father and son shook their heads. "No," said Donal. "Not that we cuid see. He seemed ferr normal—'til he gaed ower intae th' water."

Morgause decided that she had heard enough.

"I think it is clear what happened, and that you guessed right, Cormac. I think Einar was planning to play a joke, to pretend to fall in and then to emerge safely. That joke went terribly, terribly wrong. But I think that is our answer. Do you agree with me, Angus?"

"Weel, Yer Majesty," said Angus slowly, "ah cannae think o' anither explanation." The old soldier was feeling a little wrong-footed. This investigation was all happening very quickly, and he had not had a chance to discuss any of it with King Lot, who had been his commanding officer, man and boy.

Morgause was speaking again. "As you know, we plan to say farewell to Lord Einar with all ceremony this afternoon and King Lot and his sons will light the funeral pyre in his honour. My sister has arrived today from Avalon, she will officiate. I need to know now if there is any reason why we cannot do this." She paused and looked directly at Angus.

"My lord was most distressed by his cousin's death, and I need to do everything I can to help him bear it. If I can tell him that the investigation has been concluded to your satisfaction, that it was a tragic accident, but no foul play was involved, he can begin to grieve unencumbered by thoughts of revenge or redress, and we can move forwards." Angus said nothing. He had crossed his arms and was looking down at the floor, unwilling to meet the eyes of his queen.

Morgause continued, "What you do not know is that there is news of a great moment from Caer-Lundein, and King Lot must be able to give his mind to it—without any other distractions, and so I ask you again Angus. Are you satisfied?"

The sergeant at arms still remained silent, rubbing his chin as if weighing up the options. Morgause said nothing, but continued to look at him steadily, her eyes unblinking and an expression of dignified expectation on her face. Finally, he appeared to make up his mind, and slowly, raising his eyes to meet hers, gave a nod. "Aye yer majesty . . . I am satisfied."

Morgause inclined her head graciously and smiled, raising a hand in a gesture of dismissal.

"Cormac, Donal, thank you for telling us what happened, and for everything you did to try to save our beloved kinsman. You are coming tonight I hope, as our guests? I know my husband will also want to thank you."

Both man and boy blushed at her words and murmured that they had been pleased simply to serve her.

"Angus," Morgause continued, "please escort these two gentlemen to the Great Hall, where they may help themselves to refreshment; Cormac, I need speak with your wife for a moment, but she will join you very soon."

The three men departed, and Morgause and Anna said nothing until the door closed and they heard three sets of footsteps walking down the corridor towards the Great Hall.

Anna leant forward, and even though they were alone, spoke almost at a whisper, "So did you work an enchantment, Morgause? Was that why Lord Einar cast himself into the water?"

Morgause shook her head: "If there was an enchantment, it was not of my doing. As you have told me many times, what the Mazzeri decrees, will come to pass. That is enough for me. And I think it will serve neither of us well to enquire more deeply." Both women were silent for a while.

"You have been lucky, Morgause," said Anna eventually. "That could have gone a very different way indeed."

"Do you think so? I believe that you make your own luck—if you recognise the chances the Goddess sends you." Morgause reached out and poured herself a small tumbler of spiced mead. "I think I deserve this. Would you like some?"

Anna shook her head. "No, but I would thank you for some water."

Morgause waved her hand: "Help yourself."

As the older woman lifted the pitcher, Morgause leant back in her seat, and smiling raised her glass in a toast.

"Here's to Einar, who will be put to rest with all honours before the sun is set today."

"Whilst everyone is still in shock, and no one has time to really think about what happened?"

"No, Anna, whilst everyone can mourn Einar, let him go and move forward." Morgause spoke these words earnestly, giving a triumphant little smile.

"And then, we look to the future. It is Solstice next week, and even more importantly, there is news from Caer-Lundein that will make everyone forget Einar."

"News?"

"Yes, Anna. The other fox."

"You know who it was?" Anna leant forward, interested despite herself.

"Oh yes, I know exactly who the Mazzeri came for."

She paused, deliberately tantalising. "Uther Pendragon. The High King."

Anna said nothing, just stared, open-mouthed at Morgause.

At that moment there was a noise outside, the door was flung open and Lot, unshaven, dishevelled and clearly still suffering from the previous night's overindulgence, entered the room.

"They told me I'd find you here. Morgause, what's been going on?"

Morgause went straight to her husband and embraced him.

"How are you feeling, my lord? You were sleeping so soundly, and yesterday was such a distressing day, I did not want to wake you. Have you broken your fast?"

"No, and my head is pounding."

"That does not surprise me. Well, we are lucky that Anna is here with us. There is no one on Orkney who knows more of the healing arts, and I am sure she would be only too pleased to help."

Lot, who had previously not registered the presence of the local wise woman in his wife's solar, nodded to her in greeting.

"Anna," Morgause's voice was soft, and sweet as honey. "I'm sorry to delay you further, but we would be most grateful if would you go to the kitchens and make an infusion for His Majesty—fennel, chamomile and mint, I think? And anything else you feel would be helpful to ease his discomfort."

The queen reached out and touched the older woman's shoulder. "I shall ensure that Cormac is informed of your errand, so he will not worry. And Anna, one more thing, I would welcome your presence here, in my solar, this evening, after the Pyre is lit. Can I count on you?"

Anna hesitated. Eventually she said, "Yes, Your Majesty."

CHAPTER SIX

A TERRIBLE ACCIDENT

While Morgause worked, Morgan rested. Avice had provided her with a freshly laundered night shift smelling sweetly of lavender and had taken away her soiled travelling clothes. The housekeeper had promised to do what she could to restore them to some semblance of respectability, and to return at noon with linen towels and warm water.

Not wishing to risk the chance of unsettling or disturbing dreams, Morgan had chosen not to sleep, instead placing herself in a deep and restorative reverie, from which she emerged several hours later feeling strengthened and sustained.

Moving to the window, she picked up the ivory comb that Avice had placed on the table beside the bed and began to ease the tangles from her hair. It was a beautiful object, delicate, yet strongly made and decorated with copper. She recognised it as one she herself had given to Morgause some years ago and knew it to be an ancient treasure that had originally been made for the wife of the commander of the northern garrison of Vindolanda.

She wondered if it had been laid out for her because Morgause knew she would value it, or if—and, knowing her sister as she did, she thought this to be the more likely option—it had been put aside for the casual and irregular use of household guests, something not valued, and which would not be missed if it happened to inadvertently make its way into the travelling bag or knapsack of a visitor.

At first, she felt wounded by this suspicion. The comb had been sent as a Yuletide gift to the Lady of the Lake by the Chief Priestess of the sacred well at Coventina, along with other ancient and delicate artefacts designed and made for the Roman soldiers and citizens who had lived and worked there. Vivian had been delighted with the beautiful objects, some of which she displayed in Avalon's Great Hall whilst others were given as gifts to those she wished particularly to praise or honour. Morgan had at first felt a little hurt that she had not been recognised in this way, but as the months turned from winter to early spring, Vivian invited Morgan to her solar and asked her to choose something for herself to mark her birthday. There were many rare and beautiful objects to choose from, and when she could not decide between the delicately made comb and an intricately wrought cloak pin, she had been surprised, but highly delighted, when the Lady of the Lake had told Morgan that both could be hers.

The cloak pin she still had, but several years later she had sent the comb to her sister as a gift to mark the birth of Gareth, her youngest child. It had been a wrench to give it up, and she felt certain that her sister had no knowledge or understanding of the personal sacrifice it had required, or the depth of feeling the gift had been intended to convey. She had received a brief note several weeks later, containing desultory thanks, and had chided herself for being a sentimental fool in expecting anything else from Morgause.

But as she sat there, combing the tangles from her hair with the beloved comb that felt so right and natural between her fingers, she wondered if she was being entirely fair to her sister. Looking out across the loch she saw both the beauty and the isolation; the stark purity of land and sky, water and stone—but the lack of softness, warmth or comfort. Just as she, Morgan, harboured feelings of resentment towards her sister because of the comparative simplicity and naturalness of her life, for the first time she thought that perhaps Morgause resented the freedoms and powers that allowed her sister to walk the enchanted ways, to apparently effortlessly master the magics of Avalon, and to play a part in High Politics.

She realised that she should acknowledge that both of them, at a very young age, had been set upon paths that had not been of their own choosing. And perhaps, that was about to change. She remembered the confidence and authority her sister had displayed that morning, her refusal to be distracted by petty compliments, and her knowledge and understanding of both Uther's death and the reason for Morgan's visit. What had Morgause said as she welcomed her to the castle?

"You didn't think your silly fool of a sister had the means or the power to know what is going on in the big wide world, but things have changed, Morgan. Things have changed a lot."

"Yes," thought Morgan to herself. "If I am not mistaken, my sister has been dabbling in the magics, and it would seem, with some success. Perhaps we have more in common than I thought." But just as she was beginning to wonder where and how Morgause could have found anyone to help her understand and develop her insight into her powers, there was a gentle knock at the door, and Avice entered, followed by two maid servants carrying towels, a basin and a large jug of water from which pine-scented steam was enticingly rising. The three of them curtsied, and Avice placed Morgan's travelling clothes, now clean and freshly pressed, on the end of the bed.

"Is there anything else you need, my lady?"

"No, thank you, Avice." Morgan smiled her gratitude, whilst at the same time gesturing that she wished them to leave.

"Are you sure? I would be happy to stay and help you," said the housekeeper, who had known Morgan since she had been a little girl in Tintagel, and who was perhaps hoping for news of family and friends she had not seen for over twenty years.

Morgan considered. As housekeeper, there would be little that she did not know about what went on within the castle walls. "That is kind, Avice, and I am happy to accept your offer. But there is no need to keep these others from their tasks. There is much to do today, and I am sure two extra pairs of hands will be welcomed."

"Yes indeed, my lady. We are fair to run off our feet with all that has to be done." Avice turned towards the two girls who had remained in the doorway, staring goggle-eyed at the stranger. Visitors were rare in Orkney, and those who did brave the Northern Isles tended to be warriors or local lordlings, allies of King Lot and his brother, Urien. A visit from one of the enchantresses of Avalon was rare indeed.

"Now then, Elspeth." She turned to the taller of the two maid servants, a thin girl with dark hair pulled together in an untidy braid. "Go and help out in the buttery. I know Finn is losing patience with the potboys. They've damaged four casks of ale already, and he could do with someone with an iota of common sense." The girl called Elspeth giggled, nodded and ran off.

"And whit aboot me, Mistress?" The speaker was a few years older than Elspeth, short and rosy, her blonde hair neatly knotted beneath a well-laundered coif.

"Ailis, I need you to go round up the young princelings. They were at the archery butts last time I saw them, and as raggle-taggle a crew I never did see. They need to be dressed, tidied and made ready to play their parts in the ritual."

"Are they aw tae play a part? Surely master Gareth is still ower young." Ailis looked enquiringly at her mistress.

"It is not for us to question, Ailis." The older woman pursed her lips. "It is our job to obey."

"But he's ainlie seven . . . no' much more than a wee bairn." Ailis still looked unconvinced.

"That's as maybe, but that's a year older than Queen Morgause was when she first led the rituals for Solstice. I know, because I was there."

They heard a short bark of laughter from within the room, and then the voice of Morgan saying, "And I was but four when I kindled the ritual flames and led the rites on Tintagel's clifftop. Those who are called to serve the magics hold the power within them from the moment they are born, and if my sister believes her children are ready to join with us in our rituals, then I do not think it is meet for you to question her." Morgan's words were neither angry nor unkind, but they instantly quashed any further discussion, and Ailis went on her way.

Morgan had finished braiding her hair and was seated by the washstand. She had taken off her night shift and wrapped herself in one of the towels Elspeth had provided. Raising her hand, she summoned the older woman towards her.

"Now Avice, come, help me make ready—and perhaps whilst you do so, you can tell me what has been happening here since my last visit."

AS MORGAUSE HAD PREDICTED, IT was not until later that evening that the sisters had the opportunity to talk. The day had been busy and emotionally charged, but thanks to Morgause' detailed planning and hard work, all had seemed to run smoothly.

Morgan, dressed in ancient ceremonial robes leant to her by the High Priestess of the Goddess in Stromness, had officiated at the burial, leading the rituals of thanksgiving and farewell. Morgause had taken her place beside her, and together the two sisters had called upon the Goddess, thanking her for the blessing of the young man she had chosen to harvest in the prime of his life, asking for her comfort for those who loved him and who had been left behind. The two sisters had spoken the final words of the benediction together. "May the air carry your spirit gently and may fire release you to eternal joy."

After this, Lot and his sons had led the funerary procession out beyond the Firth, onto the headland where the memorial pyre was standing, a tall and somehow heroic structure, silhouetted against the pale sky. At its heart was Einar's beloved boat, which Morgause had ensured was well dowsed in pitch, and burned fiercely and steadfastly once the flaming torches had been thrust into its heart.

Indeed, as the women sat together in the warmth and comfort of Morgause's room, they were able to remark that it had all gone extremely well.

"Nothing untoward or distressing," noted Morgan.

"Unless you count Agravaine's campaign of sulks and wheedling until he was allowed to carry one of the fire-torches," commented Morgause.

"Well, you could have told him no. It did seem a little unfair to Gawaine that he had to share his moment of glory with his younger brothers." But Morgan spoke these words lightly. The last thing she wanted was to make her sister feel she was being criticised.

"It was because Gowie begged me to reconsider that I changed my mind. He said that they all loved Einar, and all wanted to honour his memory—even Gaheris and little Gareth." Morgause had an unaccustomed warmth in her voice as she pictured the earnest expression on her younger son's face as he explained to her how he felt.

"And so, the four of them walked forward together."

"The four of them walked forward together." Morgause nodded. "United as brothers, as I hope they will always remain. One day, Gawaine will be King of Orkney and the Northern Isles, and he will need his brothers to stand loyal, as Urien has always been to Lot."

Morgan listened to her sister's words and suddenly felt somewhat troubled. She had been standing on the edge of the headland, closer to the pyre than her sister. At the last moment, Agravaine had pushed ahead of his elder brother. Young Gareth, struggling to hold the heavy and fiercely burning torch had called out, asking for help. Gaheris, who was walking beside him, had simply shrugged and continued walking, but Gawaine had paused for a moment and then turned back to help his little brother.

Rather than waiting for his brothers to join him, Agravaine had pushed ahead and in the end, it had been first Agravaine and then Gaheris who thrust their torches into the pyre, catching the kindling and igniting the pitch-soaked boat. The flames were already leaping high and wild in the night sky by the time Gawaine and an exhausted Gareth had actually reached the pyre.

This, Morgan felt sure, was a portent, but until she understood how to interpret what she had seen, she felt it best to remain silent about what she had observed.

Instead, she took a sip of spiced wine, paused to appreciate the delicate combination of flavours, and then nodded her head, saying, "Urien has always been staunch in his loyalty, and steadfast in his service—both to Lot and to the Goddess. We will need this more than ever in the days to come."

"The days to come . . . yes, let us talk about the days to come." Morgause shifted in her seat, leaning in more closely to her sister, but before she could continue, there was a knock at the door. Morgan looked surprised. "Are you expecting visitors, sister? I had thought we were to converse in private."

"I have invited Anna to join us. Do you remember her? You spoke with her on your last visit. You do not mind I hope?"

Morgan cast her mind back: "Anna . . . Let me see. . . . Yes, I remember, the Wise Woman. From Corsica." She recollected the woman; graceful, with pleasing features and a distinctive voice that still retained the lilt and cadence of her birth place. She was not noble born, but she had a power and dignity that Morgan recognised and respected. Perhaps she was the person who had wrought the change in Morgause, and if her sister thought it fitting to invite her to join their conversation, she was not going to object.

"As you wish, sister. I shall be pleased to renew our acquaintance."

Morgause smiled and rose from her seat by the fire, making her way gracefully to the door. She drew back the bolt and gestured to Anna to enter.

The wise woman had changed her dress, no longer wearing the traditional homespun gown and shawl that she had worn when she had visited the castle with her husband and son earlier that day. Now she was dressed with simple elegance in an unbleached linen shift, worn beneath a finely woven overdress, which she had dyed herself with the last of the zaffaranu (or saffron) that she had brought with her from Corsica. The dress was held in place at her shoulders with two intricate bronze brooches, and at her waist she wore a leather belt, studded with stars of copper. Around her neck was a string of amber beads, and an amulet on a leather throng swung to her waist.

Morgause gestured to a chair by the fireplace. "You look well, Anna, and you have taken such trouble with your appearance. You put us both to shame!" Both sisters had changed from their ceremonial robes, and were now simply dressed in light woollen smocks, belted at the waist. Neither of them wore any jewellery, and both had plaited their hair into loose braids.

"It is out of respect, for the Goddess, and to honour the Lady Morgan." Anna gave a small curtsey to Morgan, who acknowledged her with a smile and a slight inclination of her head.

"But also, I get little opportunity to dress up, and I felt a strange and compelling desire to wear something that had not been sullied with fish scales or laundered a thousand times."

The older woman gave a small smile as she took her seat, accepting a goblet of wine from Morgause as she did so. "Thank you, Your Majesty. You must be pleased that all passed off so smoothly?"

The three women talked of the events of the day, helping themselves every now and then to a pastry or sweetmeat, and Morgause began to tell her sister of the Dream Hunters and the events she and Anna had set in chain.

Morgan was fascinated by what Anna had to say, questioning her eagerly about the Mazzeri and the magics she had learned as a young girl in Corsica. She soon realised that she was speaking to a woman whose skill and knowledge was in some respects equal to her own, and who could control and make use of magics that were deeper and more ancient than those she had learned in Avalon.

"And what of the old powers that dwell here, in Orkney? Have you been able to understand and awaken them?" she questioned, eagerly.

"I am open to the ley lines, the routes of power that connect the Stones of Orkney to the enchanted pathways and the realms beyond our day-to-day existence." Anna looked seriously at Morgan, and reached out to take her hand, holding it in hers. "I feel that they call to you too. I do not understand everything they say. I don't have the knowledge to understand or see clearly that which they seek to reveal, but yes, they are awake and they speak to me."

Morgan grasped the older woman's hand. "Yes, you are right, I do hear their voices. Their power is all around us, I can feel it, but it is just out of my reach." The two women smiled at each other, joined in a mutual understanding.

Meanwhiles, Morgause, who had initially been delighted to see how impressed her sister had been with Anna's knowledge and magics, was now feeling overshadowed and a little peeved that she was being excluded from the conversation. She got to her feet, fetching the wine, and refilling their goblets. "That's as maybe. Perhaps the next time you visit us, you may be able to spend more than a couple of days here, and you and Anna can indulge yourselves experimenting with the awakening of the ancient powers. But for now, there are more pressing matters to talk about."

Morgan let go of Anna's hand and the two women turned to Morgause, giving her their full attention.

"Now as we explained, Anna does not have complete power over the Dream Hunters. The Wild Hunt are sent to claim an individual when their time is upon them. How and why they are chosen remains a mystery, but what we do know is this." Morgause paced the room as she spoke. "I asked for Anna's assistance in calling the Wild Hunt to help me rid myself of an annoyance. She was loath to do so, but in the end, she agreed, and what I requested has come to pass."

"And at what price?" asked Morgan, who knew that nothing is given freely by the Fae folk.

"A price I was happy and willing to pay," answered Morgause, remembering with a little shudder of both fear and delight the hours she had spent with the horned, green-faced man.

"And does no one suspect foul play?"

"No, thanks again to Anna, or more accurately to her menfolk, it is believed that Einar's death was a terrible accident, a foolish joke that went tragically wrong. But what is more important is the identity of the second victim—the person I believe the Dream Hunters were really here to seek."

Morgause told Morgan of everything she and Anna had seen and recounted the vision of the death of Uther Pendragon that Gawaine had described.

"So that is how you were so well informed." Morgan gave a little smile. "It seems that at least one of your boys is gifted. I must try to spend some time with Gaheris before I leave."

"I'll believe that when I see it." Morgause poured herself another drink, offering the wine to Anna and Morgan, both of whom declined. "I don't think you have spent more than ten minutes with any of the boys on any of your meagre visits, but that is not what I want to talk about."

"Oh, and what would that be, dear sister?"

"Arthur. Our brother. The little bastard who ruined our lives." Morgause had stopped pacing and, moving away from the fireplace, returned to the chair that she had occupied earlier that day. Picking up the small dagger that she usually used to cut parchment and sharpen her quills, she pointed it at Morgan.

"You are here to ask Lot to become regent. To keep the peace and hold the throne until Merlin deems his mysterious protégé is ready, yes?" Morgan nodded her head slowly, not quite sure where this conversation was going.

"And we are supposed to do what we are told, smooth the way for the little bastard, sweet talk the Ceintish Lords, flatter the Irish and use Lot's power and influence with the Northern kingdoms? Well, why should we?" And at this, Morgause stabbed the dagger downwards, into the table, with such force that the blade penetrated the wood and stood upright, quivering slightly in the candlelight.

Anna said nothing, but she got up from her stool, and making her way round the table, put her arm gently on Morgause's shoulder. For a second, the younger woman held herself upright, not wanting to accept this silent gesture of comfort, but when Anna did not move, she relaxed and leant back, drawing solace from the wise woman who knew her well, and who had heard the hurt and anger in her voice.

Morgan collected herself, thinking carefully before she spoke. "Morgause, I have no love for our brother. You know that. But I am of Avalon. I seek and serve the will of the Goddess, and if it is her decree that Arthur should sit upon Uther's throne, then it is not for me to challenge her."

"And how do we know it is the will of the Goddess?" Morgause had regained control of herself, removing Anna's hand from her shoulder and gesturing at her—but gently and with a small smile—to go back to her seat.

"From what I know, it all seems to be about Merlin and what he wants. He was the one who gave Uther our father's face, deceiving our mother into taking him into her bed. He was the one who ensured our mother remained imprisoned in Tintagel until she gave birth to the mewling brat—and he was the one who spirited him away, keeping him safe and hidden from the world until the time is right to place him on the throne."

Morgan considered this. There was truth in what her sister had to say. She herself had been given no visions to guide her in this matter, and she realised that she had just accepted what Merlin had told her.

"So what do you suggest?"

Morgause looked at Anna. "Let us summon the Dream Hunters. If they will help me with Einar, surely, they will help to remove a person who is even more troublesome and distressing to me."

"Morgause, you are not thinking clearly. I told you before, I cannot control the Dream Hunters. You may think that spending a few hours slaking the lusts of Herne the Hunter will bind him to you, but I say to you truthfully, they will not." Anna spoke slowly, without emotion. "Neither you nor I can make Him do anything he doesn't want to do, and even if I felt that attempting to approach Him as a supplicant was the right thing to do—which I don't—I know that our chances of getting Herne to do the bidding of a mere human, however beautiful she is, is doomed to failure."

Morgan was relieved to hear these words. She had seen how worried the wise woman had been by Morgause's obvious distress and had initially been anxious that Anna would agree to help her. She had been shocked and more than a little disquieted when she had heard of the casual way in which her sister had invoked the powers of the Mazzeri, using magic almost on a whim to help her get rid of a former lover who had become troublesome to her, without any semblance of sorrow or regret.

Morgan's concern was not ethical in the conventional sense. She herself knew, and had used, enchantments to end life. She had bestowed death as a warning and a retribution upon the enemies of the Goddess and Avalon but had also used it as a gift to speed the way for those in pain or with incurable suffering. The power of life and death was hers, as it was Anna's, and both of them recognised the terrible responsibility it placed upon them. To hear Morgause talk of ending life in such a cavalier fashion once again made her realise that her sister was impetuous and untrained. It was a good thing, she mused, that Morgause would soon be in Caer-Lundein, where she, Morgan, would be able to spend more time with her, overseeing her growing experimentation with the magics.

She could tell that Morgause was about to take issue with Anna, and so hastily, she intervened. "I know little of the powers Anna conjures, but you must see that she has greater knowledge here than we do, and we should listen and respect that."

"So what do you suggest we do? Ask Lot to take on the mantle of War Duke, to put his life in danger fighting the Saxons. And if he doesn't die in battle and leave his sons fatherless, his reward is just to hand over the throne to an inexperienced bastard boy as soon as the realm is secure?"

"I think we should speak to Lot. Your husband is a respected warrior and a powerful leader. He has Urien beside him and is the only person the Northern Kings will agree to follow. We should seek his council."

"I think there is something else that we can do," Anna spoke quietly, but there was authority in her voice and the two sisters turned to listen to her.

"You asked how we know that it is the will of the Goddess that Arthur becomes High King?" Anna paused, letting her words sink in. "And you are right, Morgause, at the moment, we do not. From what I understand, we only have the word of Merlin the druid. So why should we not seek a more definite proof, a certainty that Arthur is destined to take the throne?"

Anna got to her feet, walking across to the desk, where the dagger still stood, embedded in the wooden table. She reached out, grabbing it by the pommel, and made to pull it from the table, saying as she did so in a deep, portentous voice: "Whomsoever pulleth this sword from this stone is rightwise king born of all Britain."

Feigning weakness, she appeared to be unable to pull the dagger from its place, and smiling, she looked around at the two sisters.

For a moment, they said nothing. Then Morgan spoke: "This is interesting. Please, go on. Tell us a little more about what you're proposing."

And so, Anna outlined her plan.

The three women spent several hours discussing how best to work the enchantments they would need, and it was almost dawn before they were satisfied. Finally, as the sky was just starting to turn pink over the loch, and the first of the songbirds were beginning their morning chorus, Anna was free to make her way back home, having promised to accompany Morgause and her household to Caer-Lundein.

CHAPTER SEVEN

WARD OF THE FOREST SAUVAGE

King Lot of Orkney, now also Regent of Great Britain and the Isles, was waiting for his wife. The castle of Caer-Lundein, which had been their home for nearly a year now, was large and beautiful, and he knew how much Morgause loved to linger in the riverside gardens, but they had agreed to meet with the court Seneschal at noon, to discuss the final arrangements for tomorrow's tourney and she was annoyingly, embarrassingly and utterly characteristically—late.

"Perhaps, my liege, we could discuss the feast?" The Seneschal was a short, harassed looking man, whose hair, or what was left of it, grew in pale, uneven, wispy strands from the sides of his round, moon-like face. When she had first met him, Morgause had remarked that he looked "for all the world like a dandelion clock after someone has blown on it three times," and since then, she had insisted on calling him Dandy, rather than by his given name of Dafydd.

Lot smiled at the memory: "No, Dand . . . I mean Dafydd, I think we should wait." He knew his wife prided herself upon her skills as a hostess and it would be more trouble than he wanted to consider to even suggest finalising the menus for the feast or the order of the banners without her. "Her Majesty will be here soon, I have no doubt, but perhaps we could at least confirm that the stabling is in order. We are expecting many visitors tomorrow and I must be reassured that at the very least we have provided for their horses."

Dafydd began at once to provide details of the numerous hostelries and shelters across the city that had been sequestered for this purpose and was just starting a boring but apparently essential homily relating to hay and horse feed, when the door opened, and Morgause strolled in. She was accompanied by her sister, Morgan, who had arrived from Avalon that morning. Lot had met her several times since she had visited them in Orkney some twelve months since, bearing with her the news of Uther's death, but he still did not feel that he really knew her. He was aware that she came to court frequently, to attend rituals, or to represent the interests of Avalon and the Goddess within the council, but his new duties required him to travel widely, and he not seen her for several months. He remembered his sister-in-law as short and dark, with pallid skin and strange, pale eyes. He did not remember her as beautiful, but seeing her now, standing next to his wife, Lot felt his heart miss a beat.

The two women were magnificent, like gold and silver, like the sun and the moon. Morgause, tall, and long-boned, with elegant limbs and golden skin, brown eyes and an abundant mass of tawny curls, and Morgan, delicate and elf-like with skin as pale and soft as milk and her startling blue eyes ringed with lashes as dark as the clouds of hair that she wore in a loose plait falling well below her waist.

Lot pushed back his chair and went to greet them, motioning Dafydd, who was still endlessly listing his equine arrangements, to be silent. Speaking first to Morgause, he raised her hand to his lips and kissed it. "Well, my Queen, as always, you are worth waiting for." She smiled enigmatically. She had lingered rather longer than she had intended with Lamorak, one of the young sons of King Pellinore. Nothing had happened . . . yet . . . but he had been extremely pretty. It was lucky that she had run into her sister as she was making her way across the courtyard. Lot would assume that they had been catching up together and was now unlikely to quiz her as to why she had been so inordinately late.

"See, my lord, the Lady Morgan has joined us from Avalon. As I'm sure you are aware, it is fitting that we congratulate her on her elevation. Indeed, perhaps it would be fitting that we all bow down before her. Since last she visited, my illustrious sister has been made the formal emissary of the Lady of the Lake, empowered to act on her behalf in all our rites and rituals."

♦ ♦ ♦

MORGAUSE SMILED WICKEDLY, AND LOT thought it highly unlikely that his wife would ever bow down before her younger sister.

However, King Lot understood protocol and also had a deep-rooted respect for Avalon and the Old Ways. Turning to Morgan, he bowed deeply. "It gives me joy to make you welcome here. We are all saddened by the news of Lady Vivian's continued ill health, but no one who sees you could doubt that Avalon will be well represented at the tourney, and that all honours will be given, as they should be, to the Goddess."

Morgan stepped towards him, and reaching upwards, kissed him on both cheeks. "It is my pleasure, brother. You have always been spoken of as one who respects and acclaims the Goddess. It has long been a disappointment to me that my duties have prevented me from getting to know my sister's husband as I should, as it saddens me that I have not had a chance to spend time with my nephews. Are any of your boys at court?"

Lot, who was inordinately fond of his children, beamed. "Aye, they are grand boys. They are not with us at the moment. We hope to have them with us in the autumn and keep them until next spring. But you met them last year, I believe, when they officiated in the rituals held to mark the death of my cousin Einar."

"Yes, I remember. Good, bluff lads, and very like their father."

"They are indeed," said Morgause, who was feeling a little irritated by the way her sister appeared to have captivated her husband. "But we are not here to talk over family history or past rituals, but to think about the work that we are called upon to do today. To ensure that everything is as it should be for our guests on the morrow. Morgan, do you wish to stay and discuss domestic detail, or are there other things the representative of the Lady of the Lake should be doing?"

"Sister, I am certain that you know far more than I about the ordering of a household and the contrivance of a feast—in such matters, I have no wish to interfere. And you are right, there are things that I must do before tomorrow, and it would help if I could speak with Lord Merlin. Perhaps you could direct me to his rooms?"

At once Lot called for one of the pages to accompany Morgan, and finally, nearly two hours later than he had hoped, he and his wife began to discuss their arrangements.

THE TOURNEY WAS BEING HELD both as a celebration of the Solstice and a memorial, one year after his death, for Uther Pendragon. As Regent, King Lot had been a success, bringing together the Lords of Wales and the Marches, the Scottish Isles and Lowlands and the Kings of Ireland to unite alongside Uther's traditional allies, King Ban of Brittany, the Lords of Ceint, Lindsay and Northern Britain, and the Duchies of Gewisse, Cornwall and Lyonesse. They had joined together to fight the Saxon invaders and had won many battles.

Representatives of all these Kings and fiefdoms would be present, and the castle of Caer-Lundein was full to bursting. Many could not be accommodated, and so had taken rooms in hostelries, or even pitched their tents in the fields outside the city walls. One such was Sir Ector, a knight of middle standing, holder of a castle and lands to the northwest, bordering on the Forest Sauvage, an area of wilderness, which was said to be a pathway to the realms of the Faerie.

As King Lot and Queen Morgause discussed placings and sampled figs and fine wine, Ector and his old friend Pellinore, King of the lake-lands of Listenoyse, sat upon the grass outside his tent, sharing between them a flask of rough cider and a loaf of bread.

"Ah, Ector, it is good to have a day like this, a day to do nothing but sit in the sun and drink with an old friend." Pellinore may have been a King in name, but his lands were small, and his situation was seen by most as relatively humble. He had lived not quite fifty summers and was a man who found it easy to be pleased with life. He was above average height, a little inclined to fat, with a face whose lines and wrinkles showed that he liked to smile. He had a daughter, Dindane, and three young sons, Lamorak, Aglovale and the baby, Percival. His wife had died just over a year ago, giving birth to Percival, and he had not felt any inclination to remarry.

Ector smiled and passed the flask to his old friend. They had been boys when Aurelius had died and had travelled together with Uther to the court of King Ban's father, Budic, in Brittany, where they had learned the arts of war. He was smaller than his friend and wiry, with pale brown hair and a trim beard that was now almost completely grey. Like Pellinore, he was also a widower, with one son, a boy named Kai, who was the very apple of his eye.

"Indeed, it is, and there is more of this inside the tent if you should want it. I don't plan to do anything much today. The boys have gone off to take a look at the tournament field, and we are not invited to tonight's banquet, so I feel at liberty to indulge myself."

"Oh yes, your boy . . . Kai, is it? Is this to be his first tourney?"

Ector, having just taken a large gulp of cider merely nodded.

"And Lamorak's also. He wants me to allow him to enter the jousts. I do not think I dare. He is good boy, but inexperienced, and he means too much for me to risk his life for sport."

Ector nodded in understanding. "To be honest, Kai's not much of a horseman, so I don't need to worry about the joust. He will enter the archery and the hand-to-hand, and if the field seems reasonable, I may allow him to enter the lists for the long sword."

Pellinore smiled. "Then maybe our boys will meet upon the tourney field. You could always best me with the bow."

"And you, me, with the long sword." The two old friends smiled and raised their flasks, toasting each other and their memories.

Together, they downed another couple of flagons, watching the people coming and going, and talking, in a desultory and increasingly incoherent way, about nothing in particular. Pellinore had just got to his feet and was making his way rather unsteadily behind a tree to relieve himself, when they became aware of a tall man in grey robes walking rapidly towards Ector's tent. He carried a staff, but as his stride was strong and purposeful, he clearly did not need it to assist in his progress across the field.

Pellinore could see that Ector was becoming rather flustered, and as the man drew nearer and they could make out his features, he was not a bit surprised. "That's Lord Merlin, isn't it? The druid? Counsellor to the king?"

Ector nodded, dumbly.

"But what's he doing here? Surely, he should be at the castle?"

Ector tried to get to his feet, but the cider defeated him, and he remained sprawled on the grass, looking helplessly up at the druid.

In general, Merlin was a serious man, known for his devotion to duty and overall lack of levity. Nevertheless, he had always had a bit of a soft spot for Sir Ector, and taking pity on his plight, decided to join him on the grass.

"Good Sir Ector, well met, it must be nigh on seven years since our paths last crossed. I hope you are keeping well?"

"Very well, very well indeed, my Lord Merlin . . . I do apologise that you should find me in such a muddle . . . King Pellinore and I have perhaps been a little overindulgent in the partaking of this cider the Duke of Cornwall so kindly gave us." Ector picked up the near empty flagon and held it out to the druid. "Maybe you would care to try some?"

Merlin reached out and took the flask, examining it gravely. Turning it upside down and giving it a shake, the last few drops trickled onto the grass: Merlin sighed. "Alas, I think you and your friend have ensured that there is little left for me."

Sir Ector staggered to his feet and began to weave his way unsteadily to the tent. "No, no, my lord, there is more. I warrant there is plenty for all of us."

"Peace, Sir Ector." Merlin reached out his hand and gently pulled the unsteady knight back into a seated position. "I think that you have probably had enough, and I for one need to keep a clear head this night." He paused, putting his hand on the other man's arm. "I have come for news of your ward."

"Ah, yes, my ward . . . Yes, he is good, a good boy, acting as squire to my son, Kai. They are at the tourney ground, getting to know their way around the lists."

"A squire . . . interesting . . . and does he have no ambition to be a knight?"

"Well, all the boys want to be knights, doing battle, winning glory . . . but they must first win their spurs, and Kai is the older by nearly a year you know. I thought it best that he had his chance first."

"Hmm," said Merlin, stroking his beard and looking thoughtful. "And his lessons, does he apply himself?"

"Well, he is not so bookish. Neither of the boys are if I'm honest. But he's a good soul." Sir Ector smiled fondly. "Keeps young Kai on the straight and narrow, I'll say that for him."

Merlin said nothing, and looking up noticed the position of the sun in the sky and realised that he would be wanted soon at Caer-Lundein.

"I must be gone. It was good to see you, Ector. I'm glad you are keeping well." The knight made again as if to rise, but Merlin gestured for him to remain as he was.

"No, no, stay where you are . . . Will you be at the ceremony tomorrow? In the castle courtyard?"

"Oh yes, yes, we all will. Wouldn't miss it for the world. It's going to be a wondrous spectacle by all accounts. We will see you then, my lord, and thank you for doing me the courtesy of dropping by. I apologise for being a little . . . discommoded."

The druid gave a short smile and nodded. Clapping his hand in farewell upon Sir Ector's shoulder, he nodded in acknowledgement to King Pellinore and went upon his way. He was soon lost to sight amongst the rows of tents and banners, and Pellinore, after rummaging around for another couple of flagons, went and sat down beside his old friend, eyes aflame with curiosity. "Well Ector, you sly old fox, what was all that about? You've never told me anything about being acquainted with the great Lord Merlin . . . and what's all this got to do with your ward?"

Sir Ector took the proffered flagon gratefully and raising it to his lips, drank deeply. "It's a strange story, and one I had been charged not to reveal, but given what you've seen and heard, I don't think it will do any harm to tell you the parts you don't already know."

"IT WAS A BRIGHT, CLEAR morning in February, just over twenty years ago," began Sir Ector. "There was snow on the ground, and it fair blinded you to look out across the fields—the sun was so bright. I was engaged with the steward and some of the men, looking for ewes trapped in the snowdrifts, so we could bring them back to the home farm. We had already found three—in a sorry state if I remember rightly—and had loaded them onto the cart, when one of the men pointed out someone walking towards us, over the crest of the hill.

"It was a tall man, with white hair, and a long white beard. He was wearing a white cloak, and it was hard to make him out against the snow, but what was really strange was the way he was moving. Rather than stepping over the snowdrifts like you'd expect, he seemed to glide through them, moving as easy as you or I would stroll through meadow grass in June.

"In no time at all, he had reached the bottom of the hill, crossed the stile into the field and was almost upon us. He had a heavy wooden staff in one hand, and a bundle of some sort strapped to his back.

"By now, I was standing on my own. My companions had found another one of those pitiful creatures buried deep in a snowdrift at the edge of the field and were trying to manoeuvre her onto the cart."

"Not an easy job," observed King Pellinore.

"No, sheep are remarkably stupid creatures. They don't try to co-operate even if you're attempting to help them. But this isn't really about the sheep."

"No, of course not. Please go on."

"Well, I could tell this was someone important. He had an air of great authority, and his clothes were made of the finest woollen cloth. Another odd thing, even though I had watched him make his way to us through the snowdrifts, his robe and cloak were unmarked by travel and seemed to be completely dry.

"I greeted him, wishing him the blessings of the Goddess and asking how I could be of service. 'You have a young son, I believe?' was his rather unexpected answer. I told him that I had. Kai was nearly a year old, and as lively and bonny a child as you could wish for.

"'Your son has a wet nurse?' he asked.

"I told him that was so, although my wife felt that we should be thinking of weaning the boy, and when we did, she would return to her family.

"'And she is a strong girl, and healthy?'

"I was rather surprised by the way the conversation was going, but I answered him positively, and he seemed pleased with what I had told him.

"By this time, the men had returned. They were carrying the ewe on the hurdle and began to load her onto the cart. They looked curiously at the stranger, who observed what they were doing with interest.

"He looked around him, turning to all points of the compass and tilting his head to one side as if straining to hear something. 'There are three more ewes in trouble,' he said finally. 'One over yonder, near the stile, and two on the edges of the forest.' He raised his stick and pointed towards the dark edges of the Forest Sauvage. 'I would seek them out without delay. The wolves are hungry at this time of year. Get you there with haste, as your master, and I must make our way to the castle. We have business to discuss.'

"My steward looked at me questioningly, but I could see no reason to doubt the information the stranger had given me. Although I had never met him before, I felt not only that I could trust him, but that I had to obey him. I instructed the men to look for the remaining ewes in the places the stranger had suggested, and the two of us then made our way back to the castle.

"He said little as we walked, but as soon as we arrived in the courtyard he asked to be taken to my son's nursery, or wherever we would find the wet nurse. Our arrival caused the castle hounds to set up an almighty howling, as they always do when anyone enters the courtyard and walks past their kennels. They are good creatures and the noise soon abated, but when they had quietened, I heard a strange and rather pitiful wailing coming from the bundle strapped to the stranger's back.

"'Those damned creatures have wakened him, and he is hungry,' said the stranger, sounding rather more worried than angry. There was unmistakable urgency in his voice. 'He has not eaten for several hours. Take me to the wet nurse at once if you please.'"

"You mean the bundle was a baby? He had a child strapped to his back?" asked Pellinore, downing the last of his flagon, and reaching rather unsteadily for another.

"Yes, it was a baby. As I was soon to find out, it was a little boy, and not much more than a few days old, small and scrawny, and bawling fit to burst by the time we made our way to the nursery.

"Edith, my wife, was rocking young Kai to sleep in his cradle, and Eawyn, the village girl we had engaged as a wet nurse, was sitting at the window, doing some mending.

"'Which one of you has milk for this child?' demanded the stranger, striding into the room and unstrapping the screaming bundle from his back. The commotion woke young Kai, who also began to cry, causing his mother to pick him up, all the while looking angrily at me for having allowed this intrusion. In the meanwhile, Eawyn had laid down her mending, and settled herself in the high-backed chair by the fire. Without saying a word, she held out her arms for the child, and the stranger gave him to her.

"Within seconds, he began to suck, and as his crying ceased, young Kai also became quiet, soon falling back to sleep in his mother's arms.

"The stranger looked at the two children and gave a satisfied nod.

"'I must take my leave of you now, but please, Sir Ector, walk with me for a moment.' Not quite believing what I had just heard, I followed the stranger from the room, leaving my wife and Eawyn with the children.

"The words he spoke to me were brief and to the point, telling me little about the child other than his name was Arthur and he was under the protection of the Goddess. He handed me a purse, to formally purchase his wardship, and gained my agreement that I would raise the boy alongside my own son, until such time as he came to claim him. Finally, he made me promise that I would say nothing of how he had found his way into our household.

"Then he left, without even telling me his name. He returned several times over the years, and eventually it was not possible for him to keep his identity secret from me. All England knew of Lord Merlin, advisor to Uther Pendragon, the great druid and sage.

"The last time I saw him was seven years ago, when the lads were still not long out of boyhood. But time has marched on, and those little babes are men grown. Perhaps the time is come for Arthur to find his true identity, his true family." Sir Ector sighed. "He's been a good lad, and I'll miss him if he has to leave us." He brushed a tear aside, looking sheepishly at King Pellinore, as if slightly ashamed to be caught out in such sentimentality, but his friend was lying flat on his back, a flagon of cider clasped to his chest, and snoring gently.

Ector went into the tent, returning with a blanket to cover his sleeping companion. He sat down beside him, taking the occasional sip of cider and staring at the moon, thinking about that night, all those years ago, and wondering what the druid's visit was to portend.

CHAPTER EIGHT
SOMETHING UNEXPECTED

Arthur was one of those people who are actually taller than they seem. Anyone asked to describe him would probably have said that he was a pleasant lad, of middling build, with very little in the way of distinguishing features; in fact, he stood just over six feet tall. He had pale brown hair, hazel eyes and a shy, rather diffident smile.

Growing up in the shadow of Kai, his foster brother, he had swiftly learned that he would always take second place. Kai was his parents' only child, petted, overindulged and instilled with a belief that everything he did was remarkable, and whilst no one had ever mistreated Arthur, he had learned that life was smoother and less troublesome if he stayed in the background. Consequently, by the time he had reached early manhood he had become quiet and self-effacing, finding it easier to follow than to lead.

Attending the tourney in the grounds of Caer-Lundein was the first time he had travelled any real distance from the Forest Sauvage, and as he and Kai looked around the tournament ground, wanting to see where the bouts Kai had entered for would be taking place, he was feeling more than a little overwhelmed.

"There are hundreds of people here, Kai. Do you think that many of them are going to be entering the lists?"

"Oh, I wouldn't have thought so," replied Kai. "Only knights and the nobility are allowed to take part in the tourney. Most of this lot don't look like they've got a pot to piss in. I doubt very much that we'll see churls like this sorry lot anywhere near the lists." As he spoke, he gestured dismissively towards a group of overexcited youths swigging ale from wooden tankards as they commented loudly on the merits of the two knights sparring on the practice field.

Kai was a little over medium height and well-muscled from hours practising with the bow and the long sword. He had dark blond hair, pale blue eyes and regular features which could have been pleasing had his mouth not been so frequently twisted into a sneer.

"Come on now, Arthur, stop gawping and dawdling like the village idiot. Anyone would think you've never been farther than the castle gate. We need to make haste; I want to get a squint at the competition on the archery range before we go to meet Pa for this dreary opening ceremony."

Despite his confidence and apparent world-weariness, Kai had only ever attended one tournament before, a small affair on the far side of the Forest Sauvage, and that had only been as a spectator. He was, in fact, quite nervous about what was to come over the next few days. Whilst he knew that his skills as an archer were more than passable, hand-to-hand combat and the long sword were both difficult events, and he only had experience of practice bouts with his father and the castle sergeant at arms—a grizzled old soldier who had fought alongside Uther Pendragon's brother, Aurelius, during the early Saxon campaigns.

What they saw over the next couple of hours did nothing to reassure him. Kai was not the sort of person who believed in entering any sort of game or contest simply for the experience. If he did not feel he had a chance of winning, he saw absolutely no point in taking part. The standard was high and Kai was beginning to think he would be well served if discretion became the better part of valour. Even in the practice bouts he'd just witnessed he had seen quite a few injuries, and he was now convinced that he needed to find a way to extricate himself from competing—at least in the long sword.

As the sun climbed towards midday, the two companions made their way towards the castle courtyard. They walked mainly in silence, Kai frantically trying to come up with a sensible excuse or reason which would allow him to pull out without losing face, and Arthur, who had now become acclimatised to the noise and bustle, absorbing with rapt fascination everything he saw around him.

The streets were busy, loud with the sound of hawkers and street vendors, selling sweetmeats and cakes, savoury tartlets and cheap favours, some decorated with the colours of the more well-known and successful combatants competing in the tourney over the next few days. The taverns were overflowing and the press of people only became more intense as they neared the castle. Arthur, who stood taller than his foster brother, noticed what looked like an empty space just inside the castle walls. Telling Kai what he had seen, they jostled their way through the crowd towards it, but as they approached, they realised that the space wasn't empty after all. On the small patch of grass, roped off from the rest of the courtyard, and watched over by an armed sentry, was a large stone anvil, twice the size of the one used by the blacksmiths back at Sir Ector's castle. Protruding from the anvil was a sword.

Intrigued, they moved closer to get a better look, and as they did so a man approached the enclosure. He was tall, with black hair tied in a war-plait that fell halfway down his back and dressed in half-armour, but unarmed and without a helmet. His face was bearded and battle-scarred, and when he spoke to the sentry his voice was deep and commanding.

"Let me pass, fellow; I have come to try my luck."

"What is your name, sir, and on what grounds do you base your claim?" The sentry's voice was expressionless and the words sounded formulaic.

"I am Sir Dinadan of Camdore, knight and warrior. I base my claim on three things." As Sir Dinadan began to speak, the crowds quietened, eager to hear what he had to say. "Firstly, I am of the blood royal. Uther Pendragon was my mother's cousin." There were several cheers and whistles from the crowd.

"Secondly, I have fought all my life to defend this realm." At this, a more enthusiastic round of cheers went up from the crowd, who seemed to have taken a fancy to Sir Dinadan. "And thirdly, I swear to protect Britain and its people until the day I die." At this, there was even more cheering and applause, and the sentry moved forwards, releasing the end of the rope and allowing the knight to enter.

Sir Dinadan made his way to the centre of the grass and took up his stance facing the anvil, his back to the crowds. Tightening his belt, he positioned his feet squarely, and bent once or twice from the waist, flexing his arms and rubbing his hands together as he did so. Then he leant forwards, grasping the sword firmly with both hands, and began to pull. Nothing happened. The sword did not move, and Sir Dinadan adjusted his stance, shrugging his shoulders to get more traction, and redoubled his efforts.

Arthur could see how much he was exerting himself. The muscles on his shoulders and neck stood out, strained and taut, and his breath was coming in short, laboured grunts. After a couple of minutes, the crowd had decided that they were not impressed and began to whistle and catcall until Sir Dinadan, his face red and shining with the sweat of his exertions, let go of the sword. Without saying a word, he bowed in a cursory fashion to the sentry, who saluted with equal enthusiasm before replacing the guard ropes. The crowd parted to let the silent and now shame-faced knight make his way from the scene.

"What do you think that was about?" said Arthur.

"I've no idea," replied Kai. "Some tawdry trial of strength no doubt. It's of no interest to me. Come on, if we don't get a move on, we're going to be late." Kai set off purposefully towards their agreed meeting place near the castle well, with Arthur following hesitantly, several paces behind. He'd been intrigued by what he had just witnessed and would have liked to have spoken to the sentry to find out more about it, but he knew better than to argue with Kai.

Sir Ector was waiting by the well with his friend King Pellinore, who was now accompanied by his eldest son, Sir Lamorak. Greeting both his son and his ward warmly, Sir Ector suggested that as there was still some time before the ceremony began, they could perhaps repair to an ale-house—and all were pleased to agree.

SEATED TOGETHER IN THE WINDOW seat overlooking the castle courtyard, Morgause and Morgan had witnessed Sir Dinadan's unsuccessful attempts to pull the sword from the stone.

Morgause was feeling very pleased with herself. She had spent an exhaustingly pleasurable morning with young Sir Lamorak, who appeared to combine vigour and adoration with a natural discretion. Morgause was very aware of her position and had no desire to bring shame upon her husband—or to incur his wrath. Knights such as Sir Lamorak were an entertaining diversion, but she was mindful of her position as Queen Regent, the first lady in the land, and over the past year had become rather more cautious about how and where she took her pleasures.

It was also agreeable to spend an hour or so with her sister. Over the last twelve months, Morgan had become a regular visitor to Caer-Lundein and had her own suite of rooms and permanent attendants. Vivian, Lady of the Lake, was now very frail, and found it difficult to leave her chamber. She had become increasingly reliant upon Morgan to proclaim and protect the interests of Avalon and the Goddess to the wider world.

Now that both were holding positions of power and influence, the jealousies and resentments the sisters had always felt towards each other had begun to subside. They had found that it had become possible to forge a deeper relationship, based on trust and mutual consideration, and they had both been surprised by the joy this had brought them.

As Sir Dinadan walked silently away, Morgan turned to her sister, saying, "Well, I am surprised he attempted that today. If he had succeeded, it could have caused chaos."

"Yes," agreed Morgause. "Everyone has gathered to remember the Pendragon—and to swear another year of fealty to Lot's regency. A new claimant to the throne throwing in his gauntlet now would at best have stirred up old enmities. At worst, it could have led to civil war."

"We owe Anna a deep debt of gratitude. Enchanting the sword so it could only be pulled from the stone by the one destined by the Goddess to succeed to Uther's throne was an inspired idea. How many have tried it now?"

"I think Sir Dinadan was the twelfth," replied Morgause. "Of course, I'm not counting the serial offenders—King Leodegrance has tried three times I think, and that idiot Sir Dagonet has a go once a month. But fools and braggarts apart, it has done more than almost anything else to keep the peace."

"How is she?" asked Morgan, who had not seen the Corsican wise woman since they had worked together to craft the enchantments that had placed the sword in the stone.

"Anna? Well, I think," said Morgause vaguely, conscious that it had been some months since she had received anything but official news from her old household in Orkney. She resolved that, once the tourney was over she would take pains to send messages to her boys, and to Anna, but before she could say any more, there was an urgent knocking at the door.

A young woman entered, her face pale, and eyes red with weeping.

"Nimue, what is this?" It was Morgan who spoke, getting up from the window seat and making her way towards the newcomer. The young woman was a member of her household, a little older than herself and both talented and discreet. It was unlike her to display such unrestrained emotion.

"Lady Morgan, Your Majesty, please forgive me this intrusion, for there has been some news . . . tragic news . . . from the Lake."

"From Avalon? What has happened? Tell me child."

"It is the Lady Vivian. She has left us. The Goddess has taken her . . . and Lady Morgan, I must beseech you to return without delay to Avalon."

Morgan and Morgause exchanged glances. This was not completely unexpected. Vivian had been ailing for some time, but she had been Lady of the Lake for many, many years. There would be few who could remember a time when she had not been their spiritual leader, venerated, revered and feared by all who gave service and honour to the Goddess.

Over the past year they had often found themselves discoursing upon what would happen when Vivian was no more. They recognised that her death could lead to unrest and even civil disturbance if there was any doubt or uncertainty about who would succeed her. Over the past years the new religion, the worship of the Risen God, had acquired many followers, challenging the beliefs and certainties of many. It was clear to both women that those who were uncertain about their loyalty to the old ways would need the comfort of stability and strong leadership if they were to remain confident in their faith.

Morgan, who had been Lady of the Lake in all but name for several years now, knew that it was her destiny and duty to return to Avalon, to formally take ownership of the powers she had been born and bred to wield. She would ready herself, and could leave for Avalon within the hour, but she needed to know a little more about the circumstances.

"Tell me, Nimue, who brought the news?"

The girl said nothing, and once more began to cry.

"Come, girl, control yourself. Like me, you are Avalon-trained, and that means your mind will always have dominion over your emotions. You are not a child, and however much we will mourn her passing, Vivian's death cannot be said to be unexpected." Morgan went to the girl, who was clearly trying to compose herself, and guided her to the window, motioning her to sit.

"Now that's better. Tell me, Nimue, how did you hear of Vivian's passing?" Morgan had been expecting to hear of a vision sent by the Goddess through the scrying bowl, or perhaps the arrival of a traveller from the Lake Isle who had braved the perils of the enchanted pathways. She knew that several of the elders also had the power to inhabit the minds of birds and beasts, and perhaps one of these could have been enchanted to carry the message. But neither she nor Morgause could have anticipated what Nimue was to say.

"She told me herself, or rather, it was her taibhse."

"Her taibhse? But how could that be?" A taibhse is a phantom, a spirit that can be conjured by separating the living body from its soul. When she had been a child, Morgan had helped release her mother Igraine's taibhse, and the ritual had been complex and wrought with dangers. Taibhses were also known to visit a loved one at times of death—but they could only travel to those to whom they were tied by either blood or powerful emotion.

"I'm sorry, Nimue, I don't understand. If Vivian's taibhse were to visit anyone, why would it be you?" Morgan recognised that she felt more than a little resentful. Vivian had been her guide and mentor since she had been four years old. If her taibhse was going to seek out anyone, why had it been Nimue and not herself?

The young woman gulped and took a deep breath: "Because . . . because . . . she was . . . my mother." Both Morgan and Morgause gasped in disbelief. How could this be? Vivian was sworn to the Goddess, and that meant that she had, perforce, been required to give up all hope of children and family. Morgan herself had sworn these self-same vows at sixteen, with Vivian by her side as her spiritual sponsor. She looked at Nimue. The young woman must have been at least six-and-twenty, meaning Vivian must have given birth to her when she was no longer young, at a time when she had been well established as spiritual leader and Lady of the Lake.

If this was true, if Vivian had conceived this child and carried her to term, she must have done so with the consent and protection of the most powerful in the land. This was a riddle, raising more questions than they had answers for, and which at this moment, with Nimue grieving and in shock, Morgan knew they did not have the means to solve.

"I didn't know. I'd always been told my mother died in childbirth and that I was sent to Avalon to be cared for because my father was at war." Nimue spoke quietly, her voice uncertain, as if she still did not believe the words that she was saying. "But when she came to me, just now, she said she wanted to beg my forgiveness for not acknowledging me, or loving me . . ." Her voice broke, and the tears began to fall once more: ". . . loving me as a mother should."

It was Morgause who put her arms around the girl and held her, as a mother holds a child, and let her weep. When she had been but six years old, her own mother had conjured the deep magics to send her own taibhse to provide her little daughter with guidance and protection on her voyage to the Orkney Isles.

She realised with sadness that, unlike herself, Nimue had never had a mother to hold her. She had been raised believing herself to be orphaned and unwanted, only to find out, when it was too late to do anything about it, that her mother had been there all the time, watching her, teaching her, disciplining her—but never loving her.

Nimue's tears subsided and she suddenly became aware that the woman comforting her was the Queen. Blushing, she got to her feet, stammering her apologies.

"Hush, do not speak so. The Goddess in her mercy makes sisters of us all. But I must leave you. The hour is getting late, and I should change my robe and ready myself for the tourney." Morgause reached out and touched her sister's hand. "Morgan, what will you do now?"

"I will prepare myself to depart. Nimue is right. I shall make my way to Avalon as quickly as I can." Morgan's voice was strong and certain. "I will take the enchanted pathways. There are dangers I know, but I feel confident that I can master them as I have before. It is by far the fastest way to travel—I shall be on the Lake Isle before sundown."

"Then I bid you safe passage and will wait anxiously for your news." Morgause embraced her sister, kissing her on the cheek. "I must go now, or I will be late for the ceremony. Lot forgives me many things, but I think that this would not be one of them."

Morgan looked at the other woman. "Nimue, will you come with me? It is some while since you visited the Lake Isle, and I think you would like to bid your mother a reverent farewell."

Nimue looked at her uncertainly. "You are right, Lady. It is nearly a year since I visited Avalon, but I have never walked the enchanted pathways, I'm not sure if I'm ready."

"If you trust to my protection, no harm will befall you. The dangers are to the mind, not usually to the body, and a stalwart heart will stand you in good stead." It had been Vivian who had walked beside Morgan when, as a young girl, she had taken her first steps upon the Elven pathways, the enchanted thoroughfares of the Fae that lie beneath the human realms. There were many tales told of the dangers that faced those who trespassed upon the faerie paths, to lose one's wits, or be transformed into some strange ungainly creature, or perhaps worst of all, to be placed in thrall, held captive in the Elven lands, only to be released many years later, by which time all those that one had known and loved were long since dead and gone.

But Vivian had instructed her well, teaching Morgan not only the spells and charms that gave her mastery of the enchanted pathways, but also the rules of conduct that allowed her to converse with civility and confidence with the Lords and Ladies who commanded them. She knew them well, and held them in respect, but she neither liked nor trusted them.

"Nimue, it was your mother who gave me the skills and knowledge to walk safely through the faerie realms. I feel it is only right that I now pass them on to you. Come with me. You will be safe, I promise."

And so, Nimue agreed to accompany her, and the two women went together to make their preparations for departure.

<h1 style="text-align:center">CHAPTER NINE</h1>

<h1 style="text-align:center">THE GRAND TOURNEY</h1>

having found a pleasant tavern that not only served well-kept and crafted ales, but also boasted a cook whose skill with pies and pastry were second to none, Sir Ector and his party missed the tourney's opening ceremony. By the time they returned to their tents the moon was well risen, and all of them were somewhat the worse for wear.

Sir Ector was feeling particularly emotional, hugging his friend and swearing vows of eternal comradeship, which Pellinore rather sleepily returned. He then turned to his son who was sitting inelegantly on the grass and trying, with little success, to pull off his boots. Arthur had eventually come to his rescue, and he was now gripping his foster brother's calf, laughing as he began to tug.

"Come on, you lightweight, put your back into it," taunted Kai. "You're nearly as bad as the idiot we saw at the castle trying to pull out that sword."

"I'm . . . doing . . . my . . . best," panted Arthur, giving a mighty heave, and falling over backwards as the boot finally came off.

Ector and Kai both laughed unsympathetically as Arthur, who was not used to strong ale, rolled down the slope, coming to rest at the bottom, Kai's boot clasped protectively in his arms. He lay still, looking up at the stars, and within a matter of seconds began to snore.

"Well, my boy," said Sir Ector, clumsily patting his son on the back, "tomorrow's your chance. Archery first and then the long sword. How are you feeling? Can't wait to get to the lists, I'll be bound." Kai said nothing, preferring to wiggle and pull at his second boot.

"What's this, cat got your tongue? You're not nervous are you, boy?" Sir Ector sat down awkwardly on the grass beside him. "You can't be nervous, you're a chip off the old block and you'll do us proud, lad. Everyone from the Forest Sauvage has faith in you. You know that, don't you?" Again, Kai said nothing. He was beginning to feel more than a little queasy, and just wished his father would go away, so he could get some sleep.

He still hadn't decided what he was going to do to get out of competing in the longsword, and the more he thought about entering into combat with some of the knights he had seen practising this morning, the more uncomfortable he felt.

Sir Ector reached over and patted his son rather heavily on the shoulder. "I quite envy you, boy. There's nothing like your first tourney. Oh, if I could turn back the years, I would jump at the chance." He fumbled in his robes, bringing out a small flask, which he uncorked, took a swig of and passed on to his son. "Here you are, have a nightcap. A little, tiny sip of spiced mead. That's what you need. We're going to be celebrating tomorrow, I just know it."

Kai raised his hand, trying to push away the flask, but Ector just laughed and held it closer to his face. Kai took one sniff of the strong, pungent fumes and felt his stomach cramp and then heave. Turning his head away from his father, he was copiously and violently sick.

ARTHUR WOKE BEFORE IT WAS light. His back ached and his clothes, crumpled and dew-dampened, felt uncomfortable. Making his way quietly into the tent he stepped carefully over the sleeping forms of Kai and Sir Ector and extracted a change of clothing from his pack. He dressed quickly, pulling the pale blue tabard emblazoned with falcon's wings—the crest of the Forest Sauvage—over his head. He felt excited. Today was going to be a big day. It was his first tournament, and he had an important part to play. As squire to his foster brother, it was not only his job to act as herald, announcing Kai's lands and noble lineage as he entered the lists, but also to make sure his weapons were in good order and he had everything he needed.

Bearing this in mind, Arthur decided to carry out one final check. He picked up the large leather bag that contained Kai's tourney gear and made to take it outside. As he did so, something tugged at his tabard, and looking down, he saw Kai staring at him angrily. "What are you doing with my pack, Arthur? Leave it alone."

"I thought I'd check your gear one last time, just to make sure you've got everything."

"Well, I did that last night. Just leave it alone; everything's fine." Kai sat up and stretched. "Now put it down, will you. Here, beside me."

Arthur was rather surprised by Kai's words. But he did as he was bidden. His foster brother tended to leave all practical arrangements to Arthur, and it was most unlike him to reject an offer of assistance, or to do any work for himself if it could be delegated elsewhere. Still, he reasoned, maybe he's nervous and just wants to be absolutely certain that all is as it should be.

Kai pulled the pack close to him but didn't seek to open it. His temper restored, he smiled up at his foster brother. "By the Goddess, I have a terrible thirst this morning. Fetch me a small beer, will you?"

Within a short time, everyone was awake and getting themselves ready for the tourney. Kai's armour and weapons were packed into a cart which was harnessed to Sir Ector's horse, and father and son, now dressed like Arthur in Forest Sauvage blue, declared themselves ready to depart.

King Pellinore and Lamorak soon joined them. Despite their indulgences the day before, they both looked rested and well groomed. Pellinore's horse was resplendently caparisoned in red silk, with lions rampant; Lamorak, having finally persuaded his father to allow him to enter the jousts, was bursting with excitement as the two families made their way towards the tournament field.

Although it was still not long after sun-up, there were people everywhere. Many of those who would be competing had, like Kai and Sir Lamorak, decided to arrive early, to stake their claim to a shaded spot where they could rest between their bouts. Arthur watched as squires and heralds scurried round, helping to assemble the brightly coloured awnings emblazoned with their master's sigils and coats of armour, and laying out helmets, chain-mail and weaponry upon hastily erected trestle tables.

Along each side of the field, tavern-keepers and wine merchants were constructing their stalls, and carts containing barrels of ale or cider and large flagons of wine and mead were being unloaded. Alongside these, pastry cooks and sweetmeat vendors were also setting up shop and at the far end of the field, a firepit had been dug, and a tousle-haired boy was turning the spit upon which a whole ox was slowly roasting above the glowing coals.

The field itself was divided into a number of combat areas, each dedicated to a particular event. At the very edge of the competition grounds were small, roped-off enclosures, where the wrestling and hand-to-hand fighting would take place. In the centre, marked out by an array of flags and pennants, was the joust. This was a long, rectangular stretch of the field divided by the tilt—a low wooden fence separating the two knights and preventing them from riding into each other.

Beyond this lay the archery range, which faced down towards the river, and unlike the other areas of combat, was not ringed by rows of tiered seating. The butts had been put in place for the first round; they would be moved back as the competition progressed, increasing the difficulty of the challenge, and bales of hay were being rolled into place to catch any stray arrows that fell foul of their target.

The royal boxes and seating for the nobility were situated to the right of the field, overlooking the area set aside for the long sword and with a good view of the joust. Unlike the tiered benches in other parts of the field, this area was roped off, and armed sentries were already standing guard to prevent any but the great and the good from taking a seat there. This stand had also been provided with bright silken awnings to provide protection from the sun, and pages were currently employed ensuring that the seats were furnished with cushions embroidered with a double-headed eagle, the coat of arms of Lot of Orkney.

Along the front of the royal enclosure, heralds were unfurling banners. Arthur and Kai recognised the arms of the Ceintish tribes—three black crows on a white background, and the simple black and white stripes of the kings of Brittany, but were at a loss to name the others, and had to turn to Sir Ector and King Pellinore for enlightenment. King Pellinore, who was rather fond of heraldry, was happy to oblige.

"Now the Raven in Flight is the banner of the Northern Lords, not to be confused with the raven couchant, the emblem of the lords of Norway, who are kinsmen to King Lot. The Black Boar Impaled on a Broken Spear is the banner of Sir Bedivere of Wales, and the red lions rampant represent the men of Cornwall and Lyonesse."

"And what about that one over there?" Arthur pointed to a banner that had just been unfurled, showing a silver lion with two tails, positioned rampant on a blue background.

"Oh, that is the banner of Sir Dinadan," replied King Pellinore.

"Sir Dinadan? Isn't that the knight we saw yesterday?" asked Arthur.

"I don't know," replied Kai. "And to be honest, I am not particularly interested." Both he and Lamorak were keen to make their way to the archery range. The first event would be starting in less than an hour, and they wanted to make sure they had declared their entries in good time.

Kai did well in the archery, easily beating Lamorak, whose arrow failed to find its target in the third heat. Kai continued to shoot well in both the fourth and fifth heats, securing himself a place in the final round of the competition, which was scheduled to take place in front of King Lot and Queen Morgause on the final day of the tourney.

Sir Lamorak redeemed himself in the joust, unseating three far more seasoned warriors than himself, before he was unseated in turn by Sir Bedivere. Relieved that his son had not only done well, but emerged unscathed, King Pellinore was happy to join an equally jubilant Sir Ector in a flagon or two of cider whilst Lamorak and Kai prepared themselves for the final event of the day—the longsword.

All the combatants had been assigned a space to prepare for their bouts in a makeshift pavilion that had been erected for the purpose at the edge of the field, behind the royal enclosure. Sir Lamorak had no squire, and Arthur had offered to help him put on his armour, a proposal Lamorak gratefully accepted. They were just adjusting his hauberk when Kai burst in on them.

"Arthur, what have you done with my sword?" he shouted, rushing up to Arthur and grabbing him by the scruff of his neck. "I told you not to meddle with my things. It was there last night, and now it's nowhere to be found."

"But I haven't touched your sword. I didn't even open your pack. You told me not to and I didn't." Arthur was stammering, eyes wide in disbelief as Kai pushed him backwards, sending him sprawling to the floor.

"You bastard liar. I don't believe you."

"But Kai, why would I?"

"You've always been jealous of me. Jealous because I have a father and you haven't, jealous because I know where I come from and you don't." At each word, Kai lashed out at Arthur, kicking him in his legs and stomach as he scrabbled backwards towards the tent wall.

Sir Lamorak looked on hesitantly, not sure what was going on, and uncertain if it was his place to intervene.

"But Kai, that's not true, you're my foster brother." Arthur was gazing up at Kai, who had finally stopped attacking him, unable to believe what he was hearing.

"You didn't want to be my squire, you wanted your place at the tourney, and because you couldn't have it, you've decided to spoil it for me. If I don't have a sword, I can't fight. That's what you wanted, isn't it?"

"No, Kai, it isn't. I'm sorry. I don't know what happened to your sword, but I'll find you another. I promise." And without another word, Arthur pulled himself to his feet and ran from the tent.

THE STREETS AROUND CAER-LUNDEIN WERE empty. Everyone was at the tourney, and none of the shops or taverns had felt it worth their while to open. Even the sentries had been given permission to leave their posts, and so when Arthur arrived at the entrance of the castle, red-faced and breathless, there was no one at all to be seen.

Racing into the courtyard, Arthur vaulted over the ropes that surrounded the small patch of grass and the large stone anvil. When he had rashly promised that he would provide a replacement sword for his foster brother, he had not had the faintest idea where to find one, but as he ran out of the pavilion his eye had caught the silver lion on the banner belonging to Sir Dinadan. He instantly thought of the sword sticking out of the anvil in the castle courtyard. Kai had said that it was some kind of sideshow, and the sword probably wasn't a particularly good one, but right now, that didn't matter. Kai needed a sword. He told himself that he'd bring it back after the tourney and explain what had happened to whoever was in charge. Surely in the circumstances, they would understand.

Hardly pausing for breath, he reached out and grabbed the hilt with both hands, expecting that he would need to expend considerable effort if he was to pull it from its cumbersome stone scabbard. To his surprise, the second his hand touched the pommel, he felt a gentle movement, and with no exertion at all, the sword was his.

He looked at it, first in surprise, and then in wonder. He had never seen anything like it before. It was a beautiful object, delicately crafted, with strange and intricate designs worked into the metal. It was the most perfect thing he had ever seen, and now that it was in his hands he felt a strange reluctance to part with it. But Arthur was never one to go back on his promises. He was honour-bound to take the sword back to the tourney ground and hand it over to his foster brother.

He turned, and with a single downward swipe, cut through the rope that bounded the enclosure. The sword handled well. It felt well balanced in his hand, almost as if it had become a part of him and it had sliced through the heavy tarred and plaited rope as if it had been a skein of cotton.

Arthur could tell that this sword was special, and he was certain that Kai would not want to give it up once he had handed it over. As he began to jog through the empty streets towards the tournament ground, he was thinking of ways in which he could persuade his foster brother to return the blade after the tourney. A sword like this was a prize indeed, and he would need to give it back to its true owner if he didn't want to find himself in even more trouble.

When he got to the pavilion, he found King Pellinore and Sir Ector fussing around Sir Lamorak, who had sustained a slight injury in his bout and was bleeding, although not deeply, from a cut to his arm.

Kai was standing slightly to one side, his face expressionless. Just then, a man wearing royal livery entered the pavilion, proclaiming loudly, "Call for the Forest Sauvage. Kai from the Forest Sauvage, please make your way to the lists."

Sir Ector turned to his son, "What's that, did they call you?"

"Yes, Father," said Kai, his words broken with feigned disappointment. "There is no help for it; I am going to have to forfeit."

"No, Kai, you're not." Arthur rushed towards his foster brother and handed him the sword. "I promised I'd get you a sword, and I have."

Kai looked at him in disbelief, as the official reappeared. "Final call for the Forest Sauvage. Kai from the Forest Sauvage, please make your way to the lists."

"He's over here," Sir Ector called loudly, raising his hand to attract the attention of the official, who immediately made his way towards them, and rather fussily began shepherding them towards the lists.

Sir Ector gave Arthur a pat on the back. "Well done, boy. This has been rather a rum do. I don't know where Kai's sword has got to, but whatever happened, you have more than made up for it." Arthur smiled with relief. He had been worried that his foster father might have had harsh words for him if he too had blamed him for the disappearance.

Pellinore had finished bandaging his son's wound and the four of them made their way out of the pavilion, planning to watch the contest from the side benches. It was only then that Arthur remembered it was his duty to act as Kai's herald and rushed back to the lists, arriving just in time.

As this was Kai's first competition, it was his right to enter the field before his opponent. The trumpeters had already begun to sound the fanfare announcing the bout when Arthur found Kai, looking very green about the gills, standing nervously by the entrance to the arena. Arthur noticed that he was holding the sword in such an ungainly way that it looked as if he had absolutely no idea what to do with it. Next to him was his opponent, a burly knight in battle-worn and dented armour, who exuded an air of great confidence. His shield was in place and his sword at the ready. He clearly meant business. Beside him, holding his helmet, was his squire. The lad looked a little younger than Arthur and winked at him, saying: "We thought you'd chickened out. You don't half believe in cutting it fine."

But there was no time to reply as the tourney official lifted the flap and pushed first Arthur and then Kai into the arena.

Arthur looked around him, suddenly daunted by what he had to do. He slowly made his way towards the centre of the field. There were people everywhere, faces looking down at him from the tiered benches, voices catcalling from the stands that lined the edges of the lists, eyes staring at him, arrogant and amused, from the seats within the royal enclosure. He saw two people, richly dressed, with jewelled crowns upon their heads, and thought that they must be King Lot and Queen Morgause. Next to them sat a tall man with long white hair and beard. He was wearing a white cloak, and in his hand, he held a wooden staff. There was something about him that seemed familiar, but Arthur couldn't think about that now.

Finally, after a walk that seemed to take forever, they had arrived at the centre of the Arena. Kai was standing beside him, still holding his sword and shield as if he didn't quite know how they got there, or what they were for. With a final flourish, the trumpeters brought their fanfare to a conclusion. Arthur cleared his throat.

"Your Majesties, my Lords." His voice was weak, squeaky with nerves. He heard laughter begin to break out behind him and saw the Queen Regent's lips twist in a sardonic smile. He coughed and tried again.

"Your Majesties, my Lords, ladies and gentlemen." This was better. "May I present Kai, son of Sir Ector, son of Sir Antor, son of Sir Artus, lord and master of the Forest Sauvage."

Kai stepped forward and bowed clumsily, first to the royal box, then, turning, bowed to the left, and to the right, to the applause of the crowd and the delight of Sir Ector, whose voice could be heard proclaiming. "That's my boy, that is. The pride of the Forest Sauvage."

Arthur spoke again, uttering the ritual words he had been taught by the sergeant at arms. "Your Majesties, we honour you with this sword. We pledge loyalty to you and the Goddess, and in all things seek your grace and favour." As he spoke, Kai walked slowly forwards, until he was standing directly in front of the royal box. Dropping to one knee, he bowed his head, and he raised his sword.

King Lot stood, gestured with his hand to show he accepted both the homage and the combatant, but before he could speak, to give permission for the bout to continue, the old man with white hair leapt to his feet and leant forward, pointing furiously at Kai, shouting, "This is an imposter! The sword he holds does not belong to him. He has no right to it."

Arthur saw the Queen looking at the sword, her face suddenly pale with shock. She got to her feet, also pointing at the sword and spoke, in a voice that rang throughout the arena. "That man is a thief. Guards, guards, arrest him."

CHAPTER TEN

UPON THE ENCHANTED PATHWAYS

Morgan and Nimue had left Caer-Lundein within the hour. They were dressed in travelling robes, and each carried a small haversack, but other than that, they were unencumbered. Morgan led the way, guiding her companion through small alleyways and side streets less crowded than the main thoroughfares, and within a relatively short time they had reached the Isle of Thorney. The river was shallow at this point, and they crossed with ease, making their way to Tot Hill, an ancient mound at the centre of the island.

Thorney was small and unpopulated. It lay between the River Tyburn and the River Thames and was prone to flooding in winter when the tides were high. But this was not the reason it was uninhabited. The place had a reputation for the strange and the uncanny, and although it was rich with lush and abundant grassland, few were brave enough to take their beasts across the ford to pasture them on Thorney.

Despite the soft grass and gentle slopes of Tot Hill, none who knew the place would ever spend a night there and it was whispered that any traveller foolhardy enough to do so was risking his life. Tales were told of a party of four brothers who refused to pay the price demanded for a room at the inn, choosing instead to cross the bridge and seek repose upon the island. In the morning, only one had returned, staggering across the river, weeping and raving, his wits completely gone. His hair had turned white and his face—which had been fair and unlined when he had set out the previous morning—was now wrinkled and lined as that of a man four times his age. What had become of the others, no one knew, but it was felt that they had paid a price far greater than the coin or two the innkeeper would have taken from them for a bed.

The Isle of Thorney, like the Ring of Brodgar, was a place of power. It was a sacred place, with a small shrine to the Goddess set amongst the reeds and held in particular reverence by the druids, who would often celebrate their Beltane rituals upon its shores. In such places, the walls that shield the mortal world from the realms beyond are thin, and to those who have the knowledge, a portal to the enchanted pathways is usually to be found.

However, unlike Brodgar, whose deep-seated primal magics were distasteful to the Lords and Ladies of the Fae, Tot Hill was also a gateway to the Elven halls, and thus a place of danger.

Morgan had walked slowly round the base of the hill until she found a small, circular patch of ground where the grass was a darker green than that which surrounded it. Here she stopped, making sure she did not step within the circle and warning Nimue to do likewise.

"Now it is important to understand this. The enchanted pathways were not built by the Fae. They are ancient, and created by deeper magics, far greater than anything even the Lords and Ladies can command. Indeed, in places where the Fae choose not to dwell, the pathways offer little danger to those who, like us, are trained in the magics. So, remember, it is not the paths themselves that you must guard against, but the Lords and Ladies of the Fae."

Nimue was listening, but Morgan could see that something was troubling her. "Lady, forgive me, perhaps you know that many call you 'Morgan the Fae?' They say that you count the folk of faerie as your friend, and that they even do your bidding—and yet you speak of them as if they are your enemy."

Morgan gave a sharp bark of laughter. "The Fae will never befriend any mortal, and any who believe otherwise are fools. They are as cruel as they are beautiful, and as cunning as they are cruel. But they respect power and those that wield it, and have, in their own way, a code of honour—and punish harshly those who break it."

Morgan sighed. "I have walked the pathways for many years now, and there have, on occasion, been times when Avalon's interest and the wishes of the Lords and Ladies have coincided. We have helped each other, and when it is expedient, will continue to do so. But I am not their friend and they, most certainly, are not mine. Does that answer your question?"

Nimue nodded, her face still serious but no longer troubled, and Morgan gestured once again towards the small patch of darkened grass.

"This is the gateway. We shall enter the mound in a minute, but first, I must be certain you are ready." Morgan opened her haversack and took out a small bundle of herbs and flowers. She deftly fashioned them into a posy and handed it to her companion.

"Wear this in your hair or pin it to your dress. It will give protection from all but the most vicious of their enchantments."

"What is it, Lady?" asked Nimue.

"Rowan, St. John's wort, clover and simple meadow daisy," replied Morgan, who had by now fashioned a similar bunch for herself and was plaiting it into her hair.

"Now, as I told you, there are certain rules you must follow when seeking the hospitality and goodwill of the Fae. Can you remember them?"

Nimue nodded, but a little uncertainly. "I think so. You should never accept a gift, and neither should you eat or drink anything that is offered you. You should never tell the Fae your real name, but also you should never lie to them." She looked questioningly at Morgan, who nodded, gesturing to her to continue.

"You should show gratitude when they help you, but never say the words 'Thank you' as that will place you under an obligation. Finally, no matter what you see or hear, you should never, ever leave the well-trodden ways."

Morgan nodded, her face serious. "These things sound easy out here, under the Goddess' blue sky, but once you place your feet upon the enchanted pathways there will be much to daunt and confuse you. The best advice I can give you is to hold your tongue, do not speak at all unless you have to, and when you do, make sure you weigh your words with care." She reached again into her haversack, and took out a horseshoe, a long, rusty nail and a small jar of honey. She gave the honey and the nail to her companion.

"Both of these may be of service to you. The honey is to be used as a gift. The Fae are very fond of it, and value it highly." Nimue stashed the small jar away securely in her own haversack.

"And the nail?"

"Wrap the nail in your kerchief and keep it in your pocket. You need to keep it out of sight, but within easy reach. It is only to be used in the most desperate of circumstances. The Fae cannot abide the touch of iron. It burns them like fire, and any who use it against them will become their sworn enemy. But they will be unable to hold you if you use it to resist them."

Nimue did as she was told, and Morgan wrapped the horseshoe in a small piece of cloth and placed it safely in one of the deep pockets of her travelling cloak.

"Now, are you ready? Once we stand within the ring and I cast the enchantment, there will be no going back. Are you still certain that you wish to accompany me?"

"Yes, I am sure."

"Then come with me."

The two women stepped forward together, onto the darkened grass.

NIMUE LOOKED AROUND HER IN astonishment. She was no longer standing in the sunshine on the grass of Thorney Island, but in a long corridor, high-ceilinged and lit with torches. There were no windows, but many, many doors. One, that shone like burnished copper, was so small a young child would struggle to walk beneath its threshold, whilst another, ebony-dark and studded with silver, was so tall and wide that six of the mightiest warriors could easily walk through it abreast, wearing their helms and armour.

At first Nimue thought the place was silent, but then she heard the sound of voices, faint at first, but gradually getting louder. They had begun to make their way along the corridor, Morgan walking slightly ahead of her, looking neither to left nor right. As the voices became more insistent, Morgan said quickly, "They shall soon be upon us. Now remember: You must not tell them your name, but you must not lie to them. Make sure you have thought of what you will say if they ask you to introduce yourself."

Just as she finished speaking, one of the doors opened and two figures stepped gracefully into the corridor. They were both tall, and very slender and their skin was pale blue, the colour of a starling's egg. Their eyes were large and almond shaped, with long, dark blue lashes. The woman, whose eyes were also blue, had pale hair, which seemed to float around her like a cloud. Her companion, who was now walking towards Morgan, his arms outstretched in welcome, had eyes the colour of honey, and his hair, which he wore in a long plait, was a deep, glossy green. They were both dressed in robes of deceptive simplicity, and their beauty was unearthly.

"My Lady Igrainesdottir, it does me good to see you. It has been too long since you graced us with your presence." He bowed, and taking Morgan's hand, raised it to his lips. He opened his mouth slightly to kiss it, and Nimue saw that his teeth were very white, and each of them was pointed, like a cat's.

The woman had now also reached them. Though slightly smaller than her companion, she was still easily a head taller than Morgan, and she had to bend gracefully towards her in order to kiss her, first on the left cheek, and then the right.

"You are welcome—but I see you have not come alone. Is your attendant a visitor? Or have you brought an offering?" As she spoke, the woman turned and smiled, quite terrifyingly, at Nimue.

Morgan feigned not to notice her companion's discomposure.

"Well met, my Lord Aldaron, it is indeed good to see you. As it is you my Lady Miriel, but please, I pray you, do not tease. This is my handmaid, and I have vouchsafed her safe passage."

"And what is your name, sweeting?" asked Aldaron, approaching Nimue. Taking her hand, he raised it to his lips, but he did not kiss it. Instead, he bit gently on her forefinger, not sharp enough to break the skin, but enough to startle her, and if she had not been prepared, she was certain that in her discomposure she would have given him a very different answer.

"I am called Orphan, and I give you thanks for your hospitality. I am honoured to walk upon your paths."

"You are welcome . . . Orphan. The Lady Igrainesdottir has vouched for you, and that is enough for me." Aldaron was still holding her hand. He patted it and then let it go. "But come, you talk of hospitality, and we have done nothing to honour you, to show our deep and heartfelt pleasure that you have ventured here. I pray you, please join us at the feast."

Morgan smiled a rueful smile, as if filled with the deepest regret. "I am sorry my Lord, my Lady, but we have pressing business, and I fear we cannot linger."

"This is not like you, my lady. When last you graced us with your presence, you danced the tarantella, and if my memory serves, you wore out three pairs of shoes." He spoke lightly, but there was an edge to his voice that neither Morgan nor Nimue could ignore.

The woman spoke. "You will not make me beg now, will you? You seek safe passage, and all we ask in return is that you join us at the feast. Surely you will not be so churlish as to refuse?"

"I think you give us no choice, my lady, but as I said, our business is urgent. I do not have the liberty to wear out three pairs of shoes on this occasion."

Aldaron gave his arm to Nimue, and Miriel linked hers with Morgan. In apparent amity, the four of them walked along the corridor until they came to a set of tall double doors made of burnished gold. At their approach, the doors swung open, and there was noise, light and music. They were looking down into a room in which hundreds, or maybe thousands, of people were dancing.

Some, like Aldaron and Miriel, had skin of palest blue, but they saw also faces of many shades of green, palest lilac and darkest purple. They danced with grace and elegance and seemed almost to float as they leapt in the air, turning and twirling in time to the driving, insistent melody. But not all the dancers were Lords and Ladies of the Fae. As Nimue watched, she caught sight of first one, and then another, pale, human face. Each of them was thin to the point of emaciation, and their eyes seemed to gaze ahead of them unseeingly as their bodies twitched and gyrated in time to the music.

There were men and women both, their clothes aged and ragged, their hair unkempt. Some wore no shoes, and their feet were bruised and bleeding as they danced, on and on. Nimue did not need Morgan to tell her that they were in thrall. Some would have been stolen away, others would have stumbled inadvertently upon a faerie ring or some other portal. All were now enslaved to the Elven lords, and she knew that sadly, very few would ever win their freedom.

She had been so busy staring at the dance floor that she had not realised that they had been making their way across the room to an ornate golden table, upon which was laid out a most sumptuous feast.

All manner of food was there, roast meats and baked fish, bowls of vegetables glossy with melted butter, huge wheels of cheese and loaves of fresh-made bread, dainty pies and sweetmeats, piled high on elegant platters and bowls overflowing with luscious fruit, ripe and succulent. Miriel turned to her, smiling gently, and offered her a small plate holding two plump and perfect strawberries. They smelt delicious, and without thinking, Nimue reached out and took one.

She raised it to her mouth, savouring the delectable fragrance that smelled of summer, and childhood, and happiness—she was caught up in the beauty and the pleasure, and she knew it would be even more intense once she had tasted the fruit. But just before she placed it on her tongue, just before her teeth closed upon this perfect object of her desire, she looked up and saw Miriel gazing at her in intense anticipation. She was licking her lips, and Nimue could see the sharp points of her teeth.

Suddenly, the strawberry did not smell so sweet, and she returned it to the plate, saying, "No, you are kind, but I am not hungry."

Morgan, who had been distracted by Aldaron's conversation, had not noticed what had been going on and when she heard Nimue's words she turned pale with horror. Miriel hid her disappointment well, and turned to Morgan. "Lady Igrainesdottir, you have not told us of the urgent business that has brought you to our halls."

Morgan knew that the death of the Lady of the Lake was not something she could conceal, and remembering that Vivian had been well-known to the Elven lords, she told them what had happened, and that they had to make their way to Avalon in haste.

Aldaron listened, and when she had finished said, "We forget how short a span is allotted to you mortals. It saddens me to hear of her demise."

Morgan looked at him in surprise. He seemed serious, as if the news of Vivian's departure had genuinely caused him pain. She had never before heard any of the Fae speak of sadness, particularly in connection to a human. Miriel nodded. "The Lady was a friend to us, and Avalon has long been our ally. And who is to be Lady now?"

Again, it would gain her nothing to dissemble. "I have been raised and trained to be her successor, but I must make haste. The Goddess must be served, and if I am not there to claim my place by sunrise, another must, perforce, take my inheritance."

"Then you must be gone from here with great dispatch," said Miriel, and Aldaron nodded. Whilst Morgan was making her official farewells to Miriel, Aldaron turned to Nimue, raising her hand once more to his lips.

Without warning, he bit her swift and sharp, causing a drop of blood to form upon her palm, which he licked up directly with his rough, cat-like tongue. She pulled her hand away, a shocked look on her face as he whispered in her ear. "Oh, you taste sweet, my dearest Orphan. I am truly saddened that I did not get the chance to dance with you. I shall be sure to look out for you, should you pass this way again."

MORGAN AND NIMUE MADE THEIR way back to the corridor, which now seemed very dark and quiet. Nimue did not tell Morgan what Aldaron had said and done. She was worried it might ignite her companion's anger and lead her to taking action which could delay their departure. By this time, Nimue wished for nothing more than to leave the unsettling and dangerous world of the Elven lords as quickly as she could.

Their pace was brisk and they walked in silence, meeting no more of the Fae folk on their way. Morgan supposed that some sort of message had been sent, instructing that they be allowed to make their way unimpeded. She was grateful that their dealings with the Fae had been relatively straightforward, but she also knew that Miriel and Aldaron's decision had not been made from kindness. They had put her need above their own pleasure, something the Elven folk were rarely known to do and she acknowledged to herself that she was now in debt to them. And without doubt, she was certain that they would make her pay.

Within a few hours they reached the end of the vaulted corridor, and passing through the rough stone archway that marked its boundary, found themselves standing on the edge of a deep ravine. Above them, the sky was dark and starless, and the moon hung low on the horizon, huge and yellow. On the other side of the ravine, they could see a pathway leading up into a tunnel, and beyond it, Morgan knew, was Avalon.

The rocky crags were steep, and they could see no obvious pathways down. Leaning over the edge, Nimue was unable to even see the bottom of the gorge, but they could hear, far below, the rushing of water.

"How are we to get across?" asked Nimue.

"I don't know," replied Morgan

"But you have been here before, surely you know the way."

Morgan shook her head. "Each time you walk the enchanted pathways, the route is different. The doorways to the mortal realm remain the same."

She pointed across the ravine. "I recognise the tunnel and know it leads to Avalon, but I have never before approached it from this place."

"Can you use an enchantment?"

"No," said Morgan. "There is too much old magic here. It won't allow any other spells or enchantments to work successfully. We will have to find a way to get across on foot."

They decided to look about them, and carefully, because the light was not good and the ground underfoot uneven, they made their way along the edge of the ravine. After walking for some time, they found that there were no pathways or crossings to be seen and that the rocks were becoming larger and the incline steeper. After walking for a short while longer, the path became unpassable, and they were forced to retrace their steps. This time they were more successful and soon came across a narrow stone bridge stretching out across the ravine, pale and delicate in the moonlight.

It was beautiful, and to Nimue, completely terrifying. The surface of the bridge was little more than two hands' breadth at its widest point and had no parapet. It curved up, into the sky, and at its apex seemed to reach beyond the moon.

Morgan walked towards it and placed a foot gingerly on the stonework. It held firm. She placed her other foot upon it and took two more hesitant steps. The bridge remained steady. She turned to Nimue. "This will do. It's the only way, and we must take it. Do you want to go first, or will you follow me?"

Nimue looked at the bridge in horror. "But I can't. I just can't do that."

"Well, if you don't, you are going to have to go back and beg Aldaron and Miriel for mercy, and somehow, I don't think that would end happily—for you at least."

Morgan began to walk slowly across the bridge. She made her eyes focus only on the small expanse of stone in front of her, and looking to neither left nor right she soon reached the crown. The next bit was more difficult. Going downhill put more pressure on her legs, and it was difficult to keep the steady, regular pace she needed. She stopped, closed her eyes and immediately felt as if she was going to lose her balance.

She wobbled, and heard Nimue's terrified gasp, but she was able to right herself, and soon the slope lessened and she could see the side of the ravine in front of her. Jumping jubilantly onto the ground, she waved across to

Nimue. "Come on, it's not that bad. You can do it. Just keep steady, keep your eyes open and don't look anywhere but your feet."

Uneasily Nimue approached the bridge, and placing one foot carefully upon the old stone, she took her first slow and tentative steps, repeating Morgan's words just under her breath, for reassurance. "Keep your eyes open, don't look anywhere but your feet . . . keep your eyes open, don't look anywhere but your feet . . ." Slowly but surely, she made her way forward, climbing one step at a time, lifting one foot, putting it down, lifting the other, putting it down and not looking at anything but her feet.

She had reached the crown. Morgan called jubilantly, "Well done, Nimue, you're halfway there. Now take it slowly, no need to rush; just look at your feet."

"That's what I'm doing," snapped Nimue, who was feeling both scared and irritated. She looked directly at Morgan, and as she did so, her mind fully registered the terrifying drop below her. She heard the distant sound of water, rushing over rocks, and she trembled, feeling her knees give way beneath her.

Morgan watched in horror as Nimue shuddered, swaying precariously high above her. She knew that if she called out it might make things worse and so she waited and could do nothing as Nimue fell forwards onto her knees. She was grasping onto the sides of the bridge with both hands, and her breath was coming in short, shuddering gasps. "I can't get up. Morgan, I can't," she called.

Morgan knew that if she left her there, the chances were that she would never regain her confidence and would eventually fall into the ravine. She also knew that if she tried to help her, Nimue might panic and then both of them could tumble to their deaths.

If she left her, she would be in Avalon in just a few minutes, and nobody would know what had happened. Everyone knew the enchanted pathways were treacherous, and Nimue's would be just another life that they had claimed.

Morgan looked up at the small, pathetic figure huddled at the top of the bridge. This was Vivian's daughter. Like her, she had known no other home but Avalon. Like her, she was a servant of the Goddess.

With a sigh, Morgan stepped once more upon the bridge and slowly made her way to Nimue. It took a long time to get her on her feet, but eventually, they stood together, hand in hand. Slowly, Morgan reversed her steps, walking backwards, her eyes fixed unblinkingly on Nimue's face until eventually they both jumped unsteadily from the bridge onto the edge of the ravine.

For a moment they hugged, Nimue incoherently trying to express her gratitude, but Morgan put her finger to her lips saying, "Hush Nimue, as Morgause said, the Goddess makes sisters of us all. You would have done the same for me. I need no more thanks."

She turned away from the ravine and walked towards the tunnel. A few moments later, Nimue followed her.

CHAPTER ELEVEN

YOU ARE THE KING

Arthur watched the door close, checked it was properly shut, and then sat down gingerly on the large, well-upholstered bed. He'd removed his Forest Sauvage tabard hours ago but otherwise was still dressed in his tournament gear and his feet were aching. He bent to pull off his boots, but when he'd done so, had no idea where to put them.

"Just leave them on the floor and someone will tidy them away for you." Arthur started in surprise. He had thought he was alone. The voice came from somewhere beyond the fireplace, but the speaker, whoever he was, remained concealed in the shadows. "You don't have to worry about things like that anymore. You are the king. You have rather more to concern yourself with than the disposition of your boots."

Arthur did as he was told as Merlin emerged, bearing a flagon of wine and two delicately wrought goblets. He took a seat on one of the solid benches to the side of the fireplace and gestured Arthur to join him. Pouring wine for both of them, he handed a goblet to Arthur and then raised the second in a gesture of salutation, before drinking deeply.

Arthur took a tentative sip. He had not drunk wine before, but then, he had never before been proclaimed king. It was all very bewildering.

"Well . . . Sire . . . how do you like your apartments? They belonged to your father you know, and out of respect, I instructed that they should stand empty, waiting for the day that you would claim them."

Arthur looked around him. He hadn't really given a second's thought to his surroundings, but he now saw that the walls were hung with rich, beautifully woven tapestries and that there were rugs and animal skins upon the stone flags, rather than the rushes they used in the Forest Sauvage.

"They seem very nice," stammered Arthur. "But to be honest, I'm finding it rather difficult getting used to all this."

"That is understandable." Merlin nodded sagely, one hand stroking his beard, the other pouring himself more wine. "It must indeed have been a shock to learn that only the rightful heir to Uther Pendragon could pull the sword from the stone. Mind you, if you had taken the time to read the words written below the anvil, you would, perhaps have been rather better informed." Merlin suddenly looked a little worried.

"You have been taught to read, I hope? I was very clear to Sir Ector that you should have a full, and knightly, education."

"Yes, yes, of course I can read." Arthur was a little indignant. "I was just in such a hurry to get a sword for Kai that I didn't really look."

"He's a bit of a piece of work, your foster brother. To deliberately hide his own sword and then blame the loss on the carelessness of another is not, I would suggest, the act of a man of integrity."

"Oh, Kai's alright. He just didn't want to let his father down and didn't know how to tell him he didn't want to fight. The stupid thing is, if he'd only told me, I'd have played along, and then none of this would have happened."

"Indeed," said the druid, steepling his hands, and resting his chin on them. "And then who knows how long we would have waited until the sword was freed from the stone, and you could take your rightful place on the throne of Britain." There was a moment's silence as they both thought of how events might have played out had Kai chosen to take his foster brother into his confidence.

"How did it get there in the first place?" asked Arthur.

"It is quite a long story," replied Merlin, "but in a nutshell, the Lady Morgan, she who may soon become the Lady of the Lake, and her sister, the Queen Regent Morgause, placed enchantments upon it so that only the rightful heir, chosen by the Goddess, would be able to wield it. They had an inscription carved upon it: *Whomsoever pulls this sword from this stone is rightwise king born of all Britain* and had it placed in the castle courtyard." Merlin took another sip of wine. "However, it is not, to be truthful, the right sword."

"What?" asked Arthur, completely at a loss.

"Not the right sword," repeated Merlin, a little testily. "Oh, the one you have is good enough, well made, with an impressive provenance, but the sword you are born to command is something else entirely. Its name is Caliburn, and it is a mighty blade indeed. Caliburn has long been destined to be wielded by our most mighty warrior, one who will return these Isles to peace and prosperity, and for years, I guarded it, waiting for the day when I could place it in the hands of he who was born to hold it." He looked across at Arthur, as if he was still uncertain that the person sitting with him was, in truth, the babe he had entrusted to Sir Ector all those years ago.

"But on his deathbed, Uther—your father—took it out of my keeping and placed it under the protection of Avalon. I will beseech the Lady to bestow it on you, but until she does so, you needs must make do with what you have."

"To be honest," mused Arthur, "like Kai, I'm not really that much of a swordsman, so I don't suppose it really matters."

"Arthur, Sire, you are soon to be crowned High King of all Britain. The throne is yours by right, by blood and by divine intention, but to hold it, believe me—you will have to win battles." Merlin got to his feet and began to pace about the room.

"I placed you with Sir Ector for three reasons. Firstly, he is a noble knight who honours the old ways, and I knew he would raise you to do likewise. Secondly, the Forest Sauvage is far away from anywhere. I felt it unlikely that many would visit and become curious about who you were and where you had come from. But thirdly, and perhaps most importantly, because I thought he would raise you, alongside his son, with a true knight's education and a knowledge of both chivalry and warcraft." He looked at Arthur, slumped dispiritedly on his bench by the fireside. "It would seem I was mistaken."

Arthur felt indignant, both for himself, but perhaps more for his foster father, who had always treated him with kindness and consideration. "You said yourself that Sir Ector had no idea who I was. He didn't know that I would have to be king one day. He did his best, but it wasn't always easy. The rents and tithes have been bringing in less and less, and he couldn't afford to get us tutors. We learned from him—and King Pellinore when he came to visit—and I don't think we did that badly."

Merlin looked at him and gave a small sigh. "Perhaps I was wrong to keep your identity completely hidden. Who knows? Maybe I would have done better to bring you to court when you were still a young boy and raise you as Uther's son for all to see and acknowledge." Merlin shrugged and downed his goblet. "But even a druid and enchanter with my power and standing cannot turn back time, and so we must work with what we have. We begin tomorrow."

"Begin?" questioned Arthur.

"Begin," repeated Merlin. "You have much to learn, and swordsmanship is but a small part of it. I must ready you to take your place upon the throne."

Merlin went on to explain that plans for Arthur's coronation were now underway, and before the year was out, he would formally be crowned High King of Britain and the Isles.

What he did not say was that the events of the day had been unwelcome to many, and had it not been for the diplomacy and fast thinking of King Lot, the young Arthur would have been faced with immediate, and outright rebellion.

IN THEIR CHAMBER OVERLOOKING THE castle courtyard, Lot and Morgause were engaged in heated conversation.

"I cannot believe that you have accepted the claim of that country bumpkin." Morgause was pacing frantically, her anger making it impossible for her to stay still. "You should have clapped him and that other young idiot in chains, aye and that fool—Sir Ector or whatever his name was."

"But Morgause, he pulled the sword from the stone. You saw it with your own eyes." As indeed she had . . .

AFTER THE DRAMATIC EVENTS AT the tourney, Arthur and Kai had been taken under guard to the castle courtyard, where the stone anvil now stood empty. Merlin, who had almost immediately taken the sword from the hands of the terrified Kai, returned it with all ceremony to its former resting place. He then asked Morgause if she could give assurance that the enchantments would still hold, and when she answered that they would, he proceeded to instruct one of the castle guards to attempt to remove it.

The man, tall and well built, had positioned himself beside the stone, and tried with all his might to pull out the sword. When, after several minutes of hard labour, he had been unable to make it give way, Merlin had said. "Well, it would appear the enchantments are indeed as strong as ever. Let us now ask the boy who had the audacity to wield this sword to show us how he got it."

He then had the ropes that bound Kai's hands untied and commanded him to do likewise. After trying half-heartedly, he had turned to Merlin saying. "I can't do it . . . of course I can't."

"So how did you come by the sword?"

"He gave it to me." Kai had pointed frantically at Arthur, who stood, hands bound, in the custody of the guards.

Merlin gestured to the guard, ordering him to release his prisoner, and indicated that Arthur should approach the stone.

"What is your name boy, and where do you come from?"

"My name is Arthur, sir, and I am the ward of Sir Ector of the Forest Sauvage."

"And is it true, did you pull the sword from this stone?"

"Yes, it is, sir. I meant no harm. I am squire to Kai—and he needed a sword. I'd seen this one here and thought no one would mind if I borrowed it. I always meant to return it after the tourney."

Merlin had a strange expression on his face as he said, "Well, Arthur of the Forest Sauvage, let me see what you can do."

And Arthur had reached out his hand. The moment his fingers had touched the sword's hilt, it slid smoothly from the anvil, and he brandished it, rather uncertainly in front of him.

By now a small crowd had gathered. Merlin had spoken quietly, so only Lot and Morgause could hear him.

"This is indeed Uther's son. Look at him, his height, those eyes. How could anyone doubt it? And he has taken the sword from the stone. Proof positive that he is the one chosen by the Goddess."

"Whoever he is," Lot had replied, "we need to end this circus without delay."

"This is ridiculous," Morgause had said. "Bring all this to a close, Merlin. I have had enough." She had made to move away from the court-yard, but Lot had reached out to her saying, "No, Morgause, we cannot leave. We need to see what is happening, and if trouble erupts, we must act. We are the regents of this land and its peace depends upon us."

Morgause had shrugged off her husband's hand in irritation, but she made no further move to depart.

The crowd was beginning to get restless, with shouts and calls of "impostor" and "who does he think he is" ringing loudly around the courtyard. Arthur looked nervously about him, and handed the sword back to Merlin, who returned it once more to the stone.

"Good people, listen to me." Merlin's voice was loud and strong, and it had echoed as it rang around the castle walls. "You know the enchantments that have been placed upon this stone, and you know how many good knights and true have tried their luck . . ." He had paused and looked hard at the assembled gathering, his blue eyes piercing, challenging any to naysay him. ". . . and you know that none have been successful." There was a murmuring from the crowd and many people nodded in agreement.

Merlin spoke again. "And yet today, as we gather together to remember the High King, we have seen the sword taken from the stone, by one who by right of birth and with the blessing of the Goddess, is the heir to Uther Pendragon."

There had been more shouts from the crowd:

"Who is he then?"

"Where did he come from?"

"Who will vouch for him."

Merlin was just about to reply when three men, two of them red-faced and out of breath from running, made their way into the courtyard.

One of the men had been shouting; his voice cracked and harsh with agitation. "Where is my son? Has anyone seen him? Kai, from the Forest Sauvage?" It was Sir Ector, looking frantically about him, his eyes darting to left and right as he searched the faces in the crowd for his son—or for someone who had news of him.

He had spotted the guards and was beginning to walk towards them, when he had seen first Merlin and then Kai and Arthur, standing rather shamefacedly beside the stone anvil.

He was about to run over to them when Merlin held up his hand. "Sir Ector, you could not have arrived at a more timely moment." He gestured towards Arthur. "I pray you, please relate how this man became your ward, who he is and who brought him to you."

With some stumbling and hesitation, Sir Ector had told the tale of Merlin bringing the boy to him, one cold, snowy day over twenty years ago, and that the druid had not told him whose son he was, only that he should keep him safe.

"And so, you have Sir Ector—and all the realm shall thank you for it," said Merlin, signalling to the guard, who released Kai, and then pushed Arthur towards the place where Merlin, Lot and Morgause were standing.

"Listen, and listen well," said Merlin, turning once more to face the crowd, his voice now strong and confident. "I shall tell you what only a few have ever known. Uther Pendragon had a son, born to the Lady Igraine of Cornwall, and half-brother to the noble Lady Morgause, who is today Queen Regent." There were gasps and heckles from the crowd.

"The boy was entrusted to me, and I gave him to Sir Ector for safe-keeping. Now, you see him before you, a babe grown to manhood, on the very day we gather together to celebrate and remember his father. The Goddess has sent him to us, and he has proved himself the true heir before you all." There were cheers, but still some dissenting voices, and one man had called loudly, "It's a trick! I don't believe it."

"Who speaks?" asked Merlin, and a tall man made his way to the front of the crowd. He was strong and well-muscled, although his hair and beard were shot with grey, and he was dressed in half armour. His shield was emblazoned with a silver coronet set upon a blue background.

"It is Sir Caradoc of Cornwall. He was one of my father's men," whispered Morgause to her husband.

"Ah, Sir Caradoc, it pains me that you are not prepared to take my word," Merlin spoke gently, with just a touch of reproach in his tone. "Perhaps you could examine the stone, and suggest how such a trick could be attempted? Indeed, why should you not try to pull the sword from the stone yourself."

Sir Caradoc looked apprehensively at the druid. "It is not that I doubt you did as you said, my lord, but where is the proof that this mere stripling, this humble squire, is Uther's son?"

"You have heard my story and Sir Ector's. This man is Arthur, son of Uther." Merlin's voice was harsh now, and it was clear he would brook no argument. "Now why don't you take a look at the stone?"

And with the eyes of the crowd upon him, Sir Caradoc had given the stone, and the sword, a very thorough examination. He had looked beneath it and to all sides and finally attempted to separate one from the other. He pulled with great exertion, until his face was red and the sinews on his neck and arms stood out, but it got him nowhere. Finally, he had released his grip on the sword hilt and collapsed in exhaustion on the ground.

Merlin nodded to Arthur. "Please, could I ask you to try once more." Arthur had reached out his right hand, and in one smooth gesture once more pulled the sword from the stone to the sounds of cheers, and huge applause.

Merlin had then turned to the crowd and sent them on their way and gestured to Arthur to follow him. The ancient druid had made his way into the castle.

MORGAUSE KNEW THAT SHE COULD not deny the evidence of her own eyes. She pulled her shawl more tightly around her shoulders, and looked at her husband ruefully, remembering what had happened next.

After Arthur had once more pulled the sword from the stone, she and Lot had made their way swiftly and in silence to the council chamber. There was much to discuss, but the discussion was not one which could be held in public. She was already engaging in furious and heated discussion with Lot's brother, Lord Urien, and King Ban of Brittany when Merlin, followed by a red-faced and uncertain Arthur, had entered the room.

Morgause had risen to her feet and moved towards him. She was richly dressed and although she was no longer wearing her crown, her hair was held in place with a jewelled band which glittered in the lamplight, and her eyes sparkled with a lambent flame as she looked at the nervous youth that Merlin had pushed, none too gently, in front of her. She had smiled and Arthur blushed, bending his head in embarrassed confusion. He stumbled, trying to make a bow, and Morgause, recognising that all eyes were upon her and her response to this stranger would be marked and commented upon throughout the court, had placed her hand upon his arm and smiled up at him. "Well met, sweet brother, I am your sister, Morgause. Welcome to your castle of Caer-Lundein." And she had leant towards him and kissed him on both cheeks.

Arthur's face burned, and his eyes glistened as he looked at her, as if about to brim with tears. She felt a sudden certainty that no woman had ever kissed him before. It was clear to Morgause that he had no idea what to say or to do, and she did not feel that it was in anyone's best interest to allow the spectacle to continue. She had raised her hand, addressing the council assembly, saying, "Forgive me if I presume upon our relationship, but I think, Arthur, this has all been too much for you. The King, or rather the Regent . . ." she corrected herself hurriedly, "suggests that perhaps it would be better if you get some rest tonight and meet with the council in the morning. Would you agree to this?"

Arthur had been more than delighted to agree, and although Merlin had not appeared happy with the way events were turning out, he had allowed Morgause to lead him to his chamber.

THE HOUR WAS LATE, BUT Morgause and Lot were continuing to find it hard to settle. Morgause stopped pacing and turned to face her husband, who was sitting on the window seat, looking out at the courtyard where the stone anvil still stood. Making a note that she would need to get it removed in the morning she asked, "So tell me again what happened after I left the council. You have decided that you must uphold the Bastard's claim, but what of the others? What of Cornwall and Lyonesse? What of Brittany?"

"Please, calm yourself my love. And remember before you berate me, I am not the only one to acknowledge him," said Lot. "You called him 'Sweet Brother' in front of the whole council."

"I was only doing what you asked me to do. Whatever the truth of the matter, this man, this Arthur, is my enemy. Either he is an impostor, in which case he should be hanged, or he is my bastard brother, and deserves nothing better than to be thrown to the dogs."

"Succinctly put my love. And which do you think it is?" Lot had been pouring something from a delicately made wooden flagon and passed her a small beaker. "Spiced mead. It will not make our troubles go away, but perhaps it may somehow help us decide how to address them."

Morgause took a sip of the mead and paused for a second, relishing the subtle taste upon her tongue. Even at a time like this, her senses were always open to pleasure, and the mead was good, perhaps some of the best she had ever tasted.

"In all honesty, Lot, although I am loath to admit it, I do not in my heart believe him to be an impostor." She sighed, shrugging her shoulders. "I have faith in the skill of my sister, and also in Anna. I am certain the enchantments would have held, and if that is the case, then I cannot believe that anyone, other than the chosen of the Goddess, would have been able to take the sword."

"And that, my love, is why I see I have no choice but to stand behind him." Lot was once again looking towards the courtyard. As they watched, three horsemen rode out from the stables. They all were sporting the Orcadian crest of the double-headed eagle upon their tabards and as they looked up towards the window one of the riders raised his arm in greeting. Lot returned the salute and the riders wheeled, spurring on their horses, and were gone.

"Who were they?" asked Morgause, "and where are they bound?" Lot appeared not to hear her.

"I managed to convince Cornwall and Mercia, and Wales will stand with us. I have faith in King Ban—Brittany has always allied itself to Uther, and he will not betray his old friend's son." He heaved a sigh.

"And the Irish kings and the Northern Lands, the Lords of Gewisse, Lindsay and Ceint, where do they stand?" asked Morgause.

"Ceint is undecided. Gewisse and Lindsay also." Lot turned to face her, his eyes dark with worry. "I do not know about the Irish. Five of the Northern Lords, my own kinsmen, have abandoned us outright. They will not swear fealty. I have sent envoys to talk with them, led by my brother. Those were the horsemen we just saw ride out. Perhaps they will listen to Urien when they will not listen to me."

Morgause looked at her husband, recognising his fear and anxiety. "Come my love, if we are doing what the Goddess wishes, then surely all will be well. We will gain nothing by worrying, and tomorrow, we shall see what Ceint and Gewisse have decided."

She took his hand and led him to their bed, to offer comfort and a small forgetting of the troubles that now beset them.

CHAPTER TWELVE

PLANTS AND PROPHECIES

Early the next morning, Merlin sent word to Morgause before she broke her fast, asking if he could speak with her. As a meeting place he suggested the walled physic garden, which led down to the river. Herbs and plants cultivated for their magical or healing properties were grown here, and the heavy oak door to the garden was kept locked to prevent any who were ignorant of plant lore from inadvertently doing danger to themselves or others. It was an ideal place for private conversation.

The garden was always beautiful and tranquil, but never more so than on this midsummer morning. Droplets of dew hung on the leaves and still closed flower buds, and they sparkled on the spider's webs that stretched between the trees. The just risen sun shone upon them, creating shimmering refractions of multi-coloured light.

At its centre was a circular bed, planted with yellow-flowering laburnum, used to make emetics and treat certain digestive ailments, and delicate, white-flowered ransom, sometimes known as wild garlic, used to heal wounds and provide relief to rheumatic and aching limbs. The garden's beds, intersected by sandstone pathways, radiated out from the centre like the sun's rays; here grew herbs such as sage, thyme, fennel, chamomile and rosemary, all cultivated for both their culinary and medicinal qualities. In other beds, plants with more perilous properties were to be found. One was devoted to monkshood, sometimes also known as aconite, whose delicate blue flowers when used in small doses, and with the correct preparation, will calm fevers and assuage nervous ailments, but which are fatal if taken in too large a quantity. In another grew the tall, delicately nodding pink, purple and white spikes of digitalis—or foxglove—infusions of which the castle physician used to strengthen the heart and improve blood circulation. But these plants were perilous; indeed, the touch of the leaves to the skin could cause pain and inflammation, and if administered by those unskilled in its cultivation and preparation, would likely lead to fainting, paralysis and death.

On the far side of the garden, which is where Morgause found Merlin waiting for her, were grown the plants cultivated for rituals, magics and enchantments. She was immediately aware of the heady scent of the lavender bushes, whose flowers she used in healing rituals and to bring peace and tranquillity to the heavy heart. Here also grew borage and burdock, both used for cleansing rites and to increase strength and confidence. Beyond them were dandelions and calendula, also known as marigold, for divination magics and to aid spiritual and prophetic powers. And in the shade of the tall and fragrant bay trees, whose leaves could bring visions and provide protection from evil, grew the darker plants, vervain, wormwood, henbane, deadly night-shade and lady's mantle, used for magics designed to harm and hurt.

"Good morning, Morgause," said Merlin. "Thank you for joining me. You look a little weary. I hope the events of yesterday have not caused you too much distress?" He had known her since she was a child, and when they were alone, they spoke with an informality that neither would have countenanced before the court.

"I am vexed by much of what happened yesterday, Merlin, as I'm sure you, of all people, will have realised." Morgause reached down and plucked a stem of lavender, releasing its fragrance as she rolled its woody stem and tiny petals between her fingers. "As you know, the oaths of fealty have gone unsworn, several of our Northern Allies have decided to abandon us, and I have had to deal with that benighted fool Dandy wanting me to tell him what to do with all the food that has—and will be—wasted, now the tourney has come to its sudden and unpropitious end. Is it any wonder I look weary?"

"And there is something else you have not even mentioned." Merlin looked around him with a slightly mischievous expression. "I wonder which of these delicate blossoms you would choose to harvest, should you be wanting to create an infusion for your new-found brother?"

Morgause took a seat on one of the stone benches placed against the wall and gestured to the druid to join her. "I will speak frankly with you,

Merlin. I had always thought that there could be little love lost between me and any child of Uther Pendragon. Last night I had hoped that Lot and his council would have him clapped in irons and thrown in the dungeons."

"And now you do not feel that way? What has changed your heart?"

"You may find this hard to believe, Merlin. I know you think me frivolous, too concerned with clothes and jewels and the pursuit of pleasure"

Merlin sought to speak, but she raised her hand to silence him.

"But I have been raised to honour the Goddess. When I left Tintagel, on that long, sad journey to Orkney, my mother sent her taibhse to ensure I understood the importance of Solstice and to impress upon me my duty as a queen—to always honour and respect the Goddess and uphold and work towards the fulfilment of her wishes."

Merlin looked at Morgause. She clearly had not had time this morning for her usual, more elaborate toilet and was wearing a simple homespun robe and overdress, secured at the waist with a woven belt from which hung a small pouch. She wore no jewels, and her hair fell to her waist in a simple plait. Merlin felt, rather to his surprise, that she was speaking as she was dressed, without artifice.

"Last night, Lot reminded me that Arthur could not have done what he did if it had not been what the Goddess willed. Indeed, I myself helped put the enchantments in place to ensure that would be so. And so, although it has been difficult, and I have had to battle with myself, I recognise that, like my husband, I must bow to Her wishes, and accept that this *Arthur*, wherever he has come from, is Uther's son and that the Goddess intends he be crowned king."

She smiled ruefully. "So, in answer to your question, I shall pick borage and burdock."

Merlin reached out and patted her hand. "I am pleased that you have decided to respond this way, Morgause. Arthur's path will be hard enough without having you as an enemy."

He went on to share with her the plans he intended to put in place to prepare her half-brother for his coronation and future kingship. He told her that he would propose to the council today, that the coronation take place at the festival of Alban Elfed, otherwise known as the Autumn Equinox. This was a feast day held particularly sacred by the druids, as a time of balance, before darkness overtakes light, and as a celebration of harvest and the fruitfulness of the land. Symbolically, this would be a good time for the people to accept, acknowledge and crown their new ruler. Until then Lot would be asked to remain as regent.

Alban Elfed was some months in the future, and this, Merlin told her, was necessary because there was much that would need to be done in preparation, not least of which would be the kingly education of her half-brother. Arthur would need to be coached in swordcraft and the strategies and arts of war. He would need to be given lessons in political history and geography, to understand not only current events, but also those that had preceded them, so that he could navigate the intricate alliances and enmities that contributed to the delicate balance of power. The castle sergeant at arms, Lot and Merlin themselves could act as tutors or mentors for these aspects of Arthur's education, but there were other elements that they were not so well qualified to undertake.

Merlin explained that he would shortly need to go to Avalon, to pay his respects at Vivian's funeral and to represent the Crown in offering formal congratulations to the new Lady of the Lake, who both assumed would be Morgan.

"And whilst I am there, I have other business," he mused. "I must entreat Morgan, or whomsoever is Vivian's successor, to return Caliburn to my protection."

"And what is wrong with the sword that Arthur won for himself yesterday?" asked Morgause.

"Oh, the sword that you and your sister placed enchanted in the stone is a fine weapon, and worthy of a king, but it is not the sword that Arthur is destined to wield. Uther placed Caliburn in Vivian's protection until such time his true heir appeared. Now he has, the sword should be returned."

"Did not Uther say, on his deathbed, that the sword should be given to one who rules by right, by the will of the Goddess and by the consent of the people? I am not sure that all those conditions have been fulfilled."

"How would you know what Uther said?" said Merlin, startled. "I suppose Morgan told you, a confidence she should not have shared, even with a sister. Still, I cannot make you unhear what you have heard.

"As Lot told you last night, the majority of the council has either accepted Arthur, or is minded to do so. We shall find out later this morning if the Lords of Ceint, Lindsay and Gewisse will agree to acknowledge his sovereignty. Once we have them, the rebel Northerners will stand alone."

"Aye, but until you have them," interjected Morgause, thoughtfully, "I think it unlikely that Avalon will agree to hand over the sword."

"I will deal with that difficulty if it arises. In the meantime, I must also request that the Lady sends one of her wise women to Caer-Lundein to teach Arthur. He must learn about the mysteries of the Goddess if he is to understand the role he, as king, will have to play within Her holy rituals, and to truly understand the solemnity of the oaths and promises he must make at his coronation."

Merlin told her that he planned to leave for Avalon before the week was out, and that he would be away for at least seven nights. He had been uncertain how much he could share with Morgause, knowing the deep-felt resentment she had harboured towards Uther—and by extension, to his son. This was why he had wanted to meet her, and he acknowledged to himself that he was feeling pleasantly surprised. As she sat beside him in the physic garden, calm and composed, he felt that she had achieved a sense of acceptance and purpose, recognising that Arthur's kingship was simply the fulfillment of the Goddess's will.

He asked her if, in his absence, she would be prepared to oversee the education of her half-brother in those aspects of court life at which she excelled. He would need to learn how to command the royal household, he would need to understand at least the elementary rules and ordinances of court etiquette. And he would need to be taught to dance. Smiling slightly, Morgause agreed to this. "Yes, between myself and my ladies, we will attempt to make this sow's ear resemble something more closely aligned to a silk purse. And then you shall have him crowned and we will all live happily ever after."

Involuntarily, Merlin was unable to prevent his lips from shaping a half-smile, recognising the truth in Morgause's word, and he stroked his beard ruefully. "Unfortunately, the coronation is only the first hurdle. The Goddess has vouchsafed to me visions that make it clear that the first years of Arthur's reign are unlikely to be peaceful. He will have to fight to keep his crown. That is why he must have Caliburn.

"The prophecies are clear—Arthur is destined to become High King in truth, to unite the Britannic Isles and force the invaders from our shores, but there are conditions and caveats—the first being that he must hold Caliburn in his hand and use it to give battle to his enemies."

"And the second?" asked Morgause.

"The second is more complex, and I believe, far more difficult to avert." Merlin sighed and, getting to his feet, began to pace slowly, back and forth, supporting his weight upon his staff.

"The ancient Pendragon prophecies state that the reign of Uther's son, the Once and Future King, will be brought to end if he faces in battle a noble warrior, born at Beltane within a year of his coronation."

"But Merlin, if this babe is to be born at Beltane next, it will be twenty years or more before he grows to become a warrior capable of challenging a High King. Why worry about something so far in the future?"

"Morgause, I forget that, unlike your mother and your sister, you are not Avalon trained and perhaps know little of our histories. Have you not heard of the great warrior Cú Chulainn, who first took up arms at the age of seven, or Finn MacColl, who at but six years old, excelled at hunting and swordcraft?" Morgause shook her head, once again feeling that old sense of resentment and unfairness that she had been sent to Orkney, rather than to Avalon.

Merlin continued, "Arthur has much to do if he is to secure peace within these Islands, and without amity between ourselves, we cannot hope to defend our shores from further invasions. He will need time in which to do this, and the threat of defeat within just a few years of his coronation is one that I should, and do, take seriously."

"And is this second of the prophecies widely known? Do others share your concern?"

"No, Morgause," answered Merlin. "And perhaps I should not have spoken of it to you. It was known only to myself and Vivian, and I doubt that she spoke of it even to your sister. When the time is right, I must tell Arthur, but until then, I beg of you to keep it to yourself."

Morgause nodded, saying, "I may not be well-versed in history, but I am quite able to see why a tale such as this should not be bruited abroad."

With that, Merlin had to be satisfied, and he took his leave, heading first to the Great Hall to break his fast, and then to the council chambers, where he and Lot would meet with the Lords of Lindsay, Ceint and

Gewisse to hear what they had decided, and to find out if Urien had returned with news of the rebellion from the north.

Morgause declined to accompany him, saying that she wished to remain for a while in the garden. There were indeed plants she wished to gather in order to prepare an infusion for her half-brother, but these would not be borage and burdock. Instead, she plucked stems of rosemary and jasmine and, taking a small sickle from her pouch, cut through stalks of flowering fennel.

She was beginning to formulate a plan, and if it was to work, she would need Arthur, the half-brother she had spent most of her life hating and despising, to grow rapidly to love and trust her. Jasmine signified intimacy and connection; rosemary was for loyalty and fennel for trust.

Carrying the plants carefully, not wishing to damage the delicate jasmine, Morgause returned to her chambers to prepare the infusion. Whilst it was distilling, she would compose a message to be sent to Morgan on the Lake Isle. She had little doubt that, by the time the messenger arrived, her sister would have become fully acquainted with the news of their half-brother's reappearance, but she felt it would be helpful to inform her of Merlin's impending visit and his intention to regain possession of the sword Caliburn.

She would say nothing of her half-formed plan. She needed more time to think it through, but she would ask Morgan to return to Caer-Lundein as swiftly as she could.

CHAPTER THIRTEEN
THE LADY OF THE LAKE

Vivian's body had been ritually cleansed, anointed with lavender and rose oil and dressed in ceremonial robes. At her wrists were gold bangles, and she wore an ornate torque inlaid with precious stones around her neck. Morgan was glad that the ancient tradition, in which the head of a deceased person was removed from the body in order to release its spirit, was no longer practiced. It was hard enough to look upon the face of the woman who she had loved, revered, feared and—in the last few years—protected and cared for, without thinking of it being severed from its body.

She and Nimue had arrived in Avalon travel-weary and dishevelled, just before midnight on the day of Vivian's death, but no one on the Lake Isle had been asleep. The tunnel from the enchanted pathways emerged in a small cave on the lakeside, and although the sky was heavy with clouds, the lights blazing out from the great house made it easy for them to find their way.

Morgan was greeted with reverence and shown immediately to the chamber where Vivian's body was being prepared. The air was filled with the fresh, crisp scent of pine and rosemary, and the room was ablaze with lighted candles. Three women were at work, but when Morgan and Nimue entered, they moved away from the body in silence and stood, heads bowed and hands folded, to await the words of the woman destined since childhood to inherit Vivian's mantle as Lady of the Lake.

Morgan recognised the older of the three women, and she kissed her on both cheeks. "Olwen, it is good to see you again, but sad that it should be in such circumstances."

"Welcome home, my lady. I was frightened that you would not reach us in time. Although she had been ailing for some years now, in the end Death came swiftly to her, with little warning."

"Oh, the Lady made sure a message reached me. When did Vivian ever leave anything to chance?"

They smiled, remembering the formidable woman who had provided them with guidance, leadership and inspiration for so many years.

"And now, please, seek your beds, and tell your fellows to do likewise." Morgan kindly but determinedly gestured to the women to leave the room, brushing aside their questions and offers of help: "Nimue and I will do all that has to be done. I would be grateful if you will tell everyone that I shall see you at sun-up on the lakeside and will declare then what is to be done."

When the last of the women had gone and the door had closed upon her, Morgan motioned to Nimue to approach the bed where Vivian was lying. "Come, we have work to do. Olwen and the others have done well, but we must ensure she is purified, cleansed, anointed and dressed with full honour, so her spirit can make its way joyfully to the Goddess."

Nimue approached the bed slowly, as if hesitant to look at the body of the woman she now knew to have been her mother. "Do you mean that her spirit has not left her, that it is still here, near to us, perhaps even in this room?"

"I am almost certain of it. After leaving you at Caer-Lundein, her taibhse would have returned to its physical resting place within her body, and until we have completed the rituals and blessings to release it, her spirit is earthbound and is unlikely to have strayed far."

"Morgan, is there a way to reach out to her, to her spirit, I mean?" If Morgan was startled by the question, she did not show it; she knew of such magics but also knew them to be both difficult and dangerous.

"Yes, there is a way, but it is perilous. Why would you do such a thing?"

"I would ask about my father. Everything that I had been told about who my mother was and what had happened to her turned out to be a lie. I need to know about my father—and she is the only one who can tell me."

Morgan was silent for a moment. It was Vivian herself who had taught her how to cast the enchantment that would allow the recently deceased to speak to the living. They had been together in this very room, where they often went when Vivian wished to impart knowledge that she deemed essential for a future Lady of the Lake, but which she did not believe it suitable or advisable to share with the other young women who were being schooled in Avalon. She could recall their conversation as if it had happened but days ago.

She and Vivian had already gathered the herbs that they would need for the ritual—dandelion, calendula and wormwood—and were about to begin the enchantment. Rather than a human body, the stiff grey form of the kitchen tabby lay on the table in front of them.

"And remember, child, this is not a magic you should use lightly. The spirit will have begun its journey to the realm of the Goddess and may not take kindly to being dragged back to the earthy realm."

"Could it harm me?"

"Physically, no . . . but mentally . . . yes."

"How? I do not think I would be frightened of a spirit."

"You think highly of yourself child, as well you might, but overconfidence is as dangerous as fear. Believe me when I tell you that a spirit can do many things to disturb or even destroy the one who calls it."

"Are we in danger now?"

"No, the consciousness of a cat is not sophisticated enough to do us harm. Tabby probably does not even realise she is dead, and when we call her back, it will be simply as if she had woken from her slumbers by the kitchen fire."

And so, they lit the candle and performed the rituals, and Morgan had watched in fascination as Vivian summoned the cat's spirit back into its body. It had raised its head slightly and given a little mew, but when it tried to stand, the animal found it did not have enough strength, and began to utter long, drawn-out howls of distress. The noise had been most unpleasant, and Morgan had been relieved when Vivian had snuffed out the candle, and the cat once again lay still.

Until now, she had never had cause to use the enchantment, but Morgan was also keen to know more about the circumstances surrounding Nimue's birth. She particularly wanted to know why and how Vivian had broken one of the most solemn vows she had made to the Goddess. So she told Nimue that she would try to help her but warned her that this was a spell that she had never attempted to cast on her own, and that she could not guarantee that it would work.

They were both still dressed in travelling clothes, their faces and hands dusty and grimed from the climb across the bridge. They agreed to wash and change before undertaking the enchantment and when that was done, Morgan went to the apothecary's store to fetch the herbs that they would need.

Nimue had returned to the room first and Morgan found her sitting by the bed, holding Vivian's cold and lifeless hand. She was staring intently at her face, which in death was still beautiful.

"It is strange" she said. "She is so familiar to me, and in many ways, I hold her dear. But I don't feel as if I ever really knew her. I still can't believe she was my mother."

Morgan said nothing, but as she moved to the window to extinguish the candles that stood upon the sill, and to open it, so the room would not be completely sealed, she placed her hand for a moment on the other woman's shoulder.

When all but one of the candles were doused, the room was dark, save for the fire of bay twigs and rowan that Morgan had kindled in the grate. Putting the candle on the small table beside the bed, she gave small sprigs of dandelion and calendula to Nimue saying.

"Place these on the bed, above Vivian's head and at her feet. These will help create boundaries, guiding the taibhse back to the body we are calling it to re-enter." Moving deftly, wishing to place the plants exactly as she had been instructed, Nimue did as she was bidden. Morgan then selected four delicate sprays of the bitter-smelling wormwood, handing two of them to her companion. "Now, arrange these with care, to the left and right of her head, so her eyes can see us, and her ears can hear."

Again, Nimue did as she was bid.

Finally, Morgan leant over Vivian's body, and with great gentleness and delicacy, opened her mouth, nestling the third sprig of wormwood upon her tongue. "If she is willing to speak to us, this will help her find her words."

The preparations complete, Morgan composed her mind, drawing to herself the energy she would need to work the enchantment. She emptied her thoughts of everything but Vivian and the questions only she could answer, and when she had honed this need to a single point of focus, an insistence that was almost burning in its intensity, she knew that she was ready.

She looked at Nimue questioningly, making sure that this was still what she wanted, and when the other woman gave a small nod, Morgan took the final spray of wormwood and held it to the flame:

"Across the void, I call to you

Beyond the stars, I call to you

Beneath the waves, I call to you

Vivian, return to us."

The bitter smell of burning wormwood filled the room and the candle flicked. A sudden gust of air flurried into the room from the open window.

As they watched, they saw a ripple, like a small wave of energy, run, from Vivian's feet, over her thighs, her stomach and shoulders, all the way up to her face. Slowly, the fingers on first the left hand and then the right, began to move, one by one, hesitantly tapping on the coverlet. Another wave, this time stronger and more violent, and then a shudder, and the eyes of the body on the bed sprang open.

Vivian had returned.

She retched and spat, clearing her mouth, and then tried to sit up, but like the cat from Morgan's memory she did not have the strength to lift herself. Leaning forward, Morgan gently wiped the remains of the wormwood from her chin and raised her to a more upright position.

"Thank you for returning to us. I hope we have not displeased you, Lady."

"Why have you summoned me, Morgan of Avalon?" the voice was harsh and guttural.

"There are questions we would ask, Lady, but they are few, and we will not detain you long."

"I am displeased, and discommoded. What are these questions? What would you know, Morgan of Avalon?"

It was not Morgan who answered, but Nimue. She had been standing in the shadows and now came forward. Once again, she reached out and held her mother's hand.

"You sent me your taibhse. You told me of your death, and you told me your secret. But you did not tell me everything. Who is my father?"

"Your father was a warrior. He had no wife, and neither the time nor the inclination to raise a child."

"Did you love him?"

"What a question. I carried and gave birth to his child, did I not?"

"Yes, but did you love my father?"

"You are too simplistic, child. What happened between us was not about love, but about duty."

At this, Morgan had to speak. "But what about your duty to the Goddess? The vows you made that you would have no children, that no other being would be more important, or be held above Her in your heart?"

"I did not break my vow. The Goddess remained at the core of my being and my duty to her at the centre of my heart. I was certain when I did what I did that to have this child was to follow her wishes. Merlin persuaded me that it was so, and I believed him."

"Merlin?" asked Nimue. "Is Merlin my father?"

The body on the bed made a strange noise, its mouth twisting and contorting in a strange parody of laughter: "Merlin? Ha! How could you ever think that I would sleep with Merlin, that dry old stick. No, your father was not an old, bearded druid, but a beautiful, powerful man. Your father was Uther Pendragon."

Morgan turned to Nimue. "Uther. But how can that be? He had no children but Arthur. My bastard half-brother."

"You are wrong Morgan, but this is a truth you could not be expected to know. Even Uther thought the child I carried had died in childbirth. Only Merlin and I were party to what had really happened."

And in her cracked and rasping voice, she told them.

Merlin had become consumed with his desire to understand the secrets of the Pendragon prophecies. He had gone deep into their interpretation and meaning, and had become convinced that Uther, who had only recently succeeded to the throne, was destined to be the father of a son who would wield the enchanted sword, Caliburn. This son would, by the will of the Goddess, unite the Britannic Isles, and put an end to the years of invasion and civil war. Now, at this point, Uther had no interest in taking a wife or in having children. All his thoughts were for warfare, to avenge the death of his brother, Aurelius, and to drive Vortigern and the Saxon invaders from Britain's shores.

Merlin was determined to persuade Vivian that it was her duty, as Lady of the Lake, to bear Uther a child. At first, Vivian had protested. She too had a vision regarding the prophecy, when she was a young girl being schooled on Avalon. She had seen a man she now knew to be Uther seated upon the dais at Caer-Lundein, surrounded by noble lords and warriors, with banners unfurled as though for a great celebration. She had seen him stand and hold out his hand to welcome a beautiful women clothed in white, her hair tumbling in tawny waves down her back and on her feet, a pair of swansdown slippers. Vivian was sure that this was the woman who would bear the prophesied child, but Merlin would have none of it. As the years passed and no woman seemed to catch Uther's fancy, she at last accepted Merlin's argument. At Solstice, she had led Uther in the rituals and together, they had conceived a child. But when the child was born a girl, they realised that Merlin's interpretation had indeed been at fault. Yes, the Once and Future King would be Uther's son, but it was not his father who was important, but his mother.

Uther was told his child had been born dead, and Nimue had been raised on the Lake Isle, a child of Avalon, Merlin and Vivian having agreed between themselves that she would never be told the true identity of her parents.

"But when you died your spirit, your taibhse, came to me. Why would you do that?

"Because, my daughter, at the moment of my death, the Goddess revealed to me that I had wronged you, and in her grace, gave me the opportunity to try to right that wrong. That is why I went to you and, in part, it is why I have agreed to answer these tiresome questions.

"Now snuff out that candle and let me go. I wish to be on my way."

Morgan bent low towards the bed: "I have one more question, Lady. Where is Caliburn? I brought it to you from Uther's deathbed. Where is its resting place?"

Again, the body on the bed gave a short bark of harsh laughter. "The whereabouts of Caliburn? I will say only that you shall find out on the morrow, as I always intended that you should.

"And Morgan, keep it safe. It was entrusted to you by Uther, and it is for you to give to Arthur when you deem the time is right. That is your decision, and that is the will of the Goddess. Now, I have had enough."

Morgan gently moved the pillow from her back, lying her once more upon the bed.

She held out the candle to Nimue saying. "I think it is for you to finally extinguish the flame that will put an end to Vivian's time upon this earth."

And with one hand on her mother's brow, gently stroking her fine white hair, she did so.

THE TWO WOMEN COMPLETED THE rituals of cleansing and purification and then sat, in silent vigil, until the sky began to lighten at the horizon. Morgan had not slept. Instead, she placed herself within a reverie so that when the night ended, her mind and spirit were calm and peaceful, although her body ached with tiredness.

Vivian had been one of an unbroken chain of wise women and priestesses who had served the Goddess as Lady of the Lake of Avalon. No one knew when the first lady was established, but it was said that the Goddess had decreed that the power of Avalon would wane if but one day went by without a Lady to command it.

Vivian had prepared her well, and Morgan knew what she must do to claim the title that was her birthright, and for which she had been preparing since she was four years old.

She had instructed Olwen to summon the household to the lakeside at daybreak, and before them all, as the sun rose across the waters of the Lake, she would be declared Lady of the Lake of Avalon.

CLOSING THE WINDOW AND REMOVING the sprigs of dandelion and calendula from the bed, Morgan placed a spray of fragrant lavender upon the coverlet that concealed Vivian's body. Nimue picked up their cloaks, and together the two women left the room.

"Are you not tired, my lady?" asked Nimue as they walked along the corridor, past the door of one of the three scholars' dormitories. "You have not slept for two nights, and there is still much for you to do."

"I have gone longer without sleep, Nimue. Vivian trained me to endure many privations and taught me the art of reverie, so I can calm and rest my mind, even when my body is fatigued." Morgan looked at her companion, who was now wrapping her cloak about her as protection from the lakeside breeze.

"You also have not slept, and these past few days have brought you little but unsettling news and distress. We shall bury Vivian with all honours at sunset. Until then, those who wish to honour her or say farewell may visit her chamber. During those hours, I suggest that you repair to your dormitory and find some rest."

"I shall do so my lady, but first, please permit me to say something. At Caer-Lundein, you and Queen Morgause offered me comfort and kindness, and on our journey here, you saved my life on the enchanted pathways. Last night you enabled me to ask the question that weighed heavy on my heart, causing my mother to speak to me, and tell me truly who I am." Nimue stepped back, and sank to one knee on the soft lakeside grass. The wind caught her hair, which hung loose around her shoulders, and she raised her hands towards Morgan in obeisance. There were tears in her eyes as she spoke. "Lady Morgan, all my life I have felt alone, a friendless foundling, but you have changed that. You have shown me kindness, and you have helped me discover who I am. I wish to offer you my gratitude, and my loyalty now, before you become the Lady of the Lake, so you are clear that, whilst I will always be of Avalon, my fealty is to you, and not to your office."

Morgan said nothing, but taking her hand, raised Nimue to her feet. She leant forward and kissed her gently on the brow. "Nimue, you are the daughter of Vivian and Uther Pendragon. You do not need to kneel to me, or indeed to anyone, for you are the equal of any in this land. But your words have touched me, and I thank you for them. Let us make haste—see, there are already many people gathered at the lakeside."

THE GREAT HOUSE OF AVALON STANDS on an island ringed with rushes, weeping mulberry and willow trees. It is a beautiful and verdant place, where snow and frost are seldom seen, and the rain and wind, when they come at all, are gentle. Its gardens are cared for lovingly and cultivated with care in honour of the Goddess, and beyond the house, the ground slopes gently to the lake. To the west of the island is an orchard. The trees were now in blossom, and the gentle blooms of apple and pear, cherry, quince and medlar fragranced the air, and their delicate petals, lifted from their branches by the wind, decorated the pathway that led to the lakeside and the small, crescent beach.

Here, the household was assembling. Those who dwell on Avalon are pledged to serve the Goddess. Some are scholars, young women sent to the Lake Isle to learn the craft of the magics and the healing arts in order to return to their homes and people, to lead, to mend others and to serve and protect their communities. But many who find their way to Avalon never leave the lake, happy to spend their days giving service under the watchful command of the Lady.

There were now very few remaining who could remember a time before Vivian, but all knew Morgan, who had lived among them since she had been a small child. They knew her to be not just Vivian's protégée and favourite pupil, but the daughter of Princess Igraine and sister of Morgause, Queen Regent of Britain and Queen of Orkney and the Northern Isles.

There was silence as they watched her make her way down the slope and out onto the pale strand. She was dressed simply, in a linen shift of palest green, belted at the waist with a rope of silver thread. Her feet and arms were bare and her hair, which she wore loose, was the colour of midnight. It fell to her waist, and the breeze caught it and lifted it, so it billowed gently around her like a cloak.

She walked in the shallows along the edge of the shoreline until she reached a large boulder covered with lichen, that marked the centre of the strand. Here she stopped. The sun had now risen fully above the horizon, casting a golden glow upon the water; Morgan turned to face the people who had gathered here at her command.

"Good morrow to all of you. We welcome this day in the name of the Goddess. Today, we shall give thanks for the life of Vivian, who took her leave of us yesterday, and is now making her way in spirit to the realms of the Goddess."

There was a murmur of assent from the crowd, and Morgan could see that many of the younger girls were silently weeping.

"We shall lay her to rest at sunset, but until then, any who wish to bid her farewell may do so. We will honour her memory.

But we cannot live in the past. As all you know, it was Vivian's intention and desire that I should succeed her here as Lady. I hope that I have proved to you that I am worthy of this honour, but it is a decision that I alone cannot make, and so, before you all, I will seek the blessing of the Goddess and ask if this is indeed her will."

Morgan turned once more to look out across the golden waters of the Lake. She closed her eyes and began to breathe, slowly and deeply, as she focussed her mind on what she must do. The people standing behind her on the shoreline were silent. The only sounds were the gentle lapping of the wavelets, and in the distance, the joyous cascading ripple of songbirds in the orchards, welcoming the new day.

Throwing back her head, she raised her arms to the sky.

"I am Morgan of Avalon," she cried. Her voice, strong and true, rang out across the water. "Goddess, I am your true daughter, and if it is your pleasure, I shall be Lady of this Lake." Calmly and without hesitation, Morgan placed her foot upon the water and began to walk across the surface.

The water felt firm beneath her, and although the waves splashed her ankle and the wind whipped her hair, she did not stop or falter but moved steadily onwards, until she arrived at the very centre of the lake.

Poised above the depths, she turned to face the shore. If any had doubted her, none did now, and they cheered and called her name, offering thanks and praise to the Goddess. Once more, Morgan raised her arms.

"I am Morgan of Avalon. I am daughter of the Goddess and by her command, and with her blessing, I am mistress of this island—and Lady of this Lake." Her words rang out, loud and strong, reverberating and echoing off the stone walls of the ancient buildings . . . "Lady of this Lake . . . Lady of this Lake." The branches of the weeping trees, mulberry and willow, shook and danced as they paid homage and the birds in the orchard rose together and filled the sky with a swooping, flowing murmuration, singing all the while. On the horizon appeared two white birds, swans flying together, their long necks extended, and their wings beating in serene and elegant harmony. They flew low across the lake towards Morgan holding in their beaks a cloak of silver gossamer that shimmered in the early morning sun.

The swans circled, gliding just above her with outstretched wings. Morgan reached up and took the cloak, which had once been Vivian's mantle, handed down from one Lady to the next. She raised her hand in acknowledgement, and the white birds circled once again and then flew to the lakeside, where they settled amongst the swans and geese who gathered there.

Morgan put on the cloak, fastening it carefully and prepared to return to the shore, when the water to her left became agitated. Small eddies were forming as the water roiled and churned and from beneath the waves an arm emerged, clad in purest white samite, holding a sword. Morgan recognised it at once as Caliburn, the sword that Uther Pendragon had, on his deathbed, entreated her to place under the protection of Avalon.

Its gilded hilt shone with precious stones and as she reached out and took the sword, she could see the inscription forged upon it long ago, in the ancient tongue—"*Tóg suas mé caith mé ar shiúl.*" As she reached out to take the sword, she recalled Vivian telling her that the inscription meant that Caliburn was a sword of destiny, to be used in righteous battle, but always to be restored to the Goddess.

The arm returned from whence it had come, and Morgan, clad now in the mantle that had last been worn by Vivian, and bearing Caliburn, the sword of destiny, made her way back across the waters, to the lakeshore.

She was tired and did not tarry upon the strand, speaking only to Olwen to ensure that all was being made ready for Vivian's obsequies and that someone would be sent to her chamber to keep vigil throughout the day. Gesturing to Nimue to accompany her, she began to walk rapidly towards the house when she heard a cry from the lakeside. "There are riders approaching." Looking out across the water she saw two horsemen. She did not recognise them but saw they wore the livery of King Lot of Orkney.

"Send out the barge, and offer them food and drink," she commanded, "for I do not believe they will yet have broken their fast. When they are rested, inform me, and I shall meet them in the solar."

With that, she made her way to her chamber, hoping to snatch an hour's rest, but try as she might, sleep evaded her. When finally, the messenger came to summon her, she felt so tired that it took all her strength and resolution to place one foot in front of the other.

CHAPTER FOURTEEN
THE OSSU DI PECURA

Gawaine had found this year's Solstice to be a disappointing and a lacklustre affair. His mother, father and most of the court were still in Caer-Lundein and the rituals had been led by Avice, the castle housekeeper and Finn, his father's steward.

All that the rites and ceremonies of the festival demanded had been undertaken—and to the letter, Gawaine conceded grudgingly, for Finn was a stickler for order and protocol, but the bonfire in the castle courtyard had been small, and there had been none of the excitement and revelry of previous years.

"Do you remember last time? Mother caused the bonfire to be lit upon the beach, and we stayed up all night listening to the music."

"Well, you and I did, Gowie, but have you forgotten that the two small fry fell asleep before midnight, and Mother had to get the castle guards to put them to bed?" Agravaine stretched out his foot and prodded his younger brothers in the small of the back with the pointed toe of his boot.

The boys had finished their lessons and household duties for the day, and as the sun was warm and the small wisps of cloud did not appear to promise rain, they had walked to the top of the ancient burial mound of Maeshowe. They were now lounging on the grass together, looking down over Loch Harray towards the standing stones and wondering what to do with the rest of the afternoon. It had been more than a year since Einar had died and they had learned that their father was to be King Regent, but despite their initial excitement and anticipation, not one of them had yet been to Caer-Lundein.

The year had wrought a number of changes in the brothers. Agravaine, nearing thirteen, was now a full head taller than his older brother, with a frame that although lean and wiry, was deceptively well muscled.

Gawaine, who was nearly fifteen, would never be tall but his broad shoulders and rigorous daily practice with bow, spear and long sword had already given him the physical bearing of a warrior. His face had lost the soft plumpness of boyhood and he had begun to develop a patchy and uneven stubble around his chin and upper lip. He did not like this, finding it both embarrassing and a cause of irritation and a few weeks ago he had asked Finn to teach him how to shave his face, using tallow and a sharpened flint. He knew that it would not be long before he would have to do this daily, unless he wanted to sport a red and bushy beard.

Gaheris and Gareth were now on better terms with each other, possibly because Gareth was eight and no longer slept in the nursery. He and Gaheris shared a chamber, and were in the main good companions, although Gareth was still uncomfortable with Gaheris's continued interest in the magics—which his mother's absence had done nothing to diminish.

When he could get away from Avice and his brothers, Gaheris had taken to sneaking away from the castle when he could, spending time with Anna in her small stone house by the lochside. Anna, who had two sons of her own, felt sorry for the lad, who clearly missed his mother, and she could not help but be flattered that he listened to her stories of her early life on the far away island of Corsica with such rapt attention.

He also asked her to help him to learn more about the magics and enchantments that she had brought with her, and whilst she would not involve him in the darker mysteries of the Dream Hunters, she well remembered that Morgause wanted her children to grow up with knowledge of the old ways, and so she was happy to share with him some of the less perilous secrets of the Mazzeri.

Gaheris was looking out across the loch, thinking of the last time he had visited the little stone house, and so lost in the pleasure of his memories that he did not hear Agravaine creeping up behind him. But he could not long ignore Agravaine's foot kicking him painfully in the small of his back. Letting out a sharp gasp at the pain, he looked round angrily, irritated by the look of smug condescension on his elder brother's face.

"Leave me alone, Agravaine, or I'll . . ."

"You'll what? Turn me into a frog, or one of those stupid beetles you were scrabbling about looking for in the stables . . . ?"

Gaheris reddened. Several weeks ago, Agravaine had found him down on his knees searching for beetles for Anna. She had promised to show him how to use them to cast enchantments, but only certain varieties worked, and so far, he hadn't been able to find a single one that had been any good.

"Oh, shut up. You don't know what you're talking about." Gaheris turned his back, only to feel the sharp edge of his brother's boot kicking out at him again, this time in the ribs. Furious, he turned and threw himself at his brother, his small fists flailing as he tried to land a punch on his face. But Agravaine, who now hoped to spice up a boring afternoon with a fight, only laughed.

Dodging the punches, he twisted his younger brother's arm behind his back, pushing him down onto his knees, and rubbing his face into the grass. Gaheris squealed as Agravaine twisted his arm harder, his knee now digging into the small of his brother's back. The pain was unbelievable, but almost as quickly as it started, it stopped. Gaheris felt his arm being released, and the sharp, excruciating spasms that had been running down his back to his knees stopped immediately as Agravaine was lifted up and dumped, none too gently, a few feet away from him on the coarse grass.

"Leave him alone, you great bully," said Gawaine, standing over his younger brother and looking at him contemptuously. "If you want to fight, pick on someone nearer to your own size. I'm happy to oblige." But Agravaine shook his head, having learned some time ago that whilst frequently quicker in the schoolroom, he was no match for Gawaine when it came to any form of physical activity.

Brushing the grass off his breeches, Agravaine got up and walked over to where Gareth was sitting, staring out across the loch.

"And what's on your mind, tiddler? Can you think of anything exciting for us to do on this dull and boring afternoon?"

"I was just thinking that the loch looks so nice today. I'd like to go swimming. What do you think?"

Agravaine looked down at the blue-green waters of the loch. Harray, although the largest Loch on Orkney, was also shallow, and a safe place to swim. Since the death by drowning of Einar, who all the boys had loved and who had been as close to them as any uncle, they had spent little time in the water, but on this afternoon, the sky was clear and the waters calm and tempting.

"You know what, shrimp, that's not a bad idea," said Agravaine. "How about it, Gowie?" and the brothers, all animosity forgotten, made their way to the lochshore.

They swam for a long time, jumping off rocks, and challenging each other to dive for pebbles, disturbing the brown trout who loved to idle just beneath the surface of the overgrown banks. They were enjoying themselves so much that they didn't realise it was getting cold, or that the sky was no longer clear, but filled with dark and gloomy rain clouds. It was only when first Gawaine and then Gareth felt the rain upon their backs that they realised what was happening.

The weather in Orkney is volatile. The islands are susceptible to strong winds, which bring swift changes in the weather, and as the rain began to fall in earnest, the wind whipped the waters of the lake into strong waves. Struggling to get to the shore, Gawaine saw Gareth, the youngest and slightest of his brothers, fall, and disappear beneath the waves. He did not emerge, and Gawaine realised that the pressure of the water was making it hard for his brother to get to his feet. He pushed himself against the swell, forcing himself through the waves to where he could just see the red hair and pale, freckled skin of his brother, as he attempted unsuccessfully to right himself. Grabbing him beneath the arms, he pulled him upwards, and in a second Gareth was standing in the shallows, spluttering and coughing up the brackish water. Looking to the shore, he could see that Agravaine and Gaheris were already pulling on their breeches, and reaching out for his brother's hand, he half pulled, half carried him to the grass.

The rain was falling heavily now, and the boys' clothes were soaked. They had all managed to pull on their breeches, but the thought of trying to get into the rest of their now sodden clothing struck all of them as ridiculous.

"Come on," shouted Gawaine over the wind and the driving rain. "We are going to have to make a run for home. It isn't really that far away, and to be honest, we aren't going to get any wetter."

"No," said Gaheris. "I have a better idea. Anna's house is only in the next cove. Why don't we go there? She will have a fire, and at least we will be able to get warm."

ANNA WAS ALONE WHEN THE four dripping and half-drowned boys arrived at her door. Donal and Cormac had gone over earlier that day to Conn's house, on the shores of Loch Stenness. Both their boats needed caulking, and three hands made light work, but she hoped that they'd finished and had time to cover up before the rains came, or all their efforts might well be wasted.

She had been at work in the kitchen making oatcakes when she heard the boys' urgent drumming and opened the door with her hands still floury from the batch she'd just put in the oven. As the wife and mother of fishermen, Anna was quite used to dealing with wet clothes and sodden individuals. Letting them in without fuss or question, she handed them rough linen towels and sent them into Donal's small room at the back of the house, telling them to help themselves to dry clothes.

By the time they emerged, red-faced and tousle-haired, in a mishmash of ill-fitting tunics, the oatcakes were ready. She placed them on the table alongside a crock of butter and a honeycomb dripping with sweetness and invited the boys to eat whilst she sorted out their waterlogged clothing, shaking it and hanging it out to dry by the fire.

The oatcakes disappeared in no time, and Anna could see that another batch was likely to be welcomed. As she went to the earthenware crock on the dresser, she ruffled Gaheris's damp curls. "Well, sweeting, it's been a while since you've been to see me. Have you had any news from your mother or father?"

"They sent us sweetmeats for Solstice, but they'd gone rotten by the time they arrived. Mother never thinks about things like that," Gaheris grumbled.

"I know that Finn got a message last time a ship from Caer-Lundein came to Stromness, but he wouldn't tell us what it said." Gawaine pulled at his tunic, which was really far too tight for him. "I know that they must have a lot to do. It can't be easy being regents, but we've not had any real news for months."

Anna came to join them, sitting in between Gaheris and Agravaine on the wooden settle by the fire.

"I know you must miss them, but I'm sure you will hear from them soon." She put her arm round Gaheris and gave him a hug. He turned to her. "Anna, do you think we could do that thing?"

"What thing, sweeting?"

"You know, the one you showed me, with the sheep bone. The one from Corsica."

Anna looked startled. "I thought that was our secret, Gaheris? And I don't know if it will work. Remember, when we tried it, we only searched as far as Conn's cottage."

"What are you two going on about?" asked Agravaine. "It is really quite rude of you to be talking about things the rest of us can't join in with."

Anna looked at him, uncertain of what to say next. She loved Gaheris and little Gareth and had a bit of a soft spot for Gawaine, who had often helped Donal with the arduous task of cutting, drying and stacking the peat bricks that they stored away each summer to provide fuel for the harsh months of winter. Agravaine however, usually held himself aloof. She suspected that he regarded himself as too good for the likes of her, despite his mother's friendship and familiarity, and that he would only tease his younger brother unmercifully if he knew how regularly he had been visiting her since their parents' departure. Fortunately, her quandary was cut short by Gaheris saying enthusiastically. "Anna has something even better than the scrying bowl. She's a Mazzeri, which means she can do special magic, and she showed me a way to see what people are doing, even if they're far away."

"And it shows you what people are actually doing? It's not like the scrying bowl, which shows you things that might be, or even things that have already happened?" Gawaine was not particularly proficient at any form of magic art, and he did not hold them in high regard.

"Yes," said Anna, cautiously. "The Ossu di Pecura will only show you what is, or what will be, but I am not sure if it is something that we should try, and as I said, I have only used it over small distances—on the island of Corsica, to see my family, or here on Orkney, I have sometimes used it when Cormac or my boys have been late returning home and I have wanted to make sure there was naught amiss."

"Oh, please, Anna," Gaheris pleaded. "If we can't make it, show us Caer-Lundein then at least we'll know it doesn't work on faraway places. And we would so like to know what is happening to Father and Mother." Anna looked at the faces of the boys. Even Agravaine's usually haughty expression had been replaced by a wistful longing, making him look younger and more innocent in his obvious desire to have news of his parents.

She was silent for a moment. The brothers looked up at her, and for once, their similarities were more marked than their differences. Their freckled faces had caught the sun, and their hair was still damp, making it hard to see any distinction between Gawaine's burnished curls and Gareth's auburn mane. But most of all, they all shared a look of hesitant hunger, wanting something, but not actually believing it was possible, and she recognised just how young they were and how abandoned they felt.

"Alright," she said. "We will try the Pecura. It works better in the sunlight, but a strong lamp should do. Gaheris, will you and Gawaine clear a space on the table? And you other two, please lock the door and fasten the shutters. I'm not expecting anyone else this afternoon, but if someone does chance to call, I would rather we are not disturbed."

Whilst the boys got on with the tasks she had given them, Anna lit the oil lamp and reached a leather bag down from the top shelf of the dresser. Opening it she took out something wrapped in a woollen cloth, which she carefully unwrapped. It was an old bone, almost triangular in shape, but tapering from the longest point, creating something of a handle. Gaheris told them that it had come from a sheep, and that Anna had brought it with her all the way from Corsica. The broad, flat surface of the widest part of the shoulder blade had been polished and smoothed until it was almost translucent, and when Anna held it up to the lamp, light shone through it, casting strange shadows on the table.

"Alright, boys," said Anna. "Now if we are going to do this, you must be quiet and you need to focus your mind. Gaheris has told me that your mother has shown you how to use a scrying bowl. This is a similar magic. You need to concentrate and listen to me. You must not talk, and you must not fidget. If you do, you will destroy the aura and the vision—if we are granted one—will vanish. Do you understand?"

The boys all nodded.

"Now, get yourselves into a comfortable position," They shuffled a bit and she saw Gawaine reach out for Gareth's hand. "No, there is no need to hold hands. With the Pecura, the force field is mental, not physical." Anna took a little terracotta pot of ointment from the leather bag and rubbed a small amount on her eyelids. She passed it to Gareth and indicated he should do the same. "What's in it?" asked Gawaine.

"Bay leaf and dandelion," answered Gaheris quickly. "Anna told me that Aunt Morgan brought her the bay leaves all the way from Avalon." Gawaine grunted and took the jar from Gareth, and after taking a small amount, passed it on to Agravaine. When the boys were ready, Anna sat down and positioned the bone and the lamp so that the light shone through it, the shadows projected on the empty space in the middle of the table. "Now," she said, "clear your minds and focus; look only at the shadows." As the boys looked, the shapes began to move and shimmer, dancing together like a cloud of midges over the loch in high summer. Finally, they all seemed to join in to one wheeling, shimmering cloud, and when they did so, the darkness cleared and the space on the table became illuminated by a blazing white light. Anna spoke, in a voice of certainty and command. "We are ready. Ask your question."

Gareth and Agravaine both spoke at once.

"How are our mother and father?"

"When will we go to Caer-Lundein?"

The light began to fade, turning from white to palest blue, and at its centre, small shadows began to reappear. They flickered and swirled, and as the boys watched, two of them separated and became larger and more distinct. The shadows in the background shuddered again and then cleared. To the boys' amazement they were staring into a large room, filled with people. Most of them were strangers, but at the head of the table sat two that they recognised—King Lot and Queen Morgause, their mother and father.

Unlike the last vision the boys had conjured together, in the rock pool on the day of Einar's drowning, this vision was silent. The people round the table were talking; indeed, they seemed to be arguing. Their faces looked angry, and one of the men was beating his fist upon the table as he spoke. They watched their father speak. He seemed to be trying to calm the situation down, raising his hand in a gesture of conciliation, the expression on his face that of understanding and concern. Their mother was silent, but they saw her turning towards the man who sat on their left, an old man, with white hair and a long white beard which he wore in two plaits. Her face had a strange expression, and Agravaine thought that although her mouth was not smiling, there was a sparkle in her eyes that was almost gleeful. They saw her speak, signalling to the man, who, like their father, raised his hand in a gesture of appeasement.

Then one of the others sitting at the table slammed his hands hard upon the board and pushing his chair backwards, got up and stormed out of the room. They could see that he wore the emblem of a raven and knew that he must be one of the Northern Lords. Then another man got up and appeared to be shouting something at their father and the man with white hair. He was pointing his finger at them and his face was contorted with rage. He had a golden dragon on a red background emblazoned on his chest, which Agravaine, who was good at heraldry, recognised immediately as the emblem of Gewisse. He also stormed from the room, and the boys watched their father lean forward and place his head in his hands.

The scene began to shimmer again, and the vision faded, the shadows swirling once again and reforming to show a very different prospect. Once again, they were in a large room, but this one had a high vaulted ceiling and many windows. The walls were hung with banners, and the people, who seemed to be talking animatedly as they took their seats on the rows of chairs and benches, were dressed richly in formal court dress.

As they watched, they saw the man with white hair enter the room, accompanied by a woman who wore a coronet upon her long brown hair. She was wearing a cloak of silver, and a white dress encrusted with jewels that sparkled as the light danced upon them. They did not know who she was, but something about her reminded them of Morgan, their aunt, who they had last seen on the day of Einar's funeral. She said something to the man, who nodded, and they both made their way to the far end of the hall and took their places on the dais.

Their mother came next, dressed in a dress of palest blue that shone like the summer sky. She wore a crown of gold, and her hair hung loose in soft, gentle waves that fell to her waist. As they watched, she turned and beckoned to two figures who were following behind her, and to Gawaine and Agravaine's astonishment, they saw themselves, their hair well brushed and shining, and wearing the emblem of the Eagle of Orkney emblazoned on their chests. Their mother reached out to smooth Gawaine's curls and straighten Agravaine's tunic and gave both of them a kiss upon the forehead. She led them to their seats, next to a tall, fair-haired man, and then went to join the other woman on the dais.

Then, everyone in the room rose to their feet and they saw the doors swing open to admit their father, wearing a tunic of rich purple, embroidered with flying eagles and edged with fur. His cloak billowed out behind him as he walked, and beside him was a tall youth with closely cropped dark brown hair. He was dressed simply, in a white tunic and cloak on which was embroidered a golden dragon. His head was bare, and when he looked up and saw the people on the dais, Gaheris thought that he seemed nervous and uncertain.

Their father put his arm on the other man's shoulder and said something which seemed to reassure him. The two of them began to make their way towards the dais, but as they did so the peace within the cottage was broken by a sudden eruption of noises coming from outside. Someone was trying to get in, and when the door would not open, they began to knock hard upon it and call out Anna's name.

Cormac and Donal had returned, and as Anna got up to unbolt the door, the vision shuddered, flickered and disappeared.

CHAPTER FIFTEEN
CALIBURN'S GUARDIAN

Morgan went with Nimue to the mouth of the lakeside cave and stood beside her as she carefully worked the magics to open the enchanted pathways, a look of studied concentration upon her face. After two attempts, the back wall of the cave shimmered and appeared to soften into a luminous haze as the entrance to the tunnel gradually became visible. As she watched, Morgan felt a strong sense of relief but was also aware of experiencing a level of anxiety that was unlike her usually resolute and disciplined composure. Nimue had offered to undertake the journey to Orkney without needing any persuasion, and although the younger woman was adamant that she understood and accepted the dangers, Morgan could not help but feel that she was sending an innocent to face perils that she was ill-prepared to withstand.

It had been only two days ago that the messengers from Caer-Lundein had brought news of the dramatic appearance of their half-brother, and the political unrest this had engendered. They had also relayed Morgause's messages regarding Lord Merlin's determination to regain the guardianship of Caliburn, and her urgent request that Morgan return to court as soon as the Lake Isle could spare her. Morgan had instructed that the messengers be provided with fresh horses and sent them back with her thanks and assurances that she would be with her sister within seven days.

When they had gone, she took out the sword, which she had wrapped in linen and stowed away under her bed, and summoned Nimue to her chamber. When she arrived, she was a little out of breath and Morgan gestured for her to sit and help herself to the jug of cool water infused with borage flowers that she kept on her dresser.

"It is good to see you, Nimue, but you need not have rushed. However, now you are here, I see no need to prevaricate. You heard what the messengers from my sister had to say?" Morgan looked fixedly at her. "I do not feel inclined to hand Caliburn to Lord Merlin."

"I am pleased to hear you say so, Lady. We have had little chance to speak these past few days, and I am sure that you have had much to occupy your mind." Nimue put down her goblet and walked to the window. "But I have been able to think of little but what Vivian—I still find it hard to call her 'my mother'—told us about who fathered me—and Merlin's part in all of it."

"And I take it that you don't think kindly of his actions?"

"No, I do not. He arrogantly thought that his own inaccurate interpretation of the Prophecies warranted browbeating Vivian into doing something that I'm sure she long regretted, and one which, if it had become known, could have threatened everything she worked for and held dear."

"Merlin does find it hard to acknowledge that any could be wiser than he, and he cares little for the feelings of others once he embarks upon a particular course." Morgan put her hand upon Nimue's. "His behaviour towards my own mother was equally ruthless."

The two women were silent for a moment, thinking of the role that Merlin had played in both their destinies, and the resentment they felt towards him.

"The sword is no longer Merlin's to command. He may once have had it in his keeping, but thrice now it has been given to me—by Uther on his deathbed, by Vivian, and by the Goddess herself. It is for me, and me alone to decide if—and when—my brother shall wield it."

"And do you think Merlin will accept your decision?" asked Nimue.

"I think he will appear to do so—he'll have no choice in the matter—but I am also certain that he will do anything in his power to find where the sword is being kept and find a way to avail himself of it."

"But surely it is safe here in Avalon?"

"I am not so certain. There are many here who have grown used to obeying the mighty Lord Merlin's commands without question, and he will not have any qualms about using that to his advantage. I would rather it were somewhere else altogether—and in the safekeeping of another, one whose magics are very different from Merlin's, and one whom he would find it hard to browbeat or compel to do his bidding." Morgan told Nimue of Anna, the Mazzeri, skilled in Corsican magics as deep and dark as anything Merlin could command, but completely impenetrable to him.

"Where is Anna? She is not still in this place called Corsica?"

"No, I think that would be a journey too far for even the most extensive of the enchanted pathways. She lives on the Isle of Orkney, where Morgause and King Lot have their home."

"And you wish to send her the sword, so she can conceal it?"

Morgan nodded as she sat down on the window seat and, steepling her fingers, rested her chin upon them. "Caliburn is a most precious and mystical object. If I am to send it from me, I need to be certain that I can depend on those to whom I have entrusted it.

"I have absolute faith in Anna. But I also need someone who can take it to her. Someone who I can trust absolutely, someone who understands the dangers of such a mission, and someone strong enough to withstand those dangers." Morgan looked up and met Nimue's unwavering gaze.

"What would you have me do, Lady?"

IT WAS WELL THAT MORGAN had acted as she had, for Merlin had arrived an hour or so after sunset on the following day. He had not taken kindly to her refusal to return Caliburn to his keeping. She had responded to the druid's request with formal courtesy but had been firm in her rejection of his proposal to allow the sword to be presented to Arthur at his coronation. Reluctantly, Merlin recognised that he would have to return to Caer-Lundein empty-handed. He knew that he could not afford to antagonise the new Lady of the Lake, but Morgan could see his eyes flash with anger when it became clear that, despite his best endeavours, he had not been able to bend her to his will.

He fared better with his other request. Although Morgan could not prevent herself from making a small moue of displeasure when Merlin told her that it had been arranged that her brother would be crowned at Alban Elfed, she did nothing to gainsay it.

Encouraged, he continued, ". . . and he has much to learn about what is expected of him. He has been accorded power by the grace and will of the Goddess, but his education has been woefully lacking. If he is to hold his throne, he has but a few months to become the master of many things."

"It would perhaps have been better if he had been raised in an environment more suited to his expectations. I gather he was little more than a kitchen boy in some ramshackle castle in the Forest Sauvage." Once again, Morgan detected a flash of anger in the druid's eyes, but Merlin contrived to maintain his composure.

"Oh, I think you have been misled, Lady. Sir Ector is not a wealthy knight, but he is of noble lineage, and Arthur has been his ward, foster brother to Sir Ector's own son, Kai."

"The details do not interest me, Merlin. It is clear that Uther's son is a rough stone that will need much polishing before it is fit for a crown. So, tell me what do you need from me?"

"I would ask that you send one of your wise women to court to instruct him. He will need to fully understand the part he has to play in the rituals, and I doubt he has either the knowledge or the experience to undertake what will be expected of him without personal and, perhaps, considering some of the rituals he will be called upon to lead, intimate tuition."

"I will do what I can," Morgan replied. "I agree that we need to ensure the Goddess is honoured as she should be. We cannot allow a callow and inexperienced youth to jeopardise the fruitfulness of our fields and orchards or threaten the abundance of our harvests. I will discuss the matter with the elders, and we shall send you a suitable instructor before the month is out." Morgan had then risen, indicating their meeting was over. She made her way to her own chamber, leaving a slightly mollified but still frustrated Merlin to finish his flagon of wine alone by the dying embers of the fire.

MERLIN WAS NOT HAPPY, BUT equally, he was not stupid. After having slept fitfully, he got up before dawn and made his way to the kitchens, hoping to speak with Olwen. He had known the household chatelaine since her earliest days on Avalon, and if the Lady of the Lake was the head of the Lake Isle, she was very much its heart. If he wanted to find out how things really stood, whether Morgan genuinely had the respect and loyalty of her women, Olwen was the person he needed to ask.

What she told him disturbed and infuriated him in equal measures. Asking delicately understated questions about the last stage of Vivian's illness, he was hoping to establish the level of grief and uncertainty that now existed in both the House of Avalon, and in the wider community.

He had anticipated that he would find that there was little faith in the new Lady, that people were troubled by Morgan's youth, or jealous of the privileged position she had always held. But rather than discovering the household uncertain about its future, or fuelled by doubts about its leadership, Olwen spoke of the new Lady with an almost evangelical fervency.

When she described the scene on the lakeshore where Morgan assumed Vivian's legacy and mantle, she talked of Morgan's graceful and confident statement of personal conviction and dedication to Avalon, the Goddess and her community. As she did so, Olwen beamed with a joy that was undoubtedly tempered with relief that the will of the Goddess had been so clear and unambiguous. These were difficult times, and the death of Vivian could have jeopardised the future of Avalon itself if she had been followed by one who was reticent in her convictions, or for whom there was any doubt about her rights to Vivian's mantle. But the mystical transference of power that had taken place on the waters of Avalon, where the spirit of the Lake itself had publicly bestowed the sword Caliburn upon the new Lady, was a strong and undoubted sign that Morgan was favoured by the Goddess.

Hearing this, Merlin understood that he had little hope of undermining Morgan's leadership, or suborning others to help him acquire the guardianship of the sword. As an old and experienced statesman, Merlin had come to recognise which battles to fight, and when to concede defeat. He needed to work with Morgan and so, thanking Olwen for both her time and the bread and fruit she had given him to enable him to break his fast, he hastened to the gardens where he felt certain he would encounter Morgan. She was known to make her way there every morning for an hour of quiet and contemplation to prepare her mind for the challenges each day presented.

"My Lady Morgan, forgive me for disturbing you, but would you grant me just a few moments of your time? Your brother needs me and I have tarried too long on this beauteous and enchanted Isle."

Morgan did not reply but inclined her head in assent. She gestured to a place beside her on a long granite bench set beneath the branches of espaliered apple and cherry trees which grew along the physic garden wall.

"You are welcome, as always, my Lord Merlin, but I must admit, I had thought we had said all we needed to say last night." Morgan had leant back against the wall. Her eyes were closed and her face turned to catch the warmth of the early sun. "I hope you are not going to reopen the conversation regarding the sword?"

"No, no, reluctantly, I recognise that your mind is made up on that matter." He clasped his hands, rubbing them together as if nervous or agitated and bent forwards, looking at the ground rather than at Morgan, saying quietly, "I can only hope that you will change your mind, before the situation becomes critical and all is lost."

"You made your feelings known on that point quite clearly last night," Morgan responded, in equally low and measured tones, but without opening her eyes or turning to face the old druid. "But the blade is in my gift, and I will be guided by what I know, what I see and what I hear."

"As you say, Lady. But that is not what I wish to speak to you about today. I leave this morning for Caer-Lundein. Do you wish to accompany me upon the pathways? We can travel more speedily together?"

Morgan opened her eyes and looked at Merlin. "That is a thoughtful offer, but one I shall refuse. I too intend to leave Avalon within the next few hours, but I will travel the man-made roads." He looked at her quizzically.

"I have messages and bequests from Vivian to some of the other Houses, and I am minded to take them myself, rather than entrusting them to others. I shall stay in Sarum on the morrow and then visit Wintanceaster. I hope to be in Caer-Lundein ten nights from now."

"And you shall not forget your promise to send me someone suitable to instruct your brother?"

"I give you my word, I shall attend to the matter personally. Whether I bring with me someone from the Lake Isle, or from another of our houses, I give you my assurance that Arthur will be provided with a skilled and effective instructor."

Merlin thanked her and made his way, staff in hand, to the cave on the lakeside. Morgan took an apple from her pocket and began to eat it whilst she planned all she would need to make ready before she could begin the journey to Caer-Lundein.

Waiting for her there were Morgause—and Arthur—the brother she had never met, but whom she had always loathed.

◆ ◆ ◆

IN CAER-LUNDEIN, MORGAUSE HAD SPENT several interesting and congenial hours in her chamber, and it was now growing late. The sun had set several hours ago and despite being high summer, it was an unusually dark night. There were few stars, and the moon was cloaked with heavy clouds, meaning that Sir Lamorak had been able to make his way across the courtyard to the castle gate unseen. On the whole, she was glad that he was leaving tomorrow with his father King Pellinore and those two boorish bores, Sir Ector and his son Kai.

Morgause was aware that she had recently spent too much time dallying with the pretty knight. He was a vigorous and inventive lover, but she was concerned that he was becoming too obvious in his devotion to her, and although she had been very discreet, it would be advisable that he did not gaze at her with lovesick eyes and ill-concealed longing under the watchful and potentially jealous gaze of her husband.

Lot, who had ridden out with his brother, Urien, to the lands of Lindsay in the east, was expected back any day. They had managed to persuade the lords of Ceint to recognise Arthur's claim to the throne, and if Lindsay could also be convinced to remain loyal, Lot had told her that he felt certain they could broker an uneasy peace with Gewisse and possibly also the Northlands, which should hold at least until Alban Elfed and Arthur's coronation.

She had just asked her maid Gyda to bring a flagon of spiced wine and some warm water and towels so she could refresh herself, when there was a sharp knock at the door. It was Dafydd, the castle seneschal, who she always referred to as "Dandy" because his straggles of wispy hair reminded her of a half-blown dandelion-clock.

"Well, Dandy, why are you disturbing me at this late hour? I would have thought you would have been readying yourself for your bed. The king and his counsellors are expected back presently, and there will be much for you to do on the morrow."

"Aye Your Majesty, you are r . . . r . . . right, and if truth be t . . . t . . . told, I was abed an hour ago."

"Then what roused you? Has there been some calamity?"

"No, p . . . p . . . please take my assurance that all is w . . . w . . . well." Dandy was nervously rubbing his hands. His head, which was bobbing about like a nervous pigeon's, was bent slightly sideways so he did not have to look directly at Morgause. He always found being in her presence disconcerting. She was more beautiful than anyone else he had ever known, and seeing her here, alone in her chamber, her hair down, and casually dressed in a linen shift with a shawl draped loosely around her shoulders, made him even more anxious and tongue-tied.

"So, what is it then?" asked Morgause.

"V . . . v . . . visitors, Your Majesty, from the Lake Isle. Your sister, who is now the Lady, and several members of her household. She said that you would want to be t . . . t . . . told immediately of their arrival."

"And she was right. Where is she now?"

"Her horses are being st . . . st . . . stabled. I took the liberty of showing the visitors into the great hall."

"You fool, Dandy, there will only be dregs and leavings there at this time of night. Speak to the kitchens and see that her party are refreshed and shown to their quarters. And conduct my sister to me without further delay."

As she spoke, Morgause pulled on an embroidered surcoat and reaching out for her comb, began to braid her hair. She had no wish to look like a wanton when greeting her sister. Morgan may well be the new Lady of the Lake, but she was still Queen Regent, and she was not going to allow her appearance to put her to disadvantage.

Morgan arrived at the same time as the maid arrived with the warm water and the wine, and Morgause busied herself pouring two goblets, whilst Morgan took the opportunity to wash the dust of the road from her hands and face.

"Leave us," Morgause commanded, and Dandy and the servant girl obeyed, closing the door behind them. The sisters looked at each other, and it was Morgause who opened her arms in greeting, kissing her sister on both cheeks and embracing her.

"Well, my lady, it does me good to see you. But tell me, now you are elevated, do you expect me to pay you obeisance?"

Morgan laughed and returned her sister's embrace. "Morgause, you are Queen Regent of Britain, and even when our brother places the crown upon his unworthy head, you will still be Queen of Orkney and the Northern Isles. None of this 'my lady' business when we are alone. You know I would never have you bend the knee."

Morgause smiled, and reaching out, gently touched the tip of her sister's nose. "I am glad to see you."

"And I you."

The sisters raised their goblets and toasted each other, then made their way to the settle by the fireside.

"How was the Lake Isle? And where is Nimue? Did she return with you?"

"No, I have sent her on a journey, to Anna in Orkney." Morgause looked startled at this and was about to speak when Morgan raised her finger to her lips.

"I have much to say to you, and these words are for your ears alone. Are any of your servants still within your chamber?"

"No."

"Then send word that you wish no further service until morning, and let us lock the door, so no one can disturb us."

CHAPTER SIXTEEN

A CHILD BORN AT BELTANE

Whilst Morgause went to close the door, Morgan replenished their goblets, and the two sisters settled themselves comfortably before the fire.

"I too have matters I wish to discuss with you," said Morgause, "but I can see that you're much vexed, so you must speak first. Tell me what is concerning you."

Morgan explained about Merlin and his fervent desire to secure Caliburn for Arthur. She also shared with her sister the whole truth of Nimue's parentage, a story that Morgause heard with shock and some initial disbelief, saying eventually, "Merlin has always been an irritating meddler, but I am surprised that Vivian gave in to him. The consequences for her could have been very difficult to deal with."

Morgan nodded, saying in a considered voice, "I think we should remember that she always had a fondness for Uther, and of course she had performed the rituals with him many times. The only difference on this occasion is that she did not take precautions against the birth of a child—indeed, I think it likely that she dosed herself with raspberry leaf and red clover in order to make the chances of conception more likely."

"And how did Nimue respond to this revelation?"

"To be honest, she was devastated. And she blames Merlin for browbeating her mother into believing that this betrayal of her vows was the will of the Goddess—and her duty. That is why she offered to travel the enchanted pathways to deliver Caliburn to Anna's safekeeping."

"Have you heard from her? Did she complete the journey unscathed?" Morgause had never herself walked the enchanted pathways, but she knew—and was wary of—their dangers.

"No, I have heard nothing, but I have been travelling these past few days, and it is unlikely that a messenger would know where to find me. I hope that she will send word to me here—when do you expect the next boat from Orkney?"

"I believe we are expecting the *Llyr's Daughter* to dock at the Pool of Lundein within the next day or two."

"And is Clem Trevenna still Captain?" asked Morgan. She well remembered the bluff, handsome seafarer from her early years in Tintagel. She recollected standing with her mother on the headland, watching *Llyr's Daughter* with Clem at the helm, sail out to sea. That was the voyage which had transported Morgause from her childhood home to the Isles of Orkney, where marriage to Lot, motherhood and a crown had awaited her.

"Yes, since he married Avice, ten years or so ago, he has made his home on Orkney. He is getting on in age though, and each Yuletide I expect him to say that the next journey will be his last."

"Well, let us hope he comes soon, and with news." Morgan drank deeply from her goblet. "This is pleasant wine, sister, and not too highly spiced. Where did you get it?"

"It was a gift from King Ban of Brittany. I believe it comes from the lands to the south of his kingdom, but he seems to have an almost inexhaustible supply of it and is happy to send us several barrels each summer. But we are not here to talk about wine." Morgause put down her goblet and reached out to take her sister's hand. "Did Merlin talk to you of the latest prophecy that is disturbing his composure and causing him sleepless nights?"

"No," said Morgan, looking inquiringly at her sister. "He spoke only of the need to prepare our upstart half-brother for his coronation, and to beg the services of one of my adepts, to instruct him in the part he will need to play in the rituals and ceremonies."

Morgause snorted. "Yes, he asked me to add the polish of nobility to what is little more than a rustic by-blow. I have been trying my best, and to be fair to the boy, he does seem to be willing to learn. But he was born with two left feet and does not have a natural aptitude for courtly manners or composure."

"That does not surprise me. But what of this prophecy?"

Morgause repeated the words that Merlin had spoken to her in the castle physic garden. "He said to me that it is written within those ancient scrolls he pays so much heed to, that the reign of Uther's son—who is also known for some reason as 'The Once and Future King'—will be brought to an end if he faces in battle a noble warrior, born at Beltane within a year of his coronation." Morgause looked at her sister with a sparkle in her eyes. "And the old fool is also concerned that this is a near and present danger, that Arthur may be brought low by some infantile prodigy, a warrior of less than seven summers, like the legendary Cú Chulainn."

"Do not mock or underestimate Cú Chulainn; he was a most remarkable person." Morgan got up from her seat and walked across to the window looking out to the courtyard, where the looming shape of the now empty stone anvil could just about be made out. "He trained in battle by the warrior-women of the Northern Isles and was indeed formidable. He was favoured by the Tuatha Dé Danann, and if another such as he were to wage war on our half-brother, I too would give little for Arthur's chances."

Morgause joined her sister at the window, staring out at the stone anvil they had once enchanted and which, ironically, now provided the main argument in support of Arthur's inheritance of the High King's crown. She put her arm around Morgan's waist and rested her head upon her shoulder, whispering, "It would seem to me that it would not be a bad thing if this prophecy were to be fulfilled."

"What mean you?" asked Morgan, also finding herself whispering.

"That a child should be born at Beltane, next year, and that we should take it upon ourselves to ensure that this child be fathered by none other than the soon-to-be-crowned King Arthur."

Morgan looked at her sister, the beginnings of a smile beginning to play around her lips. "You would have our brother become the begetter of his own destruction? That is elegant, and has, I believe, a certain justice.

"Now, let me see," she counted on her fingers. "To be born at Beltane, the child would need to be conceived at Lunasa, which is several weeks from now."

Morgause nodded. "Yes, and but one moon from Alban Elfed and his coronation."

"And how do you suggest we do this? If I know Merlin, he will not let the boy out of his sight if there is any chance that he may go sharing his seed at what would be, for him, an inauspicious time."

"Oh, I am sure you are right. He will allow no dalliance, no flirtations with the court ladies. But there is one whom he was actively encouraging Arthur to spend time with. One he would never suspect." Morgause looked at her sister and smiled. She shook out her hair and let the shawl drop to the floor from her shoulders, revealing the outline of her breasts and the beginning of her pale, delicate nipples, which stood hard and erect in the cool night breeze.

"But he knows you to be his half-sister," Morgan objected.

"Aye. But he is a man, and an inexperienced, naïve man at that."

"I think you read him wrong, Morgause. Had he been a sophisticated youth, one raised to seek his pleasures where he will and to think little of convention, perhaps your idea would work. But as it stands, I think he would be horrified. However beautiful you are, you are the queen and his acknowledged half-sister. It wouldn't work." She handed her sister her shawl. "Here, cover yourself—you don't want to get a chill. The night air is not warm."

Morgause felt a surge of irritation at her sister's words. But as she replaced the wrap around her shoulders, she had to recognise their wisdom. "And do you have another idea?"

"Yes." Morgan spoke slowly, and with some hesitation. "There is another whom Merlin has suggested should spend time with him. Another whom he would not suspect, and who would be well-placed to do what needs to be done."

"You mean . . . ?"

"I mean the one who will instruct him in the rituals. The one who must share with him the most intense and personal physical intimacies as part of those instructions." She looked straight into Morgause's eyes, her voice now firm and determined.

"A daughter of Avalon, sworn to obey the Goddess."

Morgause had resumed her seat by the fire, and taking a sip of wine said thoughtfully, "I presume you mean Nimue?"

"No," said Morgan firmly. "Nimue, assuming she has successfully navigated the pathways and is now safely lodged with Anna in Orkney, has done enough. Besides, this would be asking her to repeat, almost exactly, that which Merlin forced upon her mother. I would not place that burden on her." She picked up her goblet and sat next to her sister. "I mean myself."

"You?"

"Yes, Arthur has never seen me. He will have no idea who I am. If we manage it correctly, he need not even know initially that I am Lady of the Lake. I will tell Merlin that I have arranged a person to provide the instruction he requested." She looked up at Morgause. "I doubt he will ask me who she is, or where she came from. He has never been interested in detail."

"But Morgan, your vows? I thought you were sworn to the Goddess to never marry, or to have a child."

"As did Vivian, but it is clear that she and Merlin found a way around that, and if they can do it, then so can I." As she spoke, Morgan realised that this idea, which had only entered her mind a moment ago, was crystallising into something she wanted very much. She had always accepted that she would never know motherhood, never be able to suckle her child and watch him grow, but now she recognised that perhaps she had been wrong.

"But how could you raise him? You could not recognise him as your son; you would be disgraced and cast out of Avalon if the truth were to become known."

Morgan considered. "Aye, there is truth in what you say, but tell me, how would you have done it, if we had agreed to your suggestion? I can't see Lot accepting someone else's bastard at the court of Orkney."

"He would never have needed to," replied Morgause. "I would simply have told him that he had got me with child again, and the dear fool would have been delighted by such evidence of his ongoing potency and welcomed the child with open arms."

"Well, perhaps that is our answer. I will bear the child, but we will tell the world that he is yours. You will then raise him with your boys. He will be known as the youngest and the last of the sons of Lot of Orkney."

Morgause thought about this, and suddenly her scalp prickled and her blood ran cold, recollecting a night long, long ago, when she had been a child. If she remembered correctly, it had been her last night in Tintagel, and she had asked to spend it in her mother's chamber. This had been agreed, and she had gone to sleep in a small truckle bed by the side of her mother's bed.

She had been deeply asleep but had been startled awake in the middle of the night by her mother's screams. Scared, she had got out of bed and run to her mother, clinging to her and asking again and again what was wrong. It had taken Igraine some minutes before she was calm enough to cuddle her small daughter, holding her tight and whispering words of reassurance.

"Hush my sweeting. It was nothing, just a horrid nightmare."

"But what happened? Why did it make you so upset?"

And her mother had told her that it had started as a lovely dream.

"I saw you my love, a woman grown and as beautiful as the day is long. You had a pretty dress and a handsome husband, and four sturdy little red-haired sons. You looked very happy."

"So why did you cry, Mother?"

"I saw a fifth child, small and fine-boned with dark hair and blue, blue eyes, and for some reason he frightened me. I'm sorry, my darling girl. It was all very silly." Her mother had held her in her arms and rocked her gently, until Morgause had fallen back to sleep.

Five children. Her mother had seen her with five children. Four red-headed—like Gawaine and his brothers, and a fifth . . . well who could he be like? She looked at the delicate frame of her sister, her dark hair pulled into a long dark plait that fell down her back to below her waist, and looked into her large, startlingly blue eyes.

"Morgan," she said. "I've just remembered something. I need to tell you about a dream our mother had, years ago, when we were children."

Morgan poured them both another goblet of wine and they sat together talking about their plans, until the flagon was empty and the first rays of sun had slipped gently in through the window, heralding the start of a new day.

MORGAUSE WAS AWAKENED LATER THAT morning by a commotion outside her door. It sounded as if a pack of wild beasts were making merry in the corridor, and when she cautiously opened the door and put her head out to see what was happening, she found herself confronted by two quarrelling red-headed youths, who fell over the threshold in an ungainly mess of hair-pulling and punches.

She looked down at the two boys, who were now squabbling on the hearthrug. Their clothes were torn and untidy, and both looked very much in need of a wash.

"Gawaine, Agravaine, is it you? What on earth are you doing here? We did not send for you, and why are you behaving like a pair of savages? Is this any way to conduct yourselves in front of your mother and your Queen?"

The two boys stopped what they were doing and shamefacedly got to their feet. "Sorry, Mother," they both mumbled. Sighing deeply, Morgause gestured towards the table, where bread, milk, and a bowl of apples had been laid out by Gyda for her to break her fast.

"Sit down, you both look half-starved. Have something to eat and drink and then tell me how you got here, and why you have come." The boys did as they were told, and for some minutes, the only sound in the room was that of food and drink being rapidly and noisily consumed. Morgause poured herself a small tumbler of milk and joined them at the table, taking stock of the sons that she had not seen for well over a year.

She noticed that Agravaine had got taller. Built like his father, he was long and lean. Always the handsomest of her sons, she thought that he had become even more well favoured now that his face had shed itself of any remaining puppy fat.

Gawaine, on the other hand, remained short, and was still stocky. She saw with some surprise that his face was sporting a patchy but undeniable beard. To his mother, he resembled nothing so much as a young, copper-haired bear cub.

Finally, hunger assuaged, Gawaine spoke. "We came on the *Llyr's Daughter*. Anna travelled with us, and we got in first thing this morning. I'm sorry we disturbed you. Anna told us we should wait until we were clean, and be properly announced but . . ."

". . . but we wanted to see you," interrupted Agravaine. Both boys hung their heads. "We're sorry if we have displeased you."

"I am indeed displeased, and I don't know what your father will say. Where are Gaheris and Gareth? Are they about to begin brawling on my doorstep as well?"

"No, Mother, they are still at home. On Orkney."

"It is good to know I have two children who are not disobedient yahoos," but as she spoke, she bent and kissed Agravaine on the cheek, and putting her hand out, stroked Gawaine's furry cheek and ruffled his hair.

"Now tell me why you are here."

The boys explained that they had become worried because they had heard nothing of their parents for some time.

"But we send messages regularly to Avice and Finn," said Morgause. "Surely you realised that if anything concerned you, they would tell you."

"They don't tell us anything," began Gawaine.

". . . and then when that lady from Avalon turned up covered in blood, with that huge great sword, we really began to worry," added Agravaine.

". . . and when she told us that a new king had turned up and he'd pulled the sword from the stone, we thought we really needed to find out what was happening to you," said Gawaine, and he was clearly about to continue with the story when his mother raised her hand, gesturing him to be quiet.

"No more. No more. Tell me what you mean about this lady from Avalon. What happened to her? Can you tell me her name, and most importantly, does she still live?"

"Her name's Nimue, and we don't really know much about her, just that she really isn't very well. Avice is looking after her. She's moved her into the room that Aunt Morgan always has when she stays with us. Anna says she will get better."

"But what befell her, Gowie?"

"We don't know. It was horrible really." Gawaine paused, and Morgause thought he was about to cry. But he wiped his eyes, took a deep breath and managed to control himself. "Anna found her one morning, collapsed, all of a heap, and bleeding all over. Something bad had happened, but Anna brought her back to her cottage and did something to make her a bit better. She says Nimue will be all right, but she has to rest. That's why she didn't come with us. She asked Anna to come instead as she said she had a very important message for you and Aunt Morgan."

"And Mother, we knew we had to come," said Agravaine. "We saw it, saw ourselves down here."

"You mean you scryed it?" Morgause sounded dismissive. "I thought that even you two had received enough instruction to know that the scrying bowl is not necessarily an accurate predictor of the future."

And so, the boys told her about the day a few weeks before, when they had gone swimming in the loch and had turned up, half-drowned and bedraggled on Anna's doorstep. She had given them clean clothes and fresh oatcakes and, once they were warm and dry, they explained that she had agreed to show them the magic she had called the Ossu di Pecura.

"... and we saw two things, Mother," said Gawaine. "One was a lot of people arguing. You and Father were there, and an old man with a long white beard. Then a few people got very angry and stormed out."

"But you didn't look cross, Mother," added Agravaine. "It looked as if you were actually quite enjoying it."

"Father didn't though," said Gawaine. "He looked very unhappy, and when one of the men banged his fist on the table and stormed out ..."

"He was from Gewisse we think, because he was wearing the golden dragon," interrupted Agravaine.

"Well, when that happened, Father just sat there, with his head in his hands like he does when something bad happens."

"Like he did when Einar died," said Agravaine, quietly.

There was silence for a moment. Morgause thought she recognised the scene the boys had described to her. It sounded like the council meeting that had taken place the day after Arthur had pulled the sword from the stone. It had indeed ended in discord and disunity and had resulted in both Lot and his brother, Urien, journeying to the courts of lesser kings and nobles, in an attempt to get them to agree to the coronation of King Arthur. And yes, they were right; although she had hoped that she had concealed it, it was true to say that she had not been unhappy that things had gone that way. She realised that it would not do for the boys to repeat this to anyone—and least of all, not to Merlin or Arthur.

"That is very interesting, and very well described." She smiled at the boys, and both of them felt warmed by her praise and look of affection. "But you know, that was a meeting of the council and is very secret. It would not be right for you to tell anyone else what you saw. Will you promise me to speak no more of it?"

Both boys nodded eagerly and energetically. She continued. "But you said you saw two things. What was the other?"

And so the boys described the ceremony they had seen, how everyone was dressed in rich finery and that they—Gawaine and Agravaine—had been there, but not Gaheris or Gareth, and that their mother had welcomed them and shown them to their places in the Great Hall.

"That is interesting," said Morgause. "I think, weighing up all factors, your action has been rash, but I can understand why you did what you did." She smiled at the boys. "Your father is not here, but we expect him any day, and when I next see him, I will ask him not to punish you too harshly for your delinquency." And again, she gently ruffled their hair. As she did so, Agravaine caught hold of her wrist, taking her hand, he kissed it and held it to his cheek.

"Oh, Mother, we've missed you," he said, his voice low and almost broken with months of suppressed emotion. Morgause allowed her hand to remain in Agravaine's grasp for a few moments, and then she pulled away.

"And as I'm sure you know, I have missed you and your brothers. I am your mother after all. But the duties of a queen do not always allow her to remain at home." Morgause looked at her sons, a serious expression on her face. "I am sure you'll understand this when you are grown and have children of your own. But for now, you must leave me. I would speak with Anna to find out more about what has been happening on Orkney, and I think your Aunt Morgan would also like to join our conversation."

As she spoke, she opened the door and looked out into the corridor where, as expected, her maid Gyda had been waiting. She introduced the boys and asked Gyda to take them to find Dandy, and to instruct him to arrange suitable rooms and fresh clothing for them. Morgause then took her leave of her sons, telling them she would see them at sunset for supper in the Great Hall, and went swiftly in search of her sister.

CHAPTER SEVENTEEN

THE KINDNESS OF A KING, THE CRUELTY OF A LORD

As was the case so often nowadays, Arthur felt troubled. He had just received a message from Lord Merlin telling him that King Lot and his brother, Urien, had returned. The Privy Council had been summoned and would meet that morning to hear the results of their negotiations. Merlin had told him enough about the political situation for him to understand that the outcome of the discussions with the Lords of Lindsay could make the difference between relative stability and the possibility of civil war. These were worrying issues, serious and overarching, and within himself, he felt very unprepared. For the last few weeks, he had lived in an almost constant state of low-level anxiety, unsure that he would ever possess the skills and knowledge to deal with the world he had been summarily propelled into. If he was being honest with himself, he was uncertain if he even wanted to.

He thought back to the day, less than a moon ago, when he had first arrived in Caer-Lundein. He had been excited, thrilled to attend his first tourney and to see something of the world beyond the boundaries of the Forest Sauvage. He and Kai had played at jousting and questing since they had been little boys, and one day he had hoped to be made a knight. He had never imagined that his destiny was to be hailed as king, with all the daunting duties and responsibilities that seemed to entail.

His old life had not always been easy, but at least he had understood it, and felt comfortable with his place in it. That had all changed since Kai's ill-thought-out schemes had gone so spectacularly awry and he sighed deeply as he slowly got up from the bed and pulled on his boots. They were soft and comfortable, made from beautiful, perfectly tanned doeskin and far finer than anything even Sir Ector had worn back in the Forest Sauvage, but part of him hankered to replace them with the pair he had tossed on the floor at Merlin's instruction on the first night he had stayed in the castle.

Like all of his old clothes, they had been taken away by one of Caer-Lundein's army of efficient and polite servants, and he must now perforce wear fine linens, whether he liked them or not. Sighing again, he laced up his boot strings and gathered his cloak from the settle, making his way with reluctant and heavy-hearted steps to the council chamber.

He had now been at Caer-Lundein for nearly two weeks and had finally learned the ins and outs of the corridors and maze-like inter-connecting chambers of the old castle. Arthur remembered how, when he had first arrived, he had wandered the halls and passageways for hours trying to find his way to the solar, the guardroom, or simply to return to his own chamber.

On one occasion he had been found by Morgause standing outside a locked door that steadfastly refused to open when he tried the key in the lock. He had been twisting and wriggling it in the keyhole with increasing force and frustration when he heard behind him the voice of the woman he still found it hard to think of as his sister.

"Now Your Majesty, is one chamber not enough for you? Would you also like to take occupation of mine and my husband's?"

Her tone was light, and there was a smile on her lips, but it did not reach her eyes. "Your room is in the North Tower. This is the West. I must say, I am surprised that you are taking so long to get your bearings here—but perhaps it is because you have no experience of great houses. Tell me brother, how many towers did Sir Ector's house have?"

Arthur, who had been certain that the room had been his, had felt both humiliation and anger. From then on, he had made it his business to learn the geography of the castle that was now his home, walking purposefully from room to room, and when he returned to his chamber, drawing plans of the layout and marking on them the landmarks—like the war axes that hung on the wall next to the armoury—that could guide him.

He had just passed one of these—an ornate tapestry depicting the Beltane revels, which hung near the entrance to the Great Hall. There were sounds of raised voices and laughter coming from within, and the noise of tankards clinking. Obviously, the men who had returned with Lot and Urien that morning were breaking their fast and telling stories of their journey to those members of the household who had remained behind. Deciding that he did not want to run their gauntlet, Arthur turned away from the doorway and made his way instead down the small passageway to the left of the tapestry, leading directly to the council chamber.

He was the last to arrive. Some of the councillors had already taken their seats. He recognised King Ban of Brittany deep in conversation with Lord Merlin and Cador, Duke of Cornwall. Others, including Lot, Urien and the Welsh knight Sir Bedivere, were standing by the fireplace, their heads close together, talking in lowered voices.

There was only one woman present, Morgause, the Queen Regent. She was sitting at the foot of the table, in animated discussion with a tall, rather stern looking man whose name he didn't know, but who he guessed to be the Duke of Gewisse because of the golden dragon emblazoned on his red tunic. Morgause was dressed richly but simply, in a pale blue linen shift and midnight-blue overdress trimmed with ermine. Her hair had been pulled back and up, away from her face in a crown of intricate plaits, and apart from a diadem on her forehead that caught the sun's rays sending rainbow scintillations about the room, she wore no jewellery. She looked up and smiled at him.

"Good morning, Your Majesty, I trust you slept well? You certainly slept deep. We have all been gathered here awaiting your pleasure for some time. Still, it is your prerogative I suppose."

Arthur looked around the room and reddened slightly.

"I apologise, my lords. I received the message that I was needed but moments ago. Surely, if we are all here, there is no need for further delay?" He made his way to an empty seat on the near side of the table.

The men standing by the fireside also made their way to their seats, with Lot pulling back the chair at the table's head, preparing to take his usual place, when Merlin spoke:

"Nay my Lord Lot, your place is no longer here. That seat is for Arthur." The King Regent froze and for a moment said nothing. Arthur noticed that his eyes went straight to those of his wife. She held them for a moment, and he could tell that unspoken words passed between them.

Frowning, she shook her head slightly and then nodded towards the seat to his right. Following her eyes, Lot moved away from his accustomed place as the Chair of the Council to take up his newly allotted position.

Merlin then went to where Arthur—who was now feeling flustered and very uncomfortable about what had just happened—was seated and bowed low before him, his beard sweeping almost to the ground. "Your Majesty, it is for you to chair the council. I pray you, take your seat."

"But surely, King Lot is still regent . . . I have no wish to take his place prematurely. I . . . I . . . am not crowned yet," stammered Arthur.

"You are Uther's son, and the rightful King. Come, Sire, take your seat, and then we can begin."

Arthur could see that it would be even more embarrassing if he refused like a delinquent child, and so he slowly pushed back his chair and walked towards the heavy and ornately carved oak settle standing at the head of the table. Merlin then took the seat to his left, and all eyes turned expectantly to Arthur, who gave a single, panic-stricken glance to Merlin. The ancient and inscrutable druid merely folded his hands on the table in front of his beard, put his head on one side and looked back at him expectantly.

After a moment of silence, Arthur knew that he needed to say something.

"I bid you welcome, my Lords . . . and also welcome to you, my sister." Morgause nodded but did not smile. Arthur continued: ". . . Um . . . We are here to . . . um . . . find out what . . . find out about . . ." he was having terrible trouble framing his sentences. What did he want to say? And why couldn't he say it? Arthur took a deep breath and looked up into the eyes of King Ban of Brittany. The older man was looking at him kindly.

"It is indeed a daunting task to lead this council." King Ban's voice was low and carefully modulated, addressing his words to Arthur, but ensuring that all could hear what he had to say. "I well remember your father, King Uther, when he first acceded to the throne, saying to me that he would rather do battle with a thousand Saxons than attend his Cabinet." There was general laughter at this, and when it subsided, Ban continued, "Take your time, Arthur. There are many here who loved your father and who recognise you as his son."

These words had a surprising effect upon Arthur. Looking at the compassionate, intelligent face of his father's old friend, he felt for the very first time able to acknowledge who he was. His father had been Uther Pendragon. He had led and inspired many of the men who now sat round this very table, and he, Arthur, was his son, his heir. Although he had not been raised to rule, the crown was his birthright, and he owed it to his father to honour his memory and to accept his inheritance with courage and good grace. Feeling a surge of unexpected confidence, he cleared his throat and got to his feet.

"Thank you, King Ban. I will not forget those kind and wise words. Although I never met him, I know my father valued your friendship, and I am well pleased to call you comrade, and most trusted ally."

He raised his hand to salute the old warrior, before shifting slightly to his right.

"Before we begin the business of the day, I would also like to pay tribute to King Lot of Orkney, who since my father's death has ruled so ably as Regent in my stead. Much is owed to him. I thank you and your queen, my sister." He turned and raised his hand towards her in a gesture of respectful salutation, which she acknowledged with a nod of the head that sent diamonds of light dancing across the faces of the assembled council.

"And now, to business. My Lords of Orkney, Lot and Urien, pray tell us of your journey, and what befell in Lindsay."

From that point onwards, the council proceeded well. King Lot and Urien bore good news, for the Lords of Lindsay had agreed to accept Arthur as rightful heir to the throne and to attend his coronation, which the council had now formally determined would indeed take place at the feast of Alban Elfed in four moons' time. Urien was delighted to report that the only conditions demanded for this capitulation had been that their place on the council be reinstated, and that the number of representatives from Lindsay be increased from one to three.

This was agreed, with the only dissenting voice coming from the man seated next to Morgause, who Arthur had correctly deduced to be the Duke of Gewisse. He also requested an increase in representation but was mollified when Arthur promised him that this would be considered, and he laughed alongside the other Lords when Arthur brought the meeting to a close by remarking that if there were to be many more members of the council, he would need to get a bigger table.

With the business of the morning concluded, the councillors pushed back their chairs and waited for Morgause to rise before making their way to the Great Hall where meat and mead would be available. Arthur made to follow them; he had yet to break his fast and was hungry, but he felt Merlin's hand upon his wrist and saw that neither the druid nor King Lot were making any move to rise from the table.

"Well, that did not go too badly," said Merlin. "But we did not discuss the Northern Lords, and I am unable to avoid drawing the conclusion that we must still prepare for war. What say you, Lot?"

"I fear you are right. I had hoped to persuade my compatriots, but they will not be swayed." Lot pulled at his beard, a worried look upon his face. "My only hope is that they will think twice about declaring war now that Gewisse and Lindsay are ready to swear fealty, but I think we should strengthen the garrison on the northern borders and ensure we remain at all times vigilant."

This was agreed, and after a short discussion on the best way to enlist the additional troops they would require, and possible ways to fund this extra expenditure, the three of them left the room, Lot making his way to the Great Hall for refreshment, whilst Merlin and Arthur repaired to the king's solar for a meal of bread and cheese—and more discussion about the demands that now must be made upon the Treasury.

MORGAUSE HAD LEFT THE COUNCIL chamber on the arm of the Duke of Gewisse, but rather than joining him and the other nobles at the high table, she made her apologies and went instead to the South Tower and the suite of rooms that had been allocated to her sister. She still needed to find Anna. The arrival of Lot and Urien had prevented her from speaking with her earlier that morning and she was burning to find out what had happened to Nimue, and to give Morgan the latest news regarding Arthur's coronation.

She found them together in the ladies' solar, a light, pleasant room facing the castle gardens. There was a fire of fragrant apple wood burning in the hearth, and a tabby cat was stretched out in luxurious slumber on the rug. The two women were sitting at the large elmwood table with a garden trug in front of them. It was overflowing with herbs, cut flowers, leaves and small branches, and as Morgause approached, she could see they were sorting them into small, neat piles. Smiling inwardly, she remembered how as a child, Morgan's favourite pastime had been to sort the coloured threads from their mother's embroidery box, a task which Morgause had always found boring, but which had kept the young Morgan entranced for hours.

They were both so absorbed in their task that they did not notice Morgause approaching, and when she bent down to kiss her sister on the top of her head, Morgan startled and the trug fell to the floor, spilling its contents.

"Oh, Morgause, look what you've done." The note of irritation in Morgan's voice, and the way that she lengthened the letters in her sister's name, as she used to do when they argued in the nursery in Tintagel, reminded Morgause even more poignantly of their childhood. Feeling an unusual fondness for her little sister, rather than snapping back at her, she joined Anna on her hands and knees, and between them they quickly tidied up the plants and returned the trug to its place on the table.

"There now. All's fine. No need for anyone to get upset. It takes me back, seeing you sitting there, so captivated by your work. Just like . . ."

"Just like when we were children," finished Morgan.

"Do you still have Mother's embroidery box?"

"Yes," replied Morgan. "It is in my chamber, in Avalon. I would never part with it." And the two sisters smiled at each other, bound together in their memories.

Anna, who had retired to a seat by the window, now addressed Morgause.

"It is good to see you, Lady. I believe you have met with Gawaine and Agravaine. I hope that their presence does not displease you?"

"Well, I cannot pretend that I was not shocked to see them, but from what they have told me, you did right to bring them with you." Morgause beckoned to the other woman. "Come here Anna, join us. I would have news of Nimue, and of my household in Orkney."

For the next hour they listened with increasing concern as Anna told them the story of what had befallen Nimue on her journey. It had not been an easy tale for the young woman to tell, and Anna had had to piece it together over several days as she attempted to give some comfort to Nimue, whilst also working to ease the pain and shock that had overwhelmed her.

All had gone well at first. When she entered the enchanted pathways from the cave on Avalon's lakeside Nimue had been greatly relieved to not encounter the bridge that had so nearly defeated her on her previous journey. Instead, she had found herself in ancient woodlands, full of old trees, garlanded with ivy. The forest was dense, but not dark, and the sun shone through the leaves of elm, ash, and birch, creating dapples of light and casting delicate shadows upon the winding pathway. Having made sure the sword was fastened securely to her back, she made swift progress until, after about two hours of walking, she had heard in the distance the sound of a hunting horn and the baying of dogs.

This had worried her. She knew full well that only the Fae folk would be likely to be hunting upon the pathways, and the thought of encountering the likes of Aldaron or his sister Miriel filled her with apprehension. Quickening her pace, she looked around her, trying to find a place to conceal herself but in this part of the forest, the trees were young and did not grow closely together. There would be no hiding within their branches, and what shrubs and bushes there were would not have provided any sanctuary from the eager noses of the hunting hounds.

Remembering Morgan's instructions, she did not stray from the path and pressed onwards. From behind her and to her left, she heard the deep, mournful call of the horns and the hounds' frenzied, excited yapping. By now she was almost running, hoping to find the forest boundary and a more secure place of shelter, but the trees seemed to go on forever and the noise of the hunt was coming ever closer. She could hear the sound of the horses, bridles jangling, hooves pounding the forest floor. At last, the trees seemed to be thinning. She had reached the boundary and in front of her was a meadow. The path ran, straight and true, through the centre of it, and once she had reached it, Nimue picked up her skirts and ran.

But she could not outpace them. Soon the first of the hounds was upon her and behind her she heard the terrifying sound of the sharp, eager double note from the horns, telling the hunters their quarry was in sight. Out of the woods came the horses, each the mount of an Elven lord or lady. They surged forwards, their hair streaming out behind them like multi-coloured banners. Many of them held whips, which they used unsparingly on their animals, and at their head rode Aldaron.

Nimue had panicked. Rather than staying on the path, she had set out across the meadow towards a small building that she vainly hoped might give her shelter. She had run until she felt her heart and lungs could take no more, but never for one moment had she thought to lighten her burden by dropping her pack or unleashing the sword from her back. She had almost reached the door of the cottage when she caught her foot and fell full length. When she raised her head, Aldaron was standing over her.

When she reached this part of the story, Anna had fallen silent, as if uncertain how to go on. Morgan poured her a glass of water, and when the older woman had taken a mouthful, she was able to continue.

Aldaron had dismissed his companions, telling them to seek their own prey. There had been some dissent, but after heated words, the rest of the hunters had finally ridden back the way they had come, their horns once again sounding their low single note.

He had then picked Nimue up as if she had been a kitten, and taken her into the cottage, where he had tied her to the bed, using strips cut from her own clothing to secure and gag her. He had apparently taken no interest in her backpack or the sword, seeing them mainly as a hindrance to getting her on her back. He had simply cut them away from her and thrown them casually into a corner.

Then, pulling up her skirts, he had taken her, roughly and hard. As he pushed and shoved, forcing himself upon her, he ripped the gown from her shoulder and bit her, until the blood flowed. He took his time, but once he had finished, he unsheathed his knife and, going to the place where he had made the wound, slowly and carefully flayed a long straight length of her skin, taking it from her shoulder to the first joint of her forefinger. This he wrapped carefully in a handkerchief and placed in his pocket. Then he left her.

This happened the next day and the next. By the fourth sunrise, Nimue was certain that she would die. She had taken no nourishment and now had open wounds on both arms and her stomach, where he had bitten and then flayed her.

This time when Aldaron had returned, he brought with him a flask of water and a platter of food. He told her that she was proving far more entertaining than he had expected and he did not want his pleasures to be ended prematurely. Checking that all her other bonds were secure, he removed her gag and undid the binding that secured her right hand. Whilst he turned to pick up the platter and the flask of water, Nimue had plunged her hand into her pocket and stabbed Aldaron in the neck with the iron nail.

He had screamed and hissed at her, baring his teeth, his face contorted into a mask of agony, and then he had disappeared.

Nimue had withstood the temptation to eat and drink. She untied herself, and picking up her pack rebound the sword to her back. Then, slowly, painful step by painful step, she had made her way back to the path.

Luckily, she did not have far to go, and on the other side of the meadow she found herself on the stone pathway that led to the Ring of Brodgar. The roads that lead to the ancient stones are not favoured by the Elven folk, and she was able to finish her journey undisturbed. She had been uncertain if she would have the strength to open the gateway in the rock, but after several attempts she finally emerged, bleeding, shocked and exhausted.

As the sunlight found her face and she felt the breeze from the loch upon her skin, she gave thanks to the Goddess. But her strength was gone, and she had been unable to take another step. Collapsing on the coarse grass, Nimue had lain unconscious until Anna, seeking mushrooms in the early dawn, had found her. The Corsican woman had taken her back to her cottage and tended her wounds, looking after her until she was well enough to be taken to the castle where Avice could give her the seclusion and privacy so needful to her healing.

WHEN ANNA HAD FINISHED SPEAKING, she raised her beaker to her lips and drank deeply. Watching her, Morgan got to her feet and went to the dresser saying.

"Stay—after such a tale, I think we need more than water to strengthen us." She poured wine and handed it to them. The three women raised their goblets and drank. When she had finished, Morgause said, "You say Nimue needs privacy and solitude to aid with her recovery? I can understand that, and she is welcome to stay within my walls for as long as she wishes, but do you think that she will ever regain her tranquillity after such an ordeal?"

"She will always be scarred," replied Anna. "The wounds to her flesh will fade with time. She is young, and as you know, I have much experience in the healing arts, but the damage to her mind will be harder to repair."

Morgan had refilled their goblets and was now sitting on the edge of her chair, her mouth set hard, the fingers of her left hand drumming furiously and repetitively upon the table. "That Aldaron should have done this is unthinkable, and I will not hesitate to make my displeasure known when I next set my foot upon the enchanted pathways. That he dares to do this to a handmaiden of Avalon is scandal enough, but that he did so to one who is under the protection of the Lady—and thus, by definition, of the Goddess herself, is almost a declaration of war."

Morgause looked startled. "Morgan, I hope you are not thinking of returning to the lands of the Fae? I have always been troubled by what I had heard of it, and now, after what has happened to Nimue, you would be mad to return there. Who knows what this Aldaron could do to you?"

Morgan gave a short, humourless laugh. "Ha! I do not fear the Elven folk, and as for Aldaron, he will never again harm another. The wound that Nimue inflicted will have been sufficient to destroy him—and though his sister Miriel may mourn him, I think there will be few to join her."

Draining her goblet she got to her feet. "I understand that you are concerned for my welfare, Morgause. If there has been one good thing to come out of this troubled year it has been that we can finally show love for each other as sisters should." Reaching out, she laid her hand upon her sister's arm. "But if I do nothing, it will be taken as a sign of weakness—not just from me but from Avalon itself—and you can be sure that the Fae folk will be fast to exploit it. I shall journey upon the pathways this very day, and my actions there will ensure that Aldaron's crime does not go unpunished."

Morgause sought once again to dissuade her, trying to enlist Anna's voice in support in her arguments, but the older woman said she had no wish to become involved in an argument between the two sisters, and she finally gave up, saying, "You were always a stubborn one, Morgan. Even as a child, no one, not even Mother, could get you to do anything you didn't want to."

Morgan smiled ruefully. "The only person who could ever do that was Vivian. And it is also for her sake that I must do this. I sent Nimue, Vivian's daughter, into danger, and if I do not act now, the fragile relationship that Vivian fostered so carefully between Avalon and the Fae will be in tatters.

"Listen, after I have found Miriel and she has paid the price I shall demand for Aldaron's actions, I shall travel on to Orkney. I would like to see Nimue for myself, and if possible, offer her comfort."

"And the sword?" Anna looked across at Morgan questioningly. "Do you wish to know where I have concealed it?"

"No, I would rather be able to speak true when I tell Merlin that I do not know where it is to be found. I am certain you will have done all that is needed to keep it safe. Thank you for all that you have done for us." Morgan then placed her hand on Anna's forehead. "In the name of the Goddess, I bless you and your family. Long may you find favour in her sight." And so, saying she gently kissed her on the brow before turning towards her sister.

"Morgause, please, don't worry, I shall be gone no longer than three nights and I am certain that my actions will help to make the enchanted pathways safer, rather than more hazardous." She laughed. "Safe enough even for you to tread upon them one day perhaps?"

"I doubt it, sister. I can think of nothing that could ever entice me to place my feet upon those dark thoroughfares.

I understand that you will not heed my warnings, but please, for my sake, promise me you will take no unnecessary risks." She opened her arms, and the sisters held each other for a long time, dark head against copper, pale cheek against golden. Morgause put her mouth to Morgan's ear and whispered. "And make sure you return swiftly. You have a pupil needing tuition, and we have much to do if we are to ensure those lessons are to be as fruitful as we desire."

CHAPTER EIGHTEEN

MORWENNA

Arthur was sitting by himself on the grass in the walled physic garden. It was now high summer, but the glorious yellow flowers on the laburnum tree had long since vanished and he could see fallen leaves on the soil around its roots, a sure sign that autumn would soon be upon them. It was rare nowadays for him to be alone, and still more unusual for him to have an unguarded moment like this where he had a chance to simply sit, undisturbed, peaceful and uninstructed.

His days were now very busy. When he was not with Lord Merlin or King Lot discussing matters of state and policy, or attending meetings with visiting nobles, he would be closeted with Dafydd, the castle seneschal, approving plans for his coronation, or engaged in learning one of the thousand and one lessons that either Merlin or Morgause deemed it essential that he absorb and master. But despite the constant calls upon his time, and the seemingly endless and complex traditions and rules of etiquette that he needed to understand and absorb, he was not unhappy. Ever since his successful handling of the Privy Council meeting on the day of Lot and Urien's return he had felt less confused and out of his depth. As each day went by, he became more able to understand the implications and consequences of his birthright and could recognise—if only to himself—that he was becoming better equipped to face the challenges it would undoubtedly bring with it.

King Ban, who had spoken to him on that day with such kindness and understanding, had returned to his own court in Brittany some weeks ago. Before his departure Arthur had sought him out, hoping to find out more about his father, Uther, and the early years of his kingship as after the departure of the Romans. After Vortigern's invasion, Uther and his elder brother Aurelius had found shelter at the Breton court and he and Ban had become fast friends.

"He was a good man, your father, an honest king and a loyal comrade, but he had his faults, as do we all. He could be impulsive. Generous, yes, but also capricious. From boyhood he was quick to anger, and I'm afraid he often found it difficult to forgive." The old king had looked questioningly at Arthur. "I have not seen that quality in you, and to be honest, I am glad of it. To me, it would seem that you have inherited more of your mother's nature."

At this, Arthur had started. He knew little of his mother. Morgause always refused to speak of her, and Merlin would prevaricate and change the subject if he ever tried to find out more about his birth. "You knew my mother? And you think I am like her?"

Ban smiled. "I remember seeing her here, in Caer-Lundein, on the day your father made his vows of dedication to the Goddess. He had called her to sit with him on the dais, and she danced with him before all the court. I had never beheld a woman so lovely, and Uther—well—he was entranced by her." Ban had closed his eyes, and sighed deeply, as if seeing her again, a vision in his mind. "She was wearing a white dress, trimmed with swansdown, and on her head, she wore a coronet of silver roses. The Goddess herself could not have been more enchanting." He sighed again and opened his eyes. "I did not know her well, but Igraine was a gentle soul and one who, I believe, did nothing to encourage the troubles your father's love for her brought upon his kingdom."

And Ban had told him about Uther's desire for Igraine, Duchess of Cornwall and Lyonesse, and already wife to the mighty War Duke, Gorlois. His determination to possess her had splintered the alliance between the two warriors and led to bloody civil war. Eventually, Uther's men had slain Gorlois on the battlefield of Demelihoc, and Uther, with the aid of Merlin and Vivian, had carried out a great deception upon Igraine. Using their magics, they disguised the Pendragon, giving him the face and form of Gorlois, his slaughtered enemy. So enchanted, Uther had come to Tintagel castle where, believing him to be her husband, Igraine had lain with him, and made vows of love and fealty.

"...and so, you were conceived. But when your mother found out what he had done, she refused to marry Uther. On the day you were born, the Lord Merlin took you from her, and had you raised in secret. The rest you know."

Arthur had looked at Ban. "But what happened to her after that? Is she still alive, in Cornwall?"

The old king rubbed his beard and shook his head. "She is not in Cornwall. That much I know. When she rejected Uther, Tintagel became the fiefdom of her brother, Gareth, King of the Welsh Marches, and is now held by Duke Cador. As to whether she lives or died, I know not."

King Ban had been unable, or unwilling, to tell him anymore and he had returned to Brittany the day after their conversation. He had promised to return to Caer-Lundein for the coronation, and Arthur had sworn to himself that he would speak to him again, and if he could, press him further to reveal more about the father and mother he had never had the chance to know.

Ban's words had also done much to help him perceive Morgause in a different light. He now thought he understood why she had initially behaved towards him as she had. Like him, she had grown up without her mother, and in a household far from where she had been born. He recognised that it was likely that she blamed both him and his father for this.

He had not spoken to her about King Ban's revelation, not knowing how to introduce the subject and aware that she had always been unwilling to talk of their mother, but his relationship with his half-sister had changed over the past few weeks, and had become one of the things he most cherished about his new life. They met daily, frequently when the business of the council was done, and before dinner was served in the Great Hall. She would always welcome him with a chilled infusion of jasmine, rosemary and fennel, which both refreshed him and cleared his head.

He would share news with her, telling her about the questions the council had been called upon to consider, and asking for her advice on any matters that might be vexing him. He had discovered that she had a quick wit and was a remarkably astute judge of character. She was also a seemingly inexhaustible fount of knowledge about members of the court, his allies and the rebellious Northern Lords. She would tell him scandalous details about the private lives of this knight or that lady, seeming to take an inordinate amount of pleasure in his look of shocked disbelief when she revealed yet another scurrilous secret.

She had also been teaching him to dance. At first, he had hated these lessons perhaps more than any other, feeling like a coarse and clumsy oaf as she asked him to raise his leg and point his toe. But as the days passed, his confidence had grown and he now had come to enjoy learning the farandole, saltarello and pavane almost as much as he relished the time, he spent learning swordsmanship and warcraft, lessons now shared with his young nephews, Gawaine and Agravaine.

The lessons that were currently troubling him most, and which were the reason for him seeking seclusion within the walls of the physic garden, were those that had begun a week ago with the newly arrived priestess from Avalon.

He had made his way to the ladies' solar at the appointed time for his meeting with Morgause, who welcomed him with a smile. As usual, she had offered him a goblet of the herbal infusion she said she prepared only for him, but rather than the gleeman with his lyre who usually joined them, the only other occupant in the room was a slender young woman with long dark hair, simply dressed in a white linen smock and dark blue coarse-spun kirtle.

"Come, my noble brother, let me introduce you to Morwenna, who has lately joined us from the Lake Isle."

Morgause had taken his hand and led him towards the girl, who had dropped into a gentle curtsey, bowing her head before looking up at him, serious and unsmiling. He noticed that her eyes were an extraordinary shade of blue. They were framed with long, heavy lashes, and looked huge in her fine-boned and delicate face.

"It is an honour to meet you, Sire." Her voice was low and well-modulated but conveyed no emotion.

". . . Likewise, likewise . . ." replied Arthur, who was feeling a little flustered. He had been told to expect the arrival of the wise woman who was to instruct him in the rites and rituals of the Goddess, but he had been expecting a rather more matronly person. This small, serious-faced young woman seemed little older than himself.

"I trust your journey was uneventful? The roads can be hazardous at this time of year I believe," he had blustered, unable to think of anything more original to say.

"I came upon the enchanted pathways, Sire. There are indeed hazards aplenty, but by the grace of the Goddess, I myself experienced nothing untoward."

"Good . . . good . . . and do you plan to stay with us long?" Arthur had found himself almost lost for words. This calm, self-possessed woman made him feel awkward and uncomfortable, as out of his depth as he had been when he had first arrived at Caer-Lundein.

"Morwenna will be with us until your coronation. Unlike myself, she has been Avalon-trained and has been personally selected to instruct you by our sister, the Lady of the Lake." Morgause replaced the jug containing the herbal infusion on the table and made her way to the door. "I do not feel like dancing today, brother, and besides, you have improved so much, I think there is little more that I can teach you. I suggest the two of you spend this hour becoming acquainted with each other instead." She looked at the young woman and smiled.

"You will find His Majesty a willing pupil, I think Morwenna, but do not fear to scold him if he gets his lessons wrong. I have had occasion to give him many a tongue-lashing when his stubborn feet refused to master the steps I set him to learn."

"That is, perhaps, a sister's prerogative," answered Morwenna. She had looked at him directly, but there had not been even a shadow of a smile upon her lips. "I could not presume so, Your Majesty. Still, I am certain there will be no need for chastisement. I am sure the Goddess will bless our endeavours."

"Let us hope so," Morgause had replied. "There is much that depends on your stay with us being successful. But time is pressing, and I am sure you are both eager to become better acquainted. I will take my leave." And dropping a slight curtsey to Arthur, who bowed in return as she had taught him, Morgause had left the room, closing the door firmly behind her.

For some moments, neither spoke. Arthur had spent little time in the company of women. Sir Ector's wife had died soon after he had been taken into wardship, and Kai had no sisters. His early years had been isolated, and on the rare occasions they visited one of the small number of families who lived within the boundaries of the Forest Sauvage, he and Kai had always been encouraged to remain outdoors with the young squires and pages. Even when attending the rituals of the Goddess, he had had little chance to meet or speak with girls of his own age.

The wise woman of the Forest Sauvage has been a contemporary of Sir Ector's, and although Arthur and Kai had been brought up to treat her with respect, he could not remember ever being alone with her, let alone engaging her in conversation. Thus, he felt nervous and uncomfortable in the presence of this self-possessed, serious and ethereal looking young woman. The newfound confidence which enabled him to engage in easy banter with Morgause appeared to be rapidly ebbing away, and he felt himself to be becoming once more the rough-edged and ignorant country bumpkin that had first arrived at Caer-Lundein.

He moved towards the polished elmwood table, on which stood a pewter bowl, filled with delicate white roses.

"Do you mind if I sit down?"

"You are the master here, Sire. It is not for me to grant or withhold permission." Her voice was neutral, but this time her tone was not cold. Somewhat encouraged, Arthur took a seat. At first, he walked to the head of the table but decided at the last minute to choose a chair placed in the middle, along the side nearest to the window. She watched him, but did not herself move, and so he indicated with a gesture that she should take a seat across from him.

He reached for the jug and poured two more goblets of the infusion, passing one to her saying. "Try this, Morgause makes it for me. I find it very pleasant."

She accepted, took a tentative sip and when she found the taste to her liking, drank more deeply.

"She has many talents, I believe—your sister—the queen."

"Yes, I think she was not fond of me when I first arrived, but she lately has been kind, and I think we now have a good understanding."

"And has she also been teaching you?"

"Yes, all sorts of things. Things I never thought mattered or would ever have to learn."

She looked at him, an eyebrow raised questioningly.

"You know, things like who enters a room first, who should speak first at a feast. How to dance. How to eat a spitted chicken without soiling my clothes. That sort of thing."

"And have you been an apt pupil?"

"I have tried my best."

"As I hope you shall with me." Morwenna reached out and took a rose from the bowl. "What I am here to teach you is far more serious than dance steps and court etiquette. You are to be King—and as such, will have the power of life and death over your subjects. But there is one who will always surpass you, and whose powers are infinitely greater than anything you could possibly imagine." As she had been speaking, she gently pulled the petals from the flower, and they now lay in a small, fragrant pile in front of her.

"Look at the rose. Destroyed do you think?"

He said nothing, but nodded his head, unsure about what she was doing, or what would happen next.

She looked at the denuded stem. There were three thorns upon its slender length. Holding it in her right hand, she pressed the largest thorn into the forefinger of her left, until a droplet of blood emerged. Holding her finger above the petals, she let three drops fall. She then placed the stem upon the table and leant back, closing her eyes for a moment, a look of deep concentration on her face. To his astonishment, the petals began to move, slowly weaving themselves back upon their pistil until the bud had become whole again. But whereas before the flower had been a pale and creamy white, the petals were now a deep and vigorous red, the colour of heart's blood.

"How did you do that? I've never seen anything like it . . ." Arthur was staring at the rose, which Morwenna had handed to him.

"I did not do it—or rather I did, but only with the grace of the Goddess, and the power she has chosen to vest within me." Morwenna reached out and took the rose from him, placing it in the centre of the bowl.

"And will you teach me how to do things like that? How to work enchantments I mean."

"Do you think that is the business of a king? To be a parlour magician, changing the colour of roses and turning foxes into fowl?" She looked at him, and there was no warmth within her eyes. She was not teasing him as Morgause did. Instead, Arthur realised she was trying to get his measure.

"I have spent my life in Avalon, learning to serve the Goddess. Her power works through me, and you, as sovereign of this realm, needs must be as one with Her, so the spiritual and the temporal can align, for the benefit and protection of the people.

I am not here to teach you to entertain your friends or satisfy your vanity. If we are to work together, I need you to understand that although as an individual and a citizen of this realm, you are my king and make the rules that I must live by, in the deeper matters, you owe service and allegiance to the Goddess, and as her representative, you must be guided by, and obedient to me.

If we cannot reach that understanding, I cannot help you and will return this day to Avalon."

She said nothing more, just sat straight-backed, her hands folded on her lap, looking at him with her large, unblinking and startingly blue eyes.

And so, it had begun.

Arthur had stammered his agreement to the rules she had set, and they agreed to meet each morning in a small room leading off his chamber in the North Tower, a place where they could be certain of both peace and privacy.

She brought with her books from the library in Avalon, ancient tomes of hand-bound vellum, containing within them the details of the age-old rites and rituals of the magics, and these they had begun to read together. Sometimes he could not decipher the faded, spidery writing, and she would move next to him, guiding his hand and helping him to make out the words. When she did this, often he found that his arm would come to rest against hers, and he would feel the gentle warmth of her breath upon his neck and cheek as he leant in close. When first this had happened, she had pulled away when she became aware of their physical intimacy, but gradually, she had allowed her arm to linger against his and to sit close to him, so her head could rest upon his shoulder as they studied and talked together.

Soon, Arthur found that his thoughts were becoming concentrated upon Morwenna and the time he spent away from her had now seemed to be nothing but dull and wasted hours. He was entranced by the delicacy of her form and movement. The way she did everything—from drinking a cup of chilled water, to slicing herbs and flowers to prepare them for ritual use—was done with a measured and practised restraint that was both elegant and enchanting. He found himself fascinated by the soft curve of her cheek and the way she pushed her hair behind her ears when it fell, in great, tumbling sweeps of midnight, over her shoulder and onto the pages of whatever book they were studying.

They had examined the rites and rituals of Beltane, Alban Elfed and Yuletide, talking seriously and intensely of the responsibilities shared by the leader of the people and the leader of the faith. With her guidance, Arthur found that he was beginning to acquire a deeper, more fundamental understanding of the person he would need to become when he assumed the crown. He, as king, would then take on not just the right to command those who lived within his realm, but also the sworn and Goddess-given duty to protect and assure their lives, security and well-being.

The two of them spent hours discussing the vows he would make at his coronation, practising the declarations of loyalty and service that would determine his future life; actions and decisions which he would make publicly, before all his court, as his father had done over twenty years before.

They had spoken of the need to have a priestess with him when he went to war, to scry for him and provide good council, as much as to bless him and his troops in their endeavours, but there was one festival, one ritual that that had not yet been part of his instruction.

Solstice.

He had always known that the rites of the Summer Solstice were of paramount importance. Yesterday, as their lesson was drawing to an end, Morwenna had said to him: "The Solstice is a celebration of life, of fertility, of the Goddess's goodness in making our fields and bellies fruitful." She had turned her face to him, serious as always, but with eyes that met his with a gaze of passionate intensity. "It is a festival of fire, of warmth, of love and desire. It is how we honour the power that has brought us into being and taught us that our time on this earth is not just about duty and hardship—but also about pleasure."

When she'd finished speaking, she did not take her eyes from his. Instead, she did something she had never done before. Slowly, she reached out to him and touched his face. Her pale, slender fingers had gently caressed his cheek, before softly moving to stroke his mouth. The top of her forefinger had placed a slight and delicate pressure upon his lower lip and almost involuntarily, Arthur had opened his mouth, and the tip of his tongue brushed against the back of her finger, tasting the subtle beauty of her skin. Morwenna had closed her eyes, and reaching up, kissed him fiercely. He had tried to embrace her, to clasp her to him and kiss her more deeply, but as his arms reached out to encircle the delicacy of her waist, she had pulled away from him and rushed from the room without saying a word, bringing that day's lesson to an abrupt, but very definite close.

ARTHUR KNEW WHAT HAPPENED AT Solstice. It had been part of his life for as long as he could remember. They had celebrated it each year within the Forest Sauvage, and although Sir Ector had always chosen to celebrate the final elements of the ritual within the privacy of his chamber, he and Kai had known full well what they entailed.

When the Litha fires were lit, the Lord of the Land and the woman who was to him the representative of the Goddess, would make vows to each other, committing themselves to the protection of the land and its people, and beseeching the Goddess to share with them her love and bounty in the year to come. And then, together, they would consummate their vows in the oldest and most powerful of all the rituals.

Arthur leant back against the wall. The morning was silent, save for the call of a single blackbird, perched high on the branches of a nearby rowan. The berries on the graceful, silver-barked tree were just beginning to ripen, changing from pale green to a bright and vibrant red. Another marker of the turning of the year. Another sign that Alban Elfed was approaching, and he should be thinking about his duty. But when he closed his eyes, all he could see was Morwenna.

All he wanted to think about was Morwenna. Time and time again he relived the moment that she had reached up to kiss him, trying to recapture the exact sensations he had felt as she had pressed her lips to his. For a few seconds she had pushed her body close against his and he had felt the urgent beating of her heart.

Today, he knew that when she came to him, she would instruct him in the part he, as guardian of the people and custodian of the land, needs must play at Solstice. She would be his Goddess. He felt almost sick with longing, and at the same time, absolutely terrified that he would prove unworthy and fail in his duty, not just as a king—but as a man.

CHAPTER NINETEEN
THE PRACTICE GROUND

"Those are my greaves, Agravaine," said Gawaine, reaching out to retrieve his property from the pile in front of his brother. "Go get your own from the armoury, you lazy sod. These wouldn't fit you anyway—your calves are as skinny as a girl's, they'd just fall down and you'd be as vulnerable to a blow as if you weren't wearing them."

"Piss off, Gowie. At least I'm not built like a great ox—how many times is it now that you had to let out your breastplate since we've been here?" But Gawaine simply ignored his brother's jibes and continued neatly lacing his armour. Grumbling, Agravaine had hoisted himself off the bench in the courtyard and slouched unwillingly towards the armoury.

Gawaine laced up his second greave and, reaching for his helmet and shield, leant back against the wall to await his brother's return. Agravaine was annoying but he saw no reason to get him in trouble with Cerdic, the castle sergeant at arms. They would make their way to the practice yard together, and if Cerdic was annoyed by their tardiness, well, they could share the brunt of his tongue-lashing.

He did not have long to wait. Agravaine returned at a run, the greaves slung in a jumble of laces across his shoulder. He threw himself down on the bench. "Give me a hand, Gowie, I just saw Cerdic coming round the back of the stables. If we hurry, we'll make it in time." Gawaine nodded and bending down, untangled the laces and attached the armoured shin-pad to his brother's right leg, whilst Agravaine did up the left. He pulled on his breastplate but did not have time to fix it in place correctly and grabbing their shields and helmets, the two of them hastened through the archway and along the path that led into the practice yard. Slightly out of breath, they took their places at the end of the line just as the sergeant at arms, followed by a herald bearing a war-trumpet, strode onto the training ground.

The household garrison of Caer-Lundein was roughly a hundred strong and comprised of three cohorts. The first two were a small cavalry of no more than fifteen experienced horsemen, and a light-infantry platoon of thirty soldiers, who specialised in fighting with the bow and the javelin. The third cohort—some fifty-five warriors—were the heavy infantry, who fought with sword, spear and shield. Each cohort trained separately, although all had to develop some skill at archery, and today it was the turn of the heavy infantry to drill within the practice yard.

The training area was a large, open space, running the full length of the castle and walled on three sides, continuing on down to the river on the fourth. The ground was a compacted mix of earth and small stones, pressed hard to create a flat, durable surface that drained well in winter and remained useable even in the dusty months of high summer. A long, thatch-roofed stone building stood against the far wall. Here were stored the practice butts for the archers, the lances and tilts for jousting practice and the heavy wooden rude swords and quintains—life-size dummies made of wood and straw—that the heavy infantry used for much of their practice.

At Cerdic's instruction, the quintains were now being positioned in battle formation in the centre of the practice yard. Looking along the line, he caught sight of Gawaine's flushed face and took in Agravaine's rather dishevelled appearance, and he called out. "You, Orkney boys, fetch the rude swords."

They hurried to obey but needed to make three journeys before they had supplied each member of the cohort with a heavy ash-wood sword. The swords were weighted and tipped with iron, so that they handled like a real weapon, but although the tips could pierce a quintain, they were unlikely to cause any serious harm in practice combat. Agravaine looked at his scornfully. "Why are they giving us toys to play with?" he whispered to Gawaine. "At least back home we practised with real weapons." As everyone else was silent, his words carried across the enclosed training ground, causing Cerdic to turn and look hard at the red-headed brothers.

"You may be sons to Her Majesty, aye and nephews to our new-found king, but here, on the practice ground, you are soldiers." He began walking towards them, one long, heavy stride after another, until he stopped but a hair's breadth from Agravaine.

"And what must a soldier do? What is his first duty?" His voice was low, and deceptively friendly, like a kindly uncle making a polite enquiry. Agravaine said nothing.

"I asked you a question. What is the first duty of a soldier?" Agravaine hung his head, aware that all eyes were upon him.

"It is to be obedient, sir," said Gawaine, hoping to divert the sergeant at arms' attention away from his brother.

"Indeed, it is. And part of that obedience is to speak when you are spoken to, and not before." Cerdic looked at Gawaine, standing straight, breastplate polished, face sombre and concerned, and he relented.

"But loyalty is also important. As a soldier you stand shoulder to shoulder with your companions. If you cannot trust each other, cannot depend on each other, then you are lost." Turning to Agravaine he said. "You are lucky in your brother. Look to it that you return to him the allegiance that he has shown to you."

Returning to his place, Cerdic picked up his practice sword and held it high above his head, before thrusting it deep within the bowels of a quintain. He pulled it out and stabbed again. "Today we will work on the melee. Fighting in close proximity with the enemy, where your aim is to defeat him, without bringing harm to your own fellows."

Raising his sword, he pointed to sixteen or so of the assembled soldiers. He ordered them to take their places in the centre of the practice yard, where the quintains were standing like martial scarecrows. To half the men, he gave red sashes, the remainder were given blue.

They tied them in place across their chests and then stood, waiting his instruction. "Blue knights, take the north aspect; Red, you defend the south. You will fight through the quintains, and your aim is to take the other's territory—without losing your own."

Cerdic stepped back and beckoned to the herald. "Begin at the sound of his call and lay down your weapons when the second trump is sounded."

The two groups of soldiers took their places and readied themselves. At Cerdic's command, the herald raised the trumpet to his mouth, and as the note rang out, loud and harsh across the training ground, they threw themselves into action.

Gawaine and Agravaine watched as the men charged at each other, hitting out with sword and shield, obstructed by the quintains and fighting in such close proximity that it was hard for anyone to distinguish between friend and foe.

"I don't think I'd fancy doing that with a real sword," whispered Gawaine.

"But in battle we're going to have to," answered Agravaine.

"Yes, I know. But I'd rather learn the skills in a way that doesn't endanger my life. Angus never taught us anything like this back in Orkney."

"Angus was just an old fool," replied Agravaine.

"He was a good warrior. Our father trusted him with his life. But I think I'm learning more from Cerdic than ever I did back home. Arthur thinks so to. He says the sergeant at arms back in the Forest Sauvage was an old man—just like Angus."

"Where is Arthur?" asked Agravaine. "I thought we were expecting him today." Arthur's other duties meant that he sometimes had to miss a practice drill, but when he had seen him at supper in the Great Hall on the previous evening he had told them that he would join them at practice.

"I don't know," answered Gawaine. "Probably Father had some matters of state to discuss with him."

"Or Mother needed to teach him some new dance steps."

Gawaine laughed. "Poor old Arthur. I'm glad I'm not going to be a king for a very, very long time. They have to do such boring things. But look, look what's happening on the field."

Both boys looked towards the centre of the practice ground. All of the soldiers were now fighting within the quintains, leaving their allocated territory undefended. There was a lot of noise, shouts and grunts, and the thud and hammer of sword upon sword, helmet or breastplate. Whilst they fight was going on, Cerdic had silently gathered together sixteen other soldiers, giving them yellow or green sashes, and assembling them to the north and south of the quintains.

He then gestured to the herald to sound the horn, and as the red and blue cohorts stumbled away from their battlefield, many of them cut and bruised from the melee, they were captured by their yellow- and green-clad fellows and forced to their knees.

"So, my brave warriors, tell me what happened there?" Cerdic went to one of the red-sashed soldiers, a tall, well-made man in his early thirties. He had a black eye and was gingerly holding his swollen wrist to his chest.

"You, Sir Accolon, what was your mistake?"

"We left our territory undefended, sir."

"Yes, boy. Exactly. The task I gave you was to capture the other side's territory, without losing your own."

He looked at the sixteen soldiers, sitting shame-faced, battered and out of breath.

"If this had been real, those of you who did not die on the battlefield would have returned to find your lands overrun, your fields ploughed with salt and your wives and children raped or murdered. War is not just about attack. It is about defence. Never forget that."

There was silence, and then a clattering noise as one of the red-sashed soldiers dropped his sword.

"But you fought bravely, and I think now you understand a little more about what the field of battle can be like." Cerdic put out his hand to raise Sir Accolon to his feet.

"Those of you who are injured, make your way to the infirmary where the healer will find you something to ease your wounds." He pointed his rude sword at Agravaine. "These 'toys' can do a deal of damage. I'll warrant you will be glad you are not facing hard metal when it is your turn to join the melee. Now, the rest of you, take your places, and we will try again."

The second melee went slightly better than the first, with the yellows beating the greens and taking their territory, only to find that the third cohort, clad in white sashes, had taken possession of the yellow homeland, making their victory meaningless. Once again, Cerdic sent those who had been injured to the infirmary and the final two cohorts, the white and the black, got themselves into position.

Gawaine and Agravaine had both been given black sashes and despatched to the south side of the quintains. "Listen," said Agravaine, tugging insistently on his sash. "We can't all go into the melee, some of us need to remain here, to protect our territory."

"Afraid of the fight, are you?" asked a wiry, black-haired soldier.

"No," said Agravaine. "But I want to win it."

"Agravaine's right," said Gawaine. "We need to keep a small force here, maybe four of us, to deal with any who break through. The rest of us enter the melee, but I think we need to do things differently. In the other two bouts, everyone fought as an individual, each man for themselves. I think we will do better if we join together and use sheer force to push our way through them. Like the Romans did."

"What do you mean 'like the Romans did,'" asked another soldier, a tall broad-shouldered man, whose long brown hair had been pulled into a battle-plait and trailed down his back.

"Angus, our sergeant at arms back in Orkney, told us the Romans would link arms and protect each other with their shields and would march together against their enemies."

With some muttering, the black-sashed cohort agreed it wouldn't hurt to try what Gawaine was suggesting. Swiftly, Agravaine and three others were tasked to remain behind and defend the south side, whilst the others formed themselves into a tight line, shields ahead of them, and at the sound of the herald's trumpet, marched forward together.

Gawaine was positioned at the furthest end of the formation, and he hacked fiercely at any of the white-sashed warriors who sought to attack them. Protected from the front and sides, they pushed forwards, knocking down the quintains as they went, and soon they reached the north side, which to their delight, had been left undefended.

Claiming it as their territory, Gawaine slipped back along the furthest edge of the quintains, to join Agravaine and the others in defending the south side from the four white sashes who had managed to break through. Slashing at the legs of one and serving a vigorous blow to the helmet of another, Agravaine and their three companions brought the invaders to their knees.

The herald blew the final trump, and Cerdic considered them with a thoughtful look in his eyes. "So, in our final bout, we have a victor. Our black-sashed warriors managed to both win new territory and retain their own. Tell me, how did they manage it?"

"They cheated," called out one of the white-sashed soldiers, who was sitting on the ground rubbing his ungreaved legs, which were bruised from the blows Gawaine had rained upon them. "They didn't engage in hand-to-hand combat. That's cheating."

"Did I tell you that you had to engage in hand-to-hand combat?" asked Cerdic.

"No . . . but I thought . . ."

"No, my friend, you did not think. That was your problem—and the problem for each and every one of you, except for the black sashes. War is not just about strength of arms and technique. It's about tactics. I was not expecting to teach you that lesson today, but it is always a lesson worth learning." He paused, and looked thoughtfully at Gawaine and Agravaine.

"Now, those who are injured, make your way to the infirmary. The rest of you, get yourselves cleaned up and head to your tasks. Those on the black cohort—I will instruct Dafydd to broach a barrel of ale for you at supper—it's up to you if you chose to share it with your fellows."

There was a cheer at this, and everyone got up and began to make their way towards the castle. Agravaine had suffered little in the bout, but Gawaine had received a blow to his face which had bloodied his nose, and he was anxious to get to the infirmary. As they neared the gate, he felt a hand on his shoulder. It was Cerdic.

"You two, listen to me. You are two of the youngest I have ever had the dubious pleasure to teach here at Caer-Lundein, and sometimes I must admit, I have concerns about your discipline and attitude." He tapped Agravaine none too lightly on the side of his head.

"But today, you were the only ones who understood the true nature of the task I set you. You learned from mistakes of others and determined not to repeat them. Your men listened to you, and you led them well. I shall tell your father of this. It is good that he has sons he can be proud of."

With that, Cerdic left them, striding purposefully away towards the Great Hall, where he hoped to find meat and mead.

THE BOYS HAD THEN FORGOTTEN about going to the infirmary. Instead, they rushed back up the stairs of the West Tower, keen to find their mother and tell her exactly what Cerdic had said to them. They found her in her chamber, seated in front of her mirror and engaged in arranging her hair.

Full of excitement, they had burst into her room without knocking. Gawaine caught his foot on the sheepskin rug beside her bed and almost fell, catching hold of her chair to steady himself and jolting the comb from her hand, making it skid across the floor.

"Gowie, you clumsy idiot, what do you think you are doing?" Morgause got up angrily, making her way to where the comb had come to rest. She picked it up and examined it. When she was satisfied that it had not come to harm, she resumed her seat, holding the comb out to them.

"You have seen this before, and you know that it is a very, very precious thing. It is an ancient treasure made from ivory, from far-off lands. It was given to me as present. For all those reasons, I prize it, and yet you feel you have the right to cast it to the floor," and reaching out, she rapped Gawaine harshly on the knuckles.

She turned back and resumed combing her hair, looking at herself in the mirror, where the faces of her two sons were also reflected in the burnished copper.

"You are both filthy, and what have you done to your face, Gowie? Your nose is a mess."

"I'm sorry about the comb. I didn't mean it," said Gawaine, reaching out to touch his mother tentatively on the shoulder. She reached up and patted his hand briefly, before pushing it away.

"You never do, Gowie, you never do. I just wish you would put a little more thought into your actions; then you would not need to spend as much of your time apologising."

"But that's just it," said Agravaine, excitedly. "We have been thinking before we act, and Cerdic was really pleased with us. We have just come from the practice grounds, Mother, and we really want to tell you about it."

"Whatever it is, it will have to wait. There is business I must attend to, and you, Gawaine, should get someone to look at that nose. Anna is in the infirmary. She leaves tomorrow and I have asked her to take what she needs to restock the apothecary chest back home. Get clean, do your tasks, and we shall talk at supper."

With that, Morgause waved them away and returned to her task, slowly, almost hypnotically, combing her hair, and focusing all of her energy on her sister, creating a summoning to bring her to the chamber.

"You need not have summoned me," said Morgan, when she arrived at her sister's door not very many minutes later. "I also wish to speak with you, and to do so without delay."

"I am pleased to hear it, sister." Morgause got to her feet and closed the door, dropping the heavy iron lock in place. "Now, no one can disturb us, and no one can overhear us.

"Tell me, how go the lessons? Does the lovely Morwenna find favour with our brother?"

Morgan, who had arrived wearing a cloak with the hood pulled low to conceal her face, removed it and flung it on the bed. She was simply dressed in an undyed linen shift and pale green kirtle, drawn in at the waist by a plaited rope of dark green twine, interwoven with ivy leaves. Her hair hung loose around her shoulders, and she pushed it back from her face, revealing eyes that were swollen and red with recent tears.

"Oh, 'Morwenna' has indeed done her job well. She has bewitched him, as we intended, and all is now ready."

"And is it to be today? Were our calculations correct? Is now the right day, the day most likely to be blest by the Goddess with the conception of a child?"

"Aye, it is the right day."

"And the infusions of raspberry leaves and red clover?"

"They have been drunk each night since we arrived at Caer-Lundein."

"So what is the matter, Morgan? Your eyes are red, and yet you shed no tears when Vivian died. Your eyes remained dry when Anna told us all that befell Nimue. Why now do you cry?"

Morgan said nothing. She went to the window, looking down into the courtyard. In the distance she could see the archery butts being set out for practice, and the horses being led down to the river to drink. Pulling her hair over her shoulder, she divided it into three strands and began to work it into a rough braid.

"Now sister, let me do that for you." Morgause reached out her hand. "See, I have with me the comb you gave me. You know its skill. Let me help you."

"You keep the comb with you?"

"Aye, it is something I treasure, both for itself, and because of its provenance."

Morgan smiled and made her way slowly towards her sister. "You put it in my room, in Orkney, remember. After Uther died, and I visited you to tell you that Lot would be called upon to become Regent."

"Yes, I asked Avice to put it there. I knew your journey had been hard, and I wished to give you comfort."

Morgan remembered sitting in her chamber in the castle at Stromness and wondering if the comb, which had once been hers, and which it had been a struggle to give up, had been valued at all by her sister. She had suspected that Morgause had simply put it to one side to be used by random visitors, uncared for, and unloved. And she had been wrong. As she approached, Morgause got up, relinquishing her seat in front of the mirror, and the sisters leant into each other, and kissed each other gently.

"Tell me what troubles you, Morgan." Morgause stood behind her sister, freeing her hair from the rough beginnings of the braid, and separating it into long strands. Morgan's hair was heavy and soft. It smelt of lavender and rosemary. Morgause began, gently and rhythmically to draw the comb through each lock, easing out tangles, and burnishing each strand until it shone with a dark, glossy sheen.

"Tell me what troubles you, Morgan," she said again.

"There is no delicate way to put this, Morgause. I am troubled because I think we are doing wrong. What we are planning, what we intend to do this very afternoon, differs little from that which Uther, at Merlin's instigation, did to our mother."

Morgause looked up, and the sisters' eyes met within the mirror.

"Oh, I think not, Morgan. I think the circumstances are very different."

"But how, Morgause? Our mother Igraine believed the man she welcomed to her bed the night before Solstice was Gorlois, our father and her husband. She would never have welcomed the Pendragon."

"You are right. She would not, and she was tricked by Merlin's magics, not just to surrender herself, but to sue for peace and dishonour our father's memory."

"And Arthur, the child born of this deception, he believes 'Morwenna' to be a priestess of Avalon, sent here to instruct him."

"As she is." Morgause continued her slow, gentle strokes, caressing her sister's hair and staring deeply into her eyes.

"But she is also his sister. And he has fallen in love with her." Morgan lowered her eyes.

"Morgan." This time, Morgause's tone was sharp and unyielding. "Remember, this was your idea. I offered to be the one to bear the Beltane

Child and fulfill the prophecy. You rejected that suggestion and instead proposed yourself."

Morgan said nothing.

"Why this change of heart? Don't tell me you have begun to feel sorry for our bastard brother. The person who destroyed our family, the person whose father killed our father and ripped our mother's life apart. Surely you have not changed so much?"

Morgan raised her head, once again returning her sister's gaze. "No, I do not feel that. All you say is true. My concern is that we, by doing this, are resorting to exactly the same tactics deployed by Merlin and enacted by Uther. We make ourselves no better than they are."

"But we do not make ourselves worse." Morgause's voice was determined and strong but held no suggestion of anger.

"Listen, Morgan, you have been raised in Avalon, in harmony and peace, whereas I have grown up in the world. And the world is a place of war. There is one thing that Lot has taught me—that the point of war is to win. And from the moment Uther dared to try to despoil our mother, our family and his were at war. That war continues now, and if we do not do this, we will be betraying the honour of our mother and rejecting our one chance to take vengeance for the death of our father. Do you not see that?"

Morgan reached out and took her sister's hand and together they stood, reflected in the burnished surface of the mirror, magnificent in their beauty, and now with the same hard look of determined purpose shining from both the brown eyes and the blue. Morgause leant her head towards her sister, and her arm encircled her waist. Morgan leant in, resting her head upon her shoulder.

"Yes, Morgause. I do."

CHAPTER TWENTY

GIVEN BY THE GODDESS

Morgan's virginity had not been lost. Rather, it had been given, actively and willingly during the Solstice rituals that had taken place in the year of her seventeenth birthday. As a young woman raised on the Lake Isle, Morgan had been taught to respect and love her body. To care for it as gift from the Goddess, and to understand and take joy in the delights it could bring her.

She remembered with pleasure her first full participation in the rites of Solstice. Vivian had sent her to Glastenning, a small, independently held manor a day's journey from Avalon, to undertake the role of representative of the Goddess within the Solstice rituals.

"The new lord is young, but four summers older than yourself, and is pleasant to look upon," said Vivian. "His mother, Yseult, was raised here, indeed she was somewhat friendly with Igraine, your mother, and I know that Morfael has been brought up to follow the old ways."

"Is he not married?" Morgan had asked.

"No, and perhaps in acting as I am, I am doing him a disservice," replied Vivian. "From the tenor of Yseult's request, I believe she hoped that the priestess I would send could also, in time, become her son's betrothed. A reasonable thing to wish for—but that is not the fate I have in mind for you."

"Then why send me?" Morgan had asked.

"Because, my dear, I care for you, and I wish your introduction to the serious rites of Solstice and the Goddess-given pleasures of the flesh to be experiences that will help you grow both spiritually and as a woman."

And so, they had. Morgan had spent a week with Morfael and Yseult, and had developed a sincere affection for the tall, gentle young man, who was still grieving the loss of his father. From him, she had experienced her first taste of the power and exaltation of the solstice rituals, and also the more tender but no less enjoyable distraction of sharing her body willingly with another.

On the morning of her last day in Glastenning, Morfael had joined her in his mother's solar, and they broke their fast together.

"I have much to thank you for," he had said, smiling tenderly and reaching out to take her hand in his. "I was not sure if I was ready to take on the role of Lord and protector of the Glastenning manor with all its lands and people. My father was a good man—courageous and honest—and until you came to me, I doubted that I could ever aspire to be his equal." He had raised her hand to his lips. "But you have given me confidence and a certainty that I am not completely unworthy." He kissed her hand again. "Are you sure I cannot persuade you to stay, Morgan? With you at my side, we could do great things together."

But she had gently extracted her hand from his, smiling at him with affection, whilst also shaking her head in refusal. "No Morfael, that cannot be. But I cannot deny that I also have much to thank you for, and I will always think of you with affection. When I return to the Lake Isle, I shall speak with the Lady, and we shall send someone to you, who will join you in leading your rituals, and, if you find joy in each other, one day become your wife."

And she had done so. As the years had passed, she had watched with pleasure as Morfael and his Avalon-trained wife Ciara had grown to love each other and to rule the manor of Glastenning wisely and well.

Since then, Morgan had led the Solstice rituals many times and had always delighted in it. After her first experiences with Morfael, she had not taken many lovers. Her work as Avalon's emissary and Vivian's de facto deputy had left her with little time for personal pleasure, but on the rare occasion that she found a person, be they man or woman, who was interesting, intelligent and good to look upon, she had tarried a while and fully enjoyed the temporary distraction.

But now, there was Arthur, and all felt very different. Despite her conversation with Morgause, she still felt almost torn apart by the conflict raging inside her. She had grown up nursing a visceral and unwavering hatred towards her half-brother. How had it happened that she was now, and at her own instigation, planning to open herself to him, to share with him the most intimate of the Goddess' rituals? She had been taught that it was her right to bestow her body where she wished and that none could command her, and she also knew that Arthur would not have accepted her as his instructor and partner in the rituals had he known her true identity.

She was deceiving him, just as her mother had been deceived by his father. This was a conclusion she could not avoid, and one she did not find palatable. Looking honestly within herself she also recognised that, as she had come to know him, Arthur was not the monster her childhood fury had created. Instead, he was a young, innocent man, very much out of his depths but with, it seemed to her, a genuine willingness to shoulder the burdens of leadership with a glad and humble heart and to don, alongside them, the inherited mantle of a king.

Morgan was riven by doubt and knew that she needed guidance but realised that it would be futile to look to her sister, whose determination to do all she could to ensure the fulfillment of the prophecy of the Beltane Child had become an obsession. And so, as she had been taught, she prepared herself to seek counsel from the Goddess, swearing that if direction was provided, she would follow—no matter what the consequences.

Taking herself to her chamber, Morgan had bolted the door and filled a large copper basin with water. Binding her hair in a single braid, she settled herself on the floor in front of the hearth where she lit a small fire of elm wood. The tawny flames were now jumping and dancing in the grate. Reaching into the cambric pocket-bag that hung at her waist she took out the sprays of bay and calendula that she had plucked earlier in the physic garden and threw them into the flames. They crackled and hissed, releasing small plumes of a sharp, aromatic mist that swirled and surged around the copper basin.

Morgan placed her hands firmly around the basin's sides, positioning her thumbs so they rested lightly upon the rim. Letting her head fall forward on to her chest, she closed her eyes and began to concentrate on defining the counsel she was seeking and forming the question she would ask. Finally, she spoke.

"Goddess, help me, I beseech you. I am Morgan of Avalon, and I seek nothing but to do thy bidding. Show me the future, the Beltane

Child—will he come to be?" She paused, and then called out, in a harsh, broken voice.

"Goddess, tell me what you would have me do—and I swear that I shall do it."

Morgan did not move. She kept her eyes closed and head bowed, her hands gripped firmly around the basin. For a few moments, all was still, but soon she felt the basin grow warm beneath her fingers, and her ears became aware of the quiet, almost imperceptible bubble and hiss as the water within it began to roil. Raising her head, she opened her eyes and looked upon the seething surface of the water. The metal was now so hot that Morgan felt sure her flesh would burn, but she did not let go, and through her pain, she panted. "Goddess, I beseech you, show me what you would have me do."

Slowly, the surface water became still, and Morgan found she was no longer gazing into the copper depths of the basin. Instead, she was looking at a familiar, stone-walled room, as if she was standing at the doorway. The casement was open and the sun shone in, illuminating the shimmering motes of dust spinning in the air. There were rich rugs upon the floor, and she could see two women, standing with their back to her in front of a finely carved bed. She thought she could see the form of another person lying on the coverlet, but her view was obstructed and it was difficult to be certain.

Morgan realised that she was looking at the room her sister made ready for her whenever she visited the castle at Stromness—and as the surface stilled and the steam cleared, she knew without question that the two women standing in front of the bed were Morgause and Anna.

Suddenly, the picture in the water came to life, although—as usually happened with visions in the scrying bowl—she could not hear a sound. The linen hanging at the casement fluttered gently in the breeze, and the two women moved closer to the bed. The woman Morgan was certain was Morgause was holding a cloth and a crucible. She bent to her knees by the bedside and, dipping the cloth within the vessel, leant towards the figure on the bed. The other woman, Anna, bent over and adjusted the bedclothes towards the bottom end of the bed. Then, suddenly, the perspective of the vision shifted, and Morgan could now see that the figure on the bed was of a woman, lying on her back, legs apart and belly distended. Her face, obscured by a mass of tousled black hair that had sprung loose from a thick braid, was turned towards the wall.

Morgause reached out to wipe the woman's forehead, and she turned, her face distorted in agony, mouth ripped open in a scream, eyes blazing in panic and fear. Despite the distortion, Morgan had not a second's doubt that this terrified, almost hysterical creature was her future self. She had no need to hear what was happening to understand what she was seeing. She watched as Morgause and Anna helped the woman on the bed raise herself, propping her up with bolsters and pillows, working with her, in time with the contractions Morgan could see rippling through her belly.

Morgause gently pulled the hair away from her face, moistening her lips and wiping her brow, and there was a look of tenderness upon her face such as Morgan had never seen before. Then Anna looked up and said something to Morgause. Morgause reached out and placed her arm on the shoulder of the woman on the bed and then went to wash her hands before returning to the foot of the bed. Morgan saw herself reaching out and grabbing her sister's hand, holding it tight beneath her chin. The woman on the bed was panting now, her mouth opened wider to give one, long last scream, and then Anna leant forwards between the woman's legs.

Within moments, she emerged, a smile of joy upon her face, and holding out to the woman on the bed the red and purple body of a dark-haired baby boy, his mouth wide open in a lusty scream.

Morgan watched as her future self, all pain forgotten now, reached out her arms and took her baby to her breast. She looked up at her sister and her face was exultant. Morgause leant forward, gently reaching out with her forefinger to touch her sister on the nose. Then she kissed both her and the babe and stood back to allow Anna to approach.

As Morgan watched, the vision began to fade. She gazed deeper into the water, silently imploring the Goddess to allow her just one more minute, but her entreaties were in vain. Putting the basin on the floor beside her, Morgan leant back upon her heels and raised her face to the ceiling. She realised that she had been crying.

"A baby. I am to have a baby, and it is the wish and desire of the Goddess," she murmured, still unable to believe what she had seen. Hugging her arms around her she got to her feet and replaced the basin on the table. Then, closing her eyes, she raised her arms and spoke.

"Great Goddess, I thank you. You have shown me the way, and all shall be as you have shown me." Wiping her eyes to remove all traces of tears, Morgan then loosened her hair, and taking up her cloak, made her way to the little room in the North Tower where she knew Arthur awaited her.

IT WAS LATER THAN USUAL when she tapped on his door. He had almost given up on her, and to assuage his disappointment had decided to seek the cheering company of Gawaine and Agravaine. He had promised some while ago to take them to the castle falconry. It was as he was searching for his new leather gloves, made of goatskin and lined with fleece to give extra protection from the birds' keen-edged claws that he heard a gentle knock and saw the door begin to open.

He welcomed her and took her cloak, folding it as Morgause had shown him, and placing it on the heavy carved oak chest by the door. He noticed that she seemed somehow different, more distracted. Hoping to relax her, he poured a glass of mead flavoured with honey and Orkney heather. He knew she was fond of it, but although she accepted it, she took just one small sip before placing it down beside her cloak.

"I thank you Sire, but I would keep a clear head. Today, we consider the deepest and most powerful of our rituals, and even in practice or instruction, it does not do to show disrespect to the Goddess."

Arthur had mumbled an apology, and he too put down his mead. They had talked of the ritual before, and he understood the vows they would make to one another. He had some questions about the ceremony itself, and when he asked her who would take responsibility for overseeing the Solstice mysteries, Morwenna told him that she believed the Lady of the Lake herself would travel from Avalon to Caer-Lundein to celebrate his first Solstice as king in front of the court and all of his allies.

She had already tutored him on the vows that he must make, and now he knelt before her as they practised the ancient ritual together.

"Do you promise to serve the Goddess and protect Her people?"

"I do," he replied, speaking slowly and seriously.

"Do you swear to follow the paths of the Mysteries and bring homage and honour to Her shrines?"

"I do."

"Do you swear to defend Her from treachery and to oppose those who seek to cast out the Mysteries from the hearths and hearts of your lands?"

"I do, my Lady," he had said obediently, following her instructions to the letter.

Morwenna had explained to him that when they had made their vows, the final stages of the ritual would begin. They would divest themselves of the gold and silver crowns that represented the sun and the moon and would also cast aside their ceremonial robes. She told him that this part of the ritual was very ancient. It recognised that all power and rights of sovereignty and governance were a direct gift from the Goddess, a stark reminder that all our earthly status and position are not ours by right, but by the gift of Her favour.

Morwenna reached out her hand and raised him to his feet. She gave a small nod saying, "That was well done. Arthur. Are you ready to progress to the final stage of the ritual?"

"Yes, Lady, I believe I am," he replied, his voice quavering slightly, betraying the nervousness he had wished wholeheartedly to conceal: ". . . but can you tell me once again what we must do?"

"In days gone by, the Lord and Lady would stand, skyclad, before the flames of the Litha fire. Having made their vows, they would join hands, and together leap across the bonfire, an act of faith and purification."

"And then?" asked Arthur.

"And then begins the final part of the ritual, the joyful and solemn joining together of the man and the woman, to celebrate the blessing of the Goddess, to symbolise the unity of flesh and spirit that lies at the heart of all that is good, to ask, with all their hearts, that the blessing and bounty of the Goddess will remain with them and their people in the year to come."

"And must this be done with the eyes of the court upon us?" asked Arthur.

"No, not always. Many prefer to complete the ritual in the privacy of their chamber, or in a spot secluded from the eyes of others," Morwenna said gently. "But for a kingmaking, it is good that his people can see his power for themselves and know that he has the strength and potency to protect and serve his people. That is why we must practise and gain confidence that we can do this. You cannot undertake the ritual in igno-rance of what you will be called upon to do. The risk, if you should fail, would be too great."

In so saying, Morwenna untied the belt of woven twine from around her waist and pulled her kirtle to the floor. Beneath it she wore nothing but a simple shift, and this she pulled over her head, to stand naked before him.

He stared at her, and then fell to his knees, overpowered by the wonder of her. He held out his arms, and she came to him, standing before him, and reaching down, pressed his face to her belly. He put his arms around her and looked up, seeing the perfect swelling of her small, firm breasts. Her nipples, pink and tender like tiny buds, hardened as his gaze fell upon them. Reaching up, he touched one, gently at first, and then harder, and pulling himself to his feet, he took her breast into his mouth and licked and stroked until her breath came, hard and urgent.

And she helped him pull off his breeches, dragging his tunic over his head as they fell backwards together onto the bed. His mouth to hers, he entered her, and almost immediately, spent his seed.

He cried then, holding her to him, and telling her that he loved her, that she was indeed the Goddess to him, and that no woman could ever mean more to him than she did. And she was gentle, holding him as he wept, and then, sitting astride him, she kissed him on the mouth, and took him inside her one more time. She moved slowly at first. Her hair, a mid-night cloud, fell over her face and brushed his chest as her rhythm changed and she drove him onwards.

Afterwards, when both were satisfied, they fell asleep, his arm around her shoulder, her head upon his chest. But when he awoke, several hours before dawn, the sheets beside him were cold and empty and she was nowhere to be seen.

THE FOLLOWING MORNING, ARTHUR DECIDED to seek out Morgause. He wanted to talk about her sons—particularly Gawaine, of whom he was becoming very fond—but when he entered the lady's solar, he found there was no one there but Morwenna. As always, she was dressed simply in a pale blue under-smock and dark blue kirtle, held in at the waist by a knotted rope entwined with blue borage flowers. Her hair, held in place with a simple circlet of woven willow, fell in dark waves across her left shoulder and a blush had flamed on her pale cheeks when she realised who he was.

Arthur was delighted. He had been uncertain when he would see her again as they had made no arrangements on the previous day, and with a smile he opened his arms towards her. She rose slowly from her seat by the window, and walked uncertainly towards him, a strange look on her face. She rested her face upon his shoulder; he did not attempt to kiss her, happy simply to hold her close, feeling the delicacy of her fine bones, smelling the sweetness of her skin and aware of the soft but insistent beating of her heart.

They were still standing together when Morgause entered the room. As soon as Morwenna saw the Queen Regent, she ducked under Arthur's arm and making a hasty curtsey, gathered up her skirts and hurried from the room.

"Well brother, it would seem that you have been taking liberties with your teacher." Morgause reached across and rapped him sharply on the shoulder with the tip of the jewelled dagger she was accustomed to wearing upon her girdle, but her lips curled in a knowing smile, and her eyes appeared to sparkle in her enjoyment of his discomfiture. "There are rules you know, boundaries to be upheld, particularly in a relationship as ancient and symbolic as that which exists between those who wear the Crown and Lady of the Lake Isle. I hope you have been doing nothing to bring it into disrepute?"

He stammered that he had not, that he had nothing but respect for the Lady, and indeed, he had nothing but love for the woman who was her representative.

"Love, you say," said Morgause, sharply. "And what form does this 'love' take?"

Arthur realised that he had not thought much about this. Just that he knew he cared deeply for Morwenna and wanted nothing but to be in her presence, to spend his days with her.

"I'm not sure, Morgause . . ." he stammered. "I know little of her background, but what I do know pleases me greatly, and I think she has feelings for me, as I have for her."

"Are you saying you wish to marry her?" Morgause snorted derisively. She poured herself a goblet of spiced wine, which she sipped as she walked towards the window seat and settled herself comfortably amongst the cushions.

"I am afraid that will not do. Morwenna is a priestess; her role in life is to serve the Goddess. Married love is not something she has been raised to understand or recognise."

"But many of the girls who are schooled in Avalon go on to marry. Our mother, Igraine, for one."

Morgause drew in her breath at the mention of their mother's name, but for once did not end the conversation. "Our mother was a princess, schooled in Avalon, but always with the intention of making a worthy marriage and returning to the world. That is not the case with Morwenna."

Arthur's heart sagged, and pouring himself a goblet of wine, he went to join Morgause on the window seat. "What shall I do, Morgause? I know so little of such things. So much of the time, I feel confused, uncertain. I doubt myself. But, in these last few weeks, with Morwenna, I have seen another side of myself. I have more confidence, more certainty that I can do the things that you, Merlin and King Lot expect of me." He reached out and took his sister's hand in his. "And that's because of her. Because of what I am when I'm with her."

Morgause brushed his hand away. "Arthur, if she has bolstered your confidence by encouraging your understanding of what is expected of you as both a man and a king, that is a good thing. But believe me brother, although you may think me harsh, I tell you truly that you must tear from your heart and mind any thought of building a deeper relationship with Morwenna."

She left him then, and Arthur, hearing the sound of horses' hooves clip-clopping on the courtyard cobbles, looked out of the window. There was Morwenna, dressed in travelling clothes and accompanied by two of the soldiers from the castle garrison, riding out through the archway. She was leaving him.

Dropping his goblet, still half-filled with spiced red wine, upon the floor, Arthur raced out into the courtyard, but by the time he reached the archway, there was no sign of her. Slowly, unable to believe what had just happened, he made his way to his chamber in the North Tower. Pulling off his boots, he flung himself upon the bed. The smell of her skin, subtle and delicate, still lingered on the linen coverlet. He rolled on to his stomach and closed his eyes, breathing deeply, trying to suck in all that remained of her, to draw her to him and re-create her presence in his memory.

CHAPTER TWENTY-ONE
THE CORONATION

It could not be doubted that summer was over, and as Merlin walked slowly across the courtyard at Caer-Lundein, he drew his cloak tight across his shoulders to keep out the damp of the chill night air. Looking up at the crescent moon shining almost directly above him, he realised that although the lanterns were still ablaze in the Great Hall, it was almost midnight, but for him there was work to do before he could take himself to his chamber.

There were now only three days until Alban Elfed—the autumn festival that celebrates the turning of the year. It is a time when the balance between light and darkness shifts. Days shorten, and the hours of darkness lengthen. The festival is an opportunity to reflect on the blessings of summer and give thanks for the final harvest. For Merlin, as a druid, Alban Elfed was at least as important as the Summer Solstice. It symbolised the gateway of the year—a time of ending, but also a time of quickening—and it was for this reason that he had determined that Alban Elfed would also mark the coronation of the new king, whose reign, as the prophecies ordained, would herald a new resurgence for the people of Britain and the Isles.

Kings and queens, nobles and warriors, ambassadors and vassals, had been arriving in Caer-Lundein for several days now. All invited to witness the moment when the son of Uther would claim his birthright, and the Pendragon's crown would be placed upon his head. The castle could hold no more people, and many of the lower ranks were now camped out on the fields beyond the river, as they had been many months before for the great tourney. Looking out across the water, Merlin could see the flickering lights of campfires and torches, reminding him of the afternoon when he had visited Sir Ector, seeking news of his ward.

Since then, the fortunes of the family from the Forest Sauvage had changed conspicuously. Arthur had summoned his foster father and brother to court, and Sir Ector now no longer needed to pitch his tent beyond the walls. He and Kai, alongside King Pellinore and his sons Lamorak and Aglovale, had taken up lodgings in the North Tower. The three young men, together with Arthur's nephews Gawaine and Agravaine, had become firm friends, training together daily in the practice yard, where Arthur joined them whenever he could.

One thing had not changed, however. Sir Ector and his friend King Pellinore had retained their appreciation for ale and cider. As Merlin made his way through the Great Hall on his way to the council chamber, he noted the old knight with some displeasure. Red-faced and spilling ale from a tankard he was waving to and fro, Sir Ector was holding court, surrounded by a cluster of curious onlookers.

"Oh yes," he said loudly, his voice slightly slurred. "Came to me as a baby he did, still in his swaddling clothes . . ."

"And you say it was Merlin who brought him?" asked one of the visitors, a short, pale-faced warrior, whose accent suggested that he belonged to the household of King Ban of Brittany.

"Oh yes, indeed it was. Merlin, himself, as I live and breathe." As he spoke, Sir Ector waved his tankard so enthusiastically that a great rush of ale fell darkly upon the white cloak of the druid who was at that moment passing behind him. Ector gasped in a fluster of embarrassment.

"Oh, my Lord Merlin, I do apologise. Here, let me help you." Leaning forwards in an attempt to wipe away the stain with a kerchief he pulled from his pocket, the old knight only succeeded in spilling the remaining ale onto the cloak.

"I think you have done enough, Sir Ector," said Merlin. "As always, you have my gratitude for the service you performed for me so many years ago, so we shall say no more about this." Merlin gestured towards the dark stain spreading rapidly across his cloak. "But I think it is time for you and your fellows to retire. Do you not agree?" Without waiting for an answer, Merlin walked past them, muttering a few words under his breath, and passing his hand lightly over his spoiled cloak. Immediately, the stain appeared to retreat, seeping slowly backwards and in upon itself until it vanished completely.

Sir Ector looked around him sheepishly. "Great man, Merlin." He gazed with some disappointment at his empty tankard, but shrugging his shoulders said, "I think I will take his advice. Come Kai, let's to our beds, and what say you, Pellinore?"

Pellinore simply nodded in agreement, and as Merlin walked into the council chamber, the party from the Forest Sauvage began making their rather unsteady way to their lodgings.

Closing the door behind him, Merlin looked around the room. Arthur sat at the head of the table. His eyes were tired, and he was slumped slightly forward, chin resting on his balled fist. To his left sat King Lot, and King Ban of Brittany had taken the seat to his right. Both looked worried, and Ban had taken off his crown, placing it on the table in front of him, as if removing his head from its constraints might enable him to think more clearly. Only Morgause, who had arranged herself on a long, cushioned bench against the side wall, appeared to be unconcerned. Dafydd, the castle steward, was refilling her goblet.

"Ah Merlin, what has kept you so long?" she called out. "Here, try this mulled wine. It is truly delicious; yet more of our friend Ban's generosity." Looking at the French King, she blew him a kiss before raising her goblet and drinking deeply.

Merlin nodded his willingness to try the wine, and Dafydd hurried over with the flagon. When his goblet had been filled, Merlin raised it in salute, and then, taking a sip, said, "Truly excellent, King Ban; as always, we owe you great thanks. I must apologise for summoning you here at this late hour, and even more so for my tardiness, but messengers from Avalon have brought news which looks to threaten the very coronation itself."

"Please," said King Ban. "Before we begin to panic, could you explain to me the exact nature of the problem?"

The problem, it appeared, was this. Arthur's coronation was both a secular and a religious ceremony, where the new king would make his vows to lead and protect his people, and to honour and obey the commands of the Goddess. He would then be anointed, crowned and presented as High King of Britain and the Isles to his subjects and vassals. All the preparations were in place, but at the last minute, messengers had arrived from

Avalon to say the Lady of the Lake was discommoded and would be unable to attend.

"And what is the nature of this inconvenience?" asked King Ban. "It must be something very terrible to be so severe that the Lady is unable to play her accustomed and rightful place within the ceremony."

"We don't know exactly," answered Lot. "The messages from Avalon have been both brief and obscure, and the fellows despatched to bring us these missives know nothing beyond the bare fact that the Lady is unwell and has been confined to her chamber for the past seven days."

"Has there been more than one message?" asked Merlin.

"Only one actual message has been sent, but the full regalia traditionally worn by the Lady, including the sacred mantle, have also been sent to us, so that they can be worn by another," replied Lot.

"... and I am very happy to wear them," said Morgause, a cat-like smile upon her face. "The Lady is my sister, as you all know. Is there anyone more fitting to take her place?"

"I would be most happy with that as a solution," said Arthur, speaking for the first time.

"But unfortunately," said Merlin, "I am not. With the greatest respect, you, Your Majesty, have neither the knowledge nor the experience required to undertake such a responsibility."

"And whose fault is that?" questioned Morgause, throwing her goblet to the floor and rising rapidly to her feet. "You surely are not going to suggest that you represent Avalon? That would be a travesty indeed. It would be seen as a deliberate slight upon the Goddess and her holy houses." Morgause positioned herself in front of Merlin, pointing her finger directly in his face. "If anything would be likely to tip this delicate tapestry of uncertain allegiances that Lot and I have worked so hard to bind together, into rebellion—I tell you certain, it would be that!" She turned on her heel, her back to the druid as she made her way to the other end of the council chamber.

There was a moment's silence, and then Lot spoke. "Calm yourself, Morgause. I am sure that Merlin, with his great wisdom and many, many years of experience has no intention of making such a divisive suggestion." He stood, and holding out his arm, beckoned her to him. "Come, my love, you are tired, as are we all. Let us not lose our tempers." He pulled back the chair next to him and placed a velvet cushion on the seat. "Here, this will be most comfortable; sit by me now and let us hear what Merlin has to say." Morgause did as he requested, gesturing to Dafydd to pour her another goblet of mulled wine.

There was silence for a moment. Arthur looked uncertainly between Merlin and Morgause, unsure if it would be fitting for him to also say something to placate his hot-tempered half-sister, but Merlin, noticing his discomfort, shook his head slightly as he took his seat at the table. He drank deeply, draining his cup before placing it on the table in front of him and pulling two ancient scrolls from a pocket within his cloak.

"This question of Avalon is most vexing, and I have spent the last two hours searching through the documents in the archive to see if I could discover any precedent for such an occurrence."

"And have you had any joy?" asked King Lot.

"I think perhaps I have found something, but it will not please everyone," replied Merlin, casting a quick glance at Morgause.

Merlin, who had remained seated during the previous exchanges, reached out and picked up one of the ancient scrolls. Untying the ribbon, he unrolled it, his eyes darting along the lines of crabbed and faded writing. Finding his place, his finger moved across the parchment until it found the words it had been seeking.

"It relates to the coronation of King Caractacus, in ancient times, before the Romans took dominion of these lands. Here, let me read to you." Merlin cleared his throat and began to read.

Ac þa þa dæg þæs cynehalgan onwōd, wæs se wíf funden swīþe sēoc swā þæt hēo ne mihte ārīsan and forlǣtan þæt meregēat. Þā wæs ān of hire hūslīcum, nēahest tō hire on geārdæg and rīce, and geþēodod þurh þā dīore, þæt hēo onfēng þæt mǣre of þǣre Dǣde, and on hire naman, ālǣdde þæt cynehelm on þǣre heafde þæs wiðerweardes Caractacus.

When Merlin had finished, he looked up, expectantly. "Do you not agree? This is, I'm sure, the only solution."

"Merlin," said Morgause, in an extravagantly patient voice. "You must be aware that we did not understand a single word you just said. As you took pains to point out earlier, my education was somewhat lacking, but I think that neither King Ban nor my husband have any great knowledge of the ancient tongues, and as for my brother, his schooling was even less comprehensive than my own."

"Yes," said Arthur. "Sir Ector taught me hunting songs in the old language, but I had no idea what the words meant." He rubbed his forehead and tried, unsuccessfully to stifle a yawn. "Please Merlin, it is now very late. I beg you, just tell us what you have found, and how it will help us solve the problem."

"Very well. Loosely translated, here is what it says on the scroll:

But when the day of the coronation dawned, the Lady was found to be sick as to the death and could not rise and leave the Lake Isle. Accordingly, one of the maids of Avalon, closest to her in age and rank, and learned in the ways by the Goddess, did don the mantle of the Lady, and in her name, did place the crown upon the head of brave Caractacus.

Merlin once more looked around him.

"So, you see, we have a precedent from much earlier times. Another may take the place of the Lady. It has happened before. I am certain the Lady Morgan understood, which is why she ordered the ceremonial regalia be sent to us. We need only find one who is closest in age and rank, and sufficiently well-schooled in the magics to act as her proxy."

"Well, that is easy," said Morgause. "It shall be Nimue, who returned to us just one moon ago. She was schooled on the Lake Isle and holds a place of honour in my sister's household. The blood of Avalon runs in her veins."

She got to her feet and held out her hand to her husband.

"Do we all accept this as the solution?"

The others nodded and Morgause and her husband, followed by King Ban, left the room.

Arthur remained in his seat. "I am grateful for your help, Merlin. Your solution is a good one, but I am saddened that Morwenna, the priestess sent from Avalon to instruct me, could not return and play this role."

Merlin shook his head. "I know nothing of the woman. She was sent to you by the Lady, and appears to have done a good enough job, but she cannot be of high rank, or I would be aware of her." Merlin stroked his beard, ". . . and if we cannot have the Lady herself, her deputy must be, at the very least, of noble lineage."

Arthur rose to his feet, heaving a sigh. "This coronation seems to cause nothing but conflict and confusion. I shall be glad when it is over."

"I too look forward to the day when you shall rule this land as its crowned and anointed king, but I am afraid that if you hope to see an end to conflict and confusion at Alban Elfed, it is my sad duty to disabuse you."

Arthur put a hand on the old druid's shoulder. "Merlin, I hear your words and swear to always be guided by your counsel. I will always be in your debt, but I pray you, no more of this tonight. I must leave for my bed."

Arthur made his goodnights, slipping out through the side door of the Chamber so as not to be waylaid by any of the late-night revellers still remaining in the Great Hall. One by one, Merlin extinguished the lanterns and went to sit by the light of the dying fire. The child was coming, he could feel it. The Beltane Child, who carried within him death and destruction, who must be stopped—no matter what the sacrifice.

GAWAINE WAS NOT SURE IF this was the fifth or sixth visiting noble making his way to the dais and about to make a speech of homage to the new king—he just knew that he was bored. Looking up at the high table, he could see his mother, engaging in whispered conversation with Nimue, whilst his father appeared to be listening attentively to the speeches. Agravaine, sitting two seats along from him, was surreptitiously playing knucklebones with Kai, Lamorak and Aglovale. Nobody seemed to be looking at him, so Gawaine decided to take his chance. Diving beneath the table, he crawled carefully amongst the feet of the other guests until he had made his way to the end nearest the far wall. Standing up, he checked again that no one who would wish to stop him was actually watching what he was doing, and when he was certain the coast was clear, he made his way swiftly to the doorway and out into the courtyard.

It was early evening, and although it was by now past sunset, some light still remained in the sky. They had had a surprisingly warm day, and at times Gawaine had felt uncomfortably hot in the formal clothes he and Agravaine had been forced to wear for the coronation. With great relief, he pulled the heavy woollen tabard, richly embroidered with the double-headed eagle of Orkney, over his head and dropped it on the ground near the gateway to the practice yard.

Still feeling hot and sticky, he decided that what he really wanted to do was to go for a swim. Happier now, he made his way swiftly through the yard, past the equipment store and down to the river, where he took off his boots and britches and waded into the water. The river was too deep for him to stand in midstream, but the current was not strong, and the water was clear and delightfully cool. Gawaine dived deep, swimming down to the riverbed, where schools of minnow and sticklebacks, startled by his presence, darted in silver formation into the swaying banks of water weed.

On the far side of the river, two ancient willow trees dipped their branches into the water and Gawaine, not wanting to be carried downstream, lay on his back, catching hold of their branches and wrapping them round his wrists to anchor him. Looking up through the delicate pale green arch of the willows' branches he could see the red and purple tipped clouds of evening and the first of the emerging stars. Letting out a deep sigh of contentment, he moved his legs lazily, backwards and forwards, relishing the feel of the cool water on his body, and loving the peace and solitude after the busy formality of the day.

He watched the darting forms of the bats flitting low over the water in search of insects, whose presence on or just above the water also intermittently brought fish to the surface. In the stillness, he heard the gentle sound of bubbles forming and breaking as trout and perch opened and closed their mouths upon water boatmen or caddis flies. He heard night birds calling to each other across the river, and in the distance, the soft, solemn hoot of an owl. Shortly, with wings outstretched, the great bird soared across the river, coming to roost on the branches of an ancient alder.

He was just about to let go of the willow branches, planning to swim upstream and make use of the current to drift slowly back, when he heard a noise. There was a rustling on the far bank, and then a series of soft splashes, as if something—or someone—had entered the water. He stood up and moved closer to the bank under the shade of the branches. His first thought was that it had perhaps been an otter. He and his brother loved watching the sea otters at play in the salt pools and lochs of Orkney, but he had never seen those that dwelt beside the river in Caer-Lundein. He reasoned that, if he hid himself away and stayed very still, perhaps it might swim close to him.

But the silence was broken by a voice calling out across the water. "Hello Gawaine, I thought this is where you'd be when I found your tabard by the gate. I saw you escaping from the speeches and thought I'd do the same as soon as I could get away."

Gawaine saw someone swimming towards him and recognised with both pleasure and disbelief that the speaker was none other than Arthur, his newly found uncle, and as of this afternoon, the crowned and anointed King of Britain and the Isles.

"Arth . . . I mean . . . Your M . . . Majesty . . ." he stammered, suddenly unsure about the form of words he was required to use.

"Oh, let's have none of that," replied Arthur. "Your mother has schooled you well—and I must say, she has done her best with me too. Much as I hate it, there will sometimes be a need for formality, but we're family, you and me. Just call me Arthur." The new king grinned, and following Gawaine's example, turned onto his back, grabbing for a couple of willow branches to wrap round his wrists.

"But what are you doing here, Arthur? Won't you get in awful trouble for running away?"

"To be honest, after the seventh or eighth speech droning on and on about friendship and fealty, I just got so bored that I couldn't stand it anymore. I thanked whoever it was, but prevented anyone else from approaching the dais, announcing that I must attend to a call of nature."

"Well, they will play merry hell when you don't come back. Mother will be livid."

"I told old Dandy that I needed some peace and quiet, so no one will worry that I have absconded or been kidnapped. As for my sister—she has a harsh tongue on her as I know to my cost—but as of today, I am High King, and she has absolutely no authority to tell me what to do." Arthur grinned, kicking and splashing his feet with so much vigour that the wash of spray caught a low-flying bat by surprise, flipping it into the water. Immediately, Arthur let go of the willow and stood up in the shallows. Leaning forwards, he scooped the sodden little creature out of the water, placing it on the grass, where it lay still for a while, blinking its great black eyes, its small, delicate body shuddering with cold and fear.

Arthur reached out his hand and gently stroked its head with his little finger. "Look, Gawaine, it is so soft, and so beautiful." Gawaine approached, and he too reached out tentatively to stroke the tiny animal. Its fur, which was beginning to dry, was a soft, rich brown, except on its silver-grey belly. Its face, with short ears and an upturned nose, was a rosy pink. He ran his finger gently along the animal's body, and then they both stood back to watch the bat shake itself down, flicking the last of the river from its wings before flying off into the night.

"That was grand," said Gawaine. "I love animals." He gave a small sigh. "You know, it is not that I don't like being here, but I do miss home. Orkney, the lochs and the wild moors—being outside all day. The sea and the seals."

"I know what you mean," replied Arthur. "Before I came here, Kai and I would spend so much of our time in the Forest Sauvage, sometimes hunting, if the household needed venison, but mainly just being there. You know, under the trees, watching the creatures." He also gave a sigh. "I miss it too."

And both were silent for a moment, lying on their backs, wrists anchored by willow, gazing up at the midnight blue sky.

"How does it feel—to be king I mean?" asked Gawaine finally.

"I'm really not sure. To be honest, I'm terrified all the time that I'm going to do something wrong. And now I've been anointed and blessed by the Goddess, I've made all these promises, to protect my people, make the land fruitful and defend our religion." Arthur turned his head to look at Gawaine. "It's all just so big. You know, so much bigger than anything I had ever thought about. When I was growing up, I thought the best I could expect would be just to become a knight, maybe with lands and a manor of my own. But all this . . ." he repeated, "I just don't know."

"Listen, Arthur, I've always known that one day, I'll be a king when Father dies. But I'm still terrified. He does it so well, and everyone loves and respects him. Even Mother—and we all know how hard she is to please." Gawaine reached out and tentatively touched Arthur's shoulder. "I've never told anyone this, but I've always wished that Agravaine was the oldest, so he could take on the responsibility and I wouldn't have to . . ." Then he rolled over, ducking his head beneath the water. When he emerged, shaking his head and wiping his eyes, he said, "So you see, Arthur, it's not just you."

And Arthur looked at him, then reached forwards and ducked him under and for a few moments the two of them kicked and splashed, roiling the river and causing the owl, hooting indignantly at the disturbance, to take flight from the alder.

"Well, if there were any otters, this will have scared them away," panted Gawaine.

"Otters?" replied Arthur. "Oh, there are, I've seen them, a whole family. I often come out before sunrise and watch them. But they are farther upstream, near the physic garden."

"Can we take a look, do you think?" asked Gawaine. Arthur agreed, and so they set off, swimming slowly upstream. Although the current was not strong, it still took an effort to swim against it, and both were mindful of a desire to disturb the water as little as possible. They rounded the bend and saw the small, crescent beach that marked the place where the physic garden met the river.

Settling themselves in the shallows behind a leafy curtain of weeping birch and willow, they submerged their shoulders for the night air now had a chill bite to it. As they watched and waited, they talked in quiet voices, telling each other tales of their childhoods and the places where they had grown up. Each felt a growing sense of comradeship and trust in the other, a sense of friendship that neither had really felt before, and which both of them were happy to discover.

The sky was beginning to lighten when Arthur, his finger to his lips, touched Gawaine on the shoulder and pointed to the other side of the river. From a hole in the bank, a glossy head was emerging, soon to be followed by a sinuous body with a long, muscular tail which tapered like a lance.

Behind her came her children, three furry bundles with tiny pink paws and sleek nut-brown fur. For a while, they played, rolling on the sand, nipping and cuffing each other, making small whistling and chirruping noises until their mother, deciding it was time to search for breakfast, made her way to the river and swam away, her children following in the arrow of her wake.

CHAPTER TWENTY-TWO
WE SHALL HAVE A ROYAL PROGRESS

After the coronation ceremony was over, and before taking her place at the banquet, Nimue had made her way to the tiring room at the bottom of the West Tower. With some relief, she took off the silver coronet and wrapped it carefully in its lambswool cloth, before placing it back in its wooden casket. Then she removed the gossamer cloak from her shoulders and held it at arm's length, thinking of Vivian. Bending forwards, she raised the cloak to her face, breathing in the lingering and familiar smell of lavender and rosemary that her mother had favoured.

Closing her eyes, she recalled the last time she had seen her wearing that very cloak. It had been at Beltane, two or perhaps three years before her death, when Vivian still had the strength to undertake her duties as Lady of the Lake. Nimue could remember the proud way she had led the celebrations, refusing to acknowledge or betray to others any of the pain her aging body was inflicting upon her. Vivian had not always been kind, but she had been strong, and unwavering in her sense of duty and responsibility. Burying her face in the cloak, Nimue took another deep breath, wishing to bring back more memories of the remarkable woman she now knew to be her mother. But as she bent her head, she was startled by the noise of the door opening behind her.

Looking up, she saw Morgause and behind her, her handmaiden Gyda. Morgause was still wearing her coronation crown and robes, and although she looked both majestic and beautiful Nimue could tell from the look on her face that she too was eager to divest herself of them.

"Oh, let us give thanks that it is all over." Heaving a sigh, Morgause unfastened her heavy, beautifully embroidered cloak and threw it onto the settle. "Here, Gyda, come help me. This ridiculous crown has got tangled with my hair." She seated herself, and Gyda gently teased and twisted strands of her hair until the crown had been released and she was able to lift it reverently off her mistress's head, wrap it in its protective coverings and return it to the queen's jewel box. Morgause leant back in her chair and began massaging her temples. "Gyda, when you have put away my cloak, please fetch us some wine. I am parched, and I'm sure the Lady Nimue would also welcome some refreshment. We need something to sustain us before joining that collection of pompous bores in the Great Hall."

She reached out her hand, placing it on Nimue's arm. "You did well." She looked at the younger woman, seeing the strain on her face, the shadows beneath her eyes. "It cannot have been easy."

Nimue looked up at her, a tear beginning to form at the corner of her eye. She wiped it away before replying. "No, it was not. It was the first time I have been in public since . . ." She faltered, but taking a deep breath, resumed speaking, ". . . since my return to Caer-Lundein."

"It was much to ask of you . . . I realise that. But you acquitted yourself bravely. My sister would have been proud." At this point, Gyda returned, bearing a pewter jug of spiced wine and two goblets. Morgause dismissed her, and having made sure the door was closed securely, she poured out two goblets and handed one to Nimue. Morgause raised hers in tribute, before drinking deeply, delicately wiping her lips to avoid them becoming stained by the rich red wine. "We have much to thank you for, Morgan and I."

Nimue took a sip from her goblet before placing it on the table, making sure it was a safe distance from the delicate gossamer cloak. "I am bound to Avalon by unbreakable oaths and obligations. There is no need to thank me for doing my duty."

"Well, if you will not accept my thanks, at least tell me how you are feeling. Do the nightmares still continue?"

"They are becoming less frequent." Nimue gave a small smile. "Before she left, Anna prepared for me a tincture of chamomile and valerian. It has helped, and now, most nights, my sleep is dreamless."

"You know, I think, that my sister avenged you? All of Aldaron's wealth and property has been confiscated and made over to the coffers of the Lake Isle. She has told me that she intends to put it aside for you, should you one day decide that you would like to form a household of your own."

"Yes," said Nimue. "The Lady has been most kind, and I appreciate her generosity. But I would have you know that none of the blame for what happened can be ascribed to her. She warned me before I put my foot upon the enchanted pathway that my journey might be perilous, and I recognised and accepted that any risk was mine to own."

Morgause opened her mouth, but Nimue held up her hand. "Morgan saved my life and placed herself in danger to bring back the spirit of my mother. She armed me with the iron nail I used to free myself from Aldaron. I take full responsibility for any harm that befell me. I choose my own path and fully accept the consequences of my decision to take Caliburn to a safe haven."

"No, Nimue, I cannot accept that. It is not your fault that Aldaron did what he did. He was evil and perverse, an abomination in the sight of man and elf alike, and truly deserved the fate the Goddess sent him."

"I cannot disagree with that, Your Majesty. You are right to call him 'evil.' I have never experienced such terror, felt such pain . . . but I do not regret my actions, and if I had to, I would make the same choice again." Raising her goblet, she drank deeply, looking almost defiantly at Morgause.

"Well, thankfully, I think you will not have to." Morgause reached out and refilled both their goblets. "But if ever you do have cause to make another visit to the lands of Faerie, there is something you should know. We have worked a magic, myself, my sister and Anna the Mazzeri, and have laid curses upon the enchanted pathways, which will blight the lives of any who seek to bring harm to those sworn to the Goddess."

"That is good," replied Nimue. "But I have decided that I shall return to Orkney by boat when I am needed. I, for one, am in no danger of putting your magics to the test."

"You are still set upon returning when the time comes?"

"Yes, I have promised Morgan that I shall. But it will be no hardship. I love the Isles and think that I may one day wish to make my home there. But first, I have much to do in Avalon. I could not go back before the coronation—you needed me to play my part here—but I now must return to the Lake Isle and help Morgan with her preparations. She will have four months at best before the babe begins to show, and by then we must have made all the arrangements for her absence."

"And you will be her proxy once again?"

"Yes," replied Nimue. "We shall work a glamour, as Merlin did when he helped King Uther assume your father's form. All shall think that I am the Lady, and Morgan will journey north to you and Anna and remain there until she is brought to bed."

"When will you leave?" asked Morgause.

"Tomorrow, at daybreak."

"Then let us make our way to the feast." Morgause stood and held out her arm. "Come. The company may be boring, all those speeches and old men, but at least I can be certain that the food—and the wine—will be good. I shall ask Dandy to pack you a basket to take to my sister. Then at least she can partake in some way in the coronation of our brother—the illustrious father-to-be."

JUST BEFORE DAWN THE FOLLOWING morning, Merlin watched from his window in the West Tower as Nimue, accompanied by a handmaid and two soldiers from the castle garrison, rode under the archway and away. She was mounted on a great white horse, with large panniers on either side of the saddle containing gifts from Morgause to her sister. Within them, securely wrapped and swaddled to prevent any damage on the journey also lay the cloak and coronet—official regalia of the Lady of the Lake.

Merlin acknowledged somewhat grudgingly to himself that the woman brought in at the last minute because of Morgan's reported indisposition had done a good job. She had demonstrated both composure and regal bearing and had conducted the required rituals with dignity and assured knowledge. She had not disgraced Avalon. But disgrace there had been.

As soon as Nimue had entered the Great Hall, dressed in the gossamer cloak trimmed with swansdown and wearing the silver crown upon her head, he had heard whispers, and caught snippets of surprised or angry conversation as he walked beside her to the dais.

"That's not the Lady . . ."

"Does Avalon not support the new king?"

"Has this so-called son of the Pendragon lost the favour of the Lady . . . ?"

These words, and others like them, had been buzzing in his ears like persistent hornets since the previous afternoon. Thankfully, he and King Lot had managed to calm some of those most perturbed, explaining that Morgan had been too ill to attend the coronation, but that she had sent her blessings alongside her regalia. Such words, combined with lavish feasting and an apparently inexhaustible supply of wine, ale and mead, had calmed the situation last night, but Merlin felt certain that he had not heard the end of the concerns caused by the absence of the Lady of the Lake at the new king's coronation.

And now Nimue was leaving before most of the castle was awake, meaning that he could not ask her to help him assuage the fears of those troubled and doubting Lords by assuring them of Avalon's continued loyalty to the crown.

And on top of all that, mused the druid, there was Arthur.

The new king had clearly been nervous, but he had held himself well and demonstrated exactly the right blend of confidence and humility during the coronation. Whoever the girl was that Morgan had sent from Avalon to instruct him, she had done well. Arthur had made his vows in a voice that had rung out with clarity and conviction, and he had not stumbled once when making his oaths of fealty and obedience in the ancient tongue. But then, when all had been going so well, he had disgraced himself, leaving the feast on some pretext or other before the speeches had been finished, to go jackanaping with that harum-scarum Orkney boy, Gawaine.

Both the Duke of Cornwall and Aldrich, Lord of Lindsay, had been furious that they had been unable to deliver their speeches, because the king was not there to hear them, but whilst Aldrich had assumed the problem had been caused by an administrative blunder, Cador of Cornwall had perceived it as a personal affront. It had taken all of Merlin's powers of tact and diplomacy to persuade him that Arthur's behaviour was more to do with inexperience than lack of courtesy. In the end, he had promised the fiery Duke that the new king would visit Tintagel for the Yuletide festival, honouring Cornwall above all other vassals.

Musing to himself, he made his way slowly down the curved stone stairway and into the Great Hall. The visit to Cornwall was not a bad idea.

It flattered Cador's vanity, that he should be the first of the nobles to provide the new king with Yuletide hospitality, but why should it end there? Why should they not travel onwards, across the border to the Welsh Marches and the court of King Gareth—brother to Igraine, and thus uncle to the newly crowned Arthur?

As he walked into the Great Hall, Merlin's thoughts ranged widely, becoming more and more ambitious. He began to plan a Royal Progress the like of which had not been seen since the days of the Roman emperors. He would arrange pageants and spectacles, tournaments and festivals, to be held the length and breadth of the land.

Not only would this be an excellent way to introduce Arthur to his kingdom and people, but Merlin realised that it would also enable him to seek news of the Beltane Child, as every noble family in the land would be invited to the Progress and it would be an easy task to establish if they were expecting a child on, or around, May Day.

Feeling cheered, Merlin helped himself to small beer and took an apple and some cheese to a table near the fireplace. It was still early and he imagined that it would be a while before those who had indulged themselves so liberally the night before would appear, looking for cool water to clear their heads and bread to break their fast.

As he had expected there were very few people at the table. The room was quiet, most people seeming to want only to break their fast in peace, and if they did need to speak—to ask for bread to be passed or ale to be poured—they did so in soft voices, so as to not disturb the peace.

But as Merlin raised his beer to his lips, there was a great crashing and thudding in the corridor, the noise of something that sounded like pottery smashing, and a loud burst of laughter. Arthur, accompanied by Gawaine and Agravaine, burst into the hall. Behind them, and rather more sedately, came Morgause, escorted by a young knight who Merlin recognised as Sir Lamorak, and his father, King Pellinore.

"I think you've got two left feet, Gowie," said Arthur, his voice carrying through the silent room. "Old Dandy's not going to be too well pleased with you—you must have smashed at least three pitchers, and goodness knows how many beakers when you knocked over that cabinet."

"Oh, he's always been clumsy," said Agravaine, giving his brother a shove in the small of his back. "Mother says he's like a bull in a buttery."

"I wouldn't have tripped if you hadn't pushed me," said Gawaine, turning, and punching his brother hard in the stomach. Agravaine was winded, and Gawaine had just secured him in a headlock when their mother, who had been deep in conversation with Sir Lamorak, looked up.

"Boys, stop that at once. You are behaving like churls. If you do not have the manners to behave as you should in public, perhaps I shall order that you be confined to your rooms." She spoke quietly, but her voice had an edge that was sharper than a newly honed sword. "Surely, you do not wish to disturb the peace of these good people?" She gestured at the sparsely populated tables, whose inhabitants, embarrassed, made an effort to avoid her eye.

Gawaine let go of Agravaine, who instantly made to kick his brother on the shin, but was prevented by Arthur, who lifted him up by the armpits and deposited him in the nearest chair.

"Now, sister," said Arthur. "Do not be so harsh. A bit of rough and tumble is normal between brothers. And I should take some share of the blame. If I had not shied a bladder at Gowie out in the hallway, he would not have stumbled and knocked into the cabinet."

Morgause looked at him angrily but knew she could not gainsay her crowned and anointed King. She responded simply by saying, "Quite so, Your Majesty."

She turned to look at her sons, who were now sitting two seats apart from each other. "If you can manage to do so without falling over, breaking something or making a mess, go break your fast."

"Yes, Mother," they mumbled.

"And please sit somewhere else. I would have words with Lord Merlin and do not wish to be disturbed by your noise. But mind that you join me in the solar at noon. There are things I must discuss with you." So saying she sat down opposite Merlin, despatching Sir Lamorak to fetch her a goblet of water infused with rose petals and some fruit.

King Pellinore, who had provided himself with a pasty and a large jug of small beer, was already seated, and when Lamorak returned he pulled out a chair next to his father and made to sit down, but Morgause shook her head, saying, "Nay, Lamorak, this will not do."

His face fell, quite unable to hide his disappointment, and she smiled at him, placing her hand gently on his arm. "Please, indulge me. There are things I must ask of Lord Merlin—and your father—with his years of experience, may also provide good counsel. But I cannot think if I am expecting trouble. I beg you, take a seat with my boys and see if you can keep their behaviour under control."

Lamorak said that he would, as happy to please his queen as he was unhappy to leave her presence. As he began walking towards the table Gawaine and Agravaine had selected at the far side of the hall, Arthur made to join him, but Morgause caught his sleeve, "Hold fast, Sire. Could I ask that you join us?" and Arthur, slightly worried that his sister wished to raise his disappearance from the feast on the previous evening, somewhat reluctantly sat down.

AFTER THEY HAD BROKEN THEIR fast, Gawaine, Agravaine and Lamorak all made their way to the practice yard, which was markedly less busy than usual. Many of the visiting knights and even some of the castle garrison were still abed, nursing sore heads.

It was not long before Arthur joined them, and taking advantage of the unwarranted space, the four of them decided to use the morning to practise the joust. As the most experienced amongst them, Lamorak suggested they began with the half-tilt, and for several minutes, he showed the others how to hold their shield and lance correctly whilst on horseback. This wasn't easy, but both Arthur and Gawaine mastered it long before Agravaine could hold his weapon in place, protect himself with his shield and keep sufficient control of his mount to urge him along the tilt.

"Do you fancy a go at the full-tilt?" asked Gawaine.

"Yes," replied Arthur, and tying their horses' reins to the rail, they set off to fetch the quintains.

"What did Mother want with you this morning?" asked Gawaine.

"Oh, just politics stuff. Apparently, some people were not happy that my other sister, Morgan, didn't perform the ceremony yesterday. They think it means that Avalon doesn't support me."

"But Aunt Morgan is ill, Mother said so. And Nimue is Avalon trained, and really important. That's why she was sent on that secret miss . . ." As words entered his mouth, Gawaine realised that he had sworn to tell no one about the reason Nimue had been sent to Orkney, or the condition she had been in when she arrived there. Looking guiltily at Arthur, he heaved a sigh of relief. His uncle had been distracted by the sight of Agravaine, once more unseated, getting unsteadily to his feet and asking Lamorak to help him to mount his patient, long-suffering horse.

"He's not finding this easy, your brother," said Arthur. "But give him his due, he's a sport. Straight back on—and that must be his seventh fall. Now what were you saying . . . about Nimue?"

"Oh, just that I think she's quite important in Avalon."

"Well, maybe she is, but not important enough for some people . . . and . . . I also got a bit of a rap on the knuckles for deserting everyone last night."

"That's my fault," said Gawaine. "I'm sorry."

"It is not your fault," answered Arthur. "I chose to follow you, and I chose to stay out till the early hours." He leant over and ruffled the head of his nephew, who though almost as broad at the shoulder, was easily a head shorter. "And I'm glad that I did.

"Anyway, they've decided that I am having to go on what's called a Royal Progress, visiting people like the Lord of Lindsay and Duke Cador of Cornwall. I'm going to have to travel all over the country, and there are going to be banquets and celebrations, ending up with a great tourney in one of my grandfather's old castles in Caerleon, to celebrate Solstice."

They had reached the equipment store and began manhandling two of the quintains out on to the yard.

"The banquets sound a bit boring, but the tourneys should be fun. Have you ever been to one?" asked Gawaine.

"Only one." Arthur laughed. "And that turned out to have rather unexpected consequences."

"Oh yes," said Gawaine, who had been told the story of the sword in the stone by Lamorak. "Well, that can't happen again, can it? So I suppose we really should start practising. Do you think I'm old enough to enter?"

Arthur put down the quintain. "I don't think you'll be here, Gowie. That was the other thing your mother was saying to me this morning. She's planning on taking you and Agravaine back to Orkney. She told me that she was going to talk to you about it this afternoon. Your father's going to stay on here to keep an eye on things whilst I'm on this Progress, but the rest of you are going back home."

"But that's not fair. I don't want to go back and miss all the excitement."

"I thought last night you were saying how much you missed Orkney?"

"I do," said Gawaine grudgingly. "But it will all still be there when I do go back, and I'll probably never ever get another chance to go to loads of tourneys and travel if I miss out on this."

"And what about Agravaine? How do you think he'd feel?" asked Arthur.

"The same as me," said Gawaine without hesitation. "When we found out that Father was going to be Regent, he was much more excited about coming down to Caer-Lundein than I was. And he's not so keen about nature and animals. I reckon he'll be really angry if he thinks we are being sent home."

Arthur paused for a moment, as if he was not sure he should say what he was thinking. Then he made up his mind.

"Look, Gawaine, I keep on being told how precarious my position is, how I need to convince people to stand by me, that I need to prove myself and earn their loyalty. I need men I can trust, knights who will be on my side.

"You and your brother, you're my family. I haven't known you very long, but we share the same blood. If I can trust you, if you swear to be loyal, then I will do all I can to persuade Lot and my sister to let you stay."

"Do you mean that?" Gawaine's open, innocent face, flushed from the effort of heaving the quintains up the field, was wide-eyed with hope.

"Of course I do."

"Then I will swear loyalty." Gawaine, dropping the quintain, went down on one knee on the dusty, dirty floor of the practice yard.

Arthur reached out, and placed his hand on his nephew's head, saying the words that Merlin had taught him.

"Gawaine of Orkney, do you recognise me as your Sovereign Lord, second only to the Goddess?"

"I do, Sire," replied Gawaine.

"Will you swear fealty to me as your king and liege lord, to fight by my side, to defend my lands and my honour, and to take my cause as your cause, to the end of your days?"

"I will, Sire," replied Gawaine.

"Then I, Arthur Pendragon, son of Uther Pendragon, High King of Britain and the Isles, do recognise and accept you as my trusted friend and vassal. Your cause shall be my cause, and the defence of your lands and honours shall become my sworn duty."

Arthur raised Gawaine to his feet and kissed him on both cheeks as was customary.

They did not speak again as they carried the quintains back to the tilt. Both were conscious that, although the words had been spoken on the practice field, where they fought with wooden swords and tilted at men of straw, the vows they had just made were serious and binding. What they did not realise was that they would forever shape the courses of their lives.

CHAPTER TWENTY-THREE
A CHILD IS BORN IN ORKNEY

When winter came, it was one of the hardest in living memory. The rivers froze, and farmers brought their animals indoors at night, not just to shield them from the bitter winds and driving snow, but so their warm breath and bodies could add much needed heat to hearth and home. Fortunately, before the cold had bitten, the sun that had shone at Alban Elfed had continued strong through the early autumn and there had been a good harvest, so when the bite of winter meant that game became scarce in forest and field, the full granaries and barns ensured few had gone truly hungry.

Merlin told Arthur that this was good. If the year of his coronation had ended with famine, it would not have augured well for him. Despite this, things were still very unsettled. Arthur had not seen the towers of Caer-Lundein for several months now, travelling as they were from petty kingship to ancient Manor, staying three nights here and five there, meeting the nobles and walking their land.

Not wishing to place a burden upon the knights and nobles whose houses he was visiting, Arthur travelled with only a small company of soldiers, handpicked from the garrison at Caer-Lundein, and four companions: Merlin, Sir Lamorak, Kai and Gawaine.

It had proved surprisingly easy to persuade Lot and Morgause to allow their two eldest sons to remain in Caer-Lundein. Lot, in particular, had been well pleased by Cerdic's reports on their progress in the arts and crafts of war and had already been in two minds about sending them back to Orkney even before Arthur made his request.

Morgause had told Lot that he was to be a father again in the early summer, and as she had predicted, he had been delighted. This had provided further weight to the argument for the elder boys remaining with Arthur, rather than being in Orkney and adding to their mother's worries. However, neither would agree to Agravaine accompanying Gawaine on the Royal Progress. The constant squabbling between the two boys would not have been helpful, and their parents, who were not fools, had sharp enough eyes to know that it was never Gawaine who started any of the disputes. In fact, Lot wished to foster the growing friendship between Gawaine and Arthur, and he also hoped that the enforced separation would allow him to spend time with Agravaine, who he felt was becoming increasingly jealous of the popularity of his easy-going and forthright older brother.

Departing from Caer-Lundein less than four weeks after the coronation, they had stayed first with the lords of South Ceint, and had then travelled across the water, spending time with the strongholders of Ynys Weith. Moving westwards, they visited Sarum and then spent three days in the small hillfort of Camelat. They were made welcome here, and Arthur was particularly impressed with the strategic advantages of the site. From the top of the hill the surrounding countryside rolled out for miles, making it almost impossible for an invader to approach unseen, and the fort was well supplied with wood and water. He marked it as a place he intended to visit again.

Yule had been spent with Duke Cador in Cornwall. They had ridden across the causeway to the castle of Tintagel, and on the first morning of their stay, Merlin had shown Arthur the rooms his mother and her husband, the War Duke Gorlois, had inhabited, the place where he had been born. Arthur had entered the room slowly, looking about him at the faded tapestries on the wall, the embroidered coverlet on the bed.

"Were these things hers?"

"Yes," replied Merlin. "This one, the forest scene, I remember her making it when I visited Tintagel, when Morgause was but four years old and Morgan still a baby."

He had asked the druid to leave him alone in his mother's chamber, and had walked hesitantly around the room, gently touching the tapestries her fingers had made. He sat by the window, looking out to sea, as he imagined Igraine must have done and tried to find a sense of her—to catch the fleeting memory of her presence, to call her to him. But nothing came.

That night, they lit the Yule log, and the ale and mead ran like water. When supper was over, it was Gawaine who found the bean in the pudding, making him king for the night. He had ordered Merlin to sing in the voice of a cat and the old druid had complied with surprising good humour. They had gone to bed laughing, but the mood became sombre the next day when news was brought of Saxon incursions to the southwest. By midday, they were saddled and mounted, with reinforcements from Cador's garrison, riding to meet with the troops Lot had despatched from Caer-Lundein.

Arthur did not like fighting, but he found that he was good at it. With Gawaine at his right hand, wielding an axe and a hammer, and Kai and Sir Lamorak to his left, he had been invincible. The sword that he had pulled from the stone proved itself to be a worthy weapon; elegant to handle and hungry for blood. In a surprisingly short time, they put the small group of invaders to rout, and after wiping his sword clean upon the rough grass, Arthur ordered Kai and Gawaine to kneel in front of him and there, bloody and battle-stained, he knighted them. Gawaine was not yet sixteen.

From Gewisse they moved on to strongholds of North Ceint, and then farther east, celebrating Imbolc in the large, draughty halls of Aldrich, Lord of Lindsay. There had been a hunt that day, but though the riding had been good, game had been scarce. As no one had been able to bring down a stag, Aldrich had ordered the slaughter of a cow from his dairy herd; he would not suffer the shame of entertaining his king at Imbolc without an animal turning on the spit.

Arthur, who was hungry from a long day's hunting, had been pleased with his meal, and said as much to his hostess, the Lady Elaine, Aldrich's pretty, sharp-faced and heavily pregnant wife.

"I am indeed glad it is to your liking, Sire," she had answered him pointedly. "It is good the meat pleases you, if it had not, my lord would have sacrificed one of our last milk cows for no reason, and I would have been even more displeased by his decision." Arthur had been taken aback to be spoken to in this way and realised that he found it refreshing. He missed Morgause, with her mordant humour and sharp tongue, and recognised that she had a kindred spirit in the Lady of Lindsay.

"Why so, my Lady?" he had asked. "Surely there are more cows to be had?"

"Perhaps in Caer-Lundein, but here in Lindsay, there has been blight and disease, and raids from the wild men who come in boats from the north to steal our herds and our women. We now have but two cattle left to us, and I shall want milk to help me feed my own child by the time Beltane is upon us."

Arthur listened carefully, determined to talk of this to Merlin. Why could they not provide an extra garrison for the people of Lindsay, to help defend their farms from the invaders, and at the very least, send breeding stock from Caer-Lundein to help replenish their herds?

He had heard many stories like this over the past months. As he spent time travelling, becoming acquainted with the land he had vowed to protect and the people who now looked to him for leadership, he was beginning to understand the magnitude of the task that faced him.

His land was not united. The places he visited, the manors, the petty kingdoms and forest strongholds were all small, individual communities fighting for survival, frustrated and embittered by the years of war. He was learning to listen, and to think about the problems strategically. Merlin had told him a tale the Romans had told, of the ancient hero Heracles, who had been confronted with a strange monster that grew two new heads from each severed stump. The Saxons were like that monster, he thought. Each time we manage to defeat one tribe or warrior, they come back stronger. We need to find another way, as Heracles had, when he used fire to burn the stumps, so no new life could grow. We need to unite, to work together, to find a common cause.

He had smiled at his hostess and raised his goblet to her in salute. "My lady, the generosity of you and your husband will not go unnoticed. You have feasted us royally, and I shall not forget the sacrifice you have made." He gestured towards her belly. "Your child is a symbol of hope, a new generation for our Islands. I hope that you will be able to join us at Solstice, in the Welsh city of Caerleon, where I plan to welcome and bless all children born in the first year of my reign."

And at this she had smiled at him, and her sharp, cat-like face had mellowed. In place of anger, her eyes now shone with hope.

IT WAS IN THE DAYS following Imbolc that Morgan made the journey from the Lake Isle to Orkney. She had planned to leave shortly after Yuletide, but the cruel bite of winter had made her loath to leave the relative warmth of Avalon and exchange it for the bleak and bitter landscape of the Northern Isles. She had been aided in this decision by the fact that she was carrying her child high, and her shift and kirtle concealed her growing waistline for longer than either she or Nimue had anticipated.

In the past weeks, she had spent many hours alone with Nimue. The younger woman had now fully recovered her strength, and although she had been pleased to hear of the steps that Morgan had taken to ensure the enchanted pathways were now safer places for those who walked them in the name of the Goddess, she had no desire to talk about what she had endured, or to hear more about the terrible price Morgan had exacted upon the kith and kin of the Elf who had despoiled her.

Morgan respected Nimue's need to heal herself in her own way, understanding that to dwell on vengeance or to continually pick over painful memories would not restore her confidence and composure, so instead they talked of the future. They would spend hours together, exploring the complexities and subtleties of the deeper mysteries, and Morgan would tutor her in the complex geography of political loyalties and enmities Nimue would need to understand when she was called upon by Lot to join the council at Caer-Lundein. Nimue's mind was quick, and her understanding of the political complexities astute and insightful. Morgan now felt confident that she would be able to assume the role of Lady of the Lake with none being any the wiser of the imposture.

They had practised the glamour several times in the privacy of Morgan's chamber, and it had been strange to see Nimue's face and form shimmer, dissolve and reassemble, to then reappear and solidify as an exact copy of her own.

The glamour was controlled by an amulet containing a lock of Morgan's hair. It hung on a delicate silver chain, and once the spell had been performed Nimue would only reassume the appearance of her own face and body when the amulet was removed.

Not wishing to run the risk of anyone seeing Nimue in her new form before Morgan had departed, they decided that it would be safer to perform the spell at the gateway to the enchanted pathways. On the day following Imbolc, they waited until the rest of the household had gone to their beds and then made their way down to the lakeside under the cold, blue light of the winter stars. It was frosty, and the grass crackled beneath their feet. Morgan, who was taking with her nothing but her lantern and a knapsack containing herbs and medications, walked with a carved wooden staff, worried that her unaccustomed bulk could put her off balance. In her pocket she carried an iron horseshoe, although she doubted she would have need of it. There had been no trouble on the pathways in recent months.

The sand was silver in the moonlight and the water at the edge of the lake formed wavelets of frozen crystal, but it was not the cold that caused Nimue to shiver as they approached the mouth of the cave.

"There is no need for you to enter," said Morgan. "I shall go within, whilst you remain on the strand, and if any should observe us, they shall see but one person. I am known to keep strange hours. No one will think anything amiss."

Nimue nodded, and taking the amulet from her pocket, placed it around her neck as Morgan stepped back into the darkness of the cave. She reached out her hand, and together, the two women worked the enchantment.

Morgan looked at the face of the woman in front of her, illuminated in sharp relief by the brilliance of the stars. Huge eyes, of a most disconcerting blue, stared back at her. Her cheekbones were fine, and her mouth, a delicate bow of pale pink, the upper lip finely wrought, the lower soft and full. The mirror in her room, burnished copper and finely made, had not shown her such detail, and she stared in wonder as she leant forwards and cupped the other woman's face in her hands. They were exactly the same height.

She kissed her lightly on the lips and then reached out to touch the tip of the delicate, slightly upturned nose that was a mirror image of her own.

"I am forever in your debt, Nimue."

"My debt to you is just as great. We work together, Morgan, to serve the Goddess."

"Indeed, but sometimes the things she asks of us are not easy, and to serve her without complaint or question is a rare quality."

"I have had a good teacher," replied Nimue. "Now, go. You have many miles to walk upon the ancient paths, and they are expecting you before sunrise."

Morgan nodded, and reaching up, kissed Nimue once more on the forehead and gave her the blessing of the Goddess. Without saying another word, she turned and walked into the cave. Nimue listened until she could no longer hear her footsteps or the slight click of her staff on the cave floor and then made her way back to her bed.

MORGAUSE HAD DRESSED HERSELF WITH care, pulling on fleece-lined boots and winding her woollen cloak tightly about her, grateful that for once, she did not have to tie round her waist the wad of padding she had been wearing for the past month or so to simulate the appearance of pregnancy. Closing the wicket gate carefully she made her way swiftly across the courtyard and out, towards the standing stones. The night air was cold, but there was no wind, and the green and purple sky was made radiant by the otherworldly whirling of the mirrie dancers.

The ancient stones of the Ring of Brodgar were silhouetted against the ethereal green of the horizon. The sky shimmered, luminous and uncanny, and high above, in the deep heavens, glowed the aurora, now purple, then pink and finally, red. All around her the lights of the mirrie dancers sparkled and twirled, so bright and so fast that all she could see was a shimmering glitter, accompanied by the sound of rustling gossamer as they danced their magical measure across the sky. Morgause smiled and raised her hand in greeting. She loved to watch the dancers of the aurora and was pleased to have their company as she walked. As she approached the causeway, she was joined by Anna, also hooded and cloaked and carrying a bundle strapped to her back.

"I have brought a blanket for Morgan, and some bannocks. She will have eaten nothing in the lands of Faerie and may well be hungry."

Morgause said nothing, slightly annoyed that she had not thought of her sister's comfort. She had spent the earlier hours of the evening very pleasurably, entertaining visitors from the Norwegian court, relatives of Lot's dead ward and cousin Einar. They had feasted well, and had circumstances been different, she would have seriously considered offering Jarl Gunnar, the leader of the delegation, the chance to sample the pleasures of her bed. But in the end, discretion had conquered desire, and when the feast had ended, she had made her belly the excuse to retire to her chamber, leaving Gunnar to his own devices.

"No," she thought, as she pondered the annoyance she had felt at Anna's considerate gestures. "I am a queen. I have a castle to run and lands to govern. I do not have time for domestic detail. Let Anna, in her little lochside cottage deal with bannocks and the like." And with this she nodded to the other woman. "That is well thought of. I am sure Morgan will appreciate your kindness. I have been entertaining our royal visitors and have not had time to think of such things."

Anna smiled in the darkness. She had seen the handsome Jarl disembark at Stromness. "Just so, Your Majesty," she replied.

The women had crossed the causeway and now made their way to the centre of the Ring. They stopped and bowed low, in a gesture of respect to the ancient powers. The mirrie dancers flickered and sparked around their heads and then began to draw together in a shimmering cluster above the largest of the standing stones. Slowly, Morgause and Anna walked towards it. As they watched, the surface of the ancient stone began to lose its substance, its surface appearing to dissolve into a formless haze.

Behind the vapour, a tiny glow appeared, glimmering gently, but gaining strength as it moved closer. In its pale light they could see a doorway forming, and beyond it, the mouth of the tunnel. Walking towards them, lantern in one hand, staff in another, was Morgan.

She was walking slowly, and as she emerged into the weird light of the aurora, her face looked tired and strained. But she smiled when she saw the women there to meet her and opened her arms in greeting.

"Is aught wrong? Did anything befall you on the path," asked Morgause as she gently embraced her sister, feeling her belly, taut and swollen, press against her.

"No, I saw no one, but the path seemed longer than usual, the hills harder to climb, and the rocks more difficult underfoot." She smiled and touched her belly. "And he was kicking like a young colt. You did not tell me, Morgause, how inconsiderate an unborn child can be."

"Come," said Anna. "Sit for a while and rest before we walk back to the castle. There is time; it is still several hours before daybreak." In saying so, she led Morgan to one of the fallen stones, and wrapping the warm blanket around her, helped her to sit down. She placed a small package in her hand, and Morgan looked at it questioningly, before holding it to her nose, breathing in the smell of the oat bread.

"As always, you are kind, Anna. I am not hungry. These days, I eat little. He seems to fill my belly and there is but small space for food—but these are still warm, and my hands feel frozen."

She rested for a while and then the three women walked together back across the causeway and along the lochshore to the castle. As they walked, the mirrie dancers surrounded them, lighting their path. At the wicket gate, Morgan turned to look back at the stones. She raised her arms in a gesture of benediction and spoke, her voice rising clear and true on the still, cold air.

"Ancient Ones, I thank you for your welcome and ask, in the name of the Goddess, for your protection and blessing for myself and the child I bear. He will be a son of this Island, raised in the magics. Take him to your heart."

And the lights in the sky seemed to glimmer more brightly, the red and the pink all turning to deepest purple. Around them, the rustle of the mirrie dancers grew stronger and became a whispering.

"We hear you . . . we will . . . we hear you . . . we will."

MORGAN HAD NOW BEEN AT the castle in Stromness for three weeks. The only member of the household who knew of her presence was Avice, the castle housekeeper who had known both sisters since early childhood and had travelled to Orkney with Morgause on the *Llyr's Daughter*. Before leaving Tintagel, she had been entrusted by Igraine with the care and protection of her eldest daughter, and the vows Avice had made that day had never been broken.

Morgause had shared with her the plan she and Morgan had conceived. The Goddess had revealed to them that the babe would be born at Beltane, but that they must keep the birth a secret for a half-moon. The child would then be raised believing Morgause to be his mother, and Lot his father.

Morgause had not provided any other explanation and had refused to tell Avice who had fathered Morgan's child. At first, Avice had been uncomfortable about foisting the child of another upon King Lot, but in the end, she came to the conclusion that, although Morgause had not said so in so many words, the purpose of the deception was to shield Morgan. The Lady of the Lake could not be known to have a child.

Avice's deepest loyalty had always been to her first mistress, Igraine, who she had served from early childhood. As she pondered the problem each night, her husband Clem sleeping beside her, she finally decided that she would be betraying that loyalty if she refused now to give with a good heart that which was asked of her. And so, she told no one of the secret visitor and forbade any of the housemaids to even enter the corridor leading to Morgan's room.

Between them, the three women—Morgause, Anna and Avice—took care of Morgan during the last weeks of her pregnancy. At first, Morgause had forbidden her sister to leave her room, terrified that someone would see her and compromise all their plans, but then Anna, seeing how much Morgan hated being confined within the four walls of her chamber, had made a suggestion.

"You know my husband, Cormac? His aunt Mairead has but recently come to stay with us, whilst Cormac and Conn repair the thatch on her cottage. She is about your size Morgan, and not very steady on her feet. If I bring you one of her gowns, and we keep your head covered, I think no one would think it strange if the two of us were to be seen walking on the lochshore."

This was agreed, and early each morning Anna would bring the elderly woman to the castle. Avice had contrived a small sitting room for her, and she would sit contentedly by the fire, whilst Morgan, dressed in rough home-spun, with her hood up and cloak wrapped tight around her, would walk with Anna by the shores of Stenness or Harray. Sometimes, if both Cormac and Donal were out, Anna would bring Morgan into the stone cottage on the lochshore, and the two women would talk freely with each other.

"Will it hurt?" Morgan asked Anna. It was now but two days until Beltane. The weather was warm, and they were sitting side by side on an old wooden bench, polished smooth by time, and set hard up against the stone wall of the cottage. There was a slight breeze, which Morgan, who now felt uncomfortably hot most of the time, found very pleasant. It ruffled the delicate petals of the marsh-marigolds, primroses and celandine that in the last week or so had sprung up joyfully upon the banks of the loch. At the edge of the water, blue and yellow flag-iris had just begun to bloom and a little farther away, a pair of curlews were wading together in the shallows, taking small, measured steps, then digging down sharply with their long beaks, searching for shrimp and small insects.

"Yes," said Anna, "it will. There's no point pretending otherwise. The Goddess created women for both joy and suffering, and it has always seemed to me that you can't have one without the other."

Morgan had always respected the Corsican healer, but in the past few weeks, she had become increasingly aware of her wisdom and kindness.

"I am so glad I am here, and that you are with me." Morgan leant backwards, stretching her legs and pushing her aching back against the hard stone wall of the cottage. "Oh, that feels good. It is so hard to get comfortable, and I can hardly sleep at night—no matter how I position myself, it's never right, and if I do manage to drop to sleep, it won't be long before he's kicking so hard that I wake up."

"He's keen to be born, that one," said Anna, reaching out and laying her hand on the firm surface of Morgan's distended belly. "But I think you'll find he will quiet down now. Babies do, when they are getting ready to be born."

Picking up a stoneware jug and beaker from the bench beside her, she filled the beaker and handed it to Morgan.

"Here, drink this. It will help. I've been making it with the raspberry leaves you brought with you from Avalon."

Morgan took a sip. "This tastes different, more potent. Are you sure it is not too strong?"

Anna smiled. "Yes, it is more potent, but it will do you no harm. It's dangerous to drink too strong a mix in the early days, but now, we actually want to set things in motion. I've increased the concentration. We will bring some back with us to the castle, drink it tonight before you go to sleep, and in the morning when you wake."

Morgan drank deeply and then, rather unsteadily, got to her feet. Anna helped her to put on Mairead's heavy cloak, and two women made their way slowly back to the castle.

As Anna had predicted, the baby now lay still within her belly, and Morgan slept deeply that night, not waking until long past cockcrow. She felt unsettled, not hungry, but feeling she should eat; not wanting to rest but feeling the need to stay within the protective walls of the castle. Seeking distraction, she wished she had brought with her the old box of her mother's tapestry silks that she played with for hours on end as a child, but Morgause was no craftswoman, and there was nothing like it to be had in Stromness.

Unable to settle, she paced back and forth, looking out of the window at Gareth and Gaheris practising at the archery butts to the rear of the courtyard. Putting her hands to her belly, she imagined her son—the dark-haired delicate-boned boy that her mother had dreamed of—standing in that very courtyard, his cousins beside him. Perhaps Gareth would help him string his bow, and Gaheris teach him to fletch his arrows.

It was all very real now. She was going to have a baby. After all the years when she had dismissed out of hand the possibility, and all the recent months of subterfuge and waiting. Finally, she was going to have a baby, and he would be born here, in Orkney, this beautiful place of mystery and ancient power, with his family around him.

Exhausted by her pacing, and finally feeling a sense of peace, Morgan settled herself on her bed, gazing out through the casement where the sun was just beginning to turn the waters of the loch a delicate gold. Resting against the pillows, she closed her eyes and drifted into sleep, only to be woken less than an hour later by a dull ache at the base of her spine and a sharp insistent cramping in her belly.

Her pains had begun.

CLEM TREVENNA STEPPED DOWN FROM the gangplank of the *Llyr's Daughter* on to the dockside at Caer-Lundein. The port was busy. Seagulls wheeled and screamed in the sky, scanning the docks for unprotected fish barrels, but their sharp, repetitive cries were almost inaudible, overpowered by the clamour of voices. All around him was noise. Sailors, traders, agents and hawkers greeted each other, some to do business, arguing over inventories or prices, whilst others exchanged news and shared gossip.

He looked along the wharf, taking in the bright-sailed galleys from France, Germany and Denmark moored alongside the smaller barges and balingers owned by farmers and brewers from the east and west coast of England. With a practised eye he gave each boat a critical assessment and could see that some were beauties indeed—but none diminished the unwavering sense of pride he felt when he looked at the trim lines and tidy sails of the vessel he had captained for nearly thirty years. As far as Clem was concerned, he had never seen a ship that could hold a candle to the *Llyr's Daughter*.

Built to Roman design, *Llyr's Daughter* was a sleek, three-masted merchant ship, with glorious, billowing sails and an elegant, streamlined prow. She had been commissioned by Gorlois, Duke of Cornwall, and his wife, Igraine, and in her glory days, Clem had sailed her, laden with Cornish tin, over the wine-dark sea to the ports in the far south, returning with cargoes of fine glassware, wines and pottery. In the last few years, she had not sailed so far afield, making instead regular journeys between Orkney and Caer-Lundein, and the occasional trip to Denmark and Norway.

Clem had been saying for some time now that he was too old to be her Captain, and his wife, Avice, had agreed with him, saying that if he wanted to sail, he could always take a boat out on the loch. Clem had snorted at such an idea—as if sailing on the settled surface of a body of water surrounded on all sides by land could ever compare to the exhilaration of commanding a vessel upon the vast, wild waves of the open deeps. But he had decided that his aching joints and deteriorating eyesight could no longer be argued with, and the time had come to say farewell to seafaring. He doubted he would ever visit the port of Caer-Lundein again, and when he sailed her back to Stromness, it would be to hand the *Llyr's Daughter* over to her new master, his son Ronan.

It was a short, familiar walk from the dock to the riverside entrance of the castle of Caer-Lundein, and when he got there, the sentry on watch waved him through without asking to see his papers or establish the reason he sought entry. He was well known here. In the past two years there had been rarely a month when he had not been summoned to the castle to bring news of Orkney, or to bear messages to the courts of Denmark and Norway. He nodded his thanks and walked on.

Clem chose to take the path that led along the riverbank behind the physic garden, to the spot where the practice yard ran down to the water's edge. It always felt strange to be back on firm ground after many days at sea and he took care how he placed his feet on the new spring grass, trying to avoid the anemones and bluebells that were just beginning to bring forth their blooms. The pungent, evocative smell of wild garlic filled his nostrils. The small, star-shaped white flowers grew in such profusion that in a week or so's time, it would be almost impossible to walk this path without crushing them.

He could not yet see the practice yard, but he could hear it. As he rounded the corner, the soft babble of the river was drowned by the dull thud of wooden swords clashing rhythmically and repetitively against shields and breastplates. Alongside this was the sharp, measured diagonal bounce of the horses clip-clopping backwards and forwards as their riders worked to perfect the half-tilt, and above all this, the air was filled with the deep, primal grunts and shouts of the warriors practising the melee.

A man stood at the edge of the yard watching the soldiers at their tasks, his eyes, trained on one person in particular—a slender, red-headed youth, astride a sleek piebald cob. With lance in one hand and shield in the other, he used the pressure of his knees to control the horse, guiding him perfectly through a series of obstacles. Clem approached, not wishing to disturb the man, but glad that he had found him so easily—and alone.

As the horse deftly passed through the last of the obstacles and the boy dismounted with a shout of triumph, the man turned, suddenly aware of Clem's presence. The sea captain bowed, and made to bend to one knee, but the man shook his hand to dissuade him.

"Well met, Clem. I give thanks to the Goddess that you have arrived before Agravaine and I set out for Caerleon. Have you news?" He spoke quickly, eager to hear what the other had to say.

"I have, Your Majesty." Clem smiled. "You have a son, a fine boy, born two weeks after Beltane."

King Lot looked at the old sailor, who he had known for over twenty years, with an expression of delight on his face. He reached out, and the two men embraced, sharing with each other their joy.

"How is the Queen?"

"She is well."

"And what is he called, this new son of mine? I told her she could name him."

"Sire, he is called Mordred."

CHAPTER TWENTY-FOUR

CAERLEON

Like Stromness in Orkney, the flourishing riverside port of Caerleon was an ancient settlement. Long before the Romans set up their garrison there, building bathhouses, fortifying the port and constructing the huge, circular amphitheatre that dominated the landscape, Caerleon had been a wealthy community, a centre of production and trade. But unlike Stromness, Caerleon's past was not steeped in the dark mists of the ancient magics, and for Arthur, this was nothing but an advantage. He had come to recognise that the Mysteries confused and bewildered him, but a town whose long history was built on conquest and commerce was something he could understand and appreciate.

They had hired a ship in the little town of Brygstow to ferry them across the wide and sometimes challenging waters of the River Severn, arriving in Caerleon around noon, hungry and travel weary. Lord Llewellyn, who ruled the Marches of Caerleon as a vassal of Arthur's uncle, King Gareth, had sent a cart to carry their baggage, and provided horses for Merlin and Arthur. Arthur was loath to accept, offering his horse instead to Gawaine, who had sustained a nasty blow to his thigh in their most recent skirmish with the Saxons. But Merlin would not allow this, insisting that it would not be fitting for the High King to be seen trudging up the hill from the port, and reluctantly, Arthur had agreed.

A compromise was reached by finding a place for Gawaine in the cart, alongside the armour, knapsacks and trunks. Gawaine winced as he clambered on board. He had killed his man, but the blow he had taken as his foe had fallen had cut deep, catching him below his chain-mail and almost bringing him to his knees. Because he had little chance to rest and heal, the wound had been unable to close, and his leg was raw and tender. They were planning on spending at least three weeks in Caerleon—celebrating Solstice and then preparing for the long journey home, and he hoped that this would give enough time for his injury to mend.

They made their way up the paved streets, past the old Roman barracks and bathhouses, now beginning to fall into disrepair. Arthur looked around him disapprovingly.

"If those buildings are not going to be made use of, they should be demolished. This is prime land, close to the river. What think you, Merlin? Why does Lord Llewellyn not show more care? I would never allow Caer-Lundein to slide into such decay."

"We are lucky in Caer-Lundein, Sire. Many of the craftsmen, the stonemasons and artificers, remained living within the city walls when the Romans abandoned us so swiftly. That is not so in Caerleon. There are none here to mend the roads or make good the damage wrought by bad winters and the passage of time."

"Well, as I see it Merlin, the Romans are not coming back, and we need to take responsibility for the land we hold. Letting it sink into disrepair will help no one. I shall raise this with Lord Llewellyn when we dine tonight."

"Yes, Sire," replied Merlin, coughing quietly and raising his hand to his lips to conceal an involuntary smile. It was little more than a year since Arthur had pulled the sword from the stone, and the changes those months had wrought had been momentous. The raw country lad who had stood before them on the tourney ground, shabbily dressed, callow cheeked, wide-eyed and stammering, was gone. In his place was a warrior, a man who held himself with confidence, dressed in finely wrought mail, a conqueror's sword at his belt and a firmness of expression that showed him to be no stranger to command.

The last few months had been arduous and fraught with danger. The travellers were all weary and looking forward to returning to Caer-Lundein after the Solstice festivities. But Merlin was certain that they had been worth it. He felt he had been vindicated in keeping the new king away from his capital for the best part of a year—the Royal Progress had enabled Arthur to build an intensely personal and practical knowledge of the country he had been called upon to rule.

Seeing for himself the contrast between the lush, agricultural fields and orchards of Ceint or Gewisse with the marshy wetlands of Lindsay, the fishing ports and tin mines of Cornwall and Lyonesse and the rough pastures of Mercia had been as important for Arthur as meeting the people whose livelihoods depended on the land.

The new king had not been raised in luxury. From his earliest boyhood, he had known of the potential consequences of a bad harvest or a harsh winter. He had watched his foster father, noble knight though he was, work alongside his people, ploughing the fields and shepherding the lambs, and to Merlin's delight and relief, he had not suppressed or dismissed these memories as he had grown in confidence.

Instead, they had become a deep well of experience and understanding that he could draw upon, as he had done when talking with the Lady of Lindsay, finding practical ways to give comfort—and inspiring a loyalty which Merlin believed would eventually become even greater than that which had been accorded to Uther Pendragon himself.

But Merlin knew that all of this could still come to naught. For Arthur to fulfill the prophecy, to truly inherit his birthright, he would need time. The land had been broken. It required healing, and the people who for so long had been beset by invasion and war, needed to come together, united in common cause under the single banner of their king.

The Beltane Child was out there now. Merlin felt its presence. Magic had been worked, and that enchantment sought to destroy everything he had laboured for, everything he had been preparing for since he had discovered that Igraine's child was the one destined to wield Caliburn and to bring unity and prosperity to this fractured, damaged land.

The Beltane Child. Merlin knew not if it was a boy or a girl, but he had no doubt that within its tiny frame nestled the seeds of destruction. He had, as yet, told Arthur nothing of the prophecy, but if the plan Merlin had devised was to be successful, the new King could no longer remain in a state of ignorance. As they approached the gates of the castle, where Lord Llewellyn stood, arms outstretched in welcome, Merlin determined that he would broach the subject with Arthur before sunset on the following day.

THEY SPENT THE NEXT DAY resting. Myfanwy, the castle apothecary, a healer and adept of the Mysteries of Avalon, had taken one look at

Gawaine and confined him to his bed, saying that if he did not rest, there was a chance of permanent damage to his leg. Arthur and Kai had explored the fort of Caerleon without him, surprised how much they missed his bluff good humour, and when he did not join them for supper in the great hall, Arthur had determined to visit him.

The Infirmary, where Gawaine had been quartered, was a long, low, wooden building with a thatched roof, built along the far southern side of the castle grounds. Arthur crossed the courtyard and was about to go through the gate into the gardens, when he heard a voice call his name. "Arthur, I am glad I found you." Turning, Arthur was surprised to see Merlin, standing at the foot of the West Tower. "I am pleased to say that King Ban has once again supplied us with several barrels of wine for Solstice. I have just learned that they arrived here this morning and am anxious to see if they have travelled well. Will you join me?"

Arthur hesitated, explaining that he wished to check on Gawaine's well-being, but Merlin became insistent, saying that if the wine had turned to vinegar, as sometimes happened if it had not been stored appropriately, they would have very little time to find an alternative for the Solstice celebrations. Grudgingly, Arthur agreed, and they climbed the stairs together to Merlin's chamber, a small but airy and well-appointed room overlooking the site of the still magnificent Roman amphitheatre.

"What would have happened, do you think, if the Romans had not left us?" asked Arthur, accepting with a nod of thanks the pewter tankard Merlin handed to him.

"Well, the Romans left our shores because Rome itself had been invaded." Merlin leant back in his chair, taking a small sip of his wine and swallowing it slowly. He smiled. "Yes. This is good. I should have known better than to doubt Ban's vintner . . . Now where were we? Of course . . . Rome—so let us suppose that Rome had not been attacked, and there had been no need to recall the Garrisons to her aid.

"I imagine, if that had not happened, then Vortigern would not have felt confident in inviting the Angles and the Saxons to invade our lands, and things would have continued pretty much as they had for the last four hundred years."

"So, we would have had peace?" Arthur asked.

"I think it likely that there would have been no incursions, no bloody war with the Saxons. So yes, we would have had peace." Merlin leant forwards, gesturing towards the young king with his tankard. "But we would not have had sovereignty. We would have continued paying tributes to Rome, taxes on lands and harvest, even taxes on the number of children growing to adulthood in a family.

"Do not forget, Arthur, it was the Romans who benefited the most from the rich resources of this land, who exploited our tin and silver mines, enslaving our people, and then taking the fruits of their labour and trading them across the Empire. Their strength may have given us relative stability, but I ask you, at what cost?"

Arthur considered. "Peace and stability . . . the ability to live your life without fear of invasion and conquest, to sleep quiet in your bed—that may well exact a high price . . . and for many, they would see it as a price worth paying."

"Is this a conclusion you have drawn from your experiences during our travels?"

"Yes," replied Arthur. "I think people are tired of war. They want to farm their lands, and raise their children, as they did when the Romans were here. But each little kingdom, each manor, each stronghold, only sees their own problems, and so they are vulnerable."

"So what are the alternatives?" asked Merlin. "Look to another protector, another powerful invader from far-away shores, who may provide stability, but at the price of our birthright . . . Or . . . ?"

"Or . . . something very different." Arthur was speaking slowly, his thoughts developing and clarifying as he voiced them. "We become . . . our own protector. We band together, unite and work as one nation to serve a common cause. Set our enemies to flight, send them back across the sea . . ." He looked at Merlin, and drank deeply, before crashing his tankard down upon the table. "We become the Land's protector." And then he stood, one hand on the pommel of his sword.

"I become the Land's protector. That is the alternative."

And Merlin, the ancient druid, raised himself from his seat and went down on one knee before his king. "Aye, Sire, that is the alternative. That is what I have hoped for, what I have worked for all my life—and I swear to you, I will do everything in my power to make it come to pass."

Arthur raised the druid to his feet and embraced him, aware that, for the first time, Merlin, his tutor and often hardest critic, had truly acknowledged him as his king. They both took a seat at the ornately carved wooden table Merlin had been using as a desk. Like the amphitheatre, it was another remnant of the Roman occupation. Its surface, now strewn with scrolls and parchment, was intricately inlaid with marble and bronze.

"So," said Arthur, "how do we make this come to pass?"

Merlin was silent for a moment. "When attempting any task, Sire, there are two things we need to consider. The positive steps we must take, and the barriers we must overcome. We must understand and deal with both if we are to assure the success of our endeavours." Merlin leant forward, his elbows on the table, his chin resting on his clenched fists.

"As I have taught you, your birth was prophesied. You are the one destined to command the great sword Caliburn. Whoever wields that sacred blade cannot be killed in battle, and with Caliburn in your hand, you will drive the invaders from our shores."

"And where is this sword?" asked Arthur. "If it is mine by right, why can I not claim it?"

"Because, as I told you on the night you first rested at Caer-Lundein, it was taken from my hands and remains under the protection of Avalon. Only the Lady herself can bestow it upon you, and as yet, she has not been minded to do so."

"The Lady? That is my sister, Morgan," mused Arthur. "I am yet to meet her, but she is to be here, in Caerleon for Solstice, is she not? I can request it of her then."

"Aye, Sire, you can, but my instinct tells me that you will not succeed in making her part with Caliburn." Arthur opened his mouth as if to speak, but Merlin raised his hand to quiet him.

"Arthur, there is another ancient prophecy, more dreadful, and I think, more dangerous than that which deals with the sword. It is upon this that I believe we should be fixing our attention."

"What is the prophecy?" asked Arthur. "And why, Merlin, if it is so perilous, have you not spoken of it before?"

Merlin sighed and closed his eyes. For a whole minute, he sat, still and unspeaking. Finally, he said, "Because, Sire, to know the prophecy and to understand its consequences brings with it a burden that, until this night, I did not think you would be prepared—or indeed, able—to bear." Merlin spoke of the Beltane Child, a warrior of noble blood who would be born on May Day in the first year of the new king's reign and who—if they met on the field of battle—would defeat Arthur and bring about the destruction of everything he was fighting to achieve.

Arthur was silent, letting his mind absorb the words he had just heard, analysing their significance and considering their implications.

"So this, Merlin, is why we have been so interested in the children. Why we have questioned every petty king and lord of the Manor about the babes their wives have born this year."

"You grasp the point immediately, Sire." Merlin leant forward, his eyes fixed on Arthur. "Yes, we now know that there were three noble children brought into the world this Beltane. The first, just before daybreak, was a boy, born to the Lord and Lady of Lindsay.

"The second is a girl, born in Canturia, within the Ceintish fiefdoms." At this, Arthur raised his eyebrow, but Merlin shook his head, saying, "Nay, her sex cannot allow us to discount her. Think only of Queen Boudica, or the warrior women of Ynas Bray from your mother's lands in Lyonesse." At this, Arthur nodded, saying simply, ". . . and the third?"

"The final child, born just before midnight, is another boy, son to the Lord and Lady of Cilcestre, vassals of Duke Caradoc of Gewisse."

"And so, what do you propose we do? Keep the children under close observation to watch, as they grow, for any signs of rebellion or sedition?"

"That is one option," replied Merlin, "but it would be both costly, and difficult to explain. I do not think the children's parents would take kindly to having a permanent outpost of the royal household quartered on them. You would face constant questions and challenge—which could of themselves lead to the very rebellion we are seeking to avoid."

"Yes, you could be right," mused Arthur. He thought for a moment. "Well, we could make them wards of court, proclaim them to be children who have won particular royal favour, as they were born on the first Beltane of my reign—and then bring them to Caer-Lundein to be raised and schooled there. That would allow us to keep them under close watch, but also to raise them in a way that would ensure they would become true and loyal subjects."

"Yes, that is indeed another possibility, but I think it would be divisive, and cause resentment in other of our noble families as to why their sons and daughters were not so particularly favoured. It is also true that where one hopes to foster gratitude, you sow instead the seeds of envy and resentment—and neither solution would prevent one of these children becoming the focus of a plot to overthrow you."

Arthur was silent, acknowledging the truth in Merlin's words and recognising, with growing horror, their logical conclusion. It was now his turn to lean back in his chair and raise his goblet. He drank deeply, and after wiping the excess wine from his lips, rested his chin on his hand.

"Lord Merlin, I think I can guess what you are going to propose, but I may be wrong—I do not wish to misjudge you. Tell me, what do you suggest we do to resolve this problem?"

"I think there can be only one resolution, Sire, if we wish to avert the prophecy and ensure you cannot, in years to come, meet this child in battle. The child must die."

"But we do not know which child it is. There are three."

"Indeed."

Arthur stared at Merlin in horror. He went to replace his goblet on the table, but misjudged the angle and the wine spilt, rich and red over the marble inlay.

"You have gone mad, Merlin. I can think of no other explanation. You wish to murder, in cold blood, three innocent babes?" Arthur pushed his chair back, and getting to his feet, began to pace the room. "These are the children of my loyal subjects, who I have sworn to cherish and protect. What do you expect me to do? Knife them in their cradle? Spill their blood, like this wine upon the table? I repeat, Merlin. You are mad."

Merlin remained seated, his face impassive. "I understand your feelings, Arthur. Indeed, had you not responded at first exactly as you have just done, you would not be the man I believe you to be. Any normal man would shudder at the thought of doing what I believe we have to do. But you, Sire," Merlin then raised his arm and pointed directly at Arthur, "... you are not a normal man.

You are a king, chosen by the Goddess, with powers and responsibilities far greater than any of your subjects. Consider how many have died at the hands of the invaders since the Romans left us. Even now, consider how many are living in fear of the Northern marauders who plunder and pillage our eastern coast. We are talking of hundreds, possibly thousands of lives.

And you can change that. You can bring peace." Merlin stood, and made his way to Arthur, reaching out and grasping his shoulder.

"Think about it. It has been prophesied, and it can happen. You can change thousands of lives, give your people the contentment and security of home and hearth that you know they are craving. Yes, there is a cost. There is always a cost, but surely, three lives are nothing, compared to the peace of a nation?"

Arthur shook himself free of Merlin's restraining hand and made for the door. "You ask too much, Merlin. My head is bursting, and I must think. We shall talk more of this in the morning."

Merlin made no reply but went to the table and gently held his hand above the place where the wine had spilt. Slowly, it vanished, seemingly into the air itself, leaving the wood and bronze looking exactly as they had before. But the marble, once a delicate tracery of white and cream, was now dark and stained, as if with blood.

ARTHUR COULD NOT SETTLE. AFTER leaving Merlin's chamber, he had gone to his own room and thrown himself on the bed. But after a few moments, he realised that he was too agitated for rest. It was late, and the castle was silent. He thought about rousing Kai, his foster brother, but recognising that he was too unsettled to talk, he pulled on his cloak and set off across the courtyard towards the river.

He was approaching the infirmary building, when he heard the scrape of the wooden door on the stone flags and the muffled sound of two voices speaking in whispers:

"He will sleep now, and I'm happy to say the wound, though inflamed, is not infected. Come again tomorrow, Your Majesty—why not join us to break your fast?" Arthur could not see who was speaking, but recognised the calm, lilting voice of the apothecary Myfanwy.

"Thank you for your care of my son." The second speaker now came into view, crossing the threshold and stepping out onto the cobbles. "I was quite beside myself with worry. To arrive here in Caerleon hoping to surprise Gawaine and join him for a late supper, only to be told that he had been injured in battle, was not the welcome I had anticipated."

Arthur was surprised but also pleased to recognise the speaker as King Lot, who they had not expected for at least another two days.

"It must have been most distressing," replied Myfanwy. "But as you have seen, the wound, though deep, is now healing well. However, I must insist on at least another two days bed rest, and he must take care not to exert himself for some weeks to come if he is to make a full recovery."

"It shall be as you say, however hard he may entreat me. But it is late, I shall disturb you no more tonight. I am happy to accept your kind invitation, dear lady, and will be honoured to see you on the morrow."

They made their good nights, Myfanwy closing and securing the door to the Infirmary and Lot turning towards the castle—and Arthur.

"Well met, brother," said Arthur, holding out his hand in greeting. Lot grasped it in both his own, saying warmly, "Arthur, Sire, it does me good to see you. I had not thought to see you abroad so late. Were you also here to check on Gawaine?"

"No," replied Arthur. "I had planned to visit him earlier, but Merlin forestalled me. I had assumed that everyone would be asleep and so had resolved to wait until morning."

"Then why are you here?" asked Lot.

"I could ask you the same question," replied Arthur. "We were not expecting you for some days."

"As we approached the Welsh Border, we became impatient and tired of travelling. Agravaine and I knew we could cover more ground if we rode ahead of our party, laden down as they are with carts and pack horses. We arrived here about two hours ago." He smiled. "But I think we will see at least two more sunsets before the others cross the Severn."

"And my sister, Morgause? Is all well with her?"

"Yes, all is well, but she remains in Orkney. It is too soon after her childbed for her to travel." And Lot told Arthur that he now had another nephew, a boy named Mordred, born two weeks after Beltane. Arthur gave his congratulations but then looked at his brother-in-law searchingly.

"The child was born very close to Beltane. Did you not wish to avoid that time?"

"Why should I?" answered Lot, "A child is a blessing whenever the Goddess chooses to send one to us." He paused. "To be honest, this fifth child was a great surprise to me. My youngest, Gareth, has now passed eight summers, and there had been no sign of another child in all those years."

"The ways of the Goddess may often seem strange to us," said Arthur, with a cold note in his voice. "I am sure your new child will bring you joy—but I asked that question for a reason."

"Arthur, Sire, what is wrong? Your voice sounds strange?"

"I have heard tell of something tonight, and it has vexed me."

"Can I help? You are my king, but I am your senior in years, and if I can shed a light on that which has troubled you, you only have to ask."

Arthur considered. He had always found his sister's husband to be an honest man, who had never treated him within anything but courtesy. His response to the question about a Beltane Child had seemed sincere. Perhaps he too had known nothing of the prophecy. Making his mind up, Arthur spoke.

"If you are not too tired, I would appreciate your counsel. But not here in a dusty courtyard. If you will join me in my chamber, I have a flagon of spiced cider that I brought with me from Gewisse. You must be tired from your journey, and it works well at quenching a thirst."

Lot was happy to join him, and when the two men were seated, their cider warming on the hearth in front of them, Arthur told his tale.

When he finished, they were both silent. Arthur leaning forwards, chin resting on his steepled fingers; Lot sitting upright, his mouth slightly open, eyes fixed on a spot on the wall just above the tawny, dancing flames. Finally, he spoke.

"Is what you tell me true, Arthur? You have not misconstrued or misunderstood?"

"No, there has been no misunderstanding. I have never known Merlin to be more in earnest—about both the catastrophic risk to our country and people if the prophecy is fulfilled—and also, the only way to guarantee it does not come to pass."

Lot, who was still staring at the wall, said slowly, "He is asking you to sanction the slaughter of babes in their cradle." This was not a question, but a statement.

"Yes," replied Arthur.

"And how did you leave it with him? Does Merlin believe you to be aligned with his plans?"

"I told him he was mad to even consider such a course of action."

"He is clearly unbalanced to even think that the murder of these children could go unremarked or unpunished." Finally, Lot turned his gaze away from the wall and looked at his king.

"Arthur, the tales we are told as children are full of stories of those who, in a desperate desire to prevent the fulfillment of a prophecy, take actions which inexorably lead to its realisation. Do not be so rash as to become another such misguided fool." Lot reached out and laid his hand upon Arthur's arm.

"If you are party to this act, the delicate peace we have all worked so hard to sustain will be ripped asunder. And Arthur, though it pains me to say it, as I have come to love and respect you as both my wife's brother and my king, if you follow Merlin in this, I shall become the first to speak out against you. I shall be the one to lead the men of the north into battle against you." Lot leant back in his chair, his arms folded, looking to see what effect his words would have.

"Let us hope it does not come to that, brother. My lands and my people owe much to you, but you have sworn fealty to me as your High King, and the words you have just uttered cannot be seen as anything but treasonous."

At this Lot started forward, making to rise from his seat, a look of anger on his face, but Arthur held up his hand and gestured for him to sit back.

"Lot, believe me, I understand the spirit in which you spoke, and were I in your shoes, it is likely that I would feel exactly as you do. But these are matters of great moment, and I cannot leap too quickly to a decision." He stood, and walked to the window, turning his back on the seated figure.

"Merlin is a wise man and seeks only the good of our land and its people. Let me ask you a question. Did you notice, as you made your way to the castle, the crumbling buildings, the disrepair of the roads? When you sailed across the Severn, did the ship's captain tell you how Caerleon port is becoming silted up and may soon become unusable for the larger trading vessels?" Arthur turned, gazing directly at Lot. "Since the Romans left us, we have been at war, and we have not had the time, the expertise or the resources to look after our land. Towns and cities are falling into ruin, and I believe—nay, I am certain of it—that my people wish for peace, and the prosperity and contentment that would accompany it. And I believe they would be prepared to pay the price."

"And do you really believe that peace can be bought with murder?"

"I am not sure what I think. I know the outcome I am seeking, but the path I must take is still unclear to me. Listen brother, I thank you for your counsel, and I can promise you that I will not discount it, but the hour is late and I am sure that you must be longing for your bed."

"That is true." Lot rose to take his leave, but when he reached the door, he turned. "Sire, could I ask one thing? Promise me that you will not reach a decision without speaking of this to me again. Be not impetuous or foolhardy."

"Aye, I will promise this to you, but I must also seek your oath that you will speak to no one but myself upon this matter."

Lot nodded in agreement, and the two men embraced before Lot made his way to his chamber.

Both were now burdened, but the sharing of the load did not make it any lighter.

CHAPTER TWENTY-FIVE
BROTHER AND SISTER

Much troubled, sleep evaded Arthur and the sky was just beginning to lighten when he finally fell into a fitful and unsatisfactory slumber. His rest was disturbed a few short hours later by shouts from the courtyard below, accompanied by the sound of horses trotting into the courtyard, their bridles jingling. Rising from his bed, he walked rather unsteadily to the window, rubbing his eyes and stretching in an attempt to make himself feel more awake.

A small party of wayfarers had arrived, all dressed in stout boots and travelling cloaks, with bows slung across their backs. As they dismounted and looked about them, Arthur became certain that all four of the riders were women. As he watched, he saw Merlin stride out into the courtyard, one arm grasping his staff, the other held wide in welcome. He was formally dressed in a white lambswool cloak, his beard plaited ceremoniously and a circlet of oak leaves resting upon his brow. Behind him came Lord Llewellyn, finely garbed in a cloak of scarlet, a heavy gold chain around his neck.

One of the women came forward. Arthur could see that her cloak was more finely made than the others and was the deep green of holly leaves in winter, whilst her companions all wore black. She was not tall, but she held her head high and walked towards the castle with both confidence and grace. She stopped at the foot of the stairs and stood still, waiting for the druid to approach her. Arthur saw a frown pass swiftly across Merlin's face but then he moved forward and made a small, ceremonial bow. The woman responded with a dignified curtsey, before she and Merlin exchanged a formal and rather chilly embrace.

"We are pleased to welcome you, Ladies of Avalon. I hope your journey was uneventful, and you are not too tired from the road?" Merlin's voice echoed around the walled courtyard, but if the woman in the green cloak replied, Arthur could not hear her. Merlin then turned slightly to his right, resting his hand on Llewellyn's shoulder, encouraging him to move forwards as he spoke the formal words of introduction.

"My Lady, may I present Llewellyn, Lord of Caerleon.

"Lord Llewellyn, may I present the Lady Morgan, Lady of the Lake of Avalon." They bowed to each other, and Llewellyn bent to take her hand and, raising it to his lips, kissed it.

So this was his sister. Arthur leant farther out of the window, craning his neck in an effort to see more of her, but the hood of her travelling cloak was still raised, and he could see nothing of her face.

"Lady Morgan, I am sure you and your companions would welcome both rest and refreshment. Let us stable your horses and then my steward shall show you to your chambers." So saying, Lord Llewellyn clapped his hands and two stable boys came forward at a run, taking the bridles and leading the horses away. At the same time, a tall thin man with close cropped grey hair moved towards them from where he had been standing in the shadow of the doorway.

Lord Llewellyn gestured towards him. "This is Aled, steward of Caerleon castle. Please follow him; he will take you to the apartments we have prepared for your comfort. When you are rested, there is meat and mead enough for all laid out in the Great Hall." Llewellyn then offered his arm to Morgan, and with Merlin on her other side, the three of them made their way into the castle, followed closely by Aled and the three other travellers.

Arthur noticed that one of them was perhaps a head shorter than her companions, and even the bulk of her heavy travelling cloak could not disguise the slenderness of her frame. As she mounted the castle steps, she pulled back her hood and shook free her long, black hair, which was bound in a loose plait that cascaded down her back just as Morwenna's had done. Could it be her?

Pouring water from the jug on his bureau Arthur dowsed his head, the cold water chasing away any lingering remains of sleep. Rubbing his hair roughly with a linen cloth, he dragged on his tunic, breeches and boots, his fingers made clumsy with haste. Buckling his belt as he went, he ran through the corridors, seeking the chambers that had been set aside for the Lady and her household.

He had not seen Morwenna since she had ridden away from him without saying goodbye, but there had not been a day that he had not thought of her. The memory of her pale, white body, her soft skin, the dark cloud of her hair falling forwards and caressing his chest, had haunted both his dreams and his waking fantasies. He had forced himself to accept that it was likely that he would never see her again, and had tried, without success, to drive these visions from his mind.

But now it seemed that perhaps he had been wrong. Suddenly, he thought he understood. Merlin had already explained to him that, although the Lady of the Lake would officiate at Solstice, she and Arthur could not perform the final rituals together because of their close blood ties. "She will bring with her a proxy," the druid had said. "And have no fear, whoever she selects will be well-suited to the role. Morgan would not seek to bring dishonour to the Goddess."

Arthur had asked if it was likely that this would be the Lady Nimue, who had taken his sister's place at his coronation, but the colour had risen on Merlin's face and he had answered with a curt and simple, "No."

This then, could be the answer. If Morwenna was here in Caerleon, surely it must be because the Lady had selected her once more, but this time not just to be his tutor. Perhaps she, who had taken such pains to teach him the rituals, would be the one to join with him to honour the Goddess this Solstice.

By now he had reached the corridor leading to the apartments that had been made ready for the visitors from Avalon. Rounding the corner, he almost collided with Aled, the castle steward, who was explaining to one of the travellers the best way to get to the Great Hall.

Collecting himself, Aled took a step back and bowed. "May I help you, Sire?" If he was surprised to see the High King flushed, out-of-breath and alone, there was nothing in his tone to suggest it.

"Thank you, Aled, I was hoping to speak with one of the visitors from the Lake Isle. I believe she is known to me."

"Indeed, Sire. And what is her name?"

"Morwenna."

Aled considered. "Yes, Sire, I do believe that one of the ladies is indeed called Morwenna," and turning to the woman beside him, Aled asked, "Perhaps you could escort His Majesty, King Arthur, to her apartments?"

When she understood who he was, the woman gave a flustered curtsey and immediately agreed to do as Aled asked. They walked a little way along the corridor until they came to a doorway standing just a little bit ajar.

"This is Morwenna's room, Sire. I left her unpacking her belongings but a few moments ago. She is a tidy creature and does not like any form of disorder."

Arthur grinned, remembering the neat precision with which Morwenna had chopped herbs and prepared infusions when she was instructing him at Caer-Lundein—surely, this must be her. He thanked the other woman and waited until she had gone before slowly and quietly opening the door.

A woman wearing nothing but a thin linen underdress was standing there, her form illuminated by the sunlight shining through the open window. She had her back to him and was leaning over her travelling trunk, removing garments and refolding them if necessary, before placing them within the press that stood at the end of the bed. On the floor was a pale blue linen kirtle, its hem heavily stained with mud.

She was slender and graceful in her movements, bending to left and right, her arms extended as if in a dance. Her dark hair, held in its long, loose plait, swayed in time with her body. She was lovely.

Carefully and quietly, Arthur advanced into the room. Reaching out to touch her shoulder, he softly said her name, "Morwenna."

The woman turned, fear in her large, extraordinary blue eyes. Her skin was pale, dotted with a tiny sprinkle of freckles just above her nose. Her lips were full, and a delicate, delicious pink. She was beautiful—and he had never seen her before in his life.

Startled, he stepped backwards, almost falling over her discarded kirtle. They both spoke at once.

"Who are you?"

"I'm sorry . . . I'm sorry, there's been a mistake."

He reached out his hand to her, and as he did so, she screamed, "Get away from me! Who are you?"

They heard footsteps in the corridor outside and the door was flung open. Standing on the threshold was a woman, beautifully and regally dressed in a gown of lustrous green samite, held at the waist with a belt of plaited silver. A heavy silver amulet hung around her neck, and on her head was a coronet of flowers. Her eyes, blue as the sky at Solstice, were huge and framed with long, dark lashes, and her lips curved in a half-smile.

"Good morning, brother—and what fresh trouble is this?"

MORGAN INSTRUCTED THE STARTLED AND bewildered Morwenna to leave them and, snatching a fresh kirtle from her travelling trunk, she did so, closing the door sharply behind her. Making her way to the fireside, Morgan took a seat on one of the old oak chairs and settled herself comfortably. Raising her eyes to Arthur she said, "Will you not sit down? There are things we need to say to each other, and there is no need to add to our discomfort."

Arthur did not move towards the fireplace. Instead, he sank down slowly onto the bed behind him, his head cradled in his hands. He felt completely disorientated, as if he had been hit by the rough power of the tidal waves that surge up the River Severn, and was now struggling to right himself. There was a hammering pain in his head, as his mind struggled to understand what had just happened and his breath was coming in short, churning gasps. He reached forwards, clutching his stomach which heaved and roiled, and then, turning his head away from her, was violently sick upon the floor.

When his belly was empty, he wiped his mouth with the sleeve of his tunic. The pain in his head was easing and leaning forwards, elbows on his knees, he cradled his head in his hands, his fingers moving instinctively around his temples, massaging them in gentle, soothing circles.

He felt a light touch on his shoulder, and looking up, saw Morgan standing in front of him, holding out a beaker of water. He shuddered, recoiling from her touch, and when he would not take the water, she gave a small sigh and placed it on the floor beside him, before returning to her chair.

"I recommend you take a drink. Your mouth will taste foul, and it will help."

Arthur raised his head, horror and hatred in his eyes. "I want nothing you have touched."

"As you wish. There is more on the dresser. I thought simply to do my brother a service."

"What kind of abomination can you be? To sit there and speak such words, knowing how you tricked and deceived me, knowing the evil you made us do." He put his hand to his mouth, feeling the dry heaving of his stomach, worried that he was going to be sick again, but the sensation passed. Getting slowly to his feet he poured out some water and took a small sip.

"We shall talk of this once," said Morgan, "and then the subject will never again be raised between us. What I did—what we did—was as unpleasant to me at the time as the recollection of it now is to you. Do not flatter yourself that my actions were driven by desire. It was the will of the Goddess."

"I do not understand you. How can the Goddess have willed this to be? It is against all laws, against nature . . ."

"That is not strictly true, brother. Across the sea in Ireland, the kings and queens have often shared both a mother and a father, keeping the royal blood pure and untainted. And as for nature—well, our cats and dogs, our sheep and cattle—they care nothing for parentage when it comes to procreation."

"Are we not better than the beasts of the field? How can you speak so?"

"I was simply pointing out the errors in your statement. What we did was neither against nature, nor against the law of the Goddess. But these are mere semantics. It is done and will never occur between us again. My counsel to you is that you put it aside, as if it had never happened."

"But it did. You played as great and terrible a deception on me as my father did upon your mother. Is that why you did this? How much does Morgause know? She was the one who introduced you to me as 'Morwenna' . . . did you plot this together, as some type of revenge for the tribulations of your childhoods?"

Morgan was silent for a while, her hand moving involuntarily to the amulet that hung around her neck. Finally, she spoke.

"Yes, you are right when you say that your father was responsible for my father's death, and for that, I could never forgive you, but we share a mother, you, myself and Morgause. Whether we like it or not, we share blood and we share heritage. You are now the High King, and I am Lady of the Lake.

"We do not have to be fond of each other, but to govern this country effectively, we have to work together. That is why I say that it is best that we bury any memories of what occurred between us. Holding on to them, reliving them, will help neither of us."

"You have not answered my question. How much of this does Morgause know?"

Morgan considered. "My sister and I thought it would be amusing to deceive you. To pretend I was but a simple priestess. We thought it would be a great entertainment to see your face at the coronation when you realised that your tutor had been none other than the Lady of the Lake herself."

"And so, this was just some joke, a piece of unkind horseplay? You set out to make a fool of me, hoping I would falter or behave inappropriately in front of the whole court?" Arthur's voice was cold.

"Yes, we did. Morgause had been dosing you for days with jasmine and fennel, to build trust and intimacy, and you were as biddable and submissive as a lamb." Morgan shrugged. "But then, it all got rather out of hand, and we decided it would be better if I made my apologies, and instructed Nimue to officiate at the coronation. After all, there is such a thing as too much scandal."

"You really are a piece of work, aren't you? You and your sister both." Arthur poured himself more water and drank deeply this time. "I can understand why you would grow up resenting the very fact of my existence, but I can no more be blamed for what my father did to your mother than I can hold you and Morgause responsible for my own childhood, growing up ignorant of who I was, just knowing I had been abandoned."

"Oh please, don't expect me to feel sorry for you."

"I have no such expectations. I am glad that you have finally shown your true colours. I understand now that you and my sister—and, most probably her husband, Lot—have all been conspiring to undermine me. Making a fool of me at my coronation was probably not the only unpleasant joke that you had up your elegant, ceremonial sleeve."

"Arthur, let us return to what I said some ten minutes ago. We do not have to be fond of each other, but we have to work together. Whatever you may think, it is not in my interest, or in the interest of Avalon, to be in conflict with the Crown." Morgan got to her feet.

"You are right to suggest that Morgause and I should put away our childhood prejudices and resentments. We enchanted the stone anvil, she and I, so that only the one destined by the Goddess to rule as High King could release the sword. We accept that as her will, and I at least recognise that our plan to deceive you was as childish as it was unpleasant and went much further than we had intended."

She reached out to him, but he sprang backwards and her hand touched nothing but air.

"Arthur, Merlin has spoken to me of your plans to unite this land under a common cause. Listen to me, and listen seriously. You can only do this if you have the support and backing of Avalon."

"Then prove I have it. Give me the sword Caliburn. Merlin says that I am destined to wield it, and yet still you withhold it from me."

"It is for me to decide what happens to Caliburn, and as yet, you have not won the right to hold it."

"What do you mean? Merlin told me that the sword was my birthright, but only you can bestow it upon me, and despite his earnest entreaties, you have refused to do so."

"Oh, those old prophecies again. Merlin does become extremely boring on the subject." Morgan settled herself on the window seat, leaning her back against the wall, feet tucked neatly away beneath her. "But yes, he has a point. It was indeed prophesied that Igraine's son would wield the enchanted blade, but only when certain conditions were fulfilled, the most significant being that he should be the anointed High King, and rule at the wish of the People."

"But I have been anointed as High King and accepted as such by my subjects."

"By some yes, and grudgingly, eventually, by others." Morgan had taken a strand of her hair and was winding it thoughtfully around her finger, not looking at him as she spoke. "I think Lindsay, Ceint and Gewisse are still uncertain, but they trust the judgement of King Lot and will, for now, keep the peace. But the Northern Lords have refused to accept even Lot's assurances, and without their allegiance, you cannot truly claim to rule this land at the wish, and with the consent, of its people."

"But if you give me the sword, it will be proof positive that Avalon supports my reign, and my authority is endorsed by the Goddess. This, I believe, would do more to bring the Northern Lords in line than years of bloody conflict."

"That shows your naivety, Arthur. The Northern Lords are warriors, not scholars or mystics. They respect force of arms more than anything else and now they have declared against you. You will not win their loyalty until you have brought them to their knees."

"And when I have done so, will you give me Caliburn?"

Morgan looked up, her eyes bright with surprise, and a startled smile on her lips. "Aye," she said. "Should that day come, I swear by the Goddess that I will come to you, and place Caliburn in your hand."

"I shall hold you to that, Morgan," said Arthur. "But until that day, until you have proved that you can keep your word, I will neither trust, nor take counsel from you."

He made his way to the door, but before he opened it, he looked back. "You are right to say we must be seen to work together, and I will honour the Goddess, and show due respect to Her rituals and ceremonies. But please understand just how far that respect goes. I advise you to send the girl—Morwenna—back to Avalon. That was another of your unpleasant jests, and I have no wish to provide you and your sister with further opportunities for mirth. I shall select my own partner for the Solstice rituals and shall see you only on occasions where custom and propriety would be offended if we were not both to be present."

ARTHUR, FEELING HIS RAGE STILL burning ice-cold within him, went looking for Merlin. He found him in the physic garden behind the infirmary, discussing plant lore with Myfanwy. When they saw him approaching, Myfanwy took her leave, and Arthur asked Merlin if they could walk for a while by the river.

When he was certain they were completely out of earshot of anyone within the castle, Arthur turned to his companion, saying, "Merlin, I have reconsidered. I think there is much truth in what you say. I am as yet not adept in the world of high politics, but I have come to recognise that things are rarely as clear-cut as one would like them to be. And I think I have to listen only to the words of those I can trust."

They had been walking together, slowly along the riverbank, but at this, Merlin stopped and reached out, his hand on Arthur's arm. "What mean you, Sire? Who is it amongst those who give you counsel that you feel you cannot trust?"

"I do not wish to go into details, Merlin, but there are things that I have discovered today that make me question the integrity and loyalty of my sisters, and by association, King Lot."

"That is a worrying statement, Sire. The Lady Morgan plays a crucial role in the governance of this country. Without the friendship and support of Avalon, we would be lost."

Arthur nodded and patted the hand that rested on his arm. "I do not doubt that. I have guaranteed her my public respect, my obedience to the will of the Goddess, and my continued deference and participation in all of her rituals. In return, she has promised me Caliburn, when I have subdued the Northern rebels, but beyond that, there is nothing."

"You discussed Caliburn?"

"Yes, as I said. Morgan has promised that it will be mine when I win true sovereignty over all of the people of Britain."

"And did you mention the other prophecy? The Beltane Child?"

"No, Merlin, I did not. I have decided that you are right. Sometimes terrible sacrifices do have to be made, for the greater good of the nation." Arthur placed his hand on Merlin's shoulder and looked at him directly.

"We must unify this land. We must do all we can to remove the threat of invasion from these shores. I shall unite my people, and to do that, I will do everything that needs to be done, no matter what the price. There is no alternative."

CHAPTER TWENTY-SIX
THE LADY OF TYBURN

Gawaine had been discharged from the infirmary after five days of rest. His wound had healed well, and although the scar was still red and unpleasant to look at, it no longer caused him pain. He had been delighted to see his father, but his reunion with Agravaine had been less than harmonious. Gawaine had been travelling with Arthur for the best part of a year, and his experiences had changed him. He had known the terror and intensity of facing another man in battle, learning the hard and almost unbearable lesson of the uncompromising nature of war; that his own survival could often be bought only by the death of another.

He had undergone days of hard marching, with little to eat or drink, but had also been feasted royally, honoured as both kin and companion of the new king. He had slept fitfully on the cold earth, wrapped only in a blanket, and at Beltane, had lain in the arms of a sweet, green-eyed girl who had shown him for the first time how a man and a woman may honour the Goddess.

His face was now sunburned and weathered. The final plumpness of childhood had disappeared, revealing high cheekbones and a strong, finely made chin, which he now shaved almost daily. He had been knighted on the battlefield and thus had the right to bear his own arms but had chosen to retain the double-headed eagle in honour of his father.

Gawaine had left Caer-Lundein as a brave but inexperienced boy, but the person Agravaine had greeted when he and King Lot went to break their fast at the infirmary table on their first morning in Caerleon was a seasoned warrior—and a man.

When he was allowed to leave the infirmary, Agravaine had tried to engage him in their accustomed horseplay, but his brother would have none of it, treating him instead as if he were a naughty, overindulged child. He watched, with increasing jealousy and frustration, as Gawaine was included by Arthur, Lord Llewelyn and his father in discussions on battle strategies and military tactics, whilst he was dismissed and sent out to the practice yard, or even worse, to the gardens to gather herbs for the Solstice infusions.

It was thus quite unusual for Agravaine to be one of the party when Arthur rode out with his companions. Arthur had been quick to notice the division that had sprung up between his nephews, and although he had always found Gawaine to be easier company than his brother, he remembered times from his own childhood when the children of visiting Lords would come to the Forest Sauvage with their parents, and Kai would often exclude him from their games or excursions. Over the past few days, he had invited Agravaine to join them several times, but the boy, being both proud and foolish, had always said no. On this occasion however, Arthur had made the offer in front of his father, and as he knew he would, Lot had accepted with alacrity on his son's behalf.

Solstice was now but two days away, and the streets of Caerleon were thronged with visitors. Merchants and traders had travelled in from nearby towns and villages, and an impromptu market had been established in the amphitheatre where you could now buy anything from pottery to pigeons. The alehouses and taverns were full. Many had set up temporary stalls alongside the market traders, selling cider and ale to the thirsty travellers who had come from every corner of the land to celebrate Solstice—and to see with their own eyes the son of Uther Pendragon, their newly crowned and anointed king.

There was not a bed to be had at the castle, and all the taverns and hostelries were full, so a temporary encampment had been provided in the fields beyond the amphitheatre. The street vendors and hawkers, the minstrels and ale-sellers plied their trade, all of them blessing the new king for the extra coin his Solstice celebration was putting in their pockets.

Arthur and his companions were heading for the harbour to inspect the vessel he had commissioned for the Solstice banquet. He and Merlin had decided that, after the rituals had been concluded, it would be a fine thing to sail down the river and watch the sun setting over the sea. He had been awaiting the arrival of the vessel for several days, and when messages arrived at the castle to say that she had docked, he was eager to take a look at her as soon as possible.

They were all dressed in homespun tunics, wearing simple travel-worn cloaks about their shoulders. Although each had a dagger at his belt, Merlin had advised them to leave their swords at home. They wished to attract as little attention as possible. Arthur liked to go out amongst his people dressed simply and without a coat of arms to identify him. He found it interesting to hear what people were saying, to understand the things that pleased or upset them, and to get a feeling of the general mood.

But on this occasion, they did not have time to mingle amongst the makeshift stalls in the market or take a flagon of ale at the dockside tavern. When they arrived at the Wharfside, they dismounted and tied their horses' reins securely to the hitching post. Sir Kai, who could always be guaranteed to have money in his purse, gave a coin to one of the horse boys, telling him he would have another such before the afternoon was out—provided their mounts were all still waiting for them on their return.

They then made their way along the wharf, Arthur and Gawaine taking the lead, whilst Kai, Agravaine and Lamorak followed on behind them. They passed many ships as they walked; barges and balingers owned by the farmers of Cornwall and the Welsh Marches, containing barrels of ale, wine or cider, sacks of flour or barley and baskets of fresh fruits and vegetables. These were all being unloaded and checked by market-traders and tavern masters, before being carried away on handcarts. Alongside the commercial craft, there were elegant, three-masted sailing ships, like the *Wave Dancer*, which had arrived that morning, bearing on board several of the noble families invited to attend the celebrations, including the Lord and Lady of Lindsay and their household.

Arthur had greeted them at the dockside, this time wearing his coronet and cloaked in purple. Elaine, Lady of Lindsay, had allowed Arthur to take her arm and help her from the gangplank. When she was safe upon dry land she had dropped into a low and well-mademade curtsey, a smile of pleasure on her sharp-featured, cat-like face.

"It is good to see you, Sire. It seems a long time since you visited us for Imbolc."

"And have the past few months been good for you? How fares Lindsay?"

"My liege, all has gone well," answered her husband, Aldrich, Lord of Lindsay. "Since you sent the extra men to reinforce our garrison, the raiders have been beaten back—and in the past month, we have seen neither hair nor hide of them."

"And your cows?" asked Arthur, with a smile. "How is your dairy?"

"The stock you sent us yields well, Sire," answered Elaine, "and without being indelicate, the bull you provided has also been busy. We expect many calves next spring."

Arthur had been about to say his farewells and move on to greet his guests from Ceint when the Lady of Lindsay called him back. She was standing next to a young woman, from her dress, a serving maid. In her arms, she carried a small child.

"Sire, please, let me introduce you to your namesake." She took the child from his nursemaid and adjusted the blankets so his sleeping face could be seen.

"My . . . namesake?" said Arthur.

"Yes, Sire, we thought you would not mind if we named our firstborn after you, given that he was born at Beltane, in the first year of your reign," replied Elaine.

"Yes, Sire," said Aldrich. "We thought it was a sign, from the Goddess, may her will be done."

"May her will be done indeed," Arthur had said, a strange look on his face as he turned away from them.

As he looked at the *Wave Dancer*, deserted now apart from a couple of sailors who were making final checks to the rigging and sails, he thought of the child, his namesake, a small and innocent bundle whose shock of black hair had just been visible within the confines of his swaddling robes. But taking a deep breath, he forced the thought away, saying, "Where is this blasted boat? She should be easy enough to find. I have been told that the *Queen of Tyburn* is the largest and finest vessel ever to set sail out of Caer-Lundein."

They walked on, passing smaller sailing ships, single-masted vessels and a couple of galleys, but there was no sign of the *Queen of Tyburn*. Eventually, they reached the end of the wharf and had to turn back. This time, Agravaine was in the lead, walking some way ahead of Sir Kai and

Sir Lamorak, who were talking intently of the tourney that was to be held the next day. As he walked past one of the smaller sailing ships, something about her caught his eye. Her captain was standing in the bows, scanning the crowd as if he was looking for someone. The vessel was small, but neatly made, with clean lines and ornate paintings of two beautiful and very stylised eyes on each of her bows. Her name, written in small, neat letters was *Lady of Tyburn*.

Agravaine stopped in his tracks, calling out to Kai and Lamorak to make haste, but whilst he waited for them to reach him, he waved, catching the eye of the captain and calling out. "Hey—you there? Are you waiting for someone?"

"And what if I am? I can't see as how it's any of your business," came the reply. But just then, Lamorak and Kai joined Agravaine, and when they saw the ship's name, Lamorak introduced himself and asked the captain if he could come on board. Permission given, Lamorak clambered on to the deck, and after a brief conversation, the two of them disappeared into the cabin.

By the time they emerged, Arthur and Gawaine had also arrived. They all looked enquiringly at Lamorak.

"I think you need to prepare yourself for a disappointment, Sire. I'm not sure what has gone wrong, but the captain—his name's Finnian—has been waiting for King Arthur's steward. He says this is the ship that was requested."

Lamorak leant over and patted the bows.

"She is a good vessel, Sire. Finnian gave me a brief tour. There are enough berths to sleep ten people, and the galley looks big enough to prepare a meal for twelve. Everything's shipshape and in excellent condition ... but ..."

"But she is too bloody small." Arthur slapped his forehead in frustration. "I won't be able to seat even half the people we have invited. This is a mess, and the last thing I needed for my first official Solstice." Looking at Agravaine, he smiled ruefully. "Your mother would not be at all pleased; she was forever taking me to task for my lack of foresight. Still, I suppose we had better go and have a look."

They mounted the gangplank, and Lamorak led the way into the deck-house where the captain was waiting, nervously twisting a small scroll between his fingers. Lamorak introduced Arthur and his party, and after the captain had bowed deeply and mumbled about how much he was honoured, he handed the scroll to Lamorak saying, "Here you are sir. These are my orders, just see what they say . . ." Lamorak took the scroll, and having given it a quick glance, handed it back saying, "It's all in order, Sire, the papers require Captain Finnian to sail the *Lady of Tyburn* to Caerleon, where she will host a small party led by the king himself. Finnian had been given no detailed instructions. He was told these would be provided by your steward."

Arthur looked around him, an expression of despair on his face. They could all appreciate that even Merlin's magic would not be able to make the *Lady of Tyburn* accommodate more than twelve people.

It was Agravaine who came up with a solution. Jealous and unhappy that Gawaine had been invited to the banquet, whilst he had not, he now had an idea which would mean that neither of them would attend.

"Why not hold two banquets, Sire? One in Caerleon Castle, and a second, for your special guests only, on board this boat. Everything had been ordered and will be prepared as planned, but a smaller number of people will sail with you. The rest will remain in Caerleon."

Arthur thought for a moment and then clapped Agravaine on the back. "That is a very sensible solution. I shall speak to Merlin, and we will adjust our plans accordingly." He looked around him and smiled. "So, let us be going. I think we shall be expected shortly in the Great Hall, and I for one must change my clothes if I am not to disgrace myself." He waved his hand towards his foster brother. "Kai, please accompany the captain to the castle and introduce him to Aled."

They returned to the hitching post and reclaimed their horses. Kai hired a small bay cob for the captain, and they made their way back to the castle—Arthur choosing to ride alongside a jubilant and exultant Agravaine.

BY THE TIME ARTHUR MADE his entrance, dressed in a dark blue tunic embroidered with cloth of gold, coronet upon his head and doeskin breeches tucked into soft leather boots, the Great Hall was full. But as the heralds closed the doors behind him, the noise and chatter ceased as people fell silent, bowing low to greet their king.

He was accompanied by Gawaine and Agravaine, both also dressed in blue, and walking two paces behind him as he made his way to the dais.

He nodded once or twice to acknowledge greetings but did not stop until he reached his place at the centre of the table. Lord Llewellyn and his old ally King Ban were already seated, but they both rose to their feet at Arthur's approach and waited until Gawaine pulled out Arthur's chair. Arthur and Ban embraced, in a gesture of welcome and respect, then took their seats whilst Lord Llewellyn signalled to the pages to begin pouring the wine.

After Arthur had welcomed his guests and given the signal for the banquet to begin, he was about to compliment King Ban on the excellence of the wine he had supplied, when he observed Merlin standing in the shadows. Excusing himself, he rose and followed the druid into a small antechamber. He noticed that for once, Merlin looked older than his years. The skin around his eyes looked grey and drawn and he moved slowly, as if his limbs ached at every step.

"Why do you not join us at table, Merlin? We all need our meat and mead, and you particularly seem in need of nourishment. I have never seen you look so debilitated. Is aught amiss?"

Merlin gently lowered himself into a chair.

"Forgive me, Sire. I must sit. I have journeyed far today upon the enchanted pathways, and I have suffered for my exertions."

"I am sorry for that, Merlin, please take your ease. Now, as I think you will have heard, all so far has gone to plan here. Agravaine behaved exactly as we thought he would, and it is now understood that we shall hold two banquets—one on the *Lady of Tyburn*, the other here at the castle. But how did you fare? Did all go as we planned in Caer-Lundein?"

"Yes, messages will arrive tomorrow, summoning King Ban and Duke Cador to return urgently to their courts."

"And you have had a chance to speak with Lord Llewellyn and King Lot?"

"Llewellyn understands that he must remain here to host the second banquet. He regards it as an honour to act as your proxy. The Lady of the Lake has agreed to join with him at Solstice, and so she will also remain here, as the rituals will not have concluded by the time you set sail."

"And Lot? Do you know his thoughts?"

"He wishes to remain here, with his sons," replied Merlin. "I had thought that he would be difficult to persuade, but this festival also marks the anniversary of his nephew's death, and the men of Orkney wish to stay together to honour his memory at Solstice."

"All is well then?"

"Yes," replied Merlin, but despite Arthur pressing him, the old druid refused to join the feast.

Instead, he made his slow, painful way to his chamber, where he opened the shutters and sat, his chin upon his staff watching the sky darken.

CHAPTER TWENTY-SEVEN
A PLEASURE CRUISE

Elaine, Lady of Lindsay, smiled happily as she fastened the golden amulet around her neck. She wore it every Solstice, and usually it would have signified that she was preparing to join her husband in leading the rituals by their own Litha fire. But tonight, she and Aldrich would be celebrating Solstice with the king himself, chosen for this honour above almost all others.

This gave her pleasure, but she also had to acknowledge there were other reasons for her good mood. As she adjusted her belt of plaited copper, she acknowledged that it was but two moons since young Arthur had been born, and she was glad that this year, she would have no need to appear skyclad.

Aldrich, who had been sitting on the other side of the bed lacing his boots, got to his feet and looked at his wife. "You look well, Elaine. That colour becomes you."

She smiled. "I would not wish to disgrace you if we are to dine with kings."

"But one king, I believe," replied Aldrich. "I have been told King Ban has received an urgent message to return home and sailed this afternoon for Brittany."

"But could he not have waited for tomorrow?" asked Elaine. "Surely a few hours would not have made much difference?"

"I was told that if he missed the tide, conditions on the Severn would have meant he could not have set out for several days, so I believe he had no choice."

"That doesn't mean that we shouldn't go out on this boat, does it?"

"Oh no," said her husband, reassuringly. "We sail only on the River Usk, and no farther. But come, we should be on our way." Picking up the wicker basket that contained his son, Aldrich made his way down the stairs and out to the courtyard, where a finely painted cart, garlanded with willow wreaths and flowers, stood waiting to take the king's guests to the harbour.

There were already four other people aboard and both couples, like Elaine and Aldrich, had with them a small wicker basket. They introduced themselves as Godwin and Matilda, from the Manor of Canturia in Ceint, and Osgar and Winfrid, Lord and Lady of Cilcestre.

The harbour was not far, but long before they arrived, the three couples had discovered that their children were all born on the same day, and Winfrid, Matilda and Elaine were already comparing their children's capacity for sleep, debating whether it could be possible that they had already smiled their first smile.

Their husbands looked on indulgently but spoke little until Osgar said, "King Arthur seems to be serious about uniting this kingdom, creating a common cause. He spoke much of it when he visited us—did he do likewise with you?"

Godwin agreed that he had, saying that for the first time, he felt a new hope, that the new king seemed to genuinely put the good of the country and its people before his own personal prejudices or gratification. Aldrich agreed, telling the others about Arthur's visit to his court in Lindsay, and the practical steps he had immediately taken to subdue the wild marauders from the north.

"And he cares about his people," said Matilda. "Look at the blessing this afternoon, for all the children born during his reign, dedicating them to the Goddess, and swearing to serve and protect them—'for this generation and the next.'"

"For this generation and the next," they all repeated.

"And to pay such special attention to our children, those born at Beltane," said Elaine. "Who knows what this may mean for them, what honours may be in store? But whatever happens, we can tell them that they were singled out and feted by the High King, within less than two moons of their birth."

By this time, the cart had arrived at the harbour wall, and a herald was there to greet them and escort them on board the *Lady of Tyburn*.

The boat looked exquisite, its sails shimmering in the early evening breeze, resplendent with the embroidered images of a silver moon and golden sun. The handrails of the gangplank were garlanded with roses and columbines, and on the deck, which shone like burnished chestnut, stood Merlin, tall and splendid in his druid's robes, his beard divided into three plaits and a coronet of oak and ivy on his head. Behind him and dressed in regal splendour, stood Arthur, his arms outstretched in welcome.

At the far end of the deck, chairs and small tables had been arranged in the bows, protected from the sun by a richly embroidered canopy. Arthur encouraged his guests to sit, and when everyone was comfortable, asked a page boy to serve them with spiced wine. Finnian, who had been overseeing his crew as they prepared for departure, gave the orders to unfurl the sails and release the vessel from her moorings.

Merlin had taken his place in the stern, standing with his head bowed as though in contemplation. As the crew raised the gangplank and cast off the mooring rope, he raised his arms to the sky and called for the wind, which came, playfully and gradually, filling the sails, and causing the delicate silver bells at the top of each mast to chime joyously. Finnian, having carried out his final checks to ensure all was as it should be, ordered his crew to their positions and took his place at the wheel. The anchor was raised, and the *Lady of Tyburn* set sail.

It was a beautiful evening. The sun, just beginning its descent towards the horizon, cast a warm, golden glow upon the water. They were sailing towards the sunset and the light, refracted in the waters of the River Usk, which burnished the tips of the dancing waves. The wind Merlin had summoned was gentle, but the pace was good, and before long, they had left the harbour and were sailing along the river towards the Severn Estuary.

Delicate willow and weeping ash dandled their branches in the water, providing a safe haven for the nests of ducks and moorhen, and Arthur and his guests watched the water birds swim and dive in the dappled shadows. As they sailed downstream the river widened, its banks becoming overgrown with brambles and dog roses as they sailed beyond the borders of Caerleon. Only at the centre of the river was the channel deep enough for sailing ships, and Finnian, who knew the river well, kept a watchful eye on the twists and turns of the riverbank, knowing that to steer even slightly off course could result in the *Lady of Tyburn* running aground. Close to shore, sandpipers and plovers waded at the river's edge, searching for insects, shrimp and small fishes, and as they rounded a deep bend in the river, they watched a pair of grey herons gliding towards them, their eyes piercing the water as they scanned its surface for the swift flash of silver scales.

Arthur, who had been talking with Osgar and Winfrid, looked up as he saw Merlin move away from the stern. He spoke to Finnian, and at his order, the crew began to furl the sails and prepare to drop anchor.

As the page boys went amongst the guests, taking away empty goblets and beakers and offering blankets to any who were beginning to feel the slight chill of the evening breeze; a brazier was being set up on deck. Merlin arranged within it small branches of knotted oak, cut from the sacred grove just north of Tintagel, and brought to Caerleon by Cador, Duke of Cornwall. Most of his offering had been used to build the Litha pyre within the castle courtyard, but Merlin had extracted enough for the small bonfire that was to burn on board the *Lady of Tyburn*.

When the fire was built to his satisfaction, Merlin stood, silhouetted against the sky and turned to face the huge, flaming sun. He raised his staff high above his head, and it looked to those seated beneath the canopy, as if its tip was touching its fiery, shimmering surface. Throwing back his head, Merlin's voice rang out across the water.

"Great Goddess, Mistress of the Sun and Moon, grant me the gift of fire." As they watched, it seemed that both heat and light were transferring themselves from the very surface of the sun, as the tip of his staff began to glow and dance like a flaming torch.

Plunging it into the brazier, the flames of the Litha fire leaped and flickered as Merlin spoke the words that began the worship. "Lady of the Harvest and Mother of the Fields, we light the Solstice fire in your honour."

Withdrawing his staff from the brazier, its tip whole and undamaged, Merlin gestured towards Arthur. "Sire, I ask you to kneel before us, as we prepare to honour the Goddess and make our vows to her this Solstice."

Arthur rose from his seat and walked slowly across the deck towards the druid. The only sounds that could be heard were the gentle lapping of the waves and the soft sputter of the burning oak. Removing his coronet, which he held against his chest with his left hand, he knelt before Merlin, raising his right hand in a gesture of supplication. Behind him, the Lords and Ladies pushed back their chairs so they too could kneel.

When all was still, Merlin closed his eyes for a moment, head bent as if seeking guidance. Elbows to his side, he held out his hands, palms upwards and, eyes still closed, began to speak.

"Great Goddess, Holy Mother, we greet you. We thank you for your bounty and seek your forgiveness for our transgressions.

We thank you for your wisdom, which has helped guide us through these past months of change and uncertainty, and for the strength that you have given us, your children. Strength to bear the grief of loss and the pain of parting, strength to shoulder the unaccustomed burdens we must all acknowledge if we are to care for the land we hold in trust from you.

Today, we come at Solstice to seek your blessing, for heath and hearth and home. To ask that our fields and farms be fruitful and that your good-will be granted to us, helping to heal us and bring peace once again to all the lands and people of Britain, for this generation and the next."

"For this generation and the next," pledged Arthur and, after a moment, his guests repeated: ". . . For this generation and the next."

Merlin opened his eyes and leaning forwards, raised Arthur to his feet, gesturing that the others should do likewise.

The page returned with fresh goblets and flagons of wine and chilled water, and everyone was glad to drink. Arthur, who had refused a goblet of wine, accepted water, and quenched his thirst.

"Friends, as you know, this evening is not quite as we had planned it, and we have been forced through circumstance to hold two Solstice cele-brations here in Caerleon. My sister Morgan, Lady of Avalon, will light the Litha fires and lead the most solemn of the great rituals, joining with Lord Llewellyn to do homage to the Goddess, and entreat her favour in the coming year.

"Here, on the *Lady of Tyburn*, we shall sail a little farther down river and make a mooring at the mouth of the Estuary. There we shall watch the sun set on this, the longest day, as we celebrate and give thanks. But before that, I must make the solemn vows a king should make at Solstice, and by your leave, I would like a little time alone before I do so. Please, drink, enjoy the pleasures of the water, and I will rejoin you when next we drop anchor."

So saying, Arthur made his way to the cabin that had been set aside for him. Merlin once again took up his place in the stern, and when the sails were unfurled, called down the winds to speed the *Lady of Tyburn* on her way.

Beneath the canopy, Matilda had arranged herself so her seat nestled against the bows, and lifting her daughter from her cradle, held her to her breast. Elaine and Winfrid, whose children were fed by wet nurses, took out small terracotta feeding jugs, and filled them with a mixture of wine, milk and honey. Whilst the babies fed, the women talked together, pointing out the sights of the river and relishing the gentle calm of the fine summer evening.

Osgar and Godwin refilled their goblets with wine and asked Aldrich, who was drinking only water, to tell them more about the wild northern marauders that had so bedevilled his people. They had not, as yet, made incursions upon the Ceintish shores, but much had been told of their greed and ferocity and even Osgar, whose lands were many miles from the sea, was keen to hear of them. As they spoke, the shadows lengthened and the soft, haunting calls of the night birds could be heard, echoing through the trees. Soon, these were joined by the harsh shrieks of seagulls, and looking up, Godwin saw Finnian gesturing to his crew to drop anchor and secure the sails.

"Looks like we've arrived," he said, giving Osgar a gentle nudge above the ribs. His head had been drooping forward on his chest, and it had looked as if sleep was about to take him.

"Well, that's a blessing," he grumbled, drowsily. "This has all taken rather longer than I thought. I need my meat and mead."

"We've got the ritual to get through first, don't forget." Godwin grinned. "But at least, it shouldn't take long if it's only the king's vows."

Murmuring his assent, Osgar got up and went over to the women, who were still deep in conversation. The babies were all sleeping, and went quietly to their cradles, wrapped snuggly against the river's chill. As they all returned to their places under the canopy, Arthur emerged from his cabin. He had removed his cloak and embroidered tunic and was now simply dressed in a linen shirt and homespun breeches, tucked into travelling boots. His crown was nowhere to be seen, and on his head, like Merlin, he wore a coronet of oak and ivy.

Smiling, he approached them. "My friends, please do not think I seek to dishonour you. I am dressed as I was just over twelve moons ago, on the day I pulled the sword from the stone. I am a king only because the Goddess has decreed it, and I wish to approach her in humility, and give thanks."

Looking down, he noticed the empty flagon, and gesturing, called for one of the pages to refill it. As he did so, he saw Elaine give a small shiver. She was sitting close to the bow, and the breeze from the river had ruffled her hair and caused her, for a moment, to feel chill. Arthur picked up one of the blankets, and arranged it around her shoulders, holding up his hand to forestall any thanks, before making his way to the centre of the deck where Merlin awaited him.

Though the sky was still light, the first of the stars had begun to appear, and the sun was resting upon the waves. "Are you ready, Sire?" asked Merlin.

"Aye," he replied, and once again bent his knee.

Merlin stood, with one hand to his breast, placing the other upon the head of his king. Looking ahead of him, his eyes sought and held the eyes of the lords and ladies, and gestured to them to come closer, making a semicircle around the Litha fire. When everyone had found their place and was silent, he began to speak.

"People of this land, I, Merlin, Druid and Enchanter, beseech you to look with favour on this man."

Keeping his hand upon Arthur's head, he raised the other high in supplication.

"Arthur, High King and Lord of all Britain, do you promise to honour the Goddess and protect Her people?"

Arthur raised his eyes to Merlin's and, speaking loudly so that everyone gathered around the Litha fire, burning in its brazier on the deck, could hear, replied, "I do."

"Do you swear to follow the paths of the Mysteries and bring homage and honour to Her shrines?"

"I do."

"Do you swear to defend Her from dishonour and to oppose those who seek to cast out the Mysteries from the hearths and hearts of your lands?"

"I do."

"And do you promise, before these your people, to act always in good faith, and to take any steps, no matter the cost, to unify these lands and bring peace?"

"I do."

Merlin leant forwards, and raising Arthur to his feet, kissed him on both cheeks.

"Arthur Pendragon, son of Uther Pendragon, High King of this land, may the blessing of Solstice be upon you, and upon your people."

At this, a general, if slightly ragged cheer rang out from the watching lords and ladies, echoed by the captain and the crew, and at a sign from Merlin, the doors to the main cabin were thrown open. The feast was now ready and the celebrations could begin.

Whilst Arthur and Merlin made their way to the head of the table, Matilda, Elaine and Winfrid settled the babies in their berths before returning to their seats, certain that they would hear if any were to wake or cry out but hoping that the gentle rocking of the boat would lull them even more deeply asleep.

The food was plentiful and good, and the wine flowed freely, even Aldrich relaxing sufficiently to allow his goblet to be refilled more than once, and it was several hours before Merlin got to his feet, saying, "Sire, you have feasted us royally, but the hour is late, and we are keeping these good people from their beds."

Arthur looked at Merlin, disappointment on his face. "But we have yet to eat the sweetmeats that had been prepared specially for us. I received them as a gift this morning and thought they would be a perfect conclusion to the feast. Where are they?" Clapping his hands, he despatched one of the pages to the galley in search of them.

Winfrid, Elaine and Matilda shook their heads at these words. "Sire," said Matilda. "Lord Merlin is right. You have feasted us most generously, and I for one could not eat another bite." The others nodded in agreement, and when the page returned with a small tray, laden with honey-cakes and pastries, they each smiled their refusal.

Arthur selected a small honey-cake and a tiny pastry, shaped like a crescent moon and studded with hazelnuts. "Well, I shall sample these, and then yes, let us move to our beds. We need to weigh anchor early in the morning if we are to return to Caerleon for the tourney. I thank you for your company and wish you the blessings of Solstice."

At this, the others got up from the table, and after thanking Arthur and Merlin, made their way to their chambers. Arthur, looking down at the tray of sweetmeats, offered them once again to Merlin. "They are very good you know. Are you sure you won't try one?"

"I am quite sure, Sire."

Arthur looked at the page boy, who was unsuccessfully trying to conceal a yawn.

"What is your name, boy?"

"I am named Fergal, Sire."

"Here, Fergal, you take them. You have done a good job tonight." The page boy smiled delightedly, and reaching out his hand, lifted one from the plate, and at a nod from Arthur, placed it in his mouth.

"They are very good, Sire, thank you."

Arthur smiled, and reaching out, ruffled the boy's curls, before standing, and heading towards the door to his chamber.

CHAPTER TWENTY-EIGHT
THE GRUGGY ROCKS

Finnian, who had made up his bedroll on deck, always slept lightly when on board ship. The river seemed alive with noise. The calls of the night birds and the yaps and barks of the foxes all made it difficult for him to settle, and he was ill-pleased to be awakened less than two hours later by the sound of a voice, groaning as if in pain, and the noise of feet stumbling unsteadily towards him. Throwing back his blanket, he leapt to his feet, his hand going straight to the dagger at his belt. To his astonishment, he saw Arthur staggering towards the ship's rail, bent double and clutching his stomach, his white shirt stained with vomit and his face, pale in the moonlight, gaunt and twisted with pain. His eyes were wide open, their pupils vast and dilated.

Swiftly lighting a storm lantern, Finnian made his way to the bows. "Sire, what has happened? Can I help you?" He took Arthur's arm, trying to guide him to a chair, but Arthur pushed it away as he staggered to the edge of the boat where, leaning over the rail, he was violently and painfully sick. Finnian looked on in horror at the king's heaving shoulders, recoiling at the harsh, guttural sounds. He had no idea what to do.

From behind him came the noise of someone else stumbling on the deck, groaning, and crying pitiful, agonised tears. It was Fergal, the page boy Arthur had favoured at the Solstice feast with the gift of the unwanted sweetmeats. He was staggering, hand to his vomit-stained belly, as he collapsed onto the deck, legs and arms jerking violently in a series of convulsions.

"Get Merlin . . . for the sake of the Goddess . . . fetch Merlin." Arthur's voice was hoarse and strained and he gasped with pain as the agonising cramps began once again.

Finnian turned towards the sleeping quarters, but as he did so, a door opened, and Merlin appeared. Making his way swiftly on deck, he first took in the sight of the young boy, who was now lying curled up on deck, sobbing quietly to himself and grasping his stomach. Then his eyes fell upon Arthur, slumped across the bows, breathing heavily and groaning with pain. Rushing to his side, Merlin lifted the hair from Arthur's face, taking in his pallor and his huge, unnaturally dilated pupils.

"They have been poisoned," he said. "There can be no other explanation. Do you have any medicines on board?"

"No, no. I left our medicine chest at Caerleon, in the infirmary, requesting that it be replenished. I have nothing on board." Finnian ran his hands through his hair, looking frantically between the young boy and his king.

"The only hope is to administer an emetic." Merlin's voice was calm, but uncompromising. "You must take us to shore. I can gather herbs and make a medicine, but there is no time to be lost."

"But I cannot leave my ship . . . what if aught should arise?"

"What could arise, you fool?" Merlin's voice was now edged with steel. "If we do not act, the king will die. Do you want that to be upon your conscience? Wake one of your crew to keep an eye on the vessel and make ready the rowing boat. We must get to the shore."

Finnian, by now in a state of panic, did as he was told, and whilst Merlin gathered together his bag of needments, he and his sailors carried Arthur and Fergal to the rowing boat and made her ready. Within half an hour, they had reached the bank, and he had helped Merlin carry the others to a patch of soft grass. Neither had been sick again, but both were shivering, their faces convulsed with pain as they lay on their sides, arms held tight against their roiling, griping stomachs. Merlin had gone immediately in search of remedies, illuminating the tip of his staff to create a makeshift lantern.

"Shall I stay with them?" asked Finnian, following him into the undergrowth. "Surely we should not leave them alone?"

"That will be helpful," Merlin replied and handed him the waterskin that he carried at his belt. "If they will take it, give them water. I shall not be long."

Finnian did as he was bid, holding the flask first to Arthur's lips, and then to Fergal's. Both tried to push it away, but he succeeded in getting a few drops down both their throats. In a very short time, Merlin returned carrying in his hand a spray of rowan, heavy with unripened berries. Kneeling, he turned Arthur onto his back, and cradling him in his arms, opened his mouth and forced a handful of the berries onto his tongue. Gesturing for the waterskin, he raised it to Arthur's lips, urging him to drink and to swallow. After a moment, he did so and Merlin, resting him gently against a tree trunk to keep him upright, turned to the boy and repeated his actions.

After a few moments, first Arthur and then Fergal felt the cramps in their stomachs begin once again. Groaning, they rolled on their sides and were copiously and painfully sick. But this time, the sickness was cleansing, removing whatever had poisoned their bodies, and putting an end to the almost unendurable pain. Arthur opened his eyes.

"Merlin, where are we?"

"On the riverbank, Sire. How do you feel?"

"Tender, but the pain has gone. Was it poison . . . and were the others afflicted?"

"I believe it was, Sire, and no, just yourself and the young page boy."

Arthur looked at Fergal, who had once more curled up on his side, and was now weeping quietly. Reaching out, he patted his shoulder. "There, there lad, get some rest. It will all seem better in the morning."

"Shall we return to the *Lady of Tyburn*?" asked Finnian. "You may sleep better in your cabin." Arthur gave a slight, painful smile. "I think not, Captain. My sheets are somewhat stained, making my bed very unpleasant. I for one prefer the firm ground of the riverbank. But you should return to your vessel. Your crew will be worried."

Arthur and Merlin watched Finnian row back towards his ship and clamber aboard. Looking down at the sleeping Fergal, Merlin covered him with his cloak, and passed his hands slowly over his eyes, working a magic.

"Let him sleep," he said, and then, turning to Arthur, held out his hand to raise him to his feet. Reaching into his bag, he took out a homespun tunic which he passed to Arthur, who stripped himself of his stained shirt and threw it to the ground. He pulled on the new tunic gratefully and together they walked towards the river and sat down on the trunk of a fallen tree. Above them, the sky was dark, although Merlin noticed that it was just starting to lighten at the horizon, and there were few stars. The moon, half-hidden by clouds, was reflected in the rippling water, and all around them was still. Aboard the *Lady of Tyburn* everything seemed peaceful. The lantern Finnian had carried with him had been extinguished and there were no other lights.

Looking behind him to check the young page boy was still asleep, Merlin took firm hold of his staff and stood up.

"Do you feel sufficiently rested, Sire? I must admit that the effects of the nightshade were more violent than I had anticipated."

"They were indeed, and in truth Merlin, I am saddened that Lady Lindsay chose not to indulge in the sweetmeats. I would have liked the chance to get to know her better."

"She chose her fate unknowingly, as is so often the case—and do not forget, if she had accepted, perhaps the others would also have changed their minds, which would have made everything more difficult. We needed but one witness—and we have him in the boy."

Arthur nodded slowly, resting his chin on his steepled fingers.

"Now," said Merlin. "Are you ready? If we are to do this, we must act now."

"What if I say I am unwilling?"

"Then we return to Caerleon in the morning."

"All unharmed?"

"All unharmed. And in a few years' time—only the Goddess knows how many—you shall meet the Beltane Child upon the battlefield, and everything you have worked for, everything you have built, will be destroyed."

Arthur was silent, looking out at the *Lady of Tyburn*, thinking of witty Lady Elaine, with her pretty, cat-like face; of Osgar and Godwin, with their steadfast, loyal courage—and of the babes, snuggled within wicker baskets, lulled into sleep by the rocking waves.

He did not take his eyes from the ship, gently swaying at her mooring as he placed his hand on Merlin's shoulder and gripped it tightly.

"Do it," he said.

MERLIN RAISED HIS HAND TOWARDS the *Lady of Tyburn*, and pointing to the river, made a gesture as if to raise something towards him. The water around the bows became disturbed, bubbling and churning as if something was twisting and toiling beneath them and as they watched, the huge, heavy anchor rose to the surface, floating now as if it were made not of iron, but of linden-wood. With its release, the boat began to move, slowly at first, caught upon the current, moving gently downstream towards the mouth of the estuary. Raising his arms to the sky, Merlin called once again upon the winds and with a howl, he sent them, fierce and strong, down to the river, where they caught the little boat at prow and stern and carried her, faster and faster, out onto the treacherous waters of the Severn.

Finnian had woken almost as soon as the boat began to move. He had pulled up the anchor, which now weighed no more than a cushion, and realised it was useless. Completely bewildered by what was happening, he nevertheless recognised that he had to act. Rousing his crew, he ordered them to try to unfurl the sails and to lock the doors to the cabins, not wanting the panic of his passengers to hinder his attempts to regain control. Bravely, two of the men climbed the rigging to help fix the sails, but by now the *Lady of Tyburn* had been swept beyond the mouth of the Usk by the wild, raging winds. The ship pitched and tossed upon the waters, huge waves whipped up by the violence of the wind, and first one and then the other of the brave sailors lost their footing and tumbled into the waters.

In their cabin, Elaine and Aldrich clung to each other in panic as the boat heaved and shook upon the churning waves. They pounded upon the door until their knuckles bled, and the noise and disturbance woke Arthur in his cradle. Elaine reached for him and held him to her as tears ran down her face.

Next door to her, Matilda had sunk to her knees when she and Godwin had discovered their door was locked and they could not get out. Burying her head on the coverlet of her bed, she called to the Goddess to have mercy—and perhaps her prayers were answered, for as the boat roiled, she fell backwards to the floor, the heavy bedstead overturning on top of her and crushing her skull. For Matilda, unlike every other soul aboard the *Lady of Tyburn*, death at least came quickly.

On deck, Finnian and the remaining members of the crew had lashed themselves to the masts, hoping that the vessel would remain afloat when she reached the open sea, and that the storm would die down. None of them thought to open the cabins and release their terrified passengers. What could they do? There was no greater chance of survival on deck than below. But the wind did not abate. The storm carried them onwards, towards the treacherous reef of the Gruggy Rocks, barely visible above the pounding, crashing waves.

The relentless winds and pitiless currents drove the boat onwards until the *Lady of Tyburn* was driven onto the craggy outcrop, her hull splintering and her mainmast split asunder. The water, rushing into the hold, soon began to fill the cabins, and within a few short minutes, the ship disappeared beneath the waves.

She took with her the lives of her captain and his crew, two young page boys who had yet to see sixteen summers, the Lords and Ladies of Lindsay, Canturia and Cilcestre, and three tiny babes, each born at Beltane in the first year of King Arthur's reign.

AFTERMATH

When the *Lady of Tyburn* did not return to Caerleon the next morning, Lord Llewellyn despatched a search party and after several hours, they found a weak and bedraggled Arthur, accompanied by Merlin and Fergal, a young page boy, trying to make their way back to the castle along the riverside paths.

There was no sign of the *Lady of Tyburn*, but three days later, several bodies were found, washed up on the sandbanks. They were identified as Lord Aldrich and Lady Elaine of Lindsay, and their son, Arthur. A little farther down the river were found the remains of Captain Finnian, Lady Matilda and Lord Godwin of Canturia, and one of the young page boys.

No one was able to explain exactly what had happened that night. Much was made of the poisoned sweetmeats that had been sent to Caerleon as a gift for Arthur, but their provenance was unknown. It was suggested that the intention had been to poison Arthur's whole party, and it was either a trick of fate—or, as some insisted, the will of the Goddess—that the intentions of the poisoner had been so confounded.

Arthur took to his bed for some days after the tragedy, announcing that his grief for the death of his guests and their families was such that he could see no one. On the third day of his seclusion, his rest was disturbed by King Lot, who entered his chamber unannounced. Lot did not believe that the tragedy that had taken place onboard the *Lady of Tyburn* had been an accident, and true to his word, he informed Arthur that he would no longer serve or owe allegiance to him and was leaving Caerleon to join forces with the rebellious Northern Lords.

When Lot left Caerleon, neither Gawaine nor Agravaine went with him, and one of Arthur's first actions when he resumed his royal duties was to knight Sir Agravaine and make Sir Gawaine the Captain of his household.

NEW BEGINNINGS

Morgause reached up and stroked the pale, threadbare flank of the unicorn. Leaning back against the wall, the old tapestry shielded her skin from the cold, rough stone walls, giving her comfort as it had done all those years ago when she had first arrived in Orkney.

All her sons had loved the unicorn, and although Lot had urged her several times to get rid of it, she had never been able to bring herself to part with the only thing she possessed that had been given to her by her mother.

She wondered about the new child, asleep in his cradle at her feet. Would he one day love the unicorn too, and ask to be told tales of it, as her own children had done?

This was the child her mother had foreseen on the last night Morgause had slept beneath Tintagel's walls. He was here now, this tiny, delicate boy, with hair as dark as midnight and eyes as blue as the sky at Solstice, and as she gazed upon him, swaddled beneath his blankets, she wondered what else her mother had foreseen. Something had frightened her. Why else would she have woken, screaming from her sleep?

But this was not a thing to dwell on now. The babe would soon wake and need feeding, and she had much to do to prepare for her husband's homecoming. King Lot was on his way. Messengers had arrived that very morning to say that he had taken sail from Aberdon and would be in Orkney before the moon began to wane.

She walked to the window, looking out across the loch to the Ring of Brodgar, the stones standing tall, casting long shadows in the moonlight. She could see no one, and the night was quiet, save for the cry of a hunting owl. As she watched, she saw a slight distortion in the air in front of the largest of the stones and smiled to herself. Morgan was coming.

As she watched, the rough-hewn rock seemed to melt into formless vapour, beyond which glowed a pale light, revealing the doorway to the enchanted pathways. She could just make out the mouth of the tunnel and could see the outline of a figure walking purposefully towards her. Placing her lantern on the window ledge as a signal to her sister, she went to the dresser and poured two goblets of chilled water, smelling sweetly of rose petals and blue borage.

She seated herself on one of the chairs beside the cradle, gently rocking it, and listening for her sister's footsteps. The door opened quietly, and Morgan, still wearing her travelling cloak, came into the room. Morgause got to her feet and the sisters embraced. Taking off her damp and dirt-stained cloak, Morgan handed it to Morgause, who folded it and placed it on the settle.

Going to the dresser, she washed her hands in the basin, drying them with a linen cloth, before seating herself beside the cradle and taking the child in her arms.

"Hello, my darling, my beautiful Mordred," she whispered, peeling back his swaddling to look with delight upon the form of her sleeping child. He nestled against her, stirring in his sleep, and then opened his eyes. Reaching out, he caught her finger in his fist and gripped it tightly as she looked down at him.

His eyes, open and alert, seemed huge in his tiny face. Like his mother, they were fringed with long, dark lashes that swept his cheeks when he slept. He released her finger, and she stroked his face, marvelling at the softness of his skin.

This was her child, the baby she never thought she would bear, born at Beltane by the will of the Goddess. Looking down at him, she saw his hand reach for her finger, and as he grasped it to him, his mouth opened and he smiled for the first time.

ACKNOWLEDGEMENTS

The Sisters and the Sword is a dark story and, at its heart, is a tale that many retellers of the legends of Camelot chose to ignore or gloss over—the slaughter of the innocents. This element of the Arthurian legend goes back to some of the earliest versions—the Stanzaic *Morte Arthur* (1350) and the Vulgate *Mort Artu* (1210–1235). The story is also told in Sir Thomas Malory's *Le Morte d'Arthur* (1485). In more modern times, it has been touched upon by John Steinbeck, Mary Stewart, and T. H. White in their retellings but is, in the main, unknown and unacknowledged.

I discovered it during my early research for the Pendragon Prophecy series, via Marie Nelson's article "King Arthur and the Massacre of the May Day Babies" (*Journal of the Fantastic in the Arts*, Vol.11. No. 3 (43) 2000) and decided that I wanted to create my own version.

Writing *The Sisters and the Sword* had been, at times, challenging. The subject matter—incest, betrayal, and murder—is complex, and I wanted to make the motivation and behaviour of Morgause, Morgan, and Arthur understandable and credible to the reader. If I have succeeded in doing so, I would like to thank my editor, Toni Kirkpatrick, for her wise words and constructive challenge; if I have failed, the fault is my own. I would also like to thank my agent, Lindsay Guzzardo, for her faith in me and my writing.

Finally, I would like to pay tribute to the members of the Hastings Writers Group, for their ongoing friendship and support. Writing is often a lonely pastime, and I have found it invaluable to be part of a group of like-minded people who understand why you need to lock yourself away for hours at a time so you can tell a story in the way you want to tell it.